THE CONCUBINE OF SHANGHAI

Hong Ying was born into a sailor's family in Chongqing on the Yangtze River in Southwest China. An author and poet, she began her career as a full-time writer in the early 1980s having studied creative writing at Lu Xun Creative Writing Academy and Fudan University.

She is best known in the English-speaking world for her novels: *K: The Art of Love* (which won the Prix de Rome in 2005), *The Concubine of Shanghai*, *Peacock Cries* and *Summer of Betrayal*. Her autobiography, *Daughter of the River*, has been translated into twenty-nine languages and many of her works have been turned into television series and films. Her latest memoir, *Good Children of the Flowers*, a sequel to *Daughter of the River*, won *Asia Weekly*'s Top Ten Books of the Year Award in 2009. She lives in Beijing with her husband and daughter.

The Concubine of Shanghai

HONG YING

Translated by Liu Hong

PENGUIN BOOKS

PENGUIN BOOKS

Published by the Penguin Group
Penguin Books Ltd, 80 Strand, London WC2R ORL, England
Penguin Group (USA), Inc., 375 Hudson Street, New York, New York 10014, USA
Penguin Group (Canada), 90 Eglinton Avenue East, Suite 700, Toronto, Ontario, Canada M4P 2Y3
(a division of Pearson Penguin Canada Inc.)
Penguin Ireland, 25 St Stephen's Green, Dublin 2, Ireland (a division of Penguin Books Ltd)
Penguin Group (Australia), 250 Camberwell Road, Camberwell, Victoria 3124, Australia
(a division of Pearson Australia Group Pty Ltd)
Penguin Books India Pvt Ltd, 11 Community Centre, Panchsheel Park,
New Delhi – 110 017, India
Penguin Group (NZ), 67 Apollo Drive, Rosedale, North Shore 0632, New Zealand
(a division of Pearson New Zealand Ltd)
Penguin Books (South Africa) (Pty) Ltd, 24 Sturdee Avenue, Rosebank, Johannesburg 2196, South Africa

Penguin Books Ltd, Registered Offices: 80 Strand, London WC2R ORL, England

www.penguin.com

First published as *Shanghai Wang* (in Chinese) or *Lord of Shanghai*
in Taiwan by Chiu Ko Publishing Co Ltd 2004
First published in Great Britain and in the USA by Marion Boyars Publishers Ltd 2008
Published in Penguin Books 2011

1

Printed in Great Britain by Clays Ltd, St Ives plc

A CIP catalogue record for this book is available from the British Library

ISBN: 978-0-241-95067-8

www.greenpenguin.co.uk

Penguin Books is committed to a sustainable future
for our business, our readers and our planet.
The book in your hands is made from paper
certified by the Forest Stewardship Council.

Hong Ying would like to dedicate this book to
ZZ and ZT

MAIN CHARACTERS

Cassia Xiao
Madame Emerald Xin
Chang Lixiong (Master Chang)
Huang Peiyu
Yu Qiyang
Lily Chang
Xiu Fang (handmaid to Cassia)
Li Yu (handmaid to Cassia)
Lu Xianglan (Sixth Concubine)
Liu Ji (the playwright)
Zhang Hui (the actor)

NARRATOR'S ANNOUNCEMENT

This book is purely factual; the characters and plots are all based on real events. Please note that the author is well-prepared for anyone who thinks they are being slandered. See also page 352.

~ CHAPTER 1 ~

She had no time for the past. She would be willing to risk everything again to start anew. 'Anyway…' she paused to spread her long slender hand in front of me. Well sculpted, as if designed to show off, it fascinated me. When she stretched out her hand towards me my heart jumped: it had been a long cherished dream of mine to hold this hand in my own, to study it to my heart's content.

I had seen the lines on it so many times. She used to measure it against my own, making me so confused that I forgot what I was looking for, as if lost in some ancient game of strategy. The brain can transform the flesh, it can make one's very fortune manifest in the lines of one's hands. This is what people in Shanghai called 'presence' – 'taixing'. Her taixing was indeed unique: simply by focusing on the palm of her hand, I could see that she was destined to be a curse to all. The star of disaster would obstruct that of good fortune.

Worse still, I was unable to keep a calm face. I glanced up at her sweet smile – the smile that had won her the admiration of so many – and felt a sadness. One of us spoke: 'After all, every play starts with the first song.' Did I, against my better judgment, say that to comfort her; or was it she that said it, laughing at her own determination to keep going?

Her dreams were something she could not control.

She often dreamt of the morning she left home. Her heart beating fast, fearful, she had been waiting for the slow dawn to come. She had spent all night standing in the mudflats by the sea, looking to the east, worrying that the sun might not rise above that distant horizon.

She was seven when her parents died. Ever since then she had wanted to leave. So many years had passed since, in the fishing village; such dark memories should have faded by now. But she still had nightmares, and would often wake up in a cold sweat at the most terrifying moment.

If I were to make a film about her, I would start with this scene.

***

The sun was shining warmly on the Pudong Embankment, along which three men were carrying a sedan chair. In it sat an elaborately dressed middle-aged woman, her thick hair smooth and shining, with not a single strand out of place.

A large cargo ship lay in the dock, ready for repair. Half of it was covered in rust and stained by dirty water, but the other half was a glossy, newly-painted black. Hanging from the railings on the side of the ship were four foreign sailors, all bare-chested, some scrubbing at the rust, some painting vigorously. They whistled at the sudden appearance of the pretty woman.

One white sailor dropped his trousers and patted his glistening bare bottom, making vulgar noises as he did so, whilst his three companions laughed loudly.

The heavily made-up woman covered half her face with a fan to preserve her self-respect.

Underneath the bright sun and with their sweating backs bent, several peasant women were transplanting rice seedlings; one young girl lifted the back of her hand and wiped the sweat off her chin, smearing mud across her face.

A middle-aged woman hurried up, shouting: 'Come on, little Cassia!'

Cassia followed her aunt up the ridge. Suddenly the older woman turned back as if she had remembered something and grabbed Cassia's ragged straw hat, plucking a comb from her own hair as she did so. She forced the girl into a squatting position and hastily plaited her messy hair.

Now the aunt glanced over Cassia's tatty, heavily-patched clothes, wiping away the mud stains using the water from the paddy field and pulling down her rolled-up trousers. At last she looked a bit tidier. 'Let's see whether you get lucky and go to Shanghai,' the aunt muttered to the girl.

They arrived in a market, full of local produce and foreign knick-knacks being sold off by sailors: small *objects d'art*, clocks and watches. Cassia glanced around curiously as her aunt dragged her through the crowds to a large shack.

This was where horses and cattle were traded. They stood in their pens, neighing and lowing. Rowdy voices could be heard above the din as the traders bargained using elaborate hand gestures; a chaotic scene.

At the far end stood a long wooden platform. A row of small girls were standing on this stage, with a dozen adults below them, including the elaborately dressed woman in the sedan chair, still covering her nose with the fan. A tall, thin man peeped through a gap in the door and turned to warn the doorman: 'The Governor of Shanghai has just published a warning in the papers reminding everyone that the law of the Great Qing Empire forbids the trading of people. That's just for show of course, but you'd better watch out all the same.'

'Will there really be inspectors to check on us?'

'Who knows, but it's worth being careful. Does Madame Emerald want to recruit a few more girls for her Duchess Pavilion?'

'You do whatever's right by the book. We're just looking.'

Her aunt whispered to the man in charge, after which he waved his hands to a fat middle-aged man in a long traditional gown: 'Begin!' Cassia was made to stand at the end of the line of girls.

'Step forward! Turn!' the fat man commanded. 'Raise your hands! Your legs!'

The girls were not a neat looking bunch. Some were prettier

than the others; most had bound feet. They looked bewildered. Whenever a girl was approved by the adults down below, the tall thin man would take the prospective buyer to a small room at the side and start their negotiations in secret.

Soon only Cassia was left on the stage, without even an enquiry as to how much she cost.

The elaborately dressed woman had long lost interest, and her eyes glanced only briefly over Cassia: big bare feet, the gaps between her toes filled with mud. The girl's eyes were more curious than timid.

The woman stood up and complained to the man in charge: 'I came all the way from Shanghai and this is all you have to show me?' She noticed her young attendant looking intently at the girl and gave him a shove: 'Yu Qiyang, are you still with us?'

The young man recovered himself quickly. He had a handsome, innocent-looking, almost childish face. He wore a short-sleeved shirt, and held two cloth-wrapped bundles in his hands.

Now Cassia followed her aunt out of the cattle shed, the older woman grasping her collar: 'Shame on you! Nobody wants you, even as a servant girl. Even cattle have buyers!'

Her hands began to hurt from the beating she had started to deal out to Cassia, so she discarded the bamboo stick and cursed: 'Don't you want to leave us? I thought that even in your dreams you wanted to go. Now we can't sell you. You are worthless. Even cowshit can be burnt to make fire. I have wasted my time raising you!'

Cassia kept quiet, bearing the pain. 'Your uncle had it all worked out. He said you were a small girl with a big head. You will always be trouble.' She kicked her niece. 'Get out, you lousy rotten girl! If I can't sell you to someone in Shanghai, I'll sell you cheaply somewhere else.'

The entourage of sedan chairs travelled back the way it came, with the handsome young man walking at the front left hand side of the three-man-sedan. The sedan chair was carried by two men at the front, with one at the back. As he bore the most weight and they changed positions every so often, catching their breath before they pushed on. The bearers' long pigtails hung down heavily from the top of their heads.

Before long, one of the men at the front felt a tap on his shoulder. Turning, he realised that the bamboo shaft that had been resting on his shoulder had slipped off and was now being carried by somebody else. The woman swaying inside the sedan suddenly started out of her doze and was startled to see that one of the pair of porters carrying the sedan in front – apparently without any effort – was in fact a young girl. She was about to remonstrate when the girl glanced back and smiled at her. The woman tapped her stick and the sedan came to a stop.

'What on earth is this? Aren't you the one at the market today who…?'

Cassia knelt down: 'Please, Madame Emerald, I'm an orphan and have been brought up to live a tough life. I know I'm not the type you're looking for, but I'm very strong; I can work very hard.'

The older woman's eyes widened: 'How do you know my name?'

'Madame Emerald was at the market at noon today. I heard others calling your name and remembered it.'

Now Madame Emerald turned, and smiled down at another woman she had noticed who was standing next to the sedan chair, bowing.

'You really are keen to sell her, aren't you? I see that she is as strong as a man.'

'Shanghai is such a good place. Everyone dresses like Madame Emerald – so pretty!' the aunt said.

Madame Emerald glanced at the young girl, who was still kneeling on the ground, her eyes now full of tears and looking pitiful. Something stirred in her, and she said: 'Get up then. I'll break my own rule just this once! Ten pieces of silver, go on, take it.' She waved at the handsome young man who was with her: 'Yu, get them to press their fingerprints.'

'That's too little,' the aunt said: 'They say a servant girl is worth thirty pieces…'

'Then take her back.' Madame Emerald called the men by the chair to rise: 'She's only fit for rough work, you pay for what you get. Come on, let's go.'

The aunt ran up to her in a hurry: 'Please, my lady, don't be angry. Ten pieces will be fine.'

The sedan chair hurried on now and Cassia, barefoot, struggled along clutching Madame Emerald's bundles. The effort meant she often had to wipe the sweat from her face; she had cleaned it especially, but it was already smudged again. The further they travelled, the softer the green fields became. The yellow flowers of the rape seed smeared their clothing along the way, and white moths hovered around the chair.

Finally they arrived at the long bank along the Huangpu River and the sedan carriers slowed down. There were more people about as the river widened. She heard people say that they had come to Lujiazui Dock.

The Bund stood on the opposite bank of the river. The setting sun seemed to shine brighter than ever on the Victorian buildings there. A number of ships were in the middle of the river emitting clouds of smoke in fierce jets and sounding strange horns.

Putting the bundles on the ground, Cassia hitched up her trousers and stared in awe. A bamboo stick poked at her arms. It hurt, but she simply stepped aside, keeping her eyes on the river.

The dock was busy. The ferry was an iron steamboat with a giant chimney. Cassia smiled, feeling the pungent smoke on her face.

The passengers held on to their bags and other luggage, adults pulled their children along; everyone pushed past them towards the boat's landing platform.

The elaborately-dressed Madame Emerald ran her hands over her neat hair and tapped the side of her chair. The sedan was put down. She turned her face and scolded loudly: 'Cassia! Do you want us to see that you are lazy before you even get to Shanghai? Go and look after the luggage.'

This all happened in the early spring of 1907. The Emperor Xuantong hadn't yet left the throne. Everyone knew things could not carry on as they had done, but all were waiting, waiting for the beginning.

~ CHAPTER 2 ~

The so-called 'Studio' – the Duchess Pavilion on Little West Gate Street – was originally one of the residences of a famous gentleman from Songjiang, in the era of Emperor Xianfeng. A romantic, the gentleman bequeathed the building to a favourite concubine. She had originally been a prostitute and had an ambition to become a duchess; but – unexpectedly widowed – found herself with just one possession: the building the old man had left her. Poor and downtrodden, she used it to rebuild her old career, calling it the 'Duchess Pavilion', in memory of happier times.

Madame Emerald was the present owner. Whenever she talked about the building, she claimed the story was true. She even produced the old man's paintings as evidence, saying that these were left to her as presents by the would-be duchess. Songjiang was Madame Emerald's hometown and she herself had once been the Duchess Pavilion's top courtesan. Indeed, the paintings were genuine, but we will keep the name of the famous gentleman secret for now.

During the years of Emperor Tongguang's rule, parcels of land in Shanghai had begun to be awarded to foreigners as 'concessions'. A 'red light' district was quickly established, with many prosperous brothels that varied greatly in class. The Duchess Pavilion was at the top end of the market and prided itself on keeping a distance from the rest.

Situated on the border of the Chinese and foreign concessions the building had a deep purple gate, a high threshold, and heavily set, sturdy stone walls. The atmosphere was forbidding, but despite the fact that from the outside it appeared to be grand and stately, the inside of the building had long been divided into smaller apartments. All of Madame Emerald's courtesans lived on the first floor, each with her own richly decorated bedroom and sitting room. Some say the floors of certain rooms were paved with gold and silver, which in itself was enough to make the building famous in Shanghai.

The clientele were typically men of status; indeed, some came along with the specific intention of showing off that status. There was another reason why they liked frequenting the Pavilion: those who lived in the areas of Shanghai that were currently controlled by foreigners felt they were returning to a more familiar China, if only for a short time, while those from the Chinese city felt they were already halfway out of the reach of the authorities; here, they could indulge themselves in a more relaxed fashion.

Cassia maintained a smile whether she was with other people or alone. People said she had a sweet smile. She wore a servant girl's dress; with a single thick plait instead of her previous two plaits and a neat fringe across her forehead.

She'd shot up in height over the last six months. Everyone said she should have been a common maid instead; who'd ever seen such a tall servant girl? She wasn't fit to serve guests.

This proved to be a considerable headache for Madame Emerald. A servant girl cost a certain amount, but once purchased such a girl belonged to you and was totally at your mercy. But a maid was merely an employee; one had to pay her wages by the month, and she'd be free to leave whenever she wanted to. For Madame Emerald to have paid a servant girl's fee for someone who was only really fit to be a common maid wasn't such a good deal. So Cassia remained a servant girl.

In the early mornings the kitchen was busy. The two chefs, both from Suzhou, and their helpers killed chickens, ducks and fish. The blood had to be cleaned up straight away, as the first thing Madame Emerald would do after she rose was inspect the kitchen. If she found one feather or even a drop of grease, she'd fine the cook's helpers. They trod carefully, closely watching the maids as they came and went from the various rooms, in case they were punished for someone else's mistake.

Cassia was still growing, she had become annoyingly tall, but was also strong. Unlike the other servant girls, who looked for men to help them to carry heavy things, people often turned to her when Madame Emerald needed something done quickly.

By now Cassia had also learned to be less clumsy, and could hold a tea tray level while walking fast. Coming out of the kitchen, she passed through the large room where the older servant girls slept, full of envy. When would she ever get to sleep there? Her own 'bedroom' – if you could call it that – was a small room in the basement with a tiny window, narrow and crowded and shared with several other young servant girls. She had to move over onto one side of the bed to get to her sleeping space and the amount of room she was allocated was only just big enough for her to turn over whilst she was sleeping.

But compared to where she came from this was heaven. She ate well: last night's leftovers from the courtesans, after they'd been reheated, tasted as good as new to her. Madame Emerald, though she had cursed Cassia several times for growing so quickly, made her new clothes. Here, even a servant girl must dress well.

It was nearly dusk. Cassia passed along the corridor and climbed the stairs. The low whispers and songs of the courtesans mingled with the sound of teasing and flirtation. She went to the grand Phoenix Hall, where Madame Emerald herself lived. Sometimes a new customer was received there, both to show the goodwill of the hostess and to establish some sort of protocol, as befitted an establishment as grand as the Duchess Pavilion. Here the newcomer would be entertained by Madame Emerald herself and offered wine by each of the courtesans. Only if the visitor came a second time would he be allowed into the sitting room of his chosen girl. Only on the third visit might he be allowed into her bedroom.

The sun was setting and the sky was streaked with purple and blue. Street lights began to be lit. The girls in the 'studio', having woken up at noon, had spent the whole afternoon dressing. The housekeeper was busy accepting invitations, loudly shouting out the names of the girls who had been invited out, or whose appearance had been requested here in the studio, or who had been invited to a tea party. Elegantly dressed guests would arrive with myna birds, which, in response to the hustle and bustle, might suddenly caw: '*Ji Li Fa Cai*! – Be lucky! Be prosperous!'

This was the busiest time of the day at the Duchess Pavilion.

Three carriages pulled up just outside. As soon as they stopped, attendants from the front and back coaches rushed to the middle one and opened the door, to help out Chang Lixiong, the Grand Master of the Hong Brotherhood. But the man stepped out by himself and strode away, showing that he was not the sort of person who was in need of help.

Little West Gate Street was long, but not wide. Standing at one end you could not see the other: the two sides of the street were filled with pharmacies, bathhouses, inns, restaurants and grocery shops – a prosperous world. Tonight there was no wind or rain and it was even more crowded than usual.

An awkward-looking pedlar huddled close to one of Chang Lixiong's young attendants and whispered to him conspiratorially: 'Western pornography?' The young attendant shoved the pedlar away. He used a considerable amount of force and the pedlar was pushed several feet, collapsing on the ground as the pictures in his hands were scattered all around. He shouted loudly: 'Master, master, you only have to say "no" if you don't want it.'

The attendant's face did not move a muscle; he barked: 'Step aside! Watch out!', as he moved to stop the pedlar from approaching his boss.

But Chang Lixiong spoke in a soothing voice. 'There's no need to be so tough. He's only doing his job. I'm not the Governor of Shanghai, why should he be stopped?' Watching the weak pedlar's body as he crouched down, he said to his guards: 'Just make sure he hasn't any weapons on him.'

The pedlar, who had earlier been frightened by the guard, stumbled up and collected his pictures. What Chang Lixiong had said made him realise he was safe. He lowered his body, wrinkled his face into a smile and spread out the pictures in his hands: 'Master, master, please do me the favour of having a look at this… just have a look,' he urged, in a subservient voice.

It was a set of prints of Western paintings: Botticelli's *Birth of Venus,* Ingres's *The Source* and *Turkish Baths.* Either they had been sold by Western sailors, or produced by a printing house with the latest equipment. The pedlar picked out a few and handed them over.

The quality of printing was poor; so these must be the cheap copies the sailors brought over. All pictures in those days were tainted yellow and looked old.

'When Chinese and Westerners mingle, that's when trouble starts,' Madame Emerald had once said to Cassia. This incident of Chang Lixiong looking at the Western nudes was of course further evidence of the truth of this adage.

Indeed, everything started with the appearance of these pictures, although they seemed insignificant at the time.

His eyes flicked over the images briefly and Chang Lixiong waved his hands at the pedlar: 'Away, away! What rubbish. I'm only interested in the live variety.'

The Grand Master of the Hong Brotherhood was between forty and fifty years old, tall and well built and wore a long gown. Close up, one could see the hints of blue and purple in the dark silk pattern over the black base of his robe. They had been expecting him for a long time, and someone opened the door for him as soon as he reached the gate. Lifting up his gown, Chang Lixiong stepped over the high threshold.

The sound of music and laughter greeted him, mingled with the scent of perfume. 'It is Master Chang himself!' There came the sound of cheers and greetings from the women who had gathered. 'It's been so long!'

'Its been such a long time, how we've missed you!'

'Come sisters, come and attend to Master Chang!'

Madame Emerald drew open the curtains that surrounded the bed, and hooked them up on either side. Master Chang, as they called him at the Duchess Pavilion, sat by the bedside, while she herself knelt behind him on the bed and energetically massaged his back. She was still a beauty; with an oval face, high eyebrows and long almond-shaped eyes. A courtesan who, at the age of forty, could still make an old lover feel attached to her; she had not done badly.

Her jet black hair was pinned back, smooth and neat; her small feet were wrapped inside a pair of embroidered shoes, with only the toes peeking out from beneath her silk trousers. This was the feature – aside from the face of course – that a girl from the Duchess Pavilion should be most proud of; the part that the guests admired and fondled the most, and naturally the part the girls spent the most time and effort on.

Madame Emerald focused her attention entirely on Master Chang, whispering into his ears, her lips almost touching his cheeks. He listened and smiled, touching her hand.

Cassia entered through the wide-open gate of the Phoenix Hall and into the bedroom, holding a tray laden with tea. Her steps were hardly audible. The couple inside the room barely even glanced at her. She walked to the table by the bed and put the tea set down.

Madame Emerald was saying how difficult business was nowadays, with the revolutionaries and the chaos they caused.

His eyes half-closed, Master Chang enjoyed her pampering. But he was not too impressed by her words: How could business not be good when so many rich men from the South had escaped to Shanghai?

'What I meant was there are less and less guests with taste; and even fewer who are generous with their cash.'

Madame Emerald sighed:'If this is the way things are going, do you think even we courtesans will have to be revolutionised?'

Master Chang laughed: 'All right, let's all unite in the great cause.'

As Cassia bent down to the tray he heard her and opened his eyes. Noticing her unbound feet, his eyes moved up her legs and lingered on her face. Their eyes met by accident and Cassia immediately lowered her eyelids. She stood attentively. Only when Madame Emerald asked her to leave could she move. This was the house rule.

Chang Lixiong patted Madame Emerald's bottom. Was this girl new? He hadn't seen her before. He remembered that Madame Emerald had been down to the Chuansha area to look for new servant girls. He had sent his own aide Yu to be her guard.

'She is indeed a peasant girl I picked up in Chuansha,' Madame Emerald told him. 'But it's so hard to find a decent girl in the countryside these days!' She asked Cassia to step forward and show herself to Master Chang:'Look how ugly this girl is: her eyes are too big, her mouth is too wide, her legs are too long...she's just too tall.' Her fingers almost touching Cassia, she exclaimed:'The strangest thing of all is this pair of mysteriously large breasts! As ugly as can be. But to buy her I still had to pay her aunt a big pile of silver.'

Master Chang asked simply:'How old is she?'

'Well they say she's fifteen, but she doesn't look it. I've wasted my money buying this one! Look how well I fed her, now she looks all pink and healthy like a farm girl.'

'I am sixteen, my lord.' Cassia's voice was clear and loud, but she dared not look up to the two on the bed.

'Who said you could speak?' Madame Emerald hit Cassia's chest with her fan: 'I asked you to bind up your chest, how dare you let your breasts loose again?!'

As Chang Lixiong's eyes were on her, Cassia protested half-heartedly – yet somehow she didn't want to give in to Madame Emerald under such an intense stare. She licked her dry lips and said softly: 'I couldn't breathe...'

Madame Emerald interrupted her: 'If you don't want to bind your chest, then pay me back my money!' she turned to Master Chang and complained: 'I've never seen such an ugly girl. If it hadn't been for the untimely death of her parents, I wouldn't have taken her. I took pity on her, yet how can I keep such an ugly girl in my reputable house? I would like to use her as a common maid but they have to be married women. Two months ago a rich Nanjing guest took a fancy to her and I asked her to attend to him, thinking perhaps I could help her by making her one of my entertaining girls.'

'I'm sure that a cunning lady like you sorted it all out,' Master Chang teased.

Ignoring the irony in his voice, Madame Emerald carried on: the girl had fought him off, and made such a scene – as if losing her virginity was a matter of life and death – that she ended up annoying the guest, so much so that Madame Emerald herself had to ask for his forgiveness. The girl was punished by the housekeeper of course, and had all the usual beatings. Still she would not give in. She was locked up for two days, yet was still stubborn. What a fuss she had made, despite the fact that she was the humblest and most ugly girl in the house.

All this aroused Chang Lixiong's interest. He started to look at the girl in a new way.

It seemed that Master Chang was someone Madame Emerald could confide anything to. With such an understanding man, women were caught off their guard; they stepped over the line.

Now she was becoming a little too pleased with herself, boasting of how she had tamed the girl with just the one line, 'I'll send you back to the countryside tomorrow morning.' That was when the stubborn mule had broken down and begged for forgiveness.

Cassia still stood silently by her side. Her apparent indifference roused Madame Emerald's anger. 'If the guest had actually been entertained by Cassia, we'd have lost face – he'd surely think us vulgar, having a girl with such an ugly pair of feet,' Madame Emerald said and turned to Cassia: 'Take your shoes off and let Master Chang have a look at your feet.'

Cassia wanted to run, but Madame Emerald's threat was fresh in her memory. She dared not offend her further. Helplessly she took off her shoes, wriggling her toes in embarrassment. Against the shining floor her feet looked outlandishly big and ugly compared to her mistress's tiny pair, which were both as exquisite as golden lilies. She was deeply ashamed.

But next to her, Master Chang's feet were dangling over the bedside, even bigger and clumsier than her own, and covered with thick black hairs. Hers were slender and white; her nails shone; and her second toes were almost as big and neat as her big ones. Fascinated, she was in a trance.

'Isn't she destined to remain a mere servant girl, with a pair of feet like that? Look at her, she actually feels sorry for herself. Never mind her appearance, her expectations were higher than the sound of the ferry boat whistle on the Huangpu River!' Truly worried now about the girl, Madame Emerald sighed: '*Aiyaa*! Where is this all going to lead to?'

This finally drew Master Chang's attention back. 'Come on, don't take it all out on the girl,' he smiled. 'Go on, ask her to put her shoes back on.' Then Madame Emerald noticed that he had stopped staring at Cassia and had started to pinch her feet. Madame Emerald was mortified. Did he think this woman's looks were in any way comparable to hers? A beauty, who in her day had been considered Number One among the four most beautiful courtesans in Shanghai?

Madame Emerald reluctantly did as she was bid, but pointedly told him that such an ugly girl would spoil the appetite of the other guests in the house. She glanced coldly at Cassia and told her sternly to leave.

Cassia put her shoes back on and sullenly tidied up the plates. She walked to the door. Taking the tea bowl from Madame Emerald's hands, Master Chang drank the tea and watched Cassia's back absent-mindedly. Something stirred in him. The servant girl's clothes were far too small for her. They wrapped tightly around her body, making her shoulders appear too broad, though her waist seemed slender and soft. Not a conventional beauty obviously. She was a rare sight among the entertaining girls he was used to.

She had something, the innocence and toughness of a peasant girl; something he had known well when he was younger.

She reminded him of his past, he thought, there was something very familiar about her. But surely he could not be tempted so by just one glimpse of the girl? What was it that caused his heart to beat so fast?

Then he remembered: Cassia looked exactly like the Western beauty he had been looking at earlier in the pornographic picture, carrying a jug of water.

Perhaps it was because she was tall, and so her shirt clung to the small of her back like water being poured down a tree trunk. As she moved the shirt was stretched this way and that; instead of falling straight, the flow of the shirt accentuated her bottom and lower back. Her wide trousers were also flowing and her whole body wavered. She looked like a picture that was about to disappear.

Suddenly Master Chang spoke severely: 'Stop!'

Cassia had already reached the corridor. At his command she froze and hesitated. But she didn't look back.

'Wait!' Master Chang said.

Cassia, feeling helpless, lowered her head to stare at her shoes. Then she half-turned her face to the pair in the room, and raised her head and chest, her hands grasping the tray, so frightened that she could hardly breathe.

Madame Emerald had already got off the bed and now stood, about to drink from one of the teacups. She also froze, not knowing what was on Master Chang's mind.

'You said she was not fit even to be a servant girl?' Master Chang turned to Madame Emerald and said slowly: 'Then give her to me. What would you charge?'

Madame Emerald was so startled at these words that she nearly dropped the cup. But as someone who was used to the affairs between men and women she knew how irrational a man's desires could be and was ever ready to accommodate them.

She put down the cup and said in a steady voice: 'Master Chang. You've been a hero all your life. But if you are interested in sampling something a little different, be careful to choose wisely. Which other girl here is not better than her? The two other girls you favoured previously have now become very popular indeed. You could have any girl you want in Shanghai, the famous ones or the wild ones. But to seek a girl with unbound feet? You'd be the laughing stock of the Brotherhood.'

But her words trailed off, as she saw that Chang Lixiong was not listening to her at all, but had set his eyes on Cassia's nipples, hidden underneath her shirt. The look on his face was all too plain for her to see.

Flipping her sleeves, Madame Emerald changed tack and pretended to be generous: 'You are the boss around here. You want a servant girl – it couldn't be easier. Just take her.'

Master Chang replied quickly: 'I am serious. You must not eat your own words.'

She didn't believe that Master Chang had not understood the points she was making. It was just that he was pretending not to hear what he did not want to hear. She knew that while most of the time he appeared to be the strong, silent type, once his sharp ears caught a hint of weakness or a discrepancy in a conversation, he was formidable enough to break through any argument and crush his opponents with a single word. He was not a man to be crossed.

Madame Emerald's face reddened. She walked up to Cassia and studied the girl carefully. Then she moved over to Chang Lixiong, about to say something, but stopped. Finally, still smiling she said: 'Master Chang. If it pleases you, then take her home. One more servant girl to wait on one of your many wives. But don't say I haven't warned you that this girl is thick and clumsy; she might break your fine china.'

Chang Lixiong sat by the bed and put his shoes on. Then he cleared his throat. Madame Emerald stopped immediately. Master Chang was the man behind all gambling and prostitution in Shanghai. A brothel such as the Duchess Pavilion was completely dependent on him. However close his relationship was with Madame Emerald, there was no way his authority could be challenged.

'I'm not taking her home, she stays here with you. Get her a room, two maids, pay her the same as you would the other girls. Get her a complete new set of clothes, arrange the room according to her taste.'

He wasn't rude but the words came out hard and fast, without room for compromise; and they were obviously aimed at her. His commanding and severe tone of voice made Madame Emerald feel jumpy. She knew that Master Chang always meant what he said. She was not so angry that she would offend him on account of a mere servant girl. 'All right, whatever Master Chang wants.'

But now Cassia's face was turned, and she looked straight into Chang Lixiong's eyes: 'But I haven't said I am willing.'

Madame Emerald jumped up: now she had the excuse she needed. She moved as if she were about to hit the girl. How could one of her very own servant girls be so shameless?

Chang Lixiong caught her hands, flipped his jacket on, and

walked up to Cassia, talking gently: 'All right, I'm asking now, are you willing...' the voice was slow: '...or unwilling?'

Cassia's face reddened. She raised her head, dropped the tray and ran out. The tray fell on the floor, the sound of crashing not as loud as her own footsteps.

Chang Lixiong laughed uproariously.

Cassia ran through the corridor, down the stairs and straight into the dark passages. She nearly bumped straight into a young man.

But she hardly registered him and dodged out of the way just before their bodies touched. The young man watched her slender back striding away in bewilderment.

~ CHAPTER 3 ~

Madame Emerald sat down and started preparing the pipe for Master Chang. What insolence, she said, a girl that Master Chang had expressed interest in running away like that. She must be punished according to the house rules.

Chang Lixiong replied that he did not wish to force himself on her. There was no fun in that.

Madame Emerald peered at Master Chang curiously and spoke in a long, dragged-out, teasing voice: 'So, Master Chang wants taste and sentiment, in a whorehouse? You want to court her, like a foreigner? How the world changes.'

Chang Lixiong patted her face: 'All these years I've been with you. Have we not enjoyed sentiment or taste?' Madame Emerald's eyes moistened at this admission of intimacy.

He stood up and peered outside the window. Half in explanation, half in accusation, he said that actually he had been so busy lately he wouldn't ordinarily have had time to look at a girl, even if she had been Xishi, the famous beauty herself. It had been Madame Emerald's own introduction of Cassia which had aroused his interest. At this point he noticed his young aide coming up the stairs, and immediately asked Madame Emerald to leave: he needed to borrow this room to discuss something.

Madame Emerald left tactfully, feeling annoyed with herself. Dealing in flesh was what she did daily, to the extent that some newspapers called her the 'general manager of the world's beauties'. Twenty years ago, when she was considered to be Number One amongst Shanghai's four most famous courtesans, she had excelled not just because of her good looks, but also because she could elaborate on the concept of beauty, speaking with authority – what kind of woman might deserve such a title. How she must have over-exaggerated the ugliness of the serving girl to have annoyed Master Chang and caused him to make such an extraordinary demand.

Have I gone mad? She pinched her legs and asked herself if this was a bad dream.

Meanwhile, Master Chang came out to the corridor and greeted his aide, Yu Qiyang: 'Yu, what's been happening? What news do you have?'

The young man was dressed in black, his pigtail was coiled inside his hat and he wore both a gun and a dagger around his waist. He hurried towards Master Chang and bowed.

They strode into the room and closed the door. Only then did Yu speak: 'The Third Master has returned. He has brought Huang Peiyu with him from Japan. Huang says there are too many people in Inn Number 16, so he has moved to a hotel on the Carlton Road in the Foreign Concession.'

Master Chang returned to the table by the bed and said that the concession land was not necessarily safe. The foreigners had many spies. If they wanted to interfere they'd get to you straight away. Or they could ignore the Chinese authorities' extradition demand. It was the Chinese Governor's office that was weak and confused.

Yu was about to speak, but Chang Lixiong gestured for him to stop. What he had just said were merely general words of advice for his trusted aide. He returned to the business in hand: 'What does the Chief Advisor say?'

'The Chief Advisor said that Master Chang's demand – that the Qing Brotherhood submits to the Hong Brotherhood – has long been conveyed; and up until this point Huang Peiyu has said that such a demand could not even be considered. Not even his boss Sun Yat-sen, the Nationalist leader, could command the Qing Brotherhood, let alone him.'

'That sounds understandable enough,' Chang Lixiong agreed.

Yu went on to say that the Chief Advisor had sent him here to report that tonight Huang seemed to have changed his mind. He said that everything was up for negotiation now, pointing out that as long as they continued to get along with each other, the Hong Brotherhood and the Alliance Society were now a single family. And since the Qing Brotherhood obeyed the commands of the Alliance Society, it would in effect be obeying the Hong Brotherhood. Huang Peiyu had always considered himself a member of the Hong Brotherhood; in emergencies, after all, only those who were also in the Hong Brotherhood could be depended upon. He was very grateful to Master Chang for sending someone to escort him all the way from Japan to Shanghai.

'Some decent words at last.' Master Chang rose: 'But mere words. What about the details?'

He walked to the window and spoke as if he were addressing Yu, though in fact he was simply thinking aloud to himself. He knew the revolutionaries wanted to take advantage of the power of the Hong Brotherhood; he knew that they were preparing for an uprising. Finally he said to Yu Qiyang: 'You ask the Chief Advisor to watch Huang Peiyu closely, but to ease off on the negotiations. Let's see who will give in first.'

'Then I'll go to the Chief Advisor?'

'Leave it till tomorrow. Ask him to conduct another session of *Tai Chi* with our opponent.' He patted Yu's shoulders: 'Yu, you're a good man. Sit down and have a drink.'

Yu sat down cautiously: 'Yes, Master Chang.'

Chang Lixiong smiled: 'Why is it that you don't know how to relax?' he said. 'But never mind, perhaps it is a good thing for people such as ourselves always to be alert. You are seventeen years old now: why not get yourself a nice girl in this pavilion of so many beauties?'

Yu was embarrassed and said: 'Master Chang, I'm too young to marry.'

Chang Lixiong studied his aide carefully: with his elegant posture and quick wit, the young man looked more like an official than a man who deals with gangsters. He had indeed done the right thing in first taking him in and sending him to be educated.

'Good, you have a promising future.'

Yu stood up: 'I would never dare to forget what Master Chang has done for me.'

'All right, all right,' Chang Lixiong looked at him in satisfaction: 'Off you go.'

The courtyard did not quieten down until long after midnight. Cassia lay in bed but couldn't sleep. She put on her clothes and pushed the door open gently. In the moonlight, the gold fish in the pond flashed by like mysterious flames. They said that a girl had hung herself underneath that peach tree. Her ghost lingered; even during daylight no one dared to walk underneath the tree. But Madame Emerald forbade the men from cutting it down, saying that there wouldn't be any trees left if they cut one down after every death.

But Cassia felt good here. It was peaceful. She heard a cough and thought she glimpsed a shadow on the building opposite. But when she hid behind the tree and looked again it was gone.

Now she saw Master Chang coming down the stairs. Curiosity pushed her out of the darkness; she stood under a lantern, where she could be seen. Madame Emerald's voice, concerned, rang out from up the stairs: 'Travel safely, Master Chang!'

Two guards accompanied Chang Lixiong, one at the front, the other at the rear. Their carriage had long since arrived and it and the guards were now waiting just outside the door.

Upon the sight of Cassia, Master Chang paused. A few seconds passed by without a word.

Cassia remained motionless as she watched his carriage disappearing into the darkness. Then she became angry and returned to her room to lie down. Burying her face in the pillow she recalled her first day in Shanghai.

They had travelled down from the ferry and ordered a carriage at the Number 16 Inn.

Bodies pressed against each other in the bustling street. Making sure that Madame Emerald could not see her, Cassia jumped off the carriage she was travelling in and began to walk instead, looking around in curiosity. The carriages stopped often and soon Yu himself jumped off one of them.

A group of drunken, noisy Western sailors had just got off the ferry, and stumbled their way through the crowds, heading for the brothels ahead. Madame Emerald had been talking about Master Chang all the way and now Cassia could not contain her curiosity any longer: 'Who is this Master Chang?'

Madame Emerald pointed at the teahouse opposite: 'There!'

Cassia raised her head and stared: Two men were sitting by the window of the teahouse, looking down. 'But which one?', she asked again.

Madame Emerald flipped a stray piece of hair behind her ear: 'What does it matter? Master Chang is Number One in Shanghai. He's got nothing to do with you.'

All this seemed to be like a dream from long ago. Now not only had she 'something to do with him', she was going to be his woman. But this thought did not cheer her up, instead she tossed and turned in bed, weighed down with troubled thoughts.

Now it was early in the morning, and the servants were already busy. As soon as Cassia had washed, Madame Emerald appeared in the serving girls' quarter and issued a cold command: 'Follow me!'

A manservant was sweeping the courtyard, clearing the ground that was piled high with leaves that had blown off the tree. The bamboo brush made a 'shua-shua' sound on the paving slabs. The girls were not yet up and so no one was allowed to talk loudly. Although the sun had risen long ago, one could still hear the birds singing loud and clear.

Cassia was led silently on by Madame Emerald. It would not be hard to go faster than her mistress, but to remain just one step behind her required some effort.

Two clean and tidy-looking women were already waiting by the door as they pushed through it. Though they looked familiar Cassia did not recognise them. The rules of the Duchess Pavilion were such that there should be no close contact between the servant girls and handmaids, who looked after the courtesans.

Madame Emerald pointed at the taller woman, who was around twenty-eight years of age: 'This is Li Yu.' She turned her head slightly aside and glanced at the younger girl: '…and that's Xiu Fang, who is two years older than you. From now on, you two are to look after Miss Cassia.'

'Yes my lady,' Li Yu and Xiu Fang replied in unison.

At last Cassia understood that she had become a 'girl' who would be waited upon. Madame Emerald had done as Master Chang had asked. She felt light-headed; there was a warm glow in her heart.

She studied the room in which they stood. Unlike the other girls, each of whom had a sitting room and a bedroom, this was a studio room, though it appeared to be larger than the others. A screen depicting lotus flowers and birds separated the room into areas for the bed and a sitting room. A set of quilts, cushions and pillows, folded neatly, were placed at the edge of the bed. A winged mirror was hung on the dressing table by the bedside, which was well-equipped with powder, lipstick, rouge and eyebrow pencils. There were even glass chandeliers and a clock. The silk of the curtains shone brightly and their handsome trimmings hung down from the hems.

'You see, this room is much grander than the other girls' rooms,' Madame Emerald turned to Cassia: 'Isn't Muma treating you well?' Referring to herself as 'Muma', she wanted to show her friendliness.

'Thank you, Muma,' Cassia replied hurriedly.

'So don't look so gloomy; aren't you meant to be good at smiling?'

Cassia lowered her eyes and kept quiet. She wondered what price she would have to pay for such obscene luxury, and felt uneasy.

Madame Emerald laughed, ignoring the look on Cassia's face. She turned to Li Yu: 'Go and get the tailor and bring him to Cassia's room. Get him to make her a few sets of dresses. However hard up I am, we have to keep up appearances.' She paused to think: 'I wonder when Master Chang will come and claim what is his. You must be prepared. The tiger might pounce on us at any time, and when he arrives, he'll want his meat.'

The colour drained from Cassia's face. Though she knew Madame Emerald was only trying to tease her, she still felt frightened.

Madame Emerald laughed loudly: 'You know, the women Master Chang has tasted and spat out all became ten times prettier overnight. Fresh and delicious as petals, ha!'

Cassia took off her serving girl's uniform and changed into a dress of soft green and blue. She was transformed. It was as if she had become another person. She herself could hardly believe that the rich and noble-looking lady in the mirror was the same girl who had once cleaned pigsties every day.

When she was in the countryside, she'd often dealt with excrement. The smell would linger all over her body. Even after she came to the Duchess Pavilion she still had to fetch the night pots from the girls' rooms before the cart arrived to collect the night soil. The night pots had to have their lids removed before they were washed inside and out – including the lids – and then they were smoked throughout with incense, but still they smelt. Now some other servant girl had to do the task, not her.

She didn't need to do anything for herself now. The beds were made for her, her hair was done by others. But she felt uneasy and bored. Her hands rested idly, losing their purpose.

Madame Emerald advised her to study embroidery. She considered this and sent Xiu Fang to buy calligraphy equipment: paper, ink and brushes. Before her parents passed away she had received some education, but it had been a long time since she had tried writing properly. She felt nervous.

A week passed and still Master Chang did not appear. Cassia felt restless. Walking up the corridor, she glimpsed Madame Emerald eating melon seeds by herself. As she passed, Madame Emerald turned her head. She gave such a strange smile that Cassia felt even more uncomfortable than she did when her mistress retained her usual icy composure.

Li Yu, who was more than ten years older than Cassia, tried to comfort her: 'You must be patient and wait. Master Chang is the Grand Master of the Hong Brotherhood. He is such a heavyweight figure in Shanghai. Many girls aspire to get close to him but cannot. Master Chang is also a hero, a man worshipped by thousands. You will certainly be elevated above the crowds when you become his woman.'

When Cassia passed her door again, Madame Emerald called out to her: 'Get up early tomorrow. We'll go and pray in the Chenghuang temple. Take Li Yu and Xiu Fang. They can come along with us.'

The next morning the four of them took two carriages to the Chenghuang temple to pray to the Buddha.

Crowds of carriages already filled the stone-flagged road. A pleasing sound could be heard as the girls from the brothels swished their long skirts trimmed with bells.

Nearer to the temple the hot bustling street scene made the area feel like a marketplace. They jumped down from their carriages and continued on foot. Glancing beyond the showmen swallowing swords and standing on the bare bellies of children, Cassia's eyes were drawn to the food stalls that lined the street. The scent of the steamed bread filled with marinated duck could be smelt several streets away, and the stewed river snails made her mouth water.

Just then Cassia saw Yu hurrying towards them. He didn't look as if he'd just been to the temple. She thought immediately that he would know what Chang Lixiong was up to, and strode up to call him: 'Yu!'

But Yu did not hear her, and disappeared into the crowds. She turned, spotted him again and ran to catch up. He was waiting for a carriage.

'Yu…' she started, but could not carry on with what she was about to ask. It seemed that Yu Qiyang was pretending he hadn't heard her.

Her face reddened, she said that she was Cassia from the Duchess Pavilion, why hadn't he been to visit lately?

Finally Yu turned and said coldly: 'Oh, it is you, what a coincidence.' He jumped on the approaching carriage and said that he was in a hurry, before he hurried the driver on and disappeared into the crowds.

Cassia realised that Yu had deliberately ignored her. She felt humiliated and annoyed. She didn't really want to force him to tell her about Master Chang, but she hadn't reckoned that this aide to Master Chang would actually want to avoid her. Standing forlornly in the street, she did not move. Never had she felt so miserable; it was as if she'd plunged into a deep, cold well.

Her handmaid, Li Yu caught up with her: 'So there you are, I was so worried.'

Cassia forced a smile and asked if Madame Emerald had thought she'd run away? Li Yu, sharp-eyed, had caught sight of Yu disappearing around the corner, 'So you've met that child.'

Taking Cassia around the nine-bend bridge at the temple entrance, Li Yu told her all she knew about Yu Qiyang. He had been born to a courtesan in the Duchess Pavilion. No one knew who the father was. His mother lost her good looks in later life and had to leave the Pavilion for lesser institutions. They heard she became so downtrodden that she turned to streetwalking. Eventually they lost track of her. But the child remained in the Pavilion and was looked after by the handmaids who had looked after his mother. As he grew, he began to help out in the Pavilion, fulfilling the role of a 'small turtle' – a boy who ran errands in the house.

Concerned, Cassia asked: 'And his mother never reappeared?'

'She must have passed away long ago. Even before she died she must have been quite hard up and could not come and see him. Ah, no one lives for long in this business!' Li Yu sighed: 'Even in the best scenario – say when a prostitute becomes a wife – she would not dare to mention a child born in such circumstances. I fear the mother had long given up her claim to her child.'

Poor Yu. Like her, he was without a family. Cassia's anger dissipated. It might actually be quite fun to live like him, without being attached to anyone, she thought.

~ CHAPTER 4 ~

Could any night beat this? The sky was such a purplish shade of blue and the air so fresh that even long after one would remember the sensation. It bode well. On the streets and lanes off the Si Malu were numerous teahouses and restaurants, most of them serving the brothels of the area. Most displayed their own distinguishing signs, bearing the name of the establishment, and some also added the enticing-sounding names of their most popular girls, lit with red gleaming lantern shades by the gate. Amidst the colourful lanterns, guests drifted in and out of the gates with familiar ease, laughing and shouting, some in small groups.

The sounds were particularly loud in a building at the centre of the road. It was a restaurant, the large dining room of which was filled with guests. The girls who were there to sing either stood or sat, but all of their attention was focused on a famous courtesan who was in their midst wearing an embroidered green top and red dress which revealed her small bound feet beneath its trim. Playing the stringed *pipa* she sang in a clear voice, with slow and spiralling tones. Her slender fingers plucked at the strings; her soft voice whispered; each note seemed to circle the air at least three times:

'*You care for me – the paper crane who flies low; no threads bind it*
– only the autumn wind propels it.
Moonlight melts the flower, which opens and fades too soon. I beseech
you – let us be drunk tonight.'

As well as pouring the wine and putting the food onto the men's plates, the girls who were there to entertain sought to create the right atmosphere. Leaning intimately against the guests, they had to appear attentive and enchanting. Using their most seductive voices they tried their best to help the men around them shout out the couplets of the drinking song. Under the pretext of being drunk, they'd throw out flirtatious phrases and make the men laugh.

Just as the banquet started to get into full swing, Master Chang, who sat on the seat traditionally occupied by the most important guest, stood up and apologised to the host: he had business to attend to tonight and had to leave a bit early so he asked for forgiveness.

The host got to his feet, trying to detain his guest a little longer, and the fat man next to him stood too: 'You can't go, Master Chang. I've never seen you like this, leaving so early. The girls will be heartbroken without you, won't they?'

The girls shouted in unison: 'Master Chang you can't go, without you the atmosphere would be very different!'

But Chang Lixiong retreated, bowing as he went.

The guests started to whisper among themselves: what could have made Master Chang so anxious to leave?

'I heard that Master Chang's taken a fancy to a virgin?'

Someone asked the Chief Advisor, with his pock-marked face, if he knew anything, but he kept a profound silence. The man persisted: 'It's a new girl who hasn't bloomed yet, right?'

Overhearing him as he was about to depart, Master Chang laughed in agreement.

The guests started cheering: how passionate, how devoted, but what a shame he had to leave...

Master Chang declared that he was willing to drink three cups of rice wine as a penalty, and poured these himself one after another, consuming each of them in turn. Then he turned and left the table.

As he left the room, Yu Qiyang emerged from nowhere to accompany him. The two steered their way through the corridor filled with lanterns, out of the restaurant and into the well-lit street. Yu had to run to catch up with Master Chang, whose steps grew faster and faster, the back of his shirt flying in the wind.

Ever since that morning, when someone had been sent to the Duchess Pavilion with a message concerning Chang Lixiong's visit, Cassia had been in the process of being made up: bathing, changing and having her hair done. Madame Emerald had been surprised. Chang Lixiong loved to arrive unannounced: not just because he disliked fuss, but also because he did not like others to know his whereabouts. This announcement of his arrival was so unexpected that Madame Emerald knew immediately what it meant: he wanted this girl to be well-prepared.

Li Yu, Xiu Fang and Cassia were kept on their tocs. Everywhere – from window to bed, from cabinet to wall – everything was decorated red. Cassia had never worn red before and discovered that the exuberant colour really suited her. It contrasted with her youthful white skin, making it look softer and more tender.

Her lips were moist and red, with no need for balm. But Li Yu carefully made up her eyes and eyebrows, which was the first time Cassia had them done. She kept her eyes shut tight, simply putting up with the process. Yet after Li Yu had finished, she could not quite recognise herself in the mirror. Her eyes especially, shone dark and clear. Her heart was beating wild and fast. She had lost weight over the last few days, and she looked better for it.

Madame Emerald walked in, in high spirits. She glanced around: why had no candles had been lit?

Cassia, who had been sitting on the bed, jumped up to light a candle, but Madame Emerald stopped her, saying this would spoil her embroidered clothes. Xiu Fang heard them and hurried to light the candles herself. Madame Emerald walked past the screen and stared sternly at Cassia: 'Any moment now Master Chang's carriage will arrive and as soon as he does the food will be sent over here. Wait on him well and I'll reward you. But if you are disobedient, you know the rules. Remember who he is: even I have to look up to him!'

Cassia nodded nervously. With a wave of her hands, Madame Emerald left. Cassia sat down and watched the flame of the candles getting stronger, sensing the carriages racing down the big road outside, the hooves of the horses kicking and flying, the speeding carriages and their beasts enshrouded in a mass of bewildering colour. They were approaching Little West Gate; soon they would be in front of the gate of the Pavilion. Trying hard to suppress a scream, she closed her eyes and refused to look at what the others were doing around her.

Suddenly Master Chang was in the same room as her, and the red candles burned vigorously around them. Though Cassia sat on the bed, with its nets drawn all around, Master Chang quickly flipped them up and saw that she was made up elegantly and delicately, almost like a goddess. He could hardly recognise her. He stared at her and she turned her face to avoid his gaze. He leaned over to hold her and she struggled.

'Still unwilling?' he asked.

He passed a bowl of tea to her and she held it in her hands, anticipating a burst of anger. But instead of scolding her, he reached to fetch a cup for himself and drank from it. She stared at the cup in her hands, not knowing what to do next. Timidly, she said: 'I should be punished.'

'Why? What have you done wrong? You were merely born free, with a rebellious spirit,' he smiled. 'But today, you are just afraid, aren't you?'

Cassia nodded, but still she would not look up at him.

'Then we'll wait a bit more,' he said and returned to the bed.

Cassia drank her tea, feeling strange. She tiptoed back to the bed and found that Master Chang was already snoring. She flipped up the nets and gazed at his calm face. This was a man of his word. She went to blow out the candles, then sat by the bed and thought for a while. Finally she took off her shoes and climbed up to the bed, lying down next to him.

She turned to face the man, her body getting slowly closer to him, until eventually, mustering up all her courage, she put a hand on his shoulders.

The clock ticked relentlessly. Many nights passed. One night Cassia felt thirsty and climbed off the bed, put her slippers on and carefully rearranged the nets around the bed.

Going down to the kitchen, she glimpsed the moon hanging at an angle in the sky like a sickle. Near and far, everything was quiet. Though occasionally a carriage trotted by, it was as if such sounds were from another street.

Cassia carried the tea set up the stairs, each step bringing her shadow higher up the wall. Her hair flowed freely on her shoulders. It was perhaps around daybreak by now, and though many windows in the courtyard still had lights in them, the doors and windows were all tightly shut. The wine might have all been drunk; those who needed to return home might have left; but the night had no plan to draw itself to an end just yet.

Soundlessly she slipped inside the room, drank her tea and walked to the bed.

A soft light slipped through the nets and fell on the sleeping body of Master Chang, who snored quietly. Cassia rose and carefully studied his bare chest. She had noticed the tattoos on him before now, smooth as silk. Now she saw them clearly: a phoenix on the left of his chest and a dragon on the right. With the green and blue colours of the tattoos mingled together, the paws of the phoenix and the scales of the dragon made a beautiful pattern and the colour shone. Master Chang had told her that he had endured several months of bleeding to achieve this beautiful effect.

The dragon and phoenix danced slowly as his chest rose and

fell. Cassia smiled to herself and wanted to touch it, to see how deep the tattoo went and whether he was scarred by it. It was only the fear of waking him that prevented her from doing so.

He turned and the long hair that was coiled around his head fell down and covered his left cheek. She extended a hand to flip it away from him. At that moment, he suddenly rose and grabbed her arms, alert; then looked at her once and fell onto his pillow, laughing.

She rubbed her sore wrist and complained: 'You ungrateful man.'

He took her wrist and rubbed it: 'Don't be cross. A man like me has to sleep with half an eye open.'

He took the cup she brought over and rose to drink the tea. When she had finished preparing the opium, he put the cup down and inhaled a mouthful from the pipe, telling her he had many enemies out there, not to mention the government – that she should not approach him without making him aware of her presence.

'Who wants to be near you, anyway?'

She was about to fetch the needle to pierce through the blocked bowl of the pipe, but he put it aside and swept her into his arms: 'Your Madame said you were good for nothing; so why is it that I feel you are the best. You always know what I want. Even on our first night of happiness, you kept quiet. With any other girl, the fear would make them fussy and nervous.'

His words made her blush and she turned away from him and said that she had been afraid too, and that she did not know then that she would bleed.

He patted her cheek and said that she'd gasped only a little, and that too had made him look at her anew. Besides, before that day he'd hardly had time to send any messages to her and though he didn't know how she felt about it, she'd never complained, not even now. It showed that she was a dependable girl.

She thought to herself: this is a clever man, understanding how

I feel and still deliberately testing me. She said what was on her mind: 'It is my good fortune to be waiting on Master Chang; I am only too grateful for it.'

He patted her face again: 'What a sweet mouth you have, and you know how not to cause men trouble. Just as long as you don't feel I am forcing myself on you...'

He rose to drink some more tea. He usually did not want to talk when desire overtook him, as it did now, but he couldn't help himself: he wanted to make this poor little girl happier.

'Let's choose a suitable date and I will marry you,' he said, pleased with himself and drawing her into his arms.

She leaned against him and said that so long as Master Chang could come to visit her daily like this, she wanted nothing more in the world.

He promised that he would be there every day; not only that, he wanted to take her with him wherever he went.

Her finger pointing to his mouth, she said: 'What good am I, a big-footed girl?'

'You have a way of pulling me to you, here...' he pointed at his chest. 'I am thirty years older than you. How strange life is. That day, the moment I set eyes on you I liked you, and now the more I look at you the more I am satisfied. Don't you feel it? Next month, I'll get my advisor to choose a lucky date and then I will marry you, with a team of eight sedan chairs. Let's make the ceremony really grand.'

It was the second time he had mentioned it that night and only now did she believe that he really wanted to marry her. She would not be a proper wife of course, but one of his concubines. Still, he did not treat her like a prostitute.

This was so unexpected: this hero of the Hong Brotherhood actually felt her to be his soul mate. She had heard others talking about his life story, and the more she learned, the more she admired him.

Most of the Shanghai Hong Brotherhood died heroically for

their cause after the failure of the Little Knife Society's anti-Qing uprising in 1855. The surviving members had scattered to other provinces and dared not come back to Shanghai. As a result, the Hong Brotherhood – which had been in existence for nearly three hundred years – had nearly died out. It was Chang Lixiong who had re-established the Brotherhood in Shanghai, risking death and hardship, as well as deflecting several attempts to arrest him. Thanks to his efforts the Hong Brotherhood stood once more on firm ground.

She was extremely pleased with the man and thought nothing of the age difference between them. Perhaps fate had a hand and it was all meant to happen.

That tireless night, amongst the scent of the gentians, she held his hands and looked him in the eyes: 'Master Chang you are so kind to me; my only desire is to serve you for the rest of my life.'

'You are young, but wise. That's our wedding settled then. It's just a matter of time now before you'll be a bride. ' His hands held her shoulders and kept her at a distance, his eyes resting firmly upon her. Now he murmured to himself: 'How could Madame Emerald have got it so wrong?'

She kept her eyes on his for a long time, and then smiled shyly. After a while, she thought of what he'd just said and told him that perhaps it was because she was not good at singing.

'Can you sing anything at all?' he let go of her hands.

'Only the peasant ballad, "Thirteen Sales".'

'Ha! What sort of sales?'

She thought about it and replied hesitantly: 'How about "Water Chestnut?"'

'"Water Chestnut" it is. I am waiting.'

'Now you mustn't laugh, because I can't sing it properly.'

'We are in a bedroom, not a theatre!'

She hit him playfully, then dragged a peach-red silk shirt from beneath him and tossed it over her shoulders. Taking a sip of tea she straightened up and sang with undivided attention:

'The girl was harvesting red water chestnuts from the pond,
When from the bank some boy threw a skirt at her.
Oh, come on boy!
If you want to taste this water chestnut then have it,
But if you want more then forget it.
Long skirt, short skirt, my parents could buy me anything,
But I know if I wear this red skirt
Then I must give myself to you.'

It was a familiar country ballad from the Shanghai suburbs, sung in an accent similar to those of Songjiang, where Chang Lixiong came from. To his ears, the tune was even sweeter, coming out of Cassia's mouth. The long and winding melody of the song touched his heart and gave him pleasure.

Cassia had always loved singing, though in Shanghai it was only when she was washing the dishes or sweeping the floor that she dared to hum to herself. She did not want to make a fool of herself in such an elegant place, where the *pipa* reigned.

But now she saw Master Chang's eyes on her, so intoxicated and so tender, it made her sing with even greater sentiment. She hadn't realised she could make the ballad sound so full of emotion.

The singer and the listener had now both become intoxicated, and forgetting himself, Chang Lixiong picked up her left hand and patted the rhythm out gently in its palm. When she had finished, he sat up and held her tight: 'That sounds even better than the songs I heard when I was a child.'

'Master Chang…' She suddenly stopped.

'What's the matter?'

She couldn't continue, she was blushing too much.

'What's wrong?'

'I want you again,' she whispered. Turning away from him to try and hide her red face, she tried to find an excuse for herself: 'Perhaps it was the song.' But at the same time she started to feel a happy tremor within her body, and a warm flush spread from her face to her neck and then to her chest.

'I want you too, and it was all your singing!' He grasped her against his chest and fell on the pillow, tearing away the red underwear she had just put on: 'You little witch.'

Their bodies swayed in time with the arms of the clock, and however much they tried, they couldn't stop. She had never felt happier in all her life. The previous times when they had made love she had not known how to deal with what she was experiencing and felt only a little happiness. But now she already knew that this happiness belonged to her, and that so long as she wanted the man in front of her, this joy would carry her with it.

She felt as if she was riding a galloping horse; her whole body was shaking, producing spasms of pleasure. The horse galloped faster and she was taken up onto it by Master Chang. Now the horse raced over the bed, across the wall and over river after river, and then up a high hill. Ahead of them was the hilltop and the horse raced all the way up to it, unable to stop.

They both cried out loud and then flew off the horse, now floating in the air and flowing with the wind, up and down. She felt her soul had never been so at ease.

They had no idea when they floated back to earth or when they woke up. A cool breeze blew over them as she opened her eyes and found that she was sweating.

She rose to fetch a hot towel and wipe his face and body. The clock already pointed to three o'clock. He leaned closer in to look at it and then asked, strangely: 'How many times was it that you wanted me tonight?'

She said happily: 'The pleasure made me feel like I was flying.' She looked at him and asked him not to say more or she'd want them to make love again. She buried her face, as she was blushing, inside the pillow and wouldn't look up; she never knew she could feel like this, never knew the relations between men and women could be so good.

'You make me feel so happy that when I climax I wouldn't care if I died!'

He laughed loudly and said he'd never met a girl like her. She knew only too well how to enjoy a physical relationship.

Now she was really nervous. Was she that strange? What should she feel? She looked helplessly at Master Chang.

'It doesn't matter.' He laughed and took the towel and wiped her dry. 'I am different from other men. We are both different from the others. We are the same.'

'But I'm so decadent…are you sure that you still like me?' She said timidly.

'I have slept with many women in my life but none pleased me as you do. I like your personality. I like your singing. I like especially the fact that you want to fly with me as much as possible!' He said happily and patted the pillow: 'Come here, Little Cassia.'

'What is it?'

'Have a good sleep, and in your dreams tell your mother that you have found a nice man who will make you happy all your life, your worries are over.'

As soon as her head hit the pillow she fell into a deep sleep. She had never felt so carefree in all her life. Every day from now on would be as beautiful, and every night would be as lucky as this one. She didn't question why she had been granted such luck, and she didn't have to. So long as she could lean on the strong shoulders of this man, everything would be fine.

There were mirrors engraved on the bedstead and she looked at them as if in a dream. Sometimes she felt as if she could talk to dead relatives through mirrors.

When she was a little girl her mother had taken her to the temple to light the seven-star lamp. The men in the temple had told her mother that her little girl was someone that Buddha would look after: look how wondrously the lamp was lit, they had said, look at the many small sparkles of flowers.

Now, for the first time, she believed that Buddha was indeed looking upon her with kindly eyes.

Before long, the Chief Advisor arrived amidst a haze of soft drizzle, carrying an umbrella made of oiled paper. Standing by the flagstones at the edge of the courtyard, he shut the umbrella and stood it upside down to shake off the raindrops. Only then did he hand it to the housekeeper of the Duchess Pavilion. The Chief Advisor had a lucky appearance, his face wide, his eyes big; he wore a moustache. The pockmarks on his face weren't too prominent. The housekeeper took him in to a small hall at the back and fetched him a pot of Longjing tea. 'Please wait a second and I will go and report to my mistress.'

Madame Emerald arrived after the housekeeper. To avoid the rain she had walked around the courtyard to reach him.

The Chief Advisor said he needed to see Master Chang and had been to his house only to be told that nowadays he hardly ever came home. The Advisor guessed he was here.

Madame Emerald smiled: 'You know, Master Chang is besotted with a big-footed girl and will not rise before the sun is three bamboo sticks high.'

'Chang Lixiong is a lucky man; he makes us all very envious.' The Advisor asked Madame Emerald to go and report his arrival to Master Chang. He had some very urgent business to attend to and could not be delayed.

'But I cannot go and spoil his fun – I have never seen him so taken by a woman!' Madame Emerald readjusted her hair: 'If I go in, he will be annoyed. I'll send in a maid. They are used to such scenes. To be honest, I am quite disturbed by the noises those two have been making.'

The Chief Advisor smoothed his moustache and smiled tactfully. He waved his hands to show that he was not in such a hurry after all, why spoil the fun for Master Chang?

Madame Emerald asked the housekeeper who was waiting

outside to look for Xiu Fang. She invited the Chief Advisor to have some lunch and made tea for him herself. Observing the protocols carefully, the first cup was thrown away and only after she poured the second did she hand it to her guest. Glancing upstairs, she said: 'Now those two lovebirds haven't had any breakfast, nor any lunch: I don't know what they live on!'

The Advisor, who was in fact in a hurry, and whose patience wouldn't last forever, pretended he didn't understand the sullenness in her tone. After a mouthful of tea he couldn't wait any more: 'Don't you think…'

Madame Emerald knew what he was going to say next but kept a deliberate silence.

'You go and look in on him.' The Advisor decided to drop a hint or two: 'And make sure Master Chang is not too exhausted…'

But before he could finish what he was saying, and following the sound of the Chief Advisor's voice to its source, Chang Lixiong himself strode in, buttoning up his jacket. It looked as if he had indeed just been called out of bed.

But he was far from exhausted. In fact he was glowing and had a beaming smile on his face. The half-swallowed words of the Advisor and Madame Emerald didn't escape him. He laughed loudly and pointed at the Advisor: 'I see that though you've wasted half your life travelling around the world, you still don't know much about the relations between men and women! Did you think I'd be weakened?' he glared at Madame Emerald and turned to the Advisor: 'The man named Huang from Japan can't wait any longer, is that right?'

Intimidated, Madame Emerald did not dare glance back at Chang Lixiong. 'You masters discuss your own business,' she said dejectedly as she walked to the door.

'Who else has Master Chang's strength!' the Advisor hurried to say: 'I see that Master Chang was using this affair to make Huang wait. But the brother who we sent to spy on Huang has returned and says that things are starting to fall into place. Looks like there will be movement on their part after all. Huang is eager to meet with Master Chang, and he really does seem to be in a hurry. He said what we had asked for shouldn't be a problem: that he's ready to meet us face to face.'

~ CHAPTER 5 ~

In the Phoenix Hall of the Duchess Pavilion, Chang Lixiong and the Chief Advisor were sitting at the table. The Eighth Master and the three aides were standing behind them. The Third Master, who had also been summoned, entered the hall. Not yet thirty, he looked as tall and strong as Chang Lixiong himself. He was Master Chang's primary assistant whenever violence might be involved. With him were a team of assassins, all carrying daggers and handguns.

'Third Brother, there is no need to resort to arms just yet, let us all observe the rules of the Hong Brotherhood,' said the Chief Advisor. 'Is that understood by all the brothers?'

'We understand!' the aides responded in unison.

With the business discussions concluded, Master Chang walked to the end of the corridor and entered Cassia's room.

She was putting some flowers in her hair and wore a dark green dress. Many more adornments were on the dressing table, and Xiu Fang was helping her to choose amongst them. Bright sunshine filtered through the window. The lotus-and-bird screen had been moved to one side of the room by the wall and the room appeared bigger as a result.

Xiu Fang retreated discreetly, at which point Master Chang pulled out a small black parcel from underneath the mattress and opened it: it was a handgun in a holster. He uncovered the gun and loaded it with bullets, then pulled a dagger out of its leather cover – a dagger of the kind commonly used by the Hong Brothers.

Cassia went up to him. 'Are you afraid?' asked Master Chang.

Cassia shook her head and sat by him.

Master Chang smiled and told her that the dagger was traditionally used by the Grand Master of the Brotherhood for protection as the original Grand Master had started an uprising under the name of the Little Knife Society. He pointed at the handle: 'It is made of green jade. Lean the knife to the light and you will see the words, "Fight the Qing and Revive the Ming," engraved on the blade.' Suddenly he exclaimed: 'Look, the words are starting to shine, a good omen!'

Cassia leaned her head against his, fascinated.

Master Chang studied Cassia, then he nodded to himself. He walked to the door and asked Li Yu to call for Madame Emerald.

A minute or two later, Madame Emerald came over. Li Yu brought tea and a water-pipe, and then withdrew. As Master Chang smoked, he said to Madame Emerald: 'Will you teach Cassia the rules of the Hong Brotherhood, and make sure she learns them as quickly as possible?'

'You've only got one day. By tomorrow evening you two will have to put them to use – all the rules – so you must make sure she learns them by heart.'

Madame Emerald looked puzzled. 'The whole set? Do you think she can remember it all?' She fixed her eyes on Cassia and shook her head in disbelief.

'Muma, don't worry,' Cassia said loudly: 'Whatever Master Chang asks, I will do.'

Daylight had vanished in the twinkling of an eye. It was dusk the next day. As dusk fell, men from the brothels, carrying attractive prostitutes out on their backs hurried amongst the crowds, taking them to their clients. A black car braked in front of the Duchess Pavilion. A middle-aged man wearing a black hat stepped out of the car he had hired. The driver followed instructions and positioned the vehicle to one side of the road. There was no need for the man to check his pocket watch – he knew that he was on time.

There were several men with long gowns in front of the Pavilion, as well as the usual guards in their shirts with rolled-up sleeves. The atmosphere was different from usual. Yu Qiyang, sporting a new hair cut, wore a long gown that had been freshly starched. His face was stiff with nervousness.

Outside the Pavilion's great red gate, the Third Master greeted the middle-aged man. Observing protocol, the middle-aged man had brought no aides with him. The Third Master clasped his hands in front of his chest in greeting: 'Mr Huang, I have been expecting you for a long time, my master invites you in!'

Huang Peiyu nodded, but his eyes did not linger on the Third Master. He stood at the gate and glanced around in confusion. 'Why choose such a place? It's so obviously a brothel, though it calls itself a "Pavilion". The "Duchess Pavilion"!' He nearly burst out laughing as he read the sign.

The Third Master guessed his thoughts and explained carefully. The Advisor had said that, as this place was on the border between the Chinese and foreign zones, it was easy to enter and easy to leave: convenient for all. He hoped Mr Huang would thus excuse their using it as the meeting place.

Huang Peiyu was not inclined to be forgiving and his words were aggressive: 'But what you really thought was that it is a place from which you can make a quick getaway, right? Your master obviously doesn't know where I come from. He's made me wait for days. And from the look of this place it appears that he is not prepared to give me the dignity I merit.'

The Third Master knew that it was not his business to explain, and that perhaps the man would only be so rude to him and would not embarrass his master in a similar way. 'Please Mr Huang', he said, 'my master awaits.'

Huang Peiyu was thirty-six years old and was considered tall among Shanghai men. He wore a leather vest outside his long jacket. His moustache was carefully trimmed. The pigtail which hung from under his hat was obviously fake. He handed his hat to Yu Qiyang as he came towards the door. Without it he looked stylish; here was a man of experience, a man who knows his own mind. He lost his aggressiveness and adopted a gentle tone, with a slight smile. He could have passed as an elegant scholar.

Yu shot Huang Peiyu a glance and the latter immediately understood what it meant. He drew a handgun out from his chest and handed it to Yu, then raised both his hands.

Yu's search was thorough, courteous and swift, though he didn't miss any places that weapons could possibly be hidden. This was the basic training of a security guard. Afterwards he said, with extra humility: 'Mr Huang, I apologise for any offence.'

Now the Advisor strode out from within the building and clasped his hands together in greeting. He accompanied the man up the corridor. At the top of the stairs the Fifth and Eighth Masters greeted them, and together they walked to the Phoenix Hall.

As the sound of footsteps reached the door of the hall, Chang Lixiong remained standing inside with his arms raised and his hands clasped high above him in greeting. A severe and murderous look filled his eyes. He didn't speak, nor did he invite the visitor to sit down.

Huang Peiyu entered the hall and also clasped his hands together in greeting as he did so. The two men's eyes met; each seemed to be testing the inner thoughts of the other. When greeting a stranger, it was the ritual of the Hong Brotherhood to issue threats before politeness. Huang Peiyu, though long aware that he would have a tough time, had not anticipated that the Grand Master would have such a strong presence. He felt slightly intimidated and feared that tonight he would be found out. But no fear showed on his face. Several of the Hong brothers were now behind him; they could have easily crushed the man down onto the floor.

Madame Emerald was standing behind Master Chang, looking severe. Cassia, with her hair in a bun, was wearing no other decoration but a jade bracelet and a dark plain dress. She stood silently behind Madame Emerald.

'What does the guest want?' Master Chang sang out.

Huang Peiyu replied: 'To come and join the cause.'

Huang Peiyu had barely uttered the words when Master Chang asked another question: 'For what reason?'

Huang Peiyu had to reply quickly: 'For the Brotherhood.'

'Who sent you?' Master Chang did not give him a chance to think.

'Fate.'

'A Qing who wants to join the Hong is like a carp who wants to jump the dragon gate,' Master Chang said, almost threateningly.

'I've seen a golden pot filled with flowers, and I cannot imagine the Qing and the Hong being separated.'

Master Chang laughed loudly at Huang's words and the sound filled the hall. Suddenly he stopped, stood up slowly, raised his arms and did something strange. First he put both his hands in front of his chest, palms touching, then the hands parted to the left and right. Then, raising both thumbs, he held the remaining fingers in a fist. Now he threw his left hand behind his head, stretched out his right hand ahead of himself and waved it up and down three times. Then he bent his right leg forward and his left leg backward, once again his right hand waved up and down three times; and now the right hand followed the right leg, both hands withdrew back to the centre, and were pressed against each other over his left shoulder, before finally coming to rest back in their original position. His steps and gestures were smooth and gentle; they demonstrated that here was a man of immense meditative and physical power.

Huang Peiyu didn't stir, but raised his hands, his eyes on Master Chang: 'The front arch, with the arrows to the rear; the phoenix has nodded three times. Your Highness is clearly of the "big" generation. If I have offended you, please forgive me!' He turned and peered at the two women behind Master Chang: 'Why are two females present?'

Madame Emerald stretched her hands out in front of her chest, each hand creating the sign known as 'Three-and-a-half sticks of incense'. Her arms crossed in front of her chest, she stepped forward with her right leg placed in front of her left one.

Huang Peiyu smiled: 'I see, you are the Fourth Master, the Golden Phoenix. Sorry for being disrespectful.' He himself held his right hand in a fist stretched ahead, while with his left hand he made the gesture 'three-and-a-half sticks of incense'. He stretched his left arm out, then put it to the left side of his chest. Then he also executed the front arch and back arrow, and the three nods of the phoenix, before he withdrew.

Master Chang laughed again: 'Good, good. The trusted henchman of the Chief Grand Master.' He waved his hand and invited Huang Peiyu to sit down, signalling that the latter had jumped the first few hurdles and could now be treated with politeness.

They sat down, a table between them. Cassia brought over a tray of wine she had prepared earlier and put it on the table. Master Chang took the cups and spread them out in a strange pattern.

Holding the wine jar in her hand, Cassia poured the wine each time Master Chang arranged a cup. The two worked well together. Now all the cups were filled and the fragrance of the rice wine filled the room. There on the table was the 'Seven Star

Sword Formation', one of the thirty-six formations by which one could identify members of the Hong Brotherhood.

Huang Peiyu watched with no expression on his face. When Cassia had put the jar back on the tray he stretched out a hand and moved the two lower and outer cups to the middle.

He picked up the first cup and drank its contents, then, taking his time, he took the second cup and offered it to Master Chang.

There was no hesitation from Huang Peiyu and Master Chang's face relaxed. He took the cup, drank its contents, then placed it back down. He seemed to be greatly interested in seeing whether this overseas Hong Brotherhood member was able to practice the hundred-year-old protocols of the Brotherhood. He rearranged the wine cups with a smile and watched. Cassia filled up the two empty cups as Master Chang changed the position of the two full ones.

This was an extended version of the 'Seven-Star Sword

Formation', an even more complicated arrangement peculiar to the Brotherhood. Only long term initiates into the Brotherhood could remember these extended versions of the secret formations.

Everyone in the room stared at Huang Peiyu and he knew this was the last test he had to pass. The Hong Brotherhood's motto had always been, 'Fight the Qing and Revive the Ming'; those within the alliance were allowed to deny to outsiders that they were members at all, while infiltration by outsiders was absolutely forbidden. Stringent procedures were carried out so as to prevent infiltration of the organization. In contrast, the Qing Brotherhood never wanted to fight the establishment and did its best to expand. To outsiders it did the opposite of the Hong Brotherhood: it permitted them to involve themselves in the organisation and its members were obliged not to hide their identity.

Now Huang Peiyu felt a little hesitant. It seemed to him that he must not touch the two cups on either side, but he couldn't be sure. After all, he had had to learn these customs in a very short time. But by now there was no time for hesitation; he would have to take a gamble. All eyes were on his hands, they felt like tigers' eyes. In the few seconds in which he hesitated, Cassia could sense that a murderous look had passed over Master Chang's face.

Huang Peiyu felt the intensity of the eyes gazing upon him. His feet trembling, he was about to move the cup at the very end when out of the corner of his eye he caught sight of Cassia. Her eyelids flickered once and, in the same instant, he realised that he had made a mistake. He moved his hand to reach for the second cup from the end. He drank the wine and calmly moved his hand to the cup in the middle, raising it in offering to Master Chang.

Master Chang accepted the cup and smiled happily: 'Wonderful! Very good.'

Huang Peiyu took a deep breath. Cassia glanced at the sky outside. It was fast becoming dark and gloomy. It seemed soft rain was falling. Her left eyelid twitched once.

No longer suspicious of Huang Peiyu's status in the Hong

Brotherhood, Master Chang was now full of smiles, though his words were still coded: 'One hill can only house one tiger.'

Huang Peiyu said: 'Man is just a breath of air, and Buddha a stick of incense.'

Master Chang spoke fast: 'Ninety-nine is an important number, but never add one more.'

Huang Peiyu raised his hands as if to summarise: 'Anything could happen, but never doubt the visitor.'

Now Master Chang laughed, and everyone in the room could relax and breathe easily once more. Master Chang asked Huang Peiyu whether it was true that Sun Yat-sen was really a leader of the Hong Brotherhood.

Huang Peiyu leaned his body slightly forward and said that Sun Yat-sen was indeed a leader – someone who had leapt to the position of Fifth Master in the Zhigong Hall branch. He admired Master Chang and had specially sent Huang Peiyu over to greet him. The Hong Brotherhood had been around for 350 years and this was the moment to realise its goal, which, through blood and sweat, had never wavered. All patriots throughout China were depending on Master Chang to raise his hand, to lead them in their endeavour.

In response to these high expectations, Master Chang merely uttered an 'Ah...' He didn't take Huang Peiyu at his word. With determination Huang Peiyu rolled up his sleeves and bared his wrist. He turned his eyes to Madame Emerald: 'May I borrow one thing?'

Madame Emerald glanced at Master Chang and when he had nodded she drew from her sleeves a shining knife, handing it to Huang Peiyu. The latter put the knife down and took the lid of the wine jar off, then picked up the knife again and made a swift cut across his own arms. He let the blood drop on the two wine cups below, and then flipped his long sleeves over. Inviting Master Chang to pick one of them up, he himself picked up the other and together they both drunk the contents of the cups.

Master Chang stood up excitedly and waved his hands at the men outside, all leading figures of the Hong Brotherhood. They all crowded in. Master Chang told the men that Huang Peiyu was now a close confidant of his and that all who believed in the doctrines of the Hong Brotherhood were brothers. As soon as these words were said, everyone bowed to Huang Peiyu.

Master Chang then pointed at the wine glasses on the table and asked all brothers who were present to drink from them. In future they were to treat Mr Huang as if he was one of them. Huang Peiyu said he would do anything for the Brotherhood.

The Chief Advisor and the Third Master were asked by Master Chang to stay behind to discuss business with him and Huang Peiyu. The others went downstairs tactfully to begin the banquet that had been prepared for them.

That night was no different from any other night, except for one thing: Master Chang never once looked at Cassia. It was at his instruction that she was present. He told Madame Emerald to make sure Cassia was exposed to such occasions. There would be more in the days to come, and he'd need an able person to help him.

So long as the business concerned the Hong Brotherhood, Madame Emerald obeyed Master Chang unconditionally. The Hong Brotherhood included many people from all walks of life and the sources of its income came mainly from protection fees for gambling and prostitution. By appointing his courtesan lover as his Fourth Master, Master Chang had caused quite a stir. But because of the strength of his character, no one dared utter a word of discontent. Madame Emerald was grateful for this and so she taught Cassia the rules patiently. Cassia learned fast and could apply them immediately and with thoroughness. This pleased Madame Emerald who now thought of her as a clever girl. These days they got along easily.

Cassia helped Madame Emerald prepare two tables full of food in the kitchen. The brothers ate in the big hall downstairs, while inside the Phoenix Hall the four leaders sat around one table. Madame Emerald had asked the cook to make a special West Lake Sweet and Sour Fish. For the sake of discretion, all the dishes were brought over by Cassia herself. Madame Emerald helped arrange the table. The two of them looked after the men and made sure they ate well, and at the end they cleared everything away.

Once dinner had been served, Cassia went to the door and Madame Emerald warned her to wait outside and not to allow anybody else in. When the men inside wanted something, she could go and get it for them from the kitchen. If anything else was needed, she should go and fetch Madame Emerald herself from the hall downstairs

Cassia nodded and Madame Emerald took out a handkerchief to wipe the sweat away from her forehead. Cassia took three steps back to make sure the door was shut tightly. The last thing she heard the Chief Advisor say inside was: 'So, Mr Huang, shall we continue?'

It was getting dark and apart from the four people inside the secret room the brothers had finished eating and drinking and had made their way home separately. Master Chang's guards remained. Cassia, who had been waiting in the corridor outside, was so sleepy she could hardly keep her eyes open. She only woke up when the Advisor with the pock-marked face came out, to ask her to bring them some more tea.

As she stepped down the stairs, she saw that Yu was sitting in the dark beneath them though he pretended not to see her. She knew he was engaged with work and likewise pretended not to see him. Leaving the arched door to her left, she followed a small path and entered the kitchen, guided by the light from the opposite window. Yu Qiyang was a strange man, she felt. Whenever he looked at her, his eyes were cold; he was always over-polite. But once her back was turned, she felt his eyes on her, penetrating her back and making it itch.

A few nights earlier, he had fallen asleep underneath the fruit-heavy peach tree – he was unaware that it was haunted. She had nudged him so that he awoke.

'I am awake.' Yu turned, sat up and explained good-naturedly: 'People like us are only ever half asleep.'

Master Chang had stayed night after night at the Duchess Pavilion with her and she had wondered if Yu might have been unhappy about this, but she could only see deference in his eyes.

Cassia emerged from the kitchen holding a large red wooden tray, on which she carried not only the freshly-made Longjing tea, but also Suzhou-style *dim sum* and sesame buns. After hesitating slightly she went back to the kitchen and when she re-emerged there was an extra plate on the tray. As she walked past the stairs, she whispered to Yu: 'You must be hungry – this is for you.' Not caring whether he was willing to accept it, she pushed the plate of *dim sum* towards him.

It was strange how not so long ago she had disliked him because of the mysterious aloofness he'd shown her. Now that she had become his master's girlfriend, she had started to pity the young boy.

She stepped up the stairs. The courtyard was submerged in darkness. The colourful lamp that usually hung at the door was not lit tonight. She knew no clients would come today; the girls had all been told to go out if they were to entertain. The house lacked its usual atmosphere - the fragrance of wine mingled with hot breath, the singing and whisperings of lovers. Every room was lit with a dark lamp and the atmosphere was mysterious and secretive.

She held the tray in one hand and knocked on the door with the other. After a few seconds she added in a low whisper: 'It's me, Cassia.'

'Enter!' the Chief Advisor replied.

She went in. Huang Peiyu and Chang Lixiong were whispering something but suddenly they stopped. The Third Master and the

Chief Advisor stared at her. She believed she'd knocked, but still the men inside the room were reacting as if some strange creature had barged in. The atmosphere sent cold shivers down her spine. The four of them watched in silence as she put the used teacups into the tray and lay fresh cups of boiling hot tea in front of them, placing the plate of *dim sum* in the middle of the table.

Silently, Cassia bowed and withdrew, holding the tray.

Yu Qiyang walked the Advisor, who needed to leave early, to the gate. 'Yu,' ordered the Chief Advisor, 'when he's ready, drop Master Chang directly at my place; he will be staying with me tonight as we have unfinished business.'

In the courtyard, Madame Emerald leaned over to examine a pot of orchids, already in blossom, against the light that leaked from the room upstairs. Without looking up, she called to Cassia: 'How many trays of tea have they had?'

'This is only the second round,' Cassia replied. It was then that her left eyelid twitched, just as it had when Huang Peiyu was laying out the pattern of cups with Master Chang. Despite herself, she said: 'I heard they say the right eyelid jumps for wealth and the left eye jumps for misfortune. Muma, I fear something bad is about to happen.'

Madame Emerald straightened up and looked the girl directly in the eye. 'Maybe you're right. And as long as you're here it won't be the last unlucky day we'll have either,' she said bitterly.

Cassia didn't understand what she meant. She watched Madame Emerald but couldn't see her face clearly in the dark. However, she could sense that she was worried.

The night deepened and the sparrows withdrew to their nests. Huang Peiyu drew out his pocket watch and said that it was getting late. Now that the bigger picture had been decided upon, he should take his leave. The door opened and Master Chang walked him out: 'Please say to your respected master that our flesh and blood is reserved for those who value it.'

Huang Peiyu also looked solemn: 'This is our chance to revive the Han and destroy the Qing.'

'Here comes Mr Huang's car.' Yu rushed upstairs, looking anxious. He whispered softly to Master Chang: 'There are spies in the street opposite, and at the back door.'

Huang Peiyu looked startled and was about to turn, but Master Chang pulled him in and switched off all the lights in the house. He shot a glance quickly outside the window and swiftly ordered: 'Quick, let's storm out, don't give them the chance to get all of us.' Yu quickly handed Huang Peiyu back his gun.

Cassia stepped into the room and caught Master Chang's sleeves. 'Please be careful!' she said anxiously. But he merely patted her on the shoulder and strode swiftly out into the corridor. Placing one hand on the balustrade he jumped downstairs in a single step and rushed ahead.

The others quickly hurried down, taking the safety catch off their handguns as they did so.

Cassia glanced outside the window in fear. Vague shadows flitted about in the thin night air. A flash of a dark shadow walked up the wall to the roof as if on flat ground. Without a thought she rushed out of the room and down the stairs. Madame Emerald was frozen with fear at the top of the staircase. She knew well enough that now was not the time to panic, but her small feet would not carry her far. In desperation she shouted at her men: 'Hurry, go out and protect Master Chang!'

The night was still and quiet, all the shop doors were shut and the car that brought Huang Peiyu sat parked outside the door with its tyres slashed, the bloodied head of its driver resting on the steering wheel. Bullets flew at them. Master Chang withdrew and, using the doorframe for support, he fired his gun a few times, while barking orders: 'Get my carriage here! Hurry!' Now gunshots could be heard all around them. When he heard the sound of the carriage approaching, Master Chang retreated and commanded the Third Master: 'You protect Mr Huang and leave first, I will cover you.'

'No, I will cover you,' said Third Master.

'This is an emergency. Obey my orders!'

They had now retreated to the carriage that had been driven up to them. Huang Peiyu pushed the driver off and jumped onto the seat. The Third Master and Yu Qiyang jumped onto the carriage steps, shooting all the time as they did so. As Master Chang fired his gun from the back of the carriage, the horse reared, startled by the gunshots. Holding his head in his hands, the terrified driver ran off in the direction of the guns and was shot, falling to the ground with a loud cry.

Huang Peiyu grasped the reins and as he cracked the whip the horse shot out into the midst of the gunfire. Three assassins rushed forwards to try and stop it, but all were shot down as it charged out.

The sudden disappearance of the carriage left Master Chang exposed. He retreated back to the car, but within two seconds all the gunfire was centred on him. He rolled on the ground away from the car and took a bullet in the leg. He crawled his way along the side of the wall, firing back.

The cries of women could be heard in front of the darkened Duchess Pavilion. Master Chang followed the wall, trying to reach the gate. As he rose, a bullet hit the right-hand-side of his chest and he fell to the ground.

Suddenly light emerged from within the Duchess Pavilion. Cassia struggled free of Li Yu and Xiu Fang and rushed out of the gate. She stood in front of the rain of bullets aimed at Master Chang and shouted, 'Stop!'

Her left shoulder was hit and she staggered, but remained standing. 'Everybody's dead: what are you shooting for?'

Slowly the gunfire stopped. It was as if the assassins realised the woman was right. Some dark-shirted men picked up their casualties and disappeared into the lanes that led off the streets around them.

Cassia's face was bloodied; blood also dripped down her clothes.

She turned to squat in front of Master Chang, quickly pulling him to her chest. Madame Emerald rushed out also and shone a lantern on the dying man. He was covered in blood and even more blood flowed like a fountain from his chest. Cassia pressed a hand to it and the hot blood flowed from the gap between her fingers. She tried to calm herself, to stop the tears from falling.

Master Chang looked at her, his mouth open, but no words came out. Breathing was difficult for him now and the hand that held the gun stirred. His eyes were on Cassia and it looked as if he wanted to say something important to her. But he stopped breathing with his eyes still wide open.

'Master Chang!' Cassia cried, as, suddenly dizzy, she collapsed on him and lost consciousness.

In the distance Xiu Fang's voice could be heard: 'Miss, Miss!'

'Quickly – take both of them into the house,' commanded Madame Emerald.

Cassia couldn't speak and couldn't open her eyes, but she could hear the voices around her, though they were growing more and more distant. The last thing she heard was Madame Emerald saying: 'Go and get the Chief Advisor! Bring him here!'

~ CHAPTER 6 ~

Cassia lay in bed, wearing only her underwear. Li Yu had told her that Master Chang's body had been taken back to his family home that very night, and a mourning hall had now been set up. She sent Li Yu and Xiu Fang over with offerings on her behalf.

They returned to say that thanks to Master Chang's housekeeper Lao Wu, her offerings had been accepted. His concubines would probably have kicked them out of the house. Cassia knew that Master Chang had favoured her too much. She was not a concubine, not even a proper courtesan within the Pavilion. She was merely a serving girl who had been sleeping almost daily with Master Chang this last month or so. What did that make her? She pretended that she didn't know the rules; that this was why she had dared to send offerings over.

'Master Chang's house is indeed big. He has three gates altogether. I can't remember how many times we got lost in it. And so many visitors!' Li Yu said.

Cassia pretended she didn't hear. Master Chang had had another 'home'…this was something she couldn't imagine.

Master Chang's first wife was around fifty years old. Clad head to foot in an outfit appropriate for mourning, with a piece of white cloth on her head and her eyes sore and red from crying, she stood erect in front of a coffin draped with fresh flowers. The sandalwood coffin was supposed to be the most expensive in Shanghai. As was customary, the concubines did not emerge.

The Chief Advisor with the pock-marked face and several other leaders of the Hong Brotherhood were helping out around the place, and from time to time top figures of Shanghai society would send servants with offerings; some even sent gold and silver. Huang Peiyu came personally, with an elegiac couplet: 'A hero of his time, his name will never fade away; the fragrance of his legacy will not for a century decay.' The final line was, '...for he had a great vision, that was unfulfilled.'

The members of the Hong Brotherhood knelt on the floor and *kowtowed* to the coffin, then to Master Chang's wife. Then one after another they went to the two side halls. In one room the Chief Advisor and the other senior members were gathered.

Someone whispered in the Advisor's ears that it was the Qing Brotherhood's doing.

This was a matter of great importance, and it was only after he was sure of the facts that the Chief Advisor announced them to the assembled brothers. Though Qing and Hong had never cooperated, it was rare for them to attack each other. It was plain that someone else was behind all this, but they could only know for certain by capturing one or two members of the Qing Brotherhood. The Chief Advisor waved a hand: 'Third and Fifth Brothers, kill a cockerel! Let's make an offering to our elder brother. We will avenge him!'

Xiu Fang and Li Yu quietly discussed their mistress with each other: it did not seem right that she hadn't cried properly, that she simply lay there, neither sleeping, nor awake. Cassia heard them and asked herself the same question: 'Why am I not crying?'

Xiu Fang told her mistress that she must cry properly or she would never rid herself of the pain inside. 'But what I have encountered is not something I can cry about,' Cassia thought. By the evening she had managed to drink some soup.

Early the next morning, a funeral procession headed by a horse-drawn carriage emerged from the French Concession. Streams of people followed behind it. Even those who'd lived for over a hundred years had never seen such a grand ceremony. Everyone who attended wore black tops and black trousers, while white silk was draped over horses, chariots, wreaths and offerings alike.

The long procession consisted only of men, walking in straight lines to a slow march. There was something about this that made it less like a funeral procession and more like the kind of march that might accompany a declaration of war. Huang Peiyu was among those in the march, holding a pole, his face expressionless. A Taoist monk led the company, wielding an unsheathed sword. All the brothers in the brotherhood apart from the Chief Advisor wore shirts, with sharp weapons at their waist. Their faces were solemn.

Xiu Fang secretly followed behind, also wearing black. The autumn rain whipped the flags that were draped across the coffins and the paper money that was thrown in its path, some falling on the sides of the road, some on the nearby river.

Finally the rain stopped, though the sky remained dark. Several of the men who had accompanied the funeral procession returned to the Duchess Pavilion. It was now noon and the Duchess Pavilion was draped with white cloth. All the colourful lanterns had been taken down, and none of the courtesans were working that day.

Cassia attempted to get up but Xiu Fang, just back from the funeral, gently pushed her back onto the bed. She told Cassia that Master Chang was going to be buried in his hometown of Songjiang, having been escorted there by his first wife, his family and his housekeeper.

Cassia told Xiu Fang to go and have a rest. After Xiu Fang had gone, all alone in the house, Cassia put some clothes on and walked to the dressing table to look in the mirror: her face was too pale, her lips colourless. She picked up a comb and pulled it through her long black hair.

Everybody was still being kept busy. In the gunfight, two nights ago, two of the Pavilion guards had been mortally wounded, as well as the coach driver, who died in the early hours. The wound on Cassia's left shoulder had been initially treated by applying Golden Lion Hair ointment with a piece of cloth, which stopped the blood flowing. Only the next morning had the doctor had time for her. The wound was disinfected and medicine applied and a dressing was applied. 'It is lucky the bullets went through you without hurting any bones,' said the doctor, 'but you must not touch cold water and you should rest. Otherwise you will never be able to raise this arm again.'

Imagining Master Chang's body being lifted from place to place and buried somewhere she could never reach, Cassia rose in misery. She stumbled, and had to rest on the dressing table. Li Yu came in with a tray and she hurried to help Cassia back to bed.

'Why haven't you eaten for two days?'

'I have no appetite.'

Li Yu forced her to drink some soup made of lotus seeds and preserved eggs, which made her feel better. Soon the sound of a familiar footstep came from the corridor, slowly approaching the room. 'Finally, Muma's come to see me,' Cassia murmured to herself.

Madame Emerald stepped into the room and round the screen to her bed. She wore a white shirt with a white silk band on her head. Compared to the usual elaborate attire that she wore, this looked much smarter. Sitting on the bed, she asked Li Yu to go to the pharmacy and get Cassia some Chinese Angelica and red dates. She said Cassia had bled too much and needed nutrition.

When Li Yu had gone Madame Emerald moved closer to Cassia and explained that she hadn't been able to come and see her earlier because she'd been so busy over the last two days.

Seeing an odd look on her face, Cassia sat up. She said that Madame should have a good rest.

Madame Emerald pulled Cassia's right hand between hers and said that now that Master Chang was gone the two of them had to be honest. Would Cassia forgive her if she was honest for a moment?

Cassia wanted to withdraw her hand but Madame Emerald's grasp was firm.

'He was kind to you, so why shouldn't I be? But it is hard for me to treat you well. On the contrary, it is easy for me to treat you badly.' Madame Emerald had finally said something that had long been on her mind and the look on her face became softer as a result.

Madame Emerald explained that Chang Lixiong had been the person she respected most and depended upon most in her life. She had once offended the 'Number One Courtesan' in Shanghai, Lin Daiyu, who had wanted to compete with her. It was announced that whoever lost this competition must disappear from Shanghai society forever. Though it was meant to be a competition of looks and talent, it was really a competition concerning levels of extravagance. If Lin Daiyu's photo frame was gold plated, then Madame Emerald's would have to be enriched with precious stones. It was thanks to Master Chang that Madame Emerald had won the race and became the Number One of the four greatest courtesans. It was then that she had renamed herself Madame Emerald – the 'New Daiyu' – a name that she had used until this day. After that, she was able to stand upright in Shanghai society and finally take over the Pavilion. Madame Emerald's eyes reddened: 'Now you know that my fate has always been in his hands!'

It was the first time that Cassia had heard Madame Emerald talking about her love affairs and she was reminded of her own heartbreak. Master Chang was gone just like that. How quickly it had happened.

She had always felt her fate in encountering Master Chang had been too good to be true, and had had a sort of premonition that made her never dare to be too happy. Now fate had taken a cruel turn. For the first time fear gripped her. Master Chang was gone; what would happen to her now?

Taking no notice of Cassia's feelings, Madame Emerald walked up to the round table and lit a pipe of tobacco. She peered at Cassia: 'Now, when Master Chang took your virginity, he should have paid me the special fees that are due, as well as paying me for all those nights that he enjoyed your company over the last month. Because of his status this should have added up to at least 10,000 taels of silver.'

'Muma...' Cassia had heard Master Chang himself say that he'd written a cheque for 10,000 yuan to Madame Emerald, but Cassia did not want to talk about money for fear of creating bad feelings.

Madame Emerald put the pipe down and said that, indeed, Master Chang had written her a cheque; but what Cassia did not know was that about two nights ago Master Chang had said that Huang Peiyu needed money for his work and so Madame Emerald had returned the cheque to Chang, who had in turn given it to Huang Peiyu. Master Chang had said he'd go and fetch it back in a few days – but now that he was gone, there was no proof that the money was hers. Now Madame Emerald herself had ended up losing a lot of money, as well as paying for the two handmaids.

'So Muma means...'

'You know very well what I mean. Now no one in the Chang household wants to know about you and that means I will have to think of what to do with you. I cannot just put you up as if you are Mrs Chang, can I?'

'I understand. But even if I am willing, you know I cannot entertain guests. I cannot sing and I have big feet.'

Madame Emerald spoke stiffly: 'Wait a minute. You mis-understood me. Ever since you came into the Pavilion things have not gone smoothly. It was because he encountered a curse like you that Master Chang died so miserably.'

As long as she had lived, Cassia had never thought of herself in this way. She thought Madame Emerald was trying to blame her for something she hadn't done. It was only many years later that she understood what Madame Emerald had actually meant.

Madame Emerald said: 'I have been blind. I have not been able to see that you do not belong here. Your fate is too hard, so that whenever you are lucky you attract bad fortune as well!'

'Muma, I must pay for myself.' Cassia made an effort to rise and put on her shoes. Searching among her boxes and suitcases, she got all her jewellery out and laid it on the bed.

Madame Emerald teased her, with a jealous tone of voice: 'Well, well, how Master Chang must have cared for you! So much gold and silver. I myself have never had such luck.'

Cassia wrapped the jewellery up in a silk cloth, pretending she hadn't heard the older woman. She was in no mood to exchange petty words with Madame Emerald. Her despair could never be understood by this woman. She said: 'Xiu Fang and Li Yu are also here, they have been working hard to look after me and they deserve my thanks, too.'

Madame Emerald turned and indeed saw Xiu Fang and Li Yu standing beside the screen, one holding a tray, the other some soup bowls. Hearing the two women saying such words of cruelty to each other, they had frozen. Cassia knew that Li Yu and Xiu Fang had been looking after her because they adored Master Chang, and that they admired the courage she had shown when she tried to save him. She knew no words were necessary, but she wanted Madame Emerald to know how she felt.

'Muma, you've taken me out of the countryside, into Shanghai, and now you allow me to rest while I am ill. So I owe you.'

The four women were silent for a second. Downstairs there seemed to be singing, mingled with the sound of a *pipa* – a girl was playing to herself. The sky had suddenly turned a dark red and the rain, which had stopped for an hour or so, suddenly started up again, along with a wild wind. It fell in buckets from the rooftop into the courtyard.

Master Chang was indeed far-sighted. He knew what Cassia's

75

fate would be like when he had gone. Each time he had given her a new piece of jewellery she had wondered why. Now she understood. He had wanted to make sure she had a way out.

Cassia handed the silk-wrapped cloth to Madame Emerald, took the jade bracelet off her left wrist, and placed it on top of the bundle of silk cloth. 'These jewels are not enough to buy your freedom!' Madame Emerald said as she picked up the bundle and left the room.

~ CHAPTER 7 ~

A week later, Master Chang's housekeeper – a thin, smart man – arrived. With him were men carrying two boxes of silks.

All had gone smoothly, the housekeeper had said. Master Chang's Songjiang relatives helped to choose a good spot for his tomb, one with plenty of propitious associations. It had rained lightly on the day of the burial and according to the master who'd been invited to lead the ceremony this was a good omen. The blessed rain came from the East; it showed Master Chang's soul would protect everyone.

'That's good,' Madame Emerald said, as she asked him to sit down.

The housekeeper pointed at the two boxes of silk on the floor. The Pavilion had made very expensive offerings and today, the seventh day after the burial – according to tradition, the day Master Chang's soul finally departed – his first wife had asked him to come over with some silks. She was observing the tradition of sharing the offerings. She asked that Madame Emerald make some new clothes from them.

Madame Emerald presented him with tea personally and said that the first wife was being far too polite; she herself had always benefited from Master Chang's favour and was only grateful to him for this.

Cassia walked past the door and thought that it was not just to bring gifts that the housekeeper had come – he must have some other business in mind.

Very soon her suspicions were justified. Within the next few minutes, the Chief Advisor, the Third Master and other elders all arrived. The door leading to the hall was quickly shut and no one was allowed near it. Very soon, however, the people in the hall dispersed.

Yu Qiyang was among them. He looked thinner and darker. Passing the courtyard he raised his head. Cassia thought he was greeting her and nodded, but then discovered he was merely gazing at the sky. Upstairs Madame Emerald had already changed into a shirt and hurried to the top of the stairs. Outside a sedan chair was waiting.

In the afternoon the Pavilion became busy once more. The housekeeper was entertaining the guests. The plucking of some girl's fingers on the *pipa* seemed to Cassia to be playing on her heart strings. Yet she waited patiently and the lamp reflected in the mirror was forever bright. Unconsciously she was trying to imagine for whom the fingers were playing the instrument.

The housekeeper was busy registering the comings and goings at the Pavilion, singing loudly as he did so: 'Miss Shuangyu is preparing to visit the Apricot Blossom restaurant!', 'Miss Lianzhu is leaving for Lao Zheng Xing restaurant!', 'Master Wang is holding a banquet at the Garden of Abundance; he requests the pleasure of Miss Junyi's presence there!'

Cassia had never managed to make friends with the girls at the Pavilion. After Master Chang had taken her as his woman, they had at once despised her. Yet they also sought to ingratiate themselves to her and feared offending her by saying the wrong thing.

Now that Master Chang had gone, she realised that she had become a figure of controversy. The girls kept their distance. They had hidden underneath their beds during the shoot-out and afterwards had been frightened half to death by the bloodied bodies.

She must have been the oddest character ever seen in a Shanghai brothel. Now all she really cared about was what Madame Emerald made of her. What would she do with her?

Suddenly, Xiu Fang ran into the room, breathless. Cassia asked her to come to the bed. Pressing a hand to her chest, Xiu Fang said that she'd met Madame Emerald at the street corner, her face stern. 'Miss, I'm afraid that something bad is going to happen,' she said.

Cassia flipped up the nets. 'Things are drawing to their natural conclusion. It is time I left.'

'But what will happen to me if you leave?'

Cassia shook her head, thought for a while and said that she could not take her and Li Yu as she was not even sure how to manage on her own. If they stayed here, at least they wouldn't be starving. 'Perhaps one day, when my luck changes, I will need you again.'

There were tears in Xiu Fang's eyes. Sitting on the bed, Cassia said: 'It's all right, Xiu Fang. Worry about tomorrow when it comes.'

She sat by the window, hoping Madame Emerald would appear.

But she grew tired of waiting and went to bed. The room was now frighteningly dark. She opened her eyes wide, waiting for the soft small steps of the woman. However softly Madame Emerald's bound feet could tread, she'd hear them. But soon her eyes became heavy, wanting to close.

Suddenly she understood what everyone was doing. She understood why, since losing her temper the other day, Madame Emerald had completely forgotten to pursue the matter further. Cassia thought she'd seen everything and smelt all the scents, she thought she'd picked up what was going on.

A man stepped out of a dance hall and was stabbed to death as he got into his carriage. He stiffened as the knife passed through his chest. Inside a pharmacy on Si Malu Road, two men had their right arms slashed and their heads cut off – in that order. An opium den was ransacked and the five people inside it all suffocated to death.

Hardly a gunshot was heard. Overnight, the only leaders of the

Qing Brotherhood to escape were the wounded ones.

The only gunshots were inside the French Concession. The residents nearby didn't know what had happened; all they saw were people running in desperation, hotly pursued, both sides throwing knives and shooting as they ran. They had wanted to stick their heads out of the window to get a better view, but were worried about being caught by stray bullets.

The concession police patrol rushed in, shooting to disperse the gangsters, who swiftly disappeared.

The whole of Shanghai was wrapped in an atmosphere of blood and revenge. Cassia dared not sleep. As soon as her eyes were closed, she became jumpy. Around four o'clock in the morning she heard some movement downstairs, hurried to dress, got down from the bed and tiptoed out of the door.

The sky had turned fish-belly white. A cold wind blew. She had descended just two steps when she froze. Yu Qiyang sat on the stairs below her, resting against the railings. Time seemed to have returned to the night Master Chang had been fatally wounded, except for the fact Yu was not staring past her. Instead he watched her, as if he was about to say something important.

Cassia hurried down the stairs and found that he was soaked in blood and dirt. Startled, she huddled closer and studied him. Yu quickly explained that the police were after him. Sweat glistened on his forehead.

Cassia grasped his hand. She was thinking fast about how to hide him when Madame Emerald's voice rang out behind them: 'Yu, you are so naïve. You've come to the wrong place. The first incident in this clash of the Qing and Hong was right in front of the Pavilion. The police will be here any minute. Go, while the day is still young, go and hide in Number Three – hurry!'

Yu could do nothing but look at Cassia for a moment and then rushed out.

But Cassia was faster than him. Already she was by the gate, her head looking out from behind it. There was not a single shadow outside. A cat jumped diagonally onto a stone step opposite the gate, its two eyes staring nervously at them. Only then did Cassia push Yu out.

She turned to see Madame Emerald standing in front of the pot of orchids, murmuring to herself: 'Now, Master Chang, you can finally rest in peace!'

Cassia did not wish to unravel the tangle of revenge into which they had been drawn. The only thing that mattered to her was the fact that now, at last, Master Chang's soul could leave.

Cassia leaned with her back against the gate. Master Chang had indeed gone and she so wanted to go with him. She pressed her face to the gate, her hands clasping the handle, wanting to hang on to the warmth left by the hands of the departed.

The sound of horses' hooves rang clearly from the street corner. A police patrol rode past the gate.

Cassia recovered from her grief and peeped through the gap in the door. The police didn't stop, so she locked it.

Madame Emerald held out an already-soaked handkerchief, her eyes red from crying so much. She sighed a deep sigh and waved the handkerchief in her hands: 'Now the Pavilion has become a place of blood. Go! Be off with all of you! Go!'

Cassia still did not quite understand Madame Emerald's words and her tearful eyes followed the woman closely.

Madame Emerald began to mount the stairs, took two steps and turned, as if she had suddenly understood everything. 'Go. I won't ask you to pay for your freedom. Go back to Pudong, back to the countryside where you came from. Go and marry a peasant and live a peaceful life.'

Cassia didn't reply.

'No wish to go back to the countryside?' Now Madame Emerald felt the girl was being unreasonable. 'Still want to stay in Shanghai? Shanghai is not a place for peasants like you.'

Cassia said that she was no longer the girl that Madame Emerald had first picked up.

'I am only thinking of what is best for you.' Madame Emerald stood at the top of the stairs, looking at the girl by the gate: 'Now I'll have to charge you.'

Cassia walked across the courtyard and stood by the stones at its edge. Words came out of her without her thinking: 'A newspaper reporter found me today, to talk about Master Chang. I thought then that I could talk about the kinds of things that happen between a man and a woman. I held my tongue. But now I understand. If you really want to drive me back to the countryside, then I will have to talk!'

She surprised herself at this. She stared at Madame Emerald, who glared at her viciously. The atmosphere froze.

Several heads were looking through opened windows or peeping from behind curtains. Shuangyu, the Number One girl in the Pavilion, was the boldest spectator. She always loved to watch when another girl was in trouble.

'What are you staring at?' Madame Emerald didn't even glance at the window. Now anger rose quickly within her: 'Shanghai is not the place for a little peasant girl.' She was nearly screaming. Stamping her feet, she shouted: 'Off, off you go!'

Cassia suddenly knelt in front of Madame Emerald: 'If you don't want me here, then sell me to the brothels which do not mind big feet.' Thinking about how she had been pushed into such a pitiful position she felt a sudden sadness and lowered her head, but still her voice did not carry any tone of subservience.

'My virginity was taken by Master Chang; that must have been worth a little silver.'

Madame Emerald was about to hit her, but her hand stopped in mid-air. She was a woman of experience; she'd seen a lot. She knew that she shouldn't overdo things, even where revenge was concerned.

They were interrupted by an urgent knocking at the gate.

A dozen or so concession policemen, led by Chinese assistants, surged in. The sergeant claimed he was investigating the gangster gunfight of the previous night, as well as the murder that had recently occurred right outside the Pavilion. As Madame Emerald had anticipated, they suspected that the two were connected, but of course had nothing concrete to go on.

In a house with a garden on the west side of the city, the secret meeting place of the Alliance Society, several men were sitting in the garden drinking afternoon tea like Englishmen.

'Mr Huang, someone wants to see you,' a servant came in and made his announcement. Huang Peiyu was one of the group, and seemed to be reporting something to the others.

'Who is it?'

'He says he's the Chief Advisor of the Hong Brotherhood.'

Huang Peiyu stood up immediately and said to the man opposite: 'See, just as I said, he has come to seek me out.'

He followed the servant to the doorway at the front of the building and hurried from there to the gate at the entrance. Opening this outer door himself, he said: 'Well, it is the Chief Advisor himself! What an honour! Welcome! Welcome, please.'

The Chief Advisor looked sullen and forced a smile. Without resorting to formalities, he sat down and immediately stated why he had come. A young brother called Yu Qiyang had today been caught at the border of the concessions. He was running along the river and was discovered wearing bloody clothes. He was reported to a passing police patrol. 'We must ask Mr Huang to help us get over this.'

Huang Peiyu breathed easily and said in a light tone: 'Just a minor aide? What's the rush? If he has murdered someone, even better. Each side must have some fallen heads, which is only fair.'

'Though he was just one of the junior brothers,' the Advisor replied, 'he was Master Chang's loyal aide and he knows too much. If by chance he is extradited to the Chinese government, think of the tortures – I mean, no one can bear them. Several lives depend on him. If we are not careful, the whole of the Hong Brotherhood in Shanghai will be in trouble!'

Seeing that Huang Peiyu was still not convinced, and was behaving as if he were unhappy being interrupted by such trivial matters, the Advisor added, 'When Mr Huang arrived in Shanghai, it was this man who was your contact. It would be a good idea if you were not drawn into this…'

'Now I remember who this boy is.' Huang Peiyu stood up and walked several steps. After a long pause he said: 'This is a bit tricky. Where is the man right now?'

'Imprisoned in a police cell in the concessions.'

Huang Peiyu rested his hand on the advisor's wrist: 'All right, let me try to sort this out. Foreigners are not always clear about what goes on in Shanghai. It so happens I have a business associate who is English. But I have to warn you that the foreigners are greedy and your aide has got blood on his hands.'

'Money is not an issue,' said the Chief Advisor.

Huang Peiyu walked to the table and poured some tea for his visitor. A small crow landed on the window and Huang Peiyu looked up once, poured a small amount of milk and added a spoonful of white sugar. Having stirred it he respectfully handed it to the Advisor. 'Chief Advisor, come, please try some of this foreign tea.'

The Advisor took a mouthful but it was a while before he nodded and praised it.

Several Hong brothers waited outside Tilanqiao Prison. Two guards pushed open the big iron gate and out walked Yu, wearing battered clothes. His face bore a dark wound and a bruise, his hair was messy, and he sported a heavy, matted beard. A carriage was waiting outside, its exterior painted a glossy black. The door of the carriage was open, someone stretched out a hand to pull Yu in, and they embraced.

The Chief Advisor hosted a banquet at the Xin Banqi restaurant to help Yu get over the shock. All those who attended were heads of the Hong Brotherhood, among them Huang Peiyu, the Third Master, the Fifth Master and several others. When Yu re-emerged, he had washed and changed. On the table were rich dishes and vintage wines, and the waiter brought out delicacies such as 'Butterfly Sea Slug' and lobsters.

The Chief Advisor was in high spirits as he introduced the main feature of this restaurant: they cooked their food in sauces made of pork bones, fish bones and chicken bones. The dishes were authentic and perfect for nourishing one who had suffered a knife wound.

'I have long heard of these dishes and today, because of Yu Qiyang, I am able to taste them,' Huang Peiyu said, putting food on Yu's plate. 'Come, try this fish head! Look how thin you've become. Eat, eat more! You suffered in the prison; now we must nourish you.'

Yu knelt down and *kowtowed* to Huang Peiyu: 'My humble life was saved by you, and now I am indebted to you forever.'

Huang Peiyu pulled him up and raised a glass: 'A friend opens a new path while a foe builds a wall to block one's way.'

The Advisor raised his cup: 'Master Chang died, and in avenging him, our brothers from the Hong Brotherhood were not afraid of turning their knives red. You are all heroes!' He turned to Huang Peiyu: 'Thanks to Mr Huang, who gave us his support. Now the Hong Brotherhood has been revived and stands firm.'

The whole table raised their glasses in thanks to Huang Peiyu: 'It is Mr Huang who saved our face in Shanghai.'

When everyone had shared a toast, the Advisor cleared his throat and said seriously that the Hong Brotherhood could not be without a head. Before he died, Master Chang had already said that Mr Huang was of the Hong Brotherhood. It did not matter where one was from originally. Only Mr Huang could hold the fort for the Hong Brotherhood.

This was totally unexpected and the brothers were startled by it. Some lowered their heads in silence, some looked away, but nobody responded.

Huang Peiyu saw the situation and spoke in a loud voice: 'Brothers, Shanghai is the biggest port in China and only a remarkable hero like Master Chang could rule it with conviction. I am much too inferior to accept such a task.'

Still nobody spoke. The Chief Advisor said that unlike the situation inland, there had long been a disregard as to rank in the Shanghai branch of the Hong Brotherhood. Every secret society had to keep up with the times and one should not stick to ageing tradition in selecting the best person to be head.

Still none of the leaders responded. Huang Peiyu persisted in refusing the Advisor's proposal. The Advisor repeated his request until it began to sound as if they were quarrelling and the atmosphere started to get tense.

Finally Huang Peiyu stood up and nodded to everyone. The matter was too important, he said, to be decided in haste. He would like to raise a different subject. The Municipal Council of the foreign concessions was about to establish the post of Chinese Governor, for which he was to run; now he was seeking help from the Hong Brotherhood. 'If I am elected, I will be sure to look after you all. The Hong Brotherhood's base must move into the concessions if we are to stand firm; that is where the real money is. If I fail to be elected, I will retire to my hometown of Tiantai in Zhejiang and withdraw from society. By then the hefty task of being the head of the Hong Brotherhood in Shanghai could naturally be bestowed on someone more able.'

The Chief Advisor likewise stood up and urged earnestly: 'Now Mr Huang is indeed far-sighted. We can only stand firm on our ground from within the concessions! The Hong Brotherhood of Shanghai has long been in decline; only by entering the concessions can it hope to reclaim its former fame.'

Seeing that Huang Peiyu had set himself a hard task, and that they themselves needn't make a decision there and then, the leaders present started to change the subject, signalling as they did so their silent agreement to the pact.

~ CHAPTER 8 ~

It is an eventful autumn six years later. The dynasties have gone, though the Emperor still lives. The Republican revolution has finished, and yet another revolution has started. The new regime has begun, dominated by guns large and small. But the city of Shanghai has changed to such an extent that those who'd been here six years ago would barely know their way around.

As soon as the Qing Dynasty collapsed, the Brotherhoods emerged from the underground. By the end of spring 1913, their strength was greatly increased. In May, Huang Peiyu started to recruit openly from the Lao Shun Teahouse, which was run by the Hong Brotherhood. Though the revolution had been and gone, abandoning as it did many of the practises of the Qing Dynasty, those present still wore long gowns, though now they sported a range of hairstyles: some had cut their hair short, others wore hair that hung to the tips of their ears. No one wore a pigtail, the badge of the Emperor's oppression, any longer.

This was the first time that the Hong Brotherhood had openly recruited in Shanghai. Operations were more relaxed than they had been under the stern gaze of the Qing government. Then they had had to hide behind the state, or at least bribe its officials so that they turned a blind eye. Now the forming of societies was legal, they could do everything out in the open.

Lao Shun Teahouse had a grand hall. Five big candles were lit on the altar table and another row of candles, wrapped in red paper, stood in front of it. Smoke spiralled from the candles and the atmosphere was severe. The hair on the sides of the Chief Advisor's head had turned white. He wore a robe with black flowers on its blue base, with a Mandarin's padded jacket on top, and black shoes. Opening the ceremony, he sang a song of praise.

Huang Peiyu also wore a gown, but his had a pattern made up of the character for 'longevity'. He looked smarter and fitter than he had six years earlier. He sat in an armchair, with the Third and Fifth Master on either side of him, and other leaders around them. Making sure everyone had arrived, the Chief Advisor spoke loudly: 'Now the gate of the Brotherhood is open.'

Those waiting outside the hall surged in carrying red papers. The Advisor sang the song of praise that had been passed down through many generations of the Hong Brotherhood.

'On this lucky day the Hall of the Brotherhood has opened,
Heroes from all over have gathered here.
Though they were born of different mothers,
Now after oath they will all become one family, dearer than brothers.'

The men chorused the last line together: 'Dearer than brothers,' then they *kowtowed* to Huang Peiyu. The Advisor carried on with his singing:

'Let the incense be lit!'

'Kneel!'

'Question!'

Huang Peiyu cleared his throat and shot a fierce glance around the hall as he asked:

'Are you all here voluntarily, or did someone force you to join?'

'We are all here of our own accord,' replied the crowd kneeling in front of him.

'The rules of the Brotherhood are cast iron. If you violate the rules, there will be no mercy, do you understand?'

'We will be bound by the rules and swear to observe them.'

With the ceremony completed, the banqueting began. It was not until midnight, after everything was over, that Huang Peiyu and the Advisor stepped into the brightly-lit hall at the back of

the teahouse. Huang Peiyu liked the environment here at the Lao
Shun Teahouse. It was in a convenient location, near Ni Cheng
Bridge. He used it as a meeting house and place of entertainment
for the Brotherhood, believing it to be a more dignified location
than the brothel favoured by Master Chang.

He had never thought much of Master Chang, if the truth be
told. That kind of hero, with the style of an outlaw, was sure to incur
disaster. The bottom line was, now that he was in politics himself,
he understood that all politics were false, and that politicians were
only using the Brotherhood. Chang Lixiong, on the other hand,
had truly believed in the principle of 'Fight the Qing and Revive
the Ming' – a principle he paid for with his life.

Huang Peiyu took off his robe, revealing a Western shirt, belted
trousers and leather shoes. He picked up the *Da Paotai* cigarettes
on the table and the pretty and coquettish woman who had long
been waiting by him stretched out a hand and offered him the
lighter. He watched the woman's pale white neck in its pearl
necklace, and appeared to be lost in thought. The Advisor sat on
the chair and picked up a cup of tea. Huang Peiyu inhaled a
mouthful, then waved at the woman: 'You – be gone! I need to
talk business.'

The woman left obediently.

'But the Sixth Mistress has only just arrived; why has she left so
soon?' the Third Master came in and asked.

'Women will hinder our business here. The Hong Brotherhood
used to have Golden Phoenix and Silver Phoenix and so forth in
its ranks and that only caused trouble. I don't like having women
here. Master Chang himself cared too much about women.' Huang
Peiyu paused, suddenly remembering that all these men had once
been Chang Lixiong's followers. They were devoted to him now
because there was money to be had, but to criticise Master Chang
in front of them was tantamount to calling them stupid.

So he turned to the Advisor: 'As it is no longer forbidden to
form societies, I fear the Hong Brotherhood will attract men who

are less brave.' He was turning criticism into praise.

The Advisor nodded: 'Indeed, they are all men of business now.'

Huang Peiyu said that times had changed and no one could do anything about it. If in future guns and knives were needed, there was no one they could call on. He feared they must make an effort to attract leaders from the trade unions as well, so that when there were disputes between labourers and capitalists, they had people on both sides who could act as go-betweens.

The Advisor was in complete agreement. Yu stepped in as they were talking. He had changed completely from the young aide of earlier years. In order to escape punishment Huang Peiyu had sent him to Hong Kong to be educated for three years. He wore a Western suit; he looked handsome and smart, very much like a Chinese agent for a foreign business. Now he could speak passable English and dealt specifically with the foreigners in the concessions on behalf of the Hong Brotherhood.

'What did the big-nose say to you?' Huang Peiyu asked.

Yu said: 'The newly appointed chief insisted, as a new official would, on forbidding opium, gambling and prostitution.'

'Forbidding?' Huang Peiyu turned and asked in surprise: 'They never forbade these things in their own country – why on earth come to Shanghai to do so?'

Yu laughed bitterly: 'Yes, he said he wanted to forbid them, and also that if Mr Huang succeeded in putting a stop to opium, gambling and prostitution in the territory, then he would be sure to recommend that you carry on as the Chinese Governor of the Municipal Council.'

'Bastard!' Huang Peiyu rose in anger and stood facing the window, listening to the pitter-patter of the soft rain on the bamboo leaves outside. If he didn't pay attention to this foreign master, he would lose his post. Finding another Chinese governor wouldn't be hard: there were many in Shanghai who envied him.

Whatever the foreigner wanted, he had to at least pretend that he had listened wholeheartedly. Now he envied those politicians; at least they would be able to shout as loud as they wanted, 'Down with the imperialists!'

'All right, if the foreign bastard wants us to play with him, then let's play first, let's forbid prostitution – no, let's make a real sensation here: let's ban singing!' He glanced at the new recruits around the table and said to Yu: 'Make a scene, make a big scene.'

That's it, Cassia thought, that's exactly it: Lujiazui Port. Six years ago, she and Madame Emerald had waited there to board the ferry; she had watched the Shanghai Bund from across the Huangpu River. The world on the other side represented endless dreams and fantasies. That sixteen-year-old girl had the innocence of any other girl of that age – a worthless innocence, like the Shanghai sky in front of her. It wasn't as pure a blue as the fishing village in Chuansha, its chimneys spiralling smoke like a forest, but so what?

The young men and women with her wore peasant's clothes. Shouting at the top of their voices, they competed in their eagerness to talk as they watched the scene on the Bund excitedly. The crowds were getting on the ferries, carrying their luggage, shouting for the children and their mothers, all in chaos. She turned to scold her people: 'Look after your luggage! There are bad people here. Do you think Shanghai is a place where you can simply lie back and enjoy the sights?'

Watching them calm down, her face softened a bit.

For nearly a century now, it had been possible to watch a vast, international display of boats make their way dozens of miles from the mouth of the Huangpu River to Jiangnan Shipping Yard and back. How many other ports in the world could boast such a spectacular view?

Never mind the young girls and boys she had brought over

with her, any newcomer could enjoy the spectacle, for a good two hours, as the boat passed Huangpu, from Wusong Kou to the dock for Inn Number 16. Watching this great exhibition was the utmost enjoyment – this river mouth, this narrow gate through which the world entered China, this spectacular man-made wonder constructed from iron and steel.

The gigantic iron shells of the ships rotted as they were being painted; they were far inferior to a wooden junk with its wooden hull. Shanghai was an artificial invention – a great gathering of all that is man-made.

Arriving in Shanghai, Cassia had been forced to shed the 'naturally darkened skin' of a peasant girl and become a Shanghai woman – an art that involved much reinvention.

Now she must teach the same process to these youngsters, yet not everyone could live and be at ease amongst so much that was unnatural.

She turned to face the river. The sun shone on her face and she raised a hand to shield her eyes, squinting as she did so. At just over twenty years old she had become a beautiful young woman – composed, elegant and tall, with full bosoms and a thin waist. She exuded attraction. Six years ago her beauty had been the gift of youth; now it had matured.

With the Huangpu River to its east, Inn Number 16 was the centre of all water and land transport. To its west was the ruined city wall. In late winter and early spring it was low season for the shipping industry. The ticket sellers from the shipping companies came here to sell tickets in the vegetable market.

'Take the Chaori Wan and you'll get a free tube of toothpaste and a bar of soap!'

'But a ticket for the "Lafuli" comes with a towel and a pair of pillows!'

The vegetable market was nearby. Since early that morning buyers and sellers alike had shouted at the top of their voices, until the whole market was like a cage full of chickens.

Cassia waited patiently for the market to be cleared. Finally everyone was gone, though the smell of rotten vegetables still filled the air. Rubbish littered the floor and fish scales remained stuck to the stalls. Beggars were busy collecting discarded vegetable leaves, their muddy feet stepping on blackened rubbish. This was when her band started to lay out their equipment. Everyday, around this time her nerves stood on end. Each of her team of young apprentices had their own set task: some set up the stage, some beat the gong and some the drum. She stood at the centre.

She dressed like a village woman, though it was easy to see who was the leader of the troupe. She had put lipstick on her pretty lips and some pieces of jewellery hung around her neck. Her appearance attracted many passers-by. The drum was beating and the song they sang was one of the folk songs popular in the countryside of Pudong, known locally as the 'Dongxiang ballads.' The words especially appealed to the passers-by and many laughed out loud, drawing even bigger crowds:

'The watermelon sweet, the lotus root tender, it is summer
the girl and her lover were young.
Inside the bed net they lay next to each other,
doing the things that lovers do.
The girl said:
"We've practised so many kinds of love in one night,
that it feels like we've both fed the silk worms and planted the rice
seedlings."'

In front there was a piece of blue, old-looking cloth, onto which some copper coins had been thrown.

Cassia soon became tired and asked her apprentice to carry on, as she herself leaned behind the stage and glanced up at the sky, looking worried. Dark clouds had gathered here, but the other side of the sky was frighteningly bright. It was as if the sky was lopsided.

Suddenly there was a shower, and thunder, and the scores of people who had gathered as a result of their efforts dispersed. The band hurried to gather their stuff, picking up the few coins the audience had thrown and sheltering beneath the vegetable stalls.

She remained where she was, raindrops the size of beans falling on her head and face. In the time it took for her to glance about, she had become soaked. Spring had just arrived: her wet clothes stuck to her cold skin and she felt miserable. Her apprentices were calling to her, but she seemed not to hear them.

People holding umbrellas hurried past her and peered at this strange woman who did not seem to mind the rain. Some rich women sitting inside a carriage gazed haughtily as they drove past, despising this peasant girl who was not much better than a beggar. No, she had not come back to Shanghai to endure another insult, nor to test her own patience. She was even less inclined to be a street performer. The local Shanghai people called this kind of performance 'knocking on bare earth'. Those who practised it were considered scarcely better than the vagabonds who travelled from street to street with no profession to speak of. She hated having to depend on passers-by for business and struggled to make a living.

She stamped her feet and ran to the vegetable shack, saying to her apprentices inside: 'Let's not sing any more today. When the rain stops, go back to the inn, don't wander around.'

She turned to leave and several of the young girls ran after her: 'Where are you going?'

'To borrow some money. We must get inside a theatre.'

The rain became softer, and in the drizzle she hurried along the road that ran along the city wall. On this day of cold wind and miserable rain, there was hardly anyone around. Two hooligans had set themselves on her tail back at the vegetable market and now they were following her. Getting ahead by taking short cuts they blocked her way.

First, they took the money in her pocket, and then forced her into a corner. She aimed for the eyes of one and he slapped her in the face and tore at her clothes. The other, who had been keeping a look out, now ran back, seeing nobody else was around. She was thrown to the dirty, rain-soaked ground by the two men.

Unable to fight them off, it seemed her only option was to stare at the green moss on the stone wall and let them take advantage of her. But soon they started to fight with each other, each hurrying to undo their trouser belts, while keeping their eyes nervously on the streets around. Taking advantage of their preoccupation, she jumped up and tried to head butt the two of them, knocking one man to the floor.

She ran as fast as she could along the old city wall to the north, her hair loose on her shoulders. One man had given up already, out of breath, but the one who had been knocked to the ground was angry; now he took out a dagger and pursued her.

The city wall was in front of her and there was nowhere else to run or hide. She found herself running into a dead-end street. The man laughed crudely and charged towards her, brandishing the knife.

She stopped and turned back to face him. She screamed, her face like a wolf. The man stared at her and stopped. Perhaps the woman's mad, he thought. They were nearly at the city centre; maybe he did not have much to gain from a screaming woman. He left despondently.

She collapsed on the ground, exhausted, breathing heavily. After a long time she recovered. Feeling the wall with her hands she struggled up and emerged from the lane. The rain had stopped.

Suddenly she recognised the street. There was only one lane between here and The Jade Pavilion. She had unwittingly returned to the last place she had worked. Rainwater gathered and filled the lane.

There was no need to try very hard. In several minutes she was in The Jade Pavilion. Last night's colourful lamp was still alight, a girl's name written on it. She didn't knock but peeped through the gap in the gate. Everything was just as before. The girl standing beside the window in Bedroom 3 on the first floor of the half-Chinese, half-Western *shiku* house, was a stranger. Someone was plucking the strings of a *pipa* inside, singing the Suzhou tunes. Occasionally men's voices could be heard.

The rule of entertainment in the pavilions was clear: first, a tea party; then, the playing of music; then a banquet. Only when these three steps had been achieved satisfactorily could there be any talk of a union. But Cassia was too common a servant girl to be able to achieve any of the three steps.

As she stood there in front of the lanterns the harsh memories returned.

She recalled the pain during the year after Master Chang had died, after she had recovered from her wound, as well as the complications that the doctor discovered on one of his later inspections. Madame Emerald had been kind to her, she supposed. Well, she had kept her from starving, although she was isolated, even from her former handmaids, Li Yu and Xiu Fang, in a cheap room Madame Emerald had hired whilst waiting for all the unexpected problems that had arisen from her liasion with Master Chang to be resolved. At the end, Madame Emerald had been businesslike, reminding Cassia of the truths a girl in her position must accept. Cassia had not taken her advice to return to Chuansha and find a peasant husband. So be it. She was like any other discarded girl, then – like Yu's mother and many, many others before her. As Madame Emerald took away the bundle that contained everything Cassia loved, she said harshly: 'Women's joys – a home, motherhood, are not for unlucky people like you. Accept your fate. And try not to think about what might have been.'

She knelt down to beg Madame Emerald, *kowtowing* to her repeatedly until she bled, but still Madame Emerald stood there, holding the bundle, looking at her coldly. Then she turned away. Cassia fainted. When, after a long while, she came to, she went to look for Madame Emerald but found the door locked from the outside. She beat the door, screaming: 'Give me back what is mine! Give me back what is mine!' But nobody answered. At that moment, it felt as though her life was over.

A day later Madame Emerald completed the arrangements with the Jade Pavilion, whose buyer was the only one Madame Emerald had found who was prepared to overlook Cassia's big feet, because, for some unaccountable reason, she otherwise found her attractive.

Cassia had to sell herself at an even lower rate than before. The tariff of a common prostitute was as little as one yuan for drinking tea with a client, two for drinking wine and three for sleeping with them. Knowing full well that she was not as skilled as the other girls, she had wanted to reduce her fees even further, but the madame disagreed, saying: 'We are not as upmarket here as at the Duchess Pavilion, but we still have our face to save. You cannot break the rules.'

She had to be patient. Finally, when she had found a client, she tried her best to make the man realise that if he was not too fussy he might be rewarded with a very sensuous performance. She had no right at all to be choosy. If she could generate no business she would have no money to hand to her madame; then she really might sink to the bottom and wander the streets, or rent a rotten shed and become the lowest of the prostitutes. She was only a small step away from desolation.

To avoid this fate, it seemed the only option was to leave Shanghai, a thing she would never want to do. It was not that it was hell going back to the village to work in the fields – it would not kill her to do so. It was simply that she had no home to which she could return. Her only way out was to do well here.

There was a new girl at the Jade Pavilion, it was said, who might not look so refined, but who was excellent in bed. Once the news spread, clients began to accumulate; some were regulars at the Jade Pavilion and some were new.

She also learned the special language that prostitutes adopted when drinking with men – a pair of mandarin ducks, a hall filled with red decorations, two sprigs of spring blossoms, five petals of plum blossoms – flowery, decorative symbols and phrases which hinted at true love, success, beauty and other auspicious qualities in life. She took no pleasure from any of the men she encountered in bed. She thought that perhaps one day she would come across someone like Master Chang, but no one came close.

By now her longing for Master Chang had only intensified. Every scene from their lives together, every scattered drop of memory, accumulated and then began to form and reform in her mind, creating a fresh picture. If she ever tried to cut such memories off, they just reformed and returned again, one by one, as if they had a will of their own.

The last look that Master Chang had given her became even more vivid and caused her much heartache. That he had died with his eyes open bothered her very much.

But no matter how bad she felt, she never wanted to tell anyone that she had once been the lover of the Grand Master of the Hong Brotherhood.

She knew that as soon as she announced it her days would be easier, but she couldn't. She would sell her flesh but not her heart. Once when she argued with Madame Emerald she had threatened to do this, but now she understood that however low she sank, the things she held dear in her heart must not be tainted. If they were, her life would be worthless.

Then one day she was called out to entertain. She took a sedan chair to a place called the Qing Yuan Pavilion. Downstairs was a teahouse and upstairs was the brothel. This was a famous haunt of the street prostitutes; why call someone from another part of town?

It turned out that a businessman from north of Suzhou had made a bit of money and wanted to show off. Hearing of her fame, he had called her to join his banquet, along with four prostitutes he had found who slept with foreigners.

According to brothel convention, as a second-grade prostitute, she should not be mingling with common, low-grade prostitutes, but she considered such rules pointless. So long as the businessmen paid the required call-out fee, she pretended she wasn't aware of the protocol and brought her best smile to the banquet. The common prostitutes all had small feet; they could both sing and play instruments, even performing Peking Opera with a good tone.

Seeing all this had made her a little frightened. All she had to rely on was her freshness. Within five years, maybe less, her youth would be gone and she'd lose the food bowl in her hand.

She feared that, when he saw the contrast, the businessman would lose interest in her, so she tried her best to please him, acting as if she'd fallen in love with him. When the banquet was over, the businessman called a carriage to escort her home and when they got back to the Jade Pavilion she offered him fragrant tea and a small glass of heated wine. She changed into a new set of clothes to entertain him.

At last, the businessman asked to stay the night, and the madame took the opportunity to increase her fees. It was agreed that he'd pay thirty yuan a night, and that night, having been looked after well, he also tipped her a ten yuan note – a generous gesture.

The businessman became so attached to Cassia that he stayed for a whole week and wanted to buy her out; but this could only happen after he'd finished doing business in Yang Zhou. He said that he'd come back to fetch her and asked her to wait patiently for him. The madame had received several days' worth of money from Cassia's client and, aware of this higher source of income, came to congratulate her. 'To be a concubine is to enjoy a happy ending,' she said.

Cassia waited for only three days before she had a premonition. It struck her that this had been only a brief affair. He would not be coming back to buy her out. The reason was quite simple: a Yang Zhou businessman, like any other businessman, could not take a woman with such big feet as a concubine, for that would make him lose face.

She waited half a year, and not a single word came from the businessman. Eventually, she gave up. She was not the kind of person to have no plans for the future. This kind of profession could not be pursued for long; it was only a way of wasting one's youth.

The problem was that she had no other skills apart from those that her body could offer. Others could sing, but she had never learned how. Even though she began to study this, she could not reach the standard even of the common street prostitutes.

She understood that the first thing she must do was to buy herself freedom. No matter what her path ahead was, she needed to leave this place first.

Since she had no clients who wanted to buy her and no money of her own, she had to pretend to be ill, of a strange disease which meant that she vomited everything she ate. All day long she pretended she was aching all over. It was like learning to act, and once she started to play the part she became ill in reality. She soon ran up a high temperature and a fever that lasted for days.

The madame of the brothel had to drive her away. By this point, she couldn't move, but still the madame would not let her be. She threw all of Cassia's possessions on the floor and said that she had an infectious disease.

Taking only a few belongings with her, Cassia left the Jade Pavilion. That night she stumbled across the Xinyuan Inn, the cheapest place you could imagine, and asked the innkeeper for a bowl of *congee* to eat. That night she had a temperature again and her clothes, soaked through with sweat, stuck to her skin.

I am about to die and will die so miserably! Her finger desperately clutched at the bedstead. She did not fear death itself, but this fate was worse than a beggar's. This was not what she wanted.

In the second half of the night she slept and dreamt of Master Chang. He held her to his chest and said that he shouldn't have left her behind and made her suffer; that at least he should have married her as he'd promised, so that she could have some sort of reputation. He cried as he said this, and having never seen him cry in real life, she could not control her own tears. Perhaps Master Chang had never had the chance to cry in front of her; perhaps she had never had the opportunity to cry in front of him. Indeed this was the first time since he'd passed away that she had cried. She took off his clothes and found him standing near the water's edge. She pulled him up, and there by the bank the two wet bodies clasped together. She would not let him loosen his grip on her. She called out in the dream, 'I am about to fly again!' This time he took her up, and they flew high over the clouds and higher still, for hundreds and thousands of miles. It was a long time before they landed.

She cried out and awoke, her pillow wet. She had not had such a vivid dream for years. The most she'd dreamt of was Master Chang's face as his shadow faded, like that night when he had flown down the stairs in a single step. It was curious how her fever receded, how now she no longer had a headache. The illness left her.

Old people said that in such a situation, Yin and Yang would clash! To mate with a dead person would give one a terminal illness. So how was it that by mating with Master Chang she had actually been cured? For others it was forbidden, but for her it solved her problem: Master Chang was looking after her from the other world, and, seeing that she was approaching disaster, had saved her by helping her relive their good times.

Now here she was, standing in front of the Jade Pavilion, startled and covered in a cold sweat. The reality of the life that faced her there was more frightening to her than being chased by rapists. She made a decision: however high the price, she had to borrow some money and bring her troupe to an indoor theatre. She was prepared to do anything to become a success in Shanghai.

~ CHAPTER 9 ~

Dangui Number One was the top venue in the concessions, the grandest, most comfortable place of all. Others, such as the Jinxuan Teahouse and the Joy Luck Garden were also well-known and considered to be relatively dignified. All of these theatres put on Peking Opera and featured famous actors.

The Peace Pavilion, also in the bustling city centre, counted as a theatre, though its appearance did not quite match its style. Its gate had nearly collapsed for lack of maintenance. Its rent was relatively cheap compared to the other theatres. The money she'd borrowed from loan sharks was only enough to rent it out for a single month. Still, they were finally going to perform at a theatre and for once they were able to put a sign up at the gate:

'Cassia leads the Ruyi Troupe in the singing of local ballads: "Grinding the Bean Curds", "Beating Brown Sugar" and "Arbida Comes Home".'

People puzzled over the name 'Cassia'. She herself was pleased with it. It had a clear sound to it and looked good when written down.

The inside of the Peace Pavilion was even shabbier than its exterior. The only stage lighting they had was from the footlights at the front of the stage. The seats were long simple wooden benches. But there was one advantage to this theatre: its location at the corner of Zhejiang South Road, where the foreign consulates were situated, not too far from the Old City of Shanghai. So long as Shanghai remained an open port, it would be a place where people from all corners of the country mixed. People from nearby counties entered the city and quickly became so-called 'locals'; there were more 'locals' here than anywhere else.

At around four o'clock every afternoon, crowds gathered in this area. Some were people selling snacks, or performing knife-throwing tricks. There were monkey circuses and fortune-tellers. Some curious passers-by would stop and comment on the big red words, 'Local ballads', having never heard of such a genre. The bolder ones bought tickets, but in all, few came in.

Cassia had already finished putting on her make-up and now waited patiently backstage. She wore the dress of an ordinary woman from a river town: a broad jacket with buttons on the right, on her waist a small apron with many pleats. Two colourful ribbons trailed behind her back and reached halfway down her legs. Underneath the skirt she wore trousers of black cloth and embroidered cloth shoes with rounded toes. Behind the curtain several youngsters were looking out with great anxiety.

'Steady! Look after the props well: they are rented, and must not be damaged,' Cassia told them.

There still weren't many people inside, and the curtain had yet to be drawn. She asked a young girl and a boy to go on stage and sing 'Picking Lotus,' accompanied by the four-stringed *Yueqin*, and the *Bangu*, a small drum, so as to pass the time. Attracted by such alluring singing, those who had entered could not bear to leave:

> 'The sister was picking lotus in the garden; the bold young man threw a brick inside.
> Said the girl: "If it's lotus you are after, young man, I have plenty in my room.
> But if you are after romance, then come at night."'

The teasing of the two pretty young people, and their extreme flirting caused the crowds to laugh non-stop. Even those hurrying past outside were stopped in their tracks.

'A parasol tree grows outside my hall
You climb right up and jump its pink wall.

A bowl and some slippers laid out nice and neat
A moment for you to wash and warm your feet.

Draw back the curtain and lift up my quilt
Together on the pillow we'll go to where we are fulfilled.'

A well-dressed woman, who looked strangely familiar, entered the room and walked straight to the back. Distracted, Cassia did not recognise her immediately. It was only when the woman stepped closer that she saw it was Madame Emerald.

Cassia said abruptly: 'They've given me a month, it's not up yet, they can't have asked for their payment back already, can they?'

Madame Emerald shook her head.

'Then it is Muma who is worried,' Cassia said, annoyed: 'Thirty per cent monthly interest, and an annual interest rate of 3.3 times more. It's a complete swindle. You are worried I won't be able to pay the money back, that this will implicate you as a guarantor? Don't worry, I'll pay it back.'

Already showing signs of ageing, Madame Emerald didn't answer Cassia. Treading carefully with her small feet, she sat down on a wooden chair that leaned against the wall. The chair creaked and she rose, frightened: 'Will it collapse? Good heavens, who is this chair for?'

'People like me! If you are worried, then don't sit on it.'

'But I must sit. After all, I am more slender than you.'

She sat down once again, and the chair only protested once. She lowered her head and checked it. Reassured, she took out her rouge and powder puff and reapplied her make-up, then quickly she put them down and sighed:

'What a world this is! In the Duchess Pavilion we only allowed the soft *Suzhou* strings and woodwind to be played; we had taste. Now look at you. When you can't be a first class courtesan, you become a second rate prostitute, when you fail at being a second rate prostitute, you become a common prostitute, and when you can't even do that you become an actress! Not only will you be unable to pay the money back at the end of the month, but you will have to sell the whole troupe – including yourself – to a brothel to pay back the debt. Even that might not be enough!'

Cassia had no heart to form a reply to such cruel words, because inside she was indeed worried sick. From time to time she would flip the curtain up to see how many people had entered the theatre, though her face remained calm. The whole of the Ruyi Troupe was watching her and, if she showed fear, these youngsters would all be terrified.

Madame Emerald glanced at the boys and girls sitting at the edge of the stage holding *erhu* and small gongs and finally glanced back at Cassia. She shook her head: 'Not convincing at all, even as an actress! "Arbida Comes Home?" How dare you show such unrefined peasant plays here in Shanghai? You should return to your Chuansha countryside and perform it there! Then at least you might make enough to feed yourself.'

Cassia kept her silence. The words were indeed spiteful, but it was exactly the peasants who'd only just left the countryside for Shanghai that she wanted to attract.

'You are being too clever for your own good. All the stories I sang had been handed down for generations; we never made something up just like that. You have indeed taken the wrong path.' Madame Emerald sighed.

'I have no other path to take!' Enraged by Madame Emerald's words, Cassia got more and more worked up. Standing in the narrow, suffocating area backstage, she thought of the nightmarish days she had spent as a second-rate prostitute. The only thing that had been more unbearable were the two days she had spent back in her hometown in Chuansha.

Most of the people returning to her town had been the ones who had done well in business and wanted to show off. Even those who had been working as common maids would come back with gifts. She had been at a loss. Even though no one in the town knew she had become a second-rate prostitute, they certainly knew that she had been a servant girl in a brothel, hardly a respectable job. It was even more humiliating that she had returned having been fired. Still, she had held her head high and walked into the town.

Cassia's father had run a small grocery shop in town. When she was seven her parents had both died a sudden death and the grocery shop had been run by her only uncle ever since,

The town consisted of just one small street. Everything on this stone-paved street was just as it had been when she left it. But as soon as word spread that she was returning, the door of the grocery shop closed.

She knocked and told her aunt that she had not minded being sold to the brothel and that she was only returning to see her old home.

Her aunt was petite, around forty years old, and wore a floral cloth shirt. She opened the door and stood at the threshold. Pushing her husband behind her, she didn't pause or mince her words: 'It is not that we don't want to see you, it is that we dare not receive you! Go back where you came from!' She retreated, slamming the door in Cassia's face.

Cassia knocked again: 'For the sake of my dead mother, auntie, please lend me some money.'

The door opened and her aunt spoke with a sarcastic smile on her face. 'You are indeed shameless. How dare you even mention money when you haven't brought any back?'

Cassia said that she would be sure to return anything she borrowed.

Her auntie studied her and asked: 'How could you return it, with your pallid face. Let's be honest about the whole thing: from now on you are not our niece and we are no longer related.'

Cassia tried to protest: 'No, please, auntie...'

But the door clicked shut. She realised suddenly that she was surrounded by a big crowd. Whether they were old or young, none of them smiled at her. She dragged herself onto the street, staggering, and the crowd followed. The women behind her held their daughters tightly in case she might contaminate them. They whispered among themselves and stared, some spitting at her, some shouting insults along with the rotten vegetables they were throwing.

'Cheap goods!'

'Pauper! Salty radish soaked in dirty water!'

'Shameless rotten cloth that stinks all over!'

At the end of the street were the fields, ploughed by oxen. She was both thirsty and tired, but no one gave her so much as a drop to drink. She ran to the well and two young boys tried to push her in as a prank while she tried to drink from it. Although they were only trying to frighten her, she was caught unawares and nearly landed in the well. She had originally meant to lodge with an old neighbour and rest for the night before setting off again, but now she realised that the humiliation had only just begun. She hated to imagine what might happen if she stayed.

To be so poor was to be nothing but an eyesore, as far as the villagers were concerned. The only thing for her to do was to leave the village and to try and come up with a new plan in a nearby town.

Madame Emerald was shaking her head now. 'Six years ago I told you that you should marry a peasant while you were still young. You would not listen. It was all my fault that I brought you over to Shanghai. As soon as you arrived here, you became a troublemaker – and it was always me who had to sort out your problems – even when it came to throwing away your dirty linen.' Cassia's eyes stung at this injustice. She wanted to say:

'No, it was you who took my life away from me!', but as always, she restrained herself and maintained a smile.

Madame Emerald, unaware of the offence she had caused, carried on. 'Do you think it is any easier being an actress than a prostitute? Anybody who goes into the theatre must have someone to back them up; the more powerful the backer, the more popular the actress. This is something even a three-year-old would know in Shanghai. You have indeed chosen the wrong time to be an actress – you should have done it when Master Chang was still alive.'

This was indeed a good point, Cassia thought. She was a single woman leading a troupe. It was much too hard for her to fight her way in this profession, controlled as it was by the underworld.

After being humiliated in her own hometown, the only place she could call home was the town where Master Chang was buried. Songjiang was a famous, ancient river town and here, after asking several people she finally located his tomb.

The tomb, located on a bamboo-filled hill, was very grand. Lots of water had accumulated on the ground around it. Rocks and mud were piled up outside the tomb, wild grass grew rampant. It seemed his family did not attend to it often. She removed the rocks and mud and released the trapped water, letting it seep down the steep slope. She lit three sticks of incense and knelt in front of the tomb, crying silently.

A warm wind blew, and in the distance someone sang the song, 'Selling Red Water Chestnuts':

> 'Long skirt, short skirt, my parents could buy me anything. But I know
> if I wear this red skirt then I must give myself to you!'

Following the singing to its origin, she came to a teahouse by the river. A banner hung in front of it and from the inside came the sound of happy laughter. The small boat she was on turned a corner and through the open window she could see a big dark room, and there was a white cloth screen hung on one of its walls, with shadow puppets showing the monkey creating chaos in heaven, beating the heavenly soldiers and the fairies alike…

One night, in her desperate days as a second-rate prostitute, she had dreamt of herself singing peasant ballads to Master Chang, but he'd merely smiled and vanished.

Suddenly she understood. 'Hadn't Master Chang told me himself? This type of ballad is good! If others can sing the Peking Opera and the Suzhou Opera, why can't I sing the local ballads? I couldn't have sung this type of thing to my clients; that would not only lower my own status but also humiliate their taste. Madame would have punished me. But if Master Chang liked such songs, then somewhere, someone else in Shanghai must surely like them too, especially those who'd originally come from the nearby towns and countryside.' Cassia made a decision on the spot. She would set up her own kind of show. In her mind, this river town, Master Chang's hometown, had confirmed the idea that the singing of local ballads was a good one.

But it would take too long to raise the money for such a venture. How could she manage to set up such a performing troupe?

She pawned her clothes and her jewellery and got some silver for them. She paid back the rent she owed to the inn in which she lodged. Returning to the Chuansha area where she had been brought up, she picked some nice-looking peasant girls and boys from the towns and villages of the area. She selected youngsters who could sing local ballads, choosing them just as Madame Emerald had chosen her many years earlier. Of one thing she was adamant: only big-footed girls would be chosen.

She paid each family a small fee and promised that, in the future, when the troupe had earned enough money, their wages would be distributed fairly. These were sons and daughters from poor families; people who had sold their own land and now worked as labourers on the lands of rich men; people who had never thought that singing local ballads could be a way out or a way in to such a wonderful place as Shanghai. They were all more than happy to follow Cassia's plan.

'Local ballad' was a name she had thought of for this music. 'Local' was the most appropriate word: a play for the people of Shanghai themselves.

The venture had some success. It is true that the troupe managed fairly quickly to perform inside a theatre, but they were soon deep in debt. To borrow from loan sharks was akin to walking a tightrope with a noose around one's neck. If falling meant death, carrying on seemed like certain death, too. These peasant boys and girls all depended on Cassia to give them a good time in Shanghai; some even relied on her to teach them how to sing. With such high hopes, they were hard working and never tired of practising.

To save money, they moved out of the cheap Xinglong Inn in which they were staying and slept on the stage at the theatre. They often went hungry, and sometimes skipped meals. Sometimes when she went out, they kept a portion of food for Cassia. But when she came back and saw someone else still famished, she pretended that she'd eaten, and gave her share to them.

She did not want to imagine what would happen if nobody wanted to see their play. Sweat began to pour from her forehead.

'What's the matter with you? Not feeling well?!' asked Madame Emerald.

'It's nothing.' Cassia closed her eyes.

'You know what I've always thought. I counted myself as a bold woman; but you, you are even more reckless than me. I cannot help you any longer.'

Cassia could hear that the theatre was getting noisier. She opened her eyes and stepped closer to the curtain, parting it slightly to peer beyond. A lot more people had come in now, and most of the theatre was filled. She felt better immediately. It seemed her plan to attract an audience had worked. In future she might let 'Picking Lotus' be sung a little longer; perhaps she could elaborate more on its plot, thus attracting even more people.

She turned to Madame Emerald, 'Muma, please don't worry, I won't ever let it slip that I once worked at the Duchess Pavilion; I won't spoil your good reputation.'

Madame Emerald shook her head: 'Don't mention the Duchess Pavilion to me now, it has long begun to go downhill.' She stood up and came closer to Cassia. 'Can you show me how the gun wound has healed?'

Cassia looked at Madame Emerald, then took off her jacket and stripped to her underwear, revealing her left shoulder. Here, a simple image of a cassia flower was carved into the skin. Madame Emerald was frightened: 'A tattoo, on a woman?!'

Cassia lowered her head and said, 'What else would you expect me to do? Tell everyone the story of how I got the wound? How many people still remember Master Chang?'

Madame Emerald was saddened and her eyes grew red. 'A lot of water has passed under the bridge since then, that's for sure. Master Chang gave up his life, for what?' She looked closely at Cassia; visibly moved, she said: 'You have never talked about Master Chang, never taken advantage of his name. That is indeed commendable!'

But Madame Emerald had no intention of staying longer; she said she felt unsure about watching the play. As soon as the performance started, she left, as good as her word. Cassia had a peculiar feeling inside. She knew that to an expert in soft Suzhou Opera like Madame Emerald these local ballads were something to be despised, though she could not say this to her face. To her, this kind of entertainment was something cheap that peasants such as Cassia had to indulge in if they were to make a living.

Now the play began: 'Arbida Comes Home.' In it, the mother-in-law of a girl bride forbids her young daughter-in-law from going back home and visiting her own parents. The two argue.

Cassia naturally took the role of the mother-in-law, as she was the oldest in the troupe, and this role was the most important in the play.

The prelude was a verse to the tune 'Wangwang':

'The winter sun is yellow
and the woman from the Li household is thinking of chores.
Her name is Li Jiuguan
and she often goes out to sell pigs.'

The female clown acted by Cassia caused uproarious laughs throughout the theatre, but now, suddenly she felt embarrassed. This verse was indeed coarse, even she knew that. Popularity was what they were after, but still, singing 'selling pigs' in front of audiences made her feel low and common. The play finished and though the audience clapped and clapped, she felt desolate.

She felt even lower than when she was a servant girl.

~ CHAPTER 10 ~

The performance of the Ruyi Troupe was still simple: there was dialogue and singing, which together formed a story. The songs were the same old ballads. The audiences were still made up of peasants from the suburbs and nearby counties. Never forgetting their roots, they came in to listen to the songs they had grown up with. Authenticity was what Cassia could give them. Fortunately for her, the factories and shops were swallowing people daily, enabling more and more 'locals' to become Shanghai citizens.

No other local ballad troupe dared to use female actresses; the female roles were traditionally taken by men and some well-meaning people advised her that she should follow their example. Her answer was that, since she herself was female, there was no other way.

Now that they had set the precedent, many came specifically to watch the Ruyi Troupe's 'mixed sex performance'. For them, there was something tantalising, something sensational about seeing such a thing.

They were still relying on the usury loan, and their income was only enough to pay back the thirty per cent monthly interest. They only just managed to eat and not go bankrupt. They could never repay the capital, let alone make a profit. Cassia considered the matter carefully and decided to take out another high interest loan. They could never find a way out unless they achieved greater success.

After two months, they moved to the Guanyi Theatre, which was relatively well-equipped. They also recruited more staff from the Chuansha and Songjiang areas. They bought more musical instruments and made more sophisticated costumes. But even these small investments caused debtors to come demanding repayment, accusing Cassia of not paying back their rent when she had the money. This nearly made her lose face in front of the troupe. Through hard negotiation, she managed to persuade the debtors that she would make a big profit in the next few months and would then be able to repay them all. The debtors threatened that they would come back at the end of the month; by then, they said, there would be no excuse not to repay the whole sum.

The hard words they threw at her lay heavily on her heart, as heavy as a dead pig's head.

But business prospered in the Guanyi Theatre. After the hot summer the weather was pleasing. At night there were thundery showers, which ceased by the morning. The streets were washed clean; the sky was blue. People were in an exceptionally good mood. They had not had such good weather for a long time. Even those who never went out came to watch the new spectacle they'd heard so much about. Their wives and children were even more fascinated, often humming along to every tune in the show.

Cassia made a trip to Chess Street and Wang Ping Street, looking for journalists from Shenbao and Hubao, hoping that they would write features on her. None of these journalists were very enthusiastic; few even took notice of her. But she wouldn't give up. Handing over free tickets, she beseeched them to go and see her show.

Luckily for her, the Guanyi Theatre was not far from Wang Ping Street. A journalist who wrote a column for the *Saturday*, usually about Peking Opera, had for a long time been finding it hard to find something unusual to write about. Admiring this pretty woman, who had dared to introduce a new play from the countryside, impressed by her courage and with nothing else to do that evening he sauntered over to the theatre.

Perhaps because he had low expectations, he was pleasantly surprised. The singing was tuneful, the performance accomplished.

In some ways it was comparable to other ballad styles breaking into Shanghai, such as the Shaoxing 'Dijia Band' and the Ningbo ballads.

The journalist wrote a piece in which he especially praised Cassia's skills and voice. Half-teasingly he used a Western phrase to describe her in glowing colours as: 'A bright rising star.' After such a report from the hottest Shanghai entertainment journal, other publications dealing with arts and culture followed suit. Journalists surged into the theatre to interview the troupe.

The words of these journalists were conventional enough. In praising Cassia, they used frivolous tones: her appearance would 'shame the moon into disappearing behind the cloud and cause blossoms to close their petals', 'Her charm takes one's breath away!' and so on. But on one thing they all agreed: Cassia's voice was simply the best.

Local plays had prospered in the earlier days of the Republic; they had almost returned to the glorious days before Confucius deleted and edited the *Shijing – The Classic Collection of Early Poetry*.

But most local ballads failed to match the standards of Peking Opera, and their stories were repetitive. Only the local Shanghai Opera dared to go its own path. Their style of ballad, invariably known as 'Flower drum', 'Dongxiang tune' and 'Local Tanhuang' had a most humble origin, and, not content with being the grandson of Peking Opera, preferred to be related to modern plays and even to films. After all, the history of Shanghai was short; it would be strange to hear ancient people talking in Shanghai dialect.

Whatever the circumstances, the fact that Cassia dared to be original and create such a new genre was in itself courageous and commendable!

★★★

Taking a break from the Cassia's remarkable story for a moment, I put one of her old records on the gramophone. The recording quality of the period is indeed regrettable, but you can still get a taste of what the original performance must have been like. The way Cassia mixed sentimentality and gentleness in her heavily accented singing; I doubt any other singer could imitate that.

I can well imagine how many 'new migrants' watched a play such as this. The men thought of their wives; the women, tears in their eyes, would sit by the crackling sound of the radio, listening to Cassia's alluring songs until they could recite them. Those who wanted to catch a glimpse of Cassia would not give up until they had seen all her plays.

But enough! I am sorry to have strayed from my story with this mention of Cassia's alluring songs.

***

A young boy held the paper, another the glue, and within minutes new posters had appeared at the front of the Guanyi Theatre:

'Local star Cassia Xiao leading the Ruyi Troupe
will tonight perform "Grinding the Bean Curd".'

'Grinding the Bean Curd' was a story of a love triangle featuring peasant boys and girls. A good man, a bad man and a silly woman, who naturally could not distinguish between the two until it was too late. Eventually the suffering lovers were united and lived happily ever after. The best part of the play was the scene where bean curd was being ground, with its distinct rhythm, and one of the men and the woman flirted with each other. It became a popular scene.

Cassia sent someone to Madame Emerald to ask her to enquire whether her handmaids Xiu Fang and Li Yu from the old days would like to come and lend a helping hand.

The day after the message was sent, the two women came to her, each holding a bundle of cloth. At first glance they looked exactly as they used to, but on closer examination it was clear that Li Yu had wrinkles around the corner of her eyes. She had become a widow. Xiu Fang, however, had blossomed into a beautiful young woman. Cassia held their hands in hers and all six eyes were moist.

'Are you really willing to be with me?' Cassia asked.

Li Yu said that business at the Duchess Pavilion had declined like the setting sun. Madame Emerald had already decided to wash her hands of it and was looking for a way out. They were grateful Miss Cassia had remembered and trusted them and offered them somewhere else to go. Xiu Fang told Cassia that her own father had passed away half a year ago and now there was no one for her to look after at home. She was determined to live with Cassia and to carry on being her handmaid.

After Li Yu and Xiu Fang arrived, Cassia felt lighter at heart. They were reminders of her time with Master Chang. Now she had someone to consult with when she was in doubt, someone to look after her. At last everything seemed to be starting to go well.

A few days later, the theatre became unusually noisy before the play started. Cassia sensed something was not right and rushed out of her small backstage dressing room. The security guards at the gate told her anxiously that some of the fierce-looking audience members did not look as if they were here to watch a play. They had foul-smelling goods hidden in their pockets.

Cassia became nervous. Lately the papers had been talking about how the Municipal Council of the foreign concessions wanted to ban opium, gambling and prostitution. Such news was often reported, and nobody took it too seriously. One paper had denounced the local ballads which allowed men and women to mix on stage. Other troupes had boys acting the role of women. There were often obscene words in old plays, but so long as men were the players, it didn't matter; these were only plays, after all. But for men and women to be on the stage together, that was something different altogether, that would mean the words were for real – that they were really flirting! Such decadence must be stopped. In order to rescue people from moral corruption, such mixed-sex performances must be banned, otherwise chaos would descend, concluded the article. Ever since the papers had been printing this kind of opinion Cassia had felt that someone might come looking for trouble.

'Miss, drink something,' a calm looking Li Yu said, bringing her a cup of tea. Cassia knew that her trusted maid was trying to boost her spirits. She took the teacup and had a long drink, feeling calmer. Standing behind the curtain she peered into the theatre, trying to decide what to do. She glimpsed a man in the back row in dark glasses and a Western-style suit. Something about him looked familiar. She thought for a second, and called Li Yu over, exchanging a few words with her before she turned to the guard: 'Go and invite that gentleman in dark glasses backstage.'

The guard had only gone two steps when Cassia called out again: 'And if he is not willing to come, say it's an invitation from an old acquaintance from the Duchess Pavilion.'

The theatre was not big and it took the guard no time at all to reach the back row and bow respectfully to the gentleman.

'My boss invites the gentleman for a meeting backstage,' he said.

The man was aloof; not only did he refuse to come, but in a bad-tempered voice, he said: 'Go away! Don't trouble me!'

The guard then told him what Cassia had added; now the man was surprised. He thought about it and then stood up and followed the guard backstage.

Cassia put down the corner of the curtain and turned and clasped her hands happily. She walked several steps, and then stood still, waiting. When the man stepped in, she grinned: 'Yu, where have you been all these years? Are you doing so well that you don't recognise me?'

Yu Qiyang took off his glasses and asked hesitantly: 'But aren't you Cassia?' He glanced once again at the simple backstage area. 'You – aren't you the actress who sings the local ballads?'

'Yes, don't I look like it?'

Cassia took off the peasant's headscarf she used as a prop.

Yu Qiyang slapped his head as if he suddenly recognised her. He looked at Cassia, as if he was only now beginning to remember the old days. 'I'd never imagined you'd look so...' He studied her up and down but couldn't finish the sentence, as if trying to find an appropriate word. It had been a number of years since their last meeting and for a moment he was lost for words.

'But you don't look like "Young Yu" the little aide of old times – you look as if you could decide whether a person lives or dies!' Cassia's voice was especially pleasing. Unlike the Peking Opera actresses of the time, who spoke with thin shrill voices, hers was calm and rhythmic. In her high-heeled shoes, she was nearly as tall as Yu Qiyang himself.

'I'm still a footman for someone, but you...' glancing at Cassia's charming appearance and figure, Yu was tongue-tied: 'It seems you are always destined to be admired by others.'

Cassia smiled and told him to be careful with such innuendos. 'Not everyone who leaves the Duchess Pavilion has to become a common prostitute!'

Yu wrung his hands hastily; he said that that was not what he had meant, definitely not. He just could not imagine that she would turn out to be so beautiful, and her tongue so much sharper.

'So how is it that today you have time to listen to peasant singing? If there's trouble today,' Cassia leaned closer to him and said directly: 'it wouldn't be anything to do with you, would it?'

Hearing incongruous shouts from outside, she kept her eyes directly on Yu. 'Has it really come to this: the servant of the Duchess Pavilion has come out to beat the servant girl of the Duchess Pavilion?'

Yu jumped up and was about to say something when chaos broke out. Someone threw rotten eggs wrapped in black mud, creating a stench that filled the theatre. Someone else shouted: 'Men and women on the same stage! What a disgrace! Call the police!' A wooden bench was thrown onto the stage and knocked down a male musician who hadn't run fast enough. The frightened actors and actresses huddled together in the small backstage area. The audience, scared, rushed to the exit, crying and shouting. A band of men rushed aggressively up to the stage and were about to smash it up.

Yu Qiyang was in a hurry now and didn't have time to explain. Parting the actors and actresses he rushed on to the stage, and then jumped down, shouting all the time, 'Stop, away!'

They were about to smash the musical instruments and the props, but the hooligans stopped at his words, and backed away.

Cassia silently clapped her hands to herself. She finally had an opportunity to pay back the damned thirty per cent monthly interest debts. But whether she could get over this hurdle depended on what happened next.

The theatre was still chaotic, and the curtain was already drawn.

Cassia asked Li Yu to rush to Wang Ping Street and Chess Street and tell the newspapers that there had been an incident at the theatre, that hooligans had smashed the place up and injured people. As soon as they heard there was news, the papers sent journalists along, and Cassia talked to them at length. All plays should be treated equally, she said. Why didn't the police ban You Xianglan's 'Dapiguan – Smashing the Coffin', performed in the Xinxin Theatre? Why not Yao Yuyu's 'Pan Jinlian – The Concubine' in the Xianshi Roof Garden? Why not leave the local ballads alone? Is it because the local ballads were seen as common? The Municipal Council had picked on the ordinary people to bully. How many more plays would they ruin? Did they have a list of them? 'Actually there is no need to smash the theatre,' she told them, 'We'll stop working ourselves.'

The journalists saw a lone but fearless woman, who dared to stand up to a municipal council run by foreigners. She inspired sympathy and admiration. It was a good subject. The next morning all the papers printed articles with added details. Cassia's name was instantly all over the streets of Shanghai. A woman singing local Shanghai ballads had dared to challenge the foreign overlords.

Reading the papers, Cassia knew that although it looked as if she was taking a risk, she was actually creating an opportunity to reconnect with the Hong Brotherhood. She had no connection with the Brotherhood now. The new Hong Brotherhood had no Madame Emerald in it and it would be useless to use her own affair with Master Chang to make contact.

The only possible link was through Yu Qiyang. His appearance yesterday had been a godsend. In times of desperation in her mind she had often run through all her old acquaintances and had occasionally thought of this young aide of Master Chang. But Shanghai was big; where could she have begun to look for him? Even Madame Emerald had not seen Yu Qiyang since his disappearance. Now he had brought men to come and smash up the stage where she performed her play, it seemed he was still acting as a guard for someone else and still serving in the Hong Brotherhood. He could be the link she so desperately needed. She wanted to see how he would treat an old acquaintance.

Recalling their meeting last night, she walked past the place they had stood and suddenly found that her hands were trembling. He was like a dear member of a family she had thought lost, now regained; an older brother. The past had not completely disappeared. She must let anything return that was fated to return.

She had heard that the new chief of the Hong Brotherhood was the elegant-looking Huang Peiyu, the man Chang Lixiong had finally agreed to see, dying as a result. It seemed she was destined to reconnect with this underground world that only ever half revealed itself. The key to the future lay in the question of whether or not she dared to grasp this rope thrown to her in a vast sea.

That night she couldn't sleep; she couldn't stop thinking. Even as the day broke her brain was busy working. She thought of the many things which had puzzled her over the years.

Her heart beat fast, as if she'd drunk some odd herbal medicine. Still, she felt that this time she had struck gold.

Yu Qiyang stepped inside the Huang residence. The lawn was cut short and neat like a carpet, and the dark green trees were trimmed with sharp edges as if shaped by a carpenter. It looked very much like the private villas of the English aristocrats. Yu was popular with the Huang family and as soon as he entered the sitting room, the servant brought him some Longjing tea. The second and third concubines came out to greet him when they heard he'd arrived and warmly enquired about his health.

The Sixth Concubine, Lu Xianglan, made sure her voice was heard before she was visible: 'It's Yu Qiyang. Come, stay and have dinner with Master Huang. Have whatever you like, I'll get them to prepare it.' She dressed like an aristocrat, with her hair smoothed up high on her head. The second and third concubines made their excuses and left the room.

Yu stood up to greet her: 'Thank you, Sixth Mistress. I am sorry I have to decline your kind offer. I am busy tonight.'

Huang Peiyu sent his guests away and came over to meet him. The two of them walked to a meeting room at the end of the corridor. As soon as they sat down, the Sixth Concubine personally brought Yu's tea over, closing the door behind her as she left.

Yu said to Huang Peiyu: 'We wanted to pick a soft persimmon to squash; who'd have thought we'd end up pricking our fingers on a needle. This lead singer of the local peasant ballads, do you know who she was?'

'Who?'

'Cassia, the girl from the Duchess Pavilion!'

Huang Peiyu exclaimed: 'The peasant girl Master Chang consorted with?'

Yu Qiyang nodded. After a few minutes silence he said that she had refused to let the matter rest and had told the newspapers. Today, around lunchtime, she had sent someone around with a message: she wanted Master Huang to apologise to her personally.

'What's it got to do with me?'

'She saw me the other day and she understands where I came from.'

'This is a very bold actress!'

'But I don't think she really wanted your apology,' Yu added. 'She deliberately exaggerated the affair to create a stir. I think she is trying to make a bargain with you.'

Huang Peiyu's eyebrows shot up with surprise. Has this actress gone mad? If he so desired, with just a click of his fingers she'd disappear out of Shanghai without a trace.

But Yu said: 'I also think she was deliberately protecting us. She said so much to the newspapers, but she never once mentioned your name, nor the fact that I brought all those people there.'

Huang Peiyu thought for a second and spoke with a pleasant countenance: 'All right, a good man does not fight women. I will go and apologise to her. I want to see how a common actress dares to talk the way she did. I want to see what she is made of.' He rubbed his hands.

'She merely said she wanted to reason with the Municipal Council; she was adamant that it was the council that created the disturbances.' Yu added: 'It seems she is a very reasonable woman.'

Huang Peiyu listened with interest. 'Good, good. You go and find her a few more newspapers to talk to! Ask her to make a scene for us.' He thought about it and said to Yu: 'Once such a scene is created, the big-nosed-bastard will surely get off his high horse. Then we can increase the entertainment management fees we hand to the council by up to 20,000 yuan per month, which will surely make him happy.'

'I applaud the Master's clever plan,' Yu Qiyang said, and inside his heart something clicked: it seemed this Cassia could strike to the heart, in the blink of an eye. He thought of what Chang Lixiong had once said to him, that the Brotherhood offered a passable kind of order, that all the different nations' concession authorities in Shanghai knew that rather than relying on the Chinese government or the local warlords, they should count on the Brotherhood to manage security and order. After this incident, the Municipal Council would be even more convinced of the wisdom of such an approach.

Huang Peiyu turned to walk out, seemingly speaking to himself. 'I've always puzzled as to why such a man as Chang Lixiong would fancy a peasant girl and not care what others thought. How a hero like him could be attracted to her. I want to see for myself.'

A month later, in the sell-out Guanyi Theatre, a new play called 'Complaint of a Divorcee' was being performed. This was the first time a local Shanghai troupe had performed with both Western suits and traditional Chinese *qipao* as costumes. There was singing and dialogue. Before her marriage, the woman had been seduced using drugged drinks; afterwards, the husband had a lover and did not return home at night. The woman sat on a low couch and waited for the man to come home, holding a copy of the classic romantic play, 'Xixiangji: Tales from the Western Chamber.' She sang to the tune known as 'Fan Yinyang':

> *'I am like the root of the herb goldthread, soaked in bitterness,*
> *My only regret is that good looks often lead to misfortune.*
> *It is only natural that the neighbours gossip.*

> *But who'd imagine disaster striking out of nowhere:*
> *he slipped in the drug in order to ruin me.*

I feel as if dry flour had stuck to my wet hands:
how can I get out of this?'

Cassia's voice was slightly husky and melancholic. The tune originated from Jiangnan folk songs, and she sang it smooth like flowing water, giving it a special flavour.

Huang Peiyu sat watching, all the seats around him occupied by his guards. He wore a rimmed hat even inside the theatre, its edge pulled low to avoid his being recognised. He had wanted to come and laugh at the funny accents, at the farce Chang Lixiong had made by favouring a peasant girl. But the actress that he saw on stage charmed him; it was as if he'd never seen such a beautiful woman in all his life.

The plot was a complicated one. The woman, having lost her virginity, was full of regret. Cassia performed her role in such a way that she inspired much sympathy from the audience for the 'fallen' woman. The story had real passion, as well as blood and violence. The final happy scene was a hard-wrought one, and by then everyone in the theatre was in tears.

When the curtain fell, Huang Peiyu was the first to stand up to applaud. Everyone followed suit. When the curtain rose again, the woman who'd swallowed poison to kill herself and had then been revived was standing and called for the other performers to come to the front of the stage to thank the audience. Her fans came on stage, bombarding her with baskets of flowers.

Suddenly, Huang Peiyu looked serious, and raised his hand to hold his hat to his head. Then he waved a hand: 'Leave!' Not waiting for more curtain calls, he led the guards out of the theatre. Cassia glimpsed their disappearance and felt the quick beating of her heart. What was he planning to do?

The next day, after the performance, the neatly dressed Yu Qiyang came towards the stage wearing a Western suit and a hat. Cassia was taking off make-up backstage and asked Li Yu, who had come in with the message:'Do you think Yu's intentions here are for the good or not?"

Li Yu said:'It seems he is now riding high, but I don't think he means you ill.'

'Are you sure?'

Li Yu nodded,'Yesterday when he sat there watching your play, his eyes showed his admiration for you, not like Huang Peiyu, whose face was expressionless.'

'Then let the well-meaning man in.'

Yu didn't utter any pleasantries or polite words, nor did he make any excuse for smashing up the theatre during his last visit. He was acting as a messenger: 'Mr Huang Peiyu invites Miss Cassia Xiao for dinner at the Licha Hotel.'

'Oh.' Cassia turned to look at Yu Qiyang.'Will he apologise?'

His eyes differed from a month ago, when they had first met. Then he had looked pleasantly surprised; now he looked as if he was trying to keep his distance. On his face, at least, there was no expression. Cassia noticed that he was using the same techniques as he had when dealing with her six years ago.

There was an awkward silence, for Yu did not answer Cassia's question. He merely repeated the message: 'The honour of Miss Cassia Xiao's presence is requested; the car is waiting outside the theatre.'

Cassia thought for a minute, and then she said:'All right, dinner then. I need to get ready. Can you wait?'

Yu walked to the dressing table. The room was not big and the baskets of flowers sent by her fans were spread all over it. They had not yet been taken away. He had no place to stand and Cassia had not asked him to sit down. He peered into the mirror and saw that Cassia was wiping away her lipstick, as well as the dark eye shadow and eyebrows she had painted on. The face, with its messed up make-up had no expression; but occasionally her eyes glanced over to study him. Both maintained their silence; the atmosphere was forced and embarrassing. Crossing his arms, Yu said something casually: 'Who could compete with Cassia; even six years ago you were sharper than me.'

She had been waiting for him to talk. 'Sharper? Back then, even if you called me "mistress", I probably wouldn't have responded. It seems the little footman has grown up; he is much grander than before. At least now you dress as if you were somebody. And you know how to send words where they should go.'

Her sharpness surprised him and for a moment he didn't know how to respond. He wasn't sure whether he should be angry or sharp himself. He thought about it and realised neither would do, but decided he wanted to make certain what her accusation was: 'Miss Xiao, may I know how I have offended you so I can ask your forgiveness.'

'You are too reluctant to offend me,' Cassia replied.

Yu thought about it, and facing the mirror he took his hat off. His hair style was the most fashionable at the time, smoothed down with wax and shiny. Then he immediately put the hat back on. 'The world has changed,' he said.

'Indeed it has.'

Carelessly Cassia dropped her comb on the floor. Yu bent down to pick it up for her. They collided by accident. He hurried to put the comb back on the table, and she felt his eyes momentarily on her, ardent. Her heart jumped fast, but in an instant both had recovered their composure. She turned to the mirror and looked at herself, her voice unusually cool.

'Yu, will you ring Licha Hotel to ask Master Huang to wait patiently. He must at least give me a little time to take my make-up off.'

~ CHAPTER 11 ~

Huang Peiyu had invited Cassia to dine at the English-style Licha Hotel. The dining hall for Western food on the first floor there was both luxurious and sophisticated; it was rumoured to be the best in the Far East.

Cassia stepped into the grand, spacious hall as the elegantly dressed waiter drew the door open for her. Her well-tailored traditional *qipao*, which was made of cream silk with a dark pattern, suited her well. It was slit high to one side, with a tight waistline, and the cut of the garment meant that most of her shoulders were exposed. Three cape jasmine flowers adorned her permed long wavy hair and a pair of long white net gloves covered her lower arms and ran up to her elbow.

She had been to the department store to buy the '*brassieres*' that foreign women wore, thinking that they were the same thing as the cloth Madame Emerald wore to bind her own breasts. But after she tried it on with the *qipao* on top, she stood frightened in front of the mirror. Her breasts were simply too prominent; she had to abandon the bra.

She turned many eyes as she walked through the dining hall. Two Western men stood up, beside themselves. The creamy *qipao* fitted tightly around her body almost like a second skin and showed her figure off perfectly. Her beauty was pearly round and jade smooth, with her body soft and full. She had never been wrong about what to wear in what circumstances. It took some determination to have this *qipao* made with the usury loan when she could hardly afford to pay back this month's interest. But it was essential to spend this money. She knew when her theatre had been smashed that she would have to spend such a sum.

'It seems I am more "Shanghainese" than the Shanghainese,' she thought self-mockingly. 'Do not fear the wrath of heaven, only fear tripping up and spoiling my dress. I am wearing everything I own.'

A smile curled around her lips. She glided past the men as if she hadn't noticed them. Ignoring the lift, she walked up the wide white marble stairs on the right. Everyone in the hotel stared as she stepped upwards in her high heels, admiring her sinuous walk and unpretentious beauty. She knew that this was an important play she had to act in. At the corner of the stairs, she glanced around and glimpsed herself briefly in the big flower-patterned window, then continued her ascent.

Huang Peiyu was waiting impatiently in a pre-booked private room, wearing a silk gown and checking his pocket watch. He had been waiting for far too long; now he was starting to lose face. To have been slighted by a lowly actress made him angry. Just then, Cassia walked in and he looked up. Though simply dressed, she made his heart beat faster; he completely forgot the anger boiling inside him. He stood up quickly and went to pull the chair out for her. Smiling, Cassia sat down and he sat opposite her.

Huang Peiyu felt that he had never seen such a woman in his whole life: a woman who was so radiantly beautiful, and who dared to dress at once so boldly and so appropriately. For a moment, he was at a loss for words. The waiter came in, arranging teacups and napkins, breaking the awkward silence.

After the waiter withdrew, Huang Peiyu said: 'I am honoured Miss Xiao has finally granted me an audience!'

'I, too, am honoured indeed; for Master Huang has been generous enough not to take me to the police,' Cassia retorted, half-teasingly.

Seizing the topic, Huang Peiyu said that it was all a complete misunderstanding. 'If Miss Xiao would like me to apologise, then

I will be very willing to make such an announcement to any newspaper. Miss Xiao's performance was skilful and masterly and the performance of local ballads was beneficial to social morality. She should be appreciated and commended.'

Perhaps realising he had talked too much, he paused to hand her the sophisticated-looking menu, with its entries engraved in gold, and asked if she would like to have a Chinese meal or a Western one.

Cassia had not felt that he'd talked too much at all. In fact, she had been waiting for a long time to hear these words. The Huang Peiyu she saw now was far more elegant, smooth and calm than the one she had met before; he impressed her. She in turn put on a pleasing smile, and her look softened. Catching a glimpse of this, Huang Peiyu couldn't stop his heart from fluttering. Ignoring the menu, she said gently: 'For midnight snacks, I prefer Western food. Peach pudding will do.'

Huang Peiyu clapped his hands and the waiter, who had been waiting outside the door, hurried in and stood in front of their table. Huang Peiyu ordered and the waiter was sent off to arrange the dishes.

The Licha Hotel was situated at the crossing point of the Huangpu River and its main tributary, the Suzhou Creek, and had an unblocked view of the Suzhou Creek outside from its windows. Thousands of lights flickered across the river and the ships passed by like weaving needles. A bit further to the left one could glimpse the Huangpu River and the ocean liners docked at the wharf. The neon street lights outside the hotel shone right beneath their feet.

But Cassia had no time for the view. She urged Huang Peiyu to follow through on his last sentence. 'I would like to hear from Master Huang how exactly he would "appreciate" and "commend" me.'

Huang Peiyu acted as if he had thought out a plan beforehand. Perhaps he had just been pushed into it, but he was a clever man and knew by instinct what would stir the woman in front of him. He leaned slightly towards Cassia and started talking fluently.

'I have three plans. One, I have already agreed with the owner of the Xianshi Roof Garden that the Ruyi Troupe can perform there. Besides, I am helping build the One World Pleasure Park, and I believe a special "Local Ballad Hall" should be set up there so that, once the park has been built, Ruyi can perform there. There is no need for rent upfront at either venue. If you make a profit then pay us thirty per cent of the revenue; that way we both gain.'

This first point itself filled Cassia with joy. The misery she suffered on account of the loan sharks would end. But she only showed a gentle smile; she made sure she showed no sign of being overjoyed. Her smile seemed to indicate that she took for granted what Huang Peiyu had said.

'And second?' she asked.

'In my opinion, the local ballads differ from both Peking Opera and Kun Opera, and that in some ways it resembles Western plays. I am thinking of getting some students who have been abroad to come and create some new plays for you so as to improve this genre.'

These were words that touched Cassia's heart. Huang Peiyu had a taste for foreign things; he knew precisely how to please her. She was moved, and bit her lower lip. Tears nearly flowed and she had to study hard the yellow flower pattern on the edge of her teacup. After taking a few moments to calm herself, she said:

'That sounds good. What about three?' But before Huang Peiyu could reply she continued, unable to contain the words inside her. 'Our kind of plays have always been called such things as "the Huangpu tune", "the Dongxian tune" or simply "the local ballads"; they do not have a proper name at all. They shouldn't be considered peasant plays forever. What we are performing is Shanghai's native theatre: plays for the people of Shanghai.'

'Good.' Now Huang Peiyyu's own interest was aroused. 'Then

what shall we call them?'

'Kunqu is considered the noblest form of opera, the origin of all others, so we shall call ours "Shenqu", or "Shanghai opera!"' Cassia answered with confidence.

'Then we shall set up a Shenqu reform theatre club, and write a manifesto,' Huang Peiyu replied. 'How much money do you need?' It looked as if he was about to take out his cheque book.

'Master Huang's word is as good as an emperor's,' Cassia said pointedly, then, laughing happily, 'If you say you want someone – anyone – how dare they refuse?'

'That's right. If I make you the Queen of Shanghai,' Huang Peiyu said, forgetting himself, 'then you are the Queen of Shanghai.'

Cassia frowned at Huang Peiyu's boast. She picked up the teacup and drank a little from it. After a long pause, she said: 'Then who is the King of Shanghai?'

His eyes fixed on Cassia, Huang Peiyu spoke slowly: 'The whole of Shanghai knows the answer to that. It's me!'

All the way through this exchange of words, she had thought that she could play this role. It was not until Huang Peiyu threw these last few words at her that she realised she had already left the stage and taken off her make-up. For quite a while she was frozen with confusion. Then she put the teacup down, suddenly rose and left the table, her face reddening and the blush spreading to her chest. This was real life, not a play. It was not the blatant way he had pursued her that made her shy, it was all that he had said in their previous exchanges: he had praised her art, and then had appeared to offer her a business deal. There was something rude about his approach, it was worse than dealing with a client at a brothel; it hurt her pride.

'Do I leave the room or not?' she asked herself. Of course not, came the instinctive answer. She could not simply give up an opportunity which she had been waiting years for because of just one sentence.

But she had to show she maintained some pride, otherwise this man would think his money could buy anything from her. She moved to the window in anger, watching the sparkling lights on the opposite side of the Suzhou Creek, spreading all the way to the Bund and onto the Huangpu River.

Huang Peiyu was pleased with her outburst of anger. The angrier she grew, the more excited he became. 'Am I not qualified to appoint the Queen of Shanghai?'

Cassia turned back and said, with a warm smile: 'It seems you feel sure I'd agree to being appointed your Queen.'

'Since you know what I want, I hope you will think as I do!'

Huang Peiyu talked like no man she had ever met: clever, well-rehearsed, and slightly aggressive. A little annoyed, she said: 'It seems you still look upon me as the prostitute from the Duchess Pavilion – a woman for whom "selling art but not flesh" was just an empty phrase.'

'No, no, of course not. Those are totally different things.' It was only now that Huang Peiyu realised Cassia had been offended. He had been too complacent. 'I admire Miss Xiao's art; I appreciate Miss Xiao's beauty.' He paused, and said meaningfully: 'But most importantly of all, I can never forget the moment when you saved my life with just one blink of your eye – when I was spreading out the wine glasses.'

Cassia face softened. 'So you remember…'

'I will never forget it as long as I live. You saved my life.'

'I wasn't trying to help you; I was merely helping Master Chang to realise his grand plan.' She glanced briefly at Huang Peiyu, her look no longer fierce. Her eyes were wet. Blinking her eyes, she thought that not many people remembered those who'd done them favours.

Huang Peiyu's hands reached out boldly for Cassia's shoulders. Half the tattooed flower on her shoulder was revealed by the closely-cut *qipao* she wore. He gently smoothed her scar. 'The more modest you are, the more respectful I grow. Miss Xiao is a heroine; she has both courage and wisdom. Having known her, Master Chang did not live in vain. Before you arrived, I had wondered why Master Chang was so taken by you; now I understand. You have an ethereal air around you; as soon as I am near you I cannot help myself. Miss Xiao, you cannot blame me for being attracted to you.'

Huang Peiyu was indeed a clever man; she might as well be a little flexible. So she said that Master Huang was indeed true to the title 'King of Shanghai'. Thrones or women, he could conquer both. She had always admired him and had been looking forward to meeting him.

'If it is indeed so then you and I have a deep connection that cannot be broken. See how we finally came together!' He laughed loudly, apparently very happy.

'I believe in fate, too.'

'Then you agree?'

'Will you treat me well?'

'Of course. I swear I will do anything you ask – as long as it is within my power!' Now he was overjoyed, waving a hand above his head he exclaimed that he was indeed a lucky man. 'I will go and order wine! This calls for a celebration!' He hurried to the door and opened it. 'Go and fetch a bottle of your best champagne!' he said to the waiter outside.

Then, slowly, he walked back, took hold of Cassia's hands and kissed them. 'Such beautiful hands. It's too late tonight, but tomorrow I must get you a ring to express how I feel.' He smiled.

It seemed Huang Peiyu was not always as clever and understanding as he should have been. Cassia turned, her eyes lowered, and she brushed past him. She returned to the table, sat on the chair and sighed deeply.

'What's the matter?' Huang Peiyu asked.

Cassia smiled: 'A heroine? You flatter me too much. But to be your seventh concubine?! Aren't you scared I'd kill all your other wives?'

But at these words Huang Peiyu merely grew more excited. He stepped behind Cassia. 'Of course I'm scared. They are not even fit to take your shoes off for you.' His hands came up from behind the chair and his face hovered around Cassia's hair. He smelt the cape jasmine.

'You don't need to live in my house.' He rested his chin on her shoulder and spoke in an earnest tone. 'After I saw you on stage that day, I couldn't sleep all night. That has never happened to me before. Please believe me: I want to buy you the most beautiful house, and put it in your name. I will try my best to please you, my beauty.' His voice was truly sincere.

Cassia suddenly turned to face Huang Peiyu. She was smiling, but her words were sharp: 'No need to marry? That's a very good deal, isn't it? So you'd rather pay a bit more and take me as your mistress?'

Huang Peiyu immediately replied that this was not right, that she would not be his mistress.

Cassia stood up and smiled brightly. 'But that sounds good; I like being called a mistress! You don't need to explain.'

There was a light knock on the door, but they both acted as if they hadn't heard it. Cassia put her hands on his shoulders. 'Mistress sounds better than concubine. It's more romantic.' She looked as if she'd thought it all through. 'Except it's all too easy for you.'

Huang Peiyu clasped her to him. She attempted to struggle but he only clasped her tighter. 'That is arranged then,' he said. 'You are a clever woman, you know I will treat you well.'

She put his head between her two arms and let him kiss her.

Huang Peiyu asked her to spend the night with him. Smoothing her face, he said that he had no respect for convention.

Instead of answering him, Cassia kissed his ear lobe, breathing out gently. Her bold flirtation made him excited and he started to smooth her face.

'There's no rush,' Cassia whispered, stopping his probing hands, though her lips slipped from his moustache to his neck.

'No rush?' His hands had already moved from her face to her body, impatient to unbutton the *qipao*. A jewelled pin was in the way. In a mad rush he kissed her breasts through her dress as his hands kept on feeling her up and down.

The knocking continued. Finally, the waiter decided to open the door, bringing in the champagne. Hearing the click of the door, Huang Peiyu wanted to draw away from Cassia, but he merely found that, instead of loosening the grip of his hands about her waist, she merely turned and made him face the man who was entering the room.

Yu Qiyang followed directly behind the waiter, his mouth open as if he was about to speak. On taking in the scene within the room, he stopped suddenly. The waiter quickly put down the plates and the wines and Yu and the waiter withdrew. As he reached out to close the door he saw Cassia still clasping Huang Peiyu to her. She was facing him and gave him a mischievous wink.

Frightened and confused, he shut the door and put a hand to his rapidly-beating heart.

That night, Huang Peiyu booked Room 303 at the Licha Hotel. The waiter opened the double doors within, switched on the table lamp and withdrew.

They did not sleep until they were exhausted. As soon as he awoke the following morning he jumped on her again. Afterwards, watching her naked body from a slight distance, he couldn't help praising it. 'Your body is indeed modern. Now I understand what sharp eyes Master Chang had.'

She had heard similar words before, but could never understand why these men were so surprised at such things. Did they think the shape of female bodies followed changing fashions? She was washing in the bathroom in the afternoon when Huang Peiyu left. From across the door, he said to her: 'I have already booked the room for another night.'

The door clicked and she knew he'd gone.

She washed her hair, then carefully washed every trace of him from her body. She dried herself with the towel and started to brush her hair. The woman in the mirror did not look so different from the girl of six years ago. She was still herself.

Now she felt a little tired. She came out naked and lay on the bed. She couldn't wear the *qipao* any more: Huang Peiyu had torn it when he couldn't manage to unbutton it.

It wasn't early. She tried to phone the theatre to see if anybody could send over some suitable clothes. But now there was a ring at the door and she wrapped herself in a sheet and went over barefoot to answer it. It was the waiter, holding a large cardboard box.

She closed the door and opened the box. It contained a long black dress, Western in style, its collar and hems trimmed with a pattern of lotus leaves. The waiter told her that the tailor was waiting at the reception hall of the hotel; he had sent it up for her to try on. If it did not fit, he could adjust it. Huang Peiyu really did want her to dress like a Western woman. She made a noise with her nose and took the clothes into the bedroom; they fitted perfectly.

It was as if she were looking at another woman in the mirror. Apart from her hair, she looked like a foreign aristocrat; the only thing missing was a pearl necklace.

She lay on the sofa after she had sent the tailor off. Then she called a taxi to take her back to the theatre. She got ready and walked out of the door. The lift was arriving as she reached the top of the stairs. Someone walked out of it and she went in. She pressed the button for the ground floor, but the lift didn't move. She thought for a bit and then shut the iron gate. The lift descended.

Waiting for the taxi in reception, she noticed the curtains were in two layers, one cream and the second dark brown. It was a spacious, elegant room. Inside a white china vase there was a dark red cockscomb flower and on the wall was a glorious great gold-plated mirror. A blonde woman folded her dress and sat down elegantly to play in front of a luxurious-looking black grand piano.

As she got into the taxi she could still hear the echo of the music played by the blonde woman. This Western woman played 'art' but she herself sang 'ballads'. It didn't matter how much like the Western woman she was dressed. She had not got a big nose, nor a pair of deep set eyes. She spoke Chinese and sang local ballads. Why would she want to copy a Westerner?

But then again, why not? She laughed at herself; if these men felt that foreign styles were fashionable, then she would follow fashion. Wasn't this the way Shanghai itself had grown?

~ CHAPTER 12 ~

It didn't seem to take any time for Cassia to get back to the Guanyi Theatre. Stepping out of the taxi she saw Li Yu and Xiu Fang waiting for her. They said that they just knew that she'd succeeded. They could see how she seemed to have rested much better than she normally did and how like a foreigner she looked in her new dress!

Cassia smiled and walked over to hand Li Yu the folded *qipao*. Li Yu had a brief look, frowned and looked regretful. 'Should I order another of the same style?'

'Yes, but not in another pale colour.'

'What colour then?'

Cassia didn't answer as she walked off towards the dressing room. She pushed the door open and saw the carnation in front of her dressing table. Pointing at the flowers she said, 'Purple.' Xiu Fang and Li Yu stuck their tongues out.

'Yes, purple,' Cassia said delightedly to her trusted maids. 'We want red and purple, to celebrate the end of our days of poverty.' Then she thought for a second and added, '…probably. Don't say anything to the others just yet.'

She shut the door, leaned back on the chair and breathed out deeply. She took off the tight dress, put on a long robe, and started to apply her make-up. Someone knocked on the door. 'The door's open,' she said impatiently,

Yu Qiyang entered. This startled her. 'You are a rare guest here.'

'It seems I have not called at a good time,' said Yu.

'You never call at the right time,' said Cassia.

Yu pretended not to hear. 'See how well these flowers have

been cleaned up; they look fine.'

It was not until then that Cassia noticed that almost all the flowers that had previously been piled up on the floor, had been put into bottles and vases. Yu changed the topic to the purpose of his visit. Master Huang's car was waiting to fetch Cassia when the play finished. He was inviting her out for dinner.

'Isn't he coming to watch the show?'

Yu was about to say something, but stopped.

Cassia stood up and approached him. She said Master Huang had promised this afternoon that he'd go and finish some business, then come over to watch her show.

Yu was dazed; he hadn't expected Cassia to be so serious about this. But he knew that whatever he said would be wrong, and was careful to appear outwardly calm.

Cassia knew there was no point in pursuing this further. It was only the second day since they had got together, and already Huang Peiyu had broken a promise. What about the future? She had given her body to men for practical reasons, for money and power. If she didn't want to give up her pride too, she mustn't lose face. She smiled and picked up the black Western dress on the chair. Standing up she draped the dress over herself. 'Do I look good in this?'

'Of course.'

'…but I think it looks awful.' She dumped the dress on the chair.

Now it was Yu Qiyang's turn to smile, saying that if Miss Xiao would forgive the slander, it was actually he who had chosen the fabric, at Master Huang's command. 'I told the tailor your size,' Yu said. 'Perhaps it was all done in too much of a rush and the dress wasn't made as well as it should have been.'

'Oh, you have good eyes, and you know my height and size. Thanks.' Cassia wanted to offer him a way out. Of course she understood the meaning implied by Yu's words. She might have read them as an insult, but she could also interpret it as his being smart and understanding. For now, at least, she needed to flatter everyone around Huang Peiyu to get the promised cheque; only then could she afford to settle her accounts.

'Then I'll come and fetch you tonight.'

'See you tonight,' she said, and smiled.

He was already out of the door, but then he stepped back. 'I shouldn't be saying this, but I thought you'd want to know...' he said softly, as he shut the door of the dressing room.

Cassia stopped smiling and listened carefully. He said that actually it wasn't anything big, it was just that Master Huang's sixth concubine had been looking for him everywhere – from the Lao Shun Teahouse to the Municipal Council. She'd also checked with Yu Qiyang, who obviously knew nothing. Now the Second Concubine too had started a fuss, over at Huang Peiyu's house. Master Huang had often stayed out overnight before; they were used to this. Someone must have said something to the women this time for them to make all this noise.

Cassia knew well what Yu meant: that she shouldn't increase Master Huang's troubles. She looked up and thanked him.

He merely smiled. There was no point in her finding fault with him; she understood that. He had always worked hard, and with her interests in mind – perhaps a bit too hard, almost like a pimp introducing a potential client to a prostitute. It was this that she was unhappy about. But she knew well what she needed in the circumstances and that she had no right to be a sulky, fussy little woman.

She was about to say something when he opened the door and walked off. A woman's instinct cannot be suppressed. Huang Peiyu's favourite, the Sixth Concubine was sour with jealousy. Huang Peiyu had made a spur-of-the-moment decision to stay the night at the hotel, and apart from Yu and a few other guards nobody gave the same answer as to why. This was how Huang Peiyu was found out.

But Cassia needn't have worried. Huang Peiyu wasn't someone

who was easily bullied by women. His household, with its many concubines had not long been disturbed by the Sixth Concubine; she had only been married to him for half a year. Now all the other concubines had started to fight for their own status.

Now that Huang Peiyu had sent Yu to come and inform her of his intention to meet, Cassia had to simply wait and see how he would act.

At 9.30 p.m. that night, as usual, the curtain dropped and the applause rang out. Cassia ran to the dressing room. Li Yu helped her take her make-up off and rearrange her hair. Xiu Fang helped her to take off the costume of the daughter-in-law. Cassia put on her usual necklace and earrings, stepped into her high-heeled shoes, and then washed her face in a bowl of warm water, before putting some face cream on and adding some light make-up, with a touch of lipstick.

Half an hour later she stepped out of the theatre wearing a satin blue *qipao* and carrying a small leather handbag. Huang Peiyu was already waiting in his car. Seeing her coming, he got out and opened the car door for her. The driver started the engine and drove off towards the Bund. 'Where shall we go to eat?' Cassia asked excitedly.

In the rear mirror, she glimpsed Yu Qiyang and the others getting into another car.

Huang Peiyu held her hands and asked why she wasn't wearing the dress he had sent. Wasn't she satisfied with it?

'It was a bit tight,' she said, but thanked him.

'Then I shall have another one made just like the torn one, would you like that?'

'You are one step too late, I've already asked for it to be remade.'

'You've robbed me of my opportunity to please you,' Huang Peiyu teased. He patted her hand and suggested that they go to a newly-opened restaurant that belonged to the Brotherhood.

If Cassia was not tired after that, then they would take the midnight ferry for a tour of the Huangpu River. He acted as if nothing had happened, that he had not broken his earlier promise to watch tonight's performance. A man like this was accountable to no one but himself.

That night Cassia and Huang Peiyu lodged once again in the Licha Hotel. But this time they took the luxurious suite on the fourth floor, with its large arched windows facing onto the Waibaidu Bridge. There was hot water all day here and she could have a bath at any time. This alone made her happy.

Huang Peiyu looked at her and said, almost annoyed: 'Other women are not like you.'

'How so?'

'You wear a smile every day,' he said. 'You show no bitterness, you never complain. This is what I like best. I hardly ever have time to relax; if I am bothered when I am with a woman then what is the point?' He took out a golden ring, pulled Cassia's left hand to him, and put the ring on her finger.

Cassia smiled sweetly and thanked him, thinking this ring was the easiest promise to keep of all those he had given her. How many more months, or perhaps years, of flesh would she have to sell to achieve all that she wanted? She was as keen and anxious as a moth drawn towards a fire, but she had to keep calm. This was the best way of dealing with men.

Huang Peiyu spent each of the next three nights with her. On the third night, before they went to bed he told her he'd found a house with a garden on Connaught Road, in the west of Shanghai. He asked her to go and have a look, and if she was happy then she should ring him.

On the fourth day Cassia arrived at Room 407 at the agreed time, but there was no sign of Huang Peiyu. She waited impatiently in the room, occasionally walking to the window to look at the

Waibaidu Bridge. After some time, she switched the light off. She waited until 11 o'clock before the telephone rang. Without waiting to turn the light on, she picked the phone up.

'I am very sorry. I cannot come to see you tonight. There is something I have to attend to at home.'

'It doesn't matter.' Cassia understood that fire had broken out in his backyard. She might as well act as if she was being understanding; indeed, she even wanted to sound generous. 'I am used to being on my own. The bed is so big I can dream of swimming in it.'

Huang Peiyu gave a dry laugh on the other end of the phone, but it seemed he was in no mood to appreciate her joke.

'Do you like the house?'

Cassia still acted as if she was in a good mood. 'Very nice, my lord. Thank you so much.'

'I'll send over the removal company,' Huang Peiyu said.

'That's great. But you know, Master Huang, how few possessions I have. All my belongings will hardly fill a suitcase; don't make the removal company laugh at me.'

Huang Peiyu laughed. 'Go to the department store and buy some furniture,' he said; 'Make sure that all purchases are under my name. Ask the removal company to send everything over.'

'I'll arrange everything the way I think you might like it, and then invite you over for an inspection.'

'I've been very busy lately, and am so pleased you are being understanding!'

She put the phone down and sat in the darkened room for a long time. Finally she turned the light on. He was not coming; she would sleep in peace. The house would be expensive, but it was still the second easiest thing on his list to realise. She had to be patient, to wait for him to appear again. He knew well that she was waiting on his third promise.

The Ruyi Troupe could not survive on credit for much longer. Either someone had said something or these country kids had got smarter; they knew Mistress Xiao was doing her best to win a good future for the troupe. All of them muttered magic words like 'Xianshi Roof Garden' and 'The One World'. They dared not utter such words in front of her, though she could see from their eyes how much more eager and anxious they were than her. She had to move out first, to go and live in luxury. This was what she minded most and found hardest to explain.

The hotel room was wallpapered in a classical floral pattern. The bed was not big, but it was soft. An enormous, carved Western-style dressing table faced the window. Two sofas were sat opposite each other. Curtains trailed inside brown wooden shutters. Waibaidu Bridge was extremely quiet and, by now, so was the Suzhou Creek. A few lights flickered on the opposite bank and were reflected in the water. The sky was starless; dark clouds weighed it down.

A man breaking his promise. She watched the gloomy sky and felt there would probably be more days like this one from now on, moments such as the one just now when she stepped out of the lift and entered this room alone. She had walked past long corridors and turned a couple of corners. The floor had been waxed and shone bright against her lonely figure. Only she knew how her high-heels sounded, as if they were stepping on her heart. What was the point of staying here? She searched for her shoes.

There was no taxi. The hotel porter told her the English Commercial Central Taxi Company ran an all-night service, but when he phoned them they told him that no taxis would now be available for quite a while. She might as well walk, she thought.

She had not walked for some time. She felt odd in the night wind. She had crossed the Waibaidu Bridge many times, but now there was no one else around, and not a car to be seen. It was dead quiet. She recalled the first night she'd spent with Huang Peiyu: they had drunk the champagne and entered the room, both of their faces red. Cassia had drunk a bit more than Huang Peiyu.

Outside, the veranda, the river and the ferries; inside, the lamps and the double beds; all were dreamlike. She remembered taking off her high-heeled shoes, stepping from the chair to the desk and standing on the windowsill. Huang Peiyu carried her from the window and dropped her on the bed.

'I was merely thinking of having a dip in the river, what are you going to do to me then?' She was drunk, and pinched Huang Peiyu's nose.

Huang Peiyu had said: 'You will see.'

Now Cassia looked back. The veranda protruded elegantly out from the room by the street overlooking the river, revealing the curtain flapping gently in the soft wind, the light seeping through it. By now she had walked exactly eighty steps and was standing right in the middle of the Waibaidu Bridge. Another eighty steps and she had reached the other end of the bridge. She followed the Suzhou Creek to her right. Cassia had gradually grown used to the city after all these years in Shanghai. She had walked through numerous streets and lanes and had become more familiar with this gigantic city than she was with her own hometown.

To the south she entered a lane that was clouded with a sweet fragrance. The moon poked out between the clouds and spread a little light on the stone-paved road. The night deepened. Night watchmen could be heard banging their sticks to remind people of the passing of the time. Turning into another lane she saw that someone had set up a bamboo bed and was sleeping outside, snoring. From this lane she entered another street.

'White sugar – lotus porridge!'

'Osmanthus flower – mung bean soup!'

The pedlar's voice sounded familiar and warm, and the long echo fell on the words 'sugar' and 'flower'. She followed the sound and saw a pedlar spreading out his fare. At her appearance he invited her warmly to taste a little. She was hungry, and asked for a bowl of mung bean soup. She'd always had a soft spot for it. Compared to so many more expensive delicacies, it was mung bean soup that most relaxed and invigorated her.

Half-an-hour later she entered a lane and knocked at the front door of a house. Li Yu was surprised to see her at such a late hour.

'He is busy,' Cassia said briefly.

This was an ordinary Shanghai citizen's house. It had three storeys altogether and the Ruyi Troupe had hired four rooms spread across two of them. Only Cassia had a room all to herself; the other rooms were occupied either all by men or all by women. The first room one came to on entering the house was a shared kitchen. Iron pots and bamboo containers were piled up on the shelf.

The two of them passed through the kitchen and followed each other up a small, narrow, dark stairway. They twisted and turned their way up to the second floor and walked straight into her room. It was small but very tidy. Two vases of roses on the windowsill made the room seem homely. It was nice to be back at her own house. Cassia collapsed on the bed and Li Yu came over to massage her neck, back and shoulders, saying things to make her laugh. If her mistress found it hard to sleep, she teased, she'd go and find a man to entertain her.

'There's no need, I have deliberately walked away from him,' Cassia said. 'Think about it. Even when we are in the heat of things he was able to walk away. I must not put up with everything he does, not like his other women. He'd tire of me quickly if I was like that. If he comes looking for me, just say I am not here.'

At noon the next day Li Yu understood the meaning of Cassia's words. She heard a knocking at the door and went downstairs. Other occupants of the house had already opened the door and now she saw Huang Peiyu standing outside. It was drizzling. 'Has the mistress come back?' he asked.

Li Yu didn't say anything and went back upstairs. She wanted to see how anxious Huang Peiyu would get. 'Is she not in?' he asked again, following her up, 'Or has she gone out and not come back yet?'

Li Yu walked on, pretending she hadn't heard. Xiu Fang was

standing on the stairs and singing a line or two from one of their plays. She said warmly: 'My mistress is in her boudoir.' She took a step down and asked Huang Peiyu if she should wake her mistress up.

Huang Peiyu shook his head. He had never encountered a situation like this. He thought for a second, then said he'd wait for her to wake up; may he wait in the mistress's room? Neither maid dared to stop him.

He entered the room and sat by the bed. Cassia embraced him, wrapping herself in the quilt. 'Look, you woke me up,' she said. 'Why are you here? Why are you so wet?' She took off Huang Peiyu's jacket, wiped his hair dry with a towel, pushed him down on the bed and put a quilt over him. He had been thinking about her; he had looked for her at the hotel and found her gone. He had then gone to do his business at the Municipal Council; now he had found her here.

On the way here it had started to rain, so he had got wet.

Cassia apologised to him, saying she had not been able to sleep by herself last night and so she had come back here. She would have waited if she had known he'd eventually go back to the hotel.

She thought again and wondered if he had wanted to know if she was alone in bed, whether in the hotel or in her own room. Perhaps he had wanted to surprise her. This was a suspicious man who trusted no one.

Cassia noticed he looked a bit odd; perhaps he was genuinely not feeling very well. She felt his forehead and thought that he might have a temperature. 'Have you got a headache?'

'A small one,' Huang Peiyu admitted.

She asked him to sleep by himself, then got up and dressed herself. She said to Li Yu: 'Perhaps Master Huang has caught a cold. Go and make a bowl of strong ginger soup.' She sat next to him and looked after him carefully, wiping away his sweat and feeding him the ginger soup.

He fell asleep and she remained by his side. It was not until it was time for her to prepare to perform that she woke him up and sent him home.

Apart from going to the Municipal Council in the foreign concessions, every day Huang Peiyu tried to visit the special room that was kept for him at the Lao Shun Teahouse. His time there varied from as long as six hours to a mere half-an-hour. He called it 'tea time'. But in fact he spent most of this time gambling.

His office at the back of the teahouse faced a stand of bamboo plants. There were too many people in his own house and the gossip of the women was unbearable. He was, after all, an educated man; he liked to come here to practise calligraphy and occasionally to solve other people's troubles. These included the buying and selling of opium, disputes between gambling houses, ransoms for brothels, thefts of jewellery, murder and arson, and police arrests for which bribes needed to be arranged.

But the biggest business in the back room of the Lao Shun Teahouse was gambling. This was Shanghai's biggest gambling house. It was not open to the public; only by application and through recommendation could one become a member. The gambling games practised there were a combination of the Chinese and the Western: *Mahjong* and domino games, fruit machines and large roulette wheels around which noisy gamblers gathered. The most popular game was Blackjack, which revealed its winners and losers instantly.

When a big player appeared, Huang Peiyu would often be there in person, acting as the game's dealer. He alone was powerful enough to enable the loser to admit defeat. This gambling house was Huang Peiyu's biggest source of income.

Whenever Huang Peiyu was hosting the gambling, Yu Qiyang stood behind him, acting as a guard. At certain key moments he'd drop some subtle hint, but only with his eyes; never with a hand gesture.

Every night, starting at around 10 p.m., Huang Peiyu's gambling house was filled with people. Around each roulette table sat crowds of gamblers. On this night, Huang Peiyu, handsomely dressed and with a pipe in the corner of his mouth, was playing with great interest. The chips on the table were piled as high as a small hill. The other gamblers looked nervous.

Cassia slipped behind Huang Peiyu. He turned and saw her and looked pleased. In a flash he pushed all his chips out and put them on the centre and the four edges of Number 22.

The whole table stared at this with great surprise. Yu whispered gently: 'Master?'

Huang Peiyu stretched out a hand to pat Cassia's; he took no notice of Yu. Men on neighbouring tables also craned their necks to watch the big show that Huang Peiyu was putting on. A large crowd gathered. The dealer was about to flash the sign when a guest said: 'May I have a go?'

The croupier eyed Huang Peiyu, who waved a hand generously. 'Please, any ball will do.'

Cassia walked up a few steps. Instead of picking up the ball, she bent down and blew on it: 'Twenty-two, my age. Master Huang's life and property all rest on me.'

This caused loud laughter all around and the atmosphere relaxed a little. But the ball shot out immediately and everyone held their breath. The hands of some holding the edge of the wheel began to tremble.

The ball circled a few times around the wheel, about to fall, and then staggered downwards. Finally, it came to rest on number twenty-two.

'Magical, magical!' the crowds chorused.

One man who'd lost his bet would not admit defeat. 'If you don't mind, Master Huang, I'd like to take the table apart and examine it from the inside.'

Huang Peiyu waved his hands generously, but his words were

not lightweight: 'Of course, go ahead. But if you disassemble it and find no trick there, you will have to buy a new one to replace it. Business must not be interrupted.'

At this he turned and put one hand behind Cassia's back. He started walking her to a room further inside. 'Someone told me that your Yin is too strong, that it will cause men trouble. Today I deliberately wanted to test it. But as soon as you arrived I won a big sum! I don't believe in such rubbish anyway. That sum is yours.'

Cassia smiled sweetly. 'If Yang is smooth then Yin will be smooth. My Yin is helping your Yang.' But her private thoughts were far less calm, 'Thank goodness. Tomorrow the Ruyi Troupe will be able to pay back their debts and the troupe members can be given their wages!'

The next day Cassia received her invitation from the Xianshi Roof Garden Theatre, inviting her over to discuss the contract regarding the Ruyi Troupe's move there. Just as had been predicted, no deposit was due, and the rent would be divided with a thirty-seventy split. Finally Cassia had overcome the shadow of the usury loan; finally she was seeing the realisation of the promise she'd most desired.

But one thing still bothered her about Huang Peiyu. Several days earlier, when he had come to her house looking for her, she had wondered if he really desired her.

~ CHAPTER 13 ~

Since moving into her strange little foreign house at 54 Connaught Road, Cassia felt that winter barely existed. It was as if the season had jumped straight from autumn's end in one year to the start of spring in the next. Ever since she was small, she had suffered in winter, her fingers frozen like carrot sticks. Not this year. This showed how well she felt: everything had gone as she had wished.

The house itself was not very big but it was extremely elegant. There were two stories. Downstairs was a large hall with a bedroom on both sides, and a kitchen. Xiu Fang and Li Yu lived here. Upstairs there was a master bedroom with an *en suite* bathroom and two other rooms. The house had its own boiler behind the kitchen. By burning coal one could make enough hot water for several baths.

Now Cassia could enjoy a toilet that flushed and her own bath. It was a great luxury to have a bath each day before bed. To a girl who had been used to planting rice seedlings in paddy fields awash with shit, this hot water that had come to her all too easily was something she couldn't quite get used to.

In a room upstairs, Xiu Fang, her hair curled, the fringe on her forehead twisted inwards using hair oil, was looking proud as a crane. She put Cassia's winter clothes into a leather box and made a special trip to the shops to buy camphor balls. Then she went to Wang Ping Street and bought newspapers, both major and minor ones, from the boys who sold them there. When she returned home, she went immediately to wrap the camphor balls in pieces of cloth, which she tucked into the pile of clothes to ward off insects.

The vase on the wooden tea table was filled with a few canna lillies. Xiu Fang sat on the sofa and opened a newspaper, looking for news of Cassia. Nowadays her name appeared almost daily in each and every newspaper. Then Xiu Fang exclaimed out loud.

Cassia was in the bathroom, next to the bath tub, washing her hair. The noise of running water prevented her from hearing what Xiu Fang was shouting about. Carrying her newspaper, Xiu Fang walked into the bathroom and pointed something out to her.

Cassia had long ceased to be excited by such things, but Xiu Fang remained constantly thrilled.

★★★

Indeed I myself, when I read these papers in the archives, was as delighted as Xiu Fang. I could imagine how women of the time might talk about Cassia, listening to her songs and going over images of her.

★★★

The popular magazine *The Boudoir* had a big photo of her holding the latest style of telephone and wearing a Western evening dress, with a long wavy perm. The lead article was about how she dressed and made herself up. Clothes were made for her and she gave them life.

The Five Continent Pharmacy's 'Capsules with essence of fish liver oil' and 'Ginseng substitute paste' featured an advertisement with Cassia wearing leathers, the picture of a rich married woman, stylishly poised, modern and attractive.

Her face even appeared on the front of Guanshengyuan Food Ltd's mooncake boxes, where she was called the 'Number One Flower' of Shanghai.

For the completion of the reinforced concrete bridge on Sichuan Road, on which a tramline was laid, the concession authorities invited Cassia, the famous actress, to cut the ribbons.

Cassia, the 'Queen of Shanghai Shenqu', was likewise invited to cut the ribbon at the opening of the Great Shanghai Pleasure Ground.

When there were floods in Hubei and Hunan, Cassia led three days of charity performances with her play, 'Embroidering the Pocket Bag'. Other stars and rich tycoons responded and in total 20,000 yuan were made, and donated to the affected area. Every newspaper reported the event. She wore a dark *qipao* and stood next to stars of Peking Opera and Kunqu, smiling serenely.

The bells of the trams that creaked along the noisy Nanjing Road rang pleasingly when they stopped to pick up passengers: Cassia had become a famous 'celebrity' across the ten miles of the foreign concessions.

Her parents had passed away sixteen years earlier. This Qing Ming, at last, Cassia felt she had the dignity to return home and sweep their graves.

Her old Chuansha hometown was still the same old seaside town. Their two cars rode one after another to the graves outside the town. Someone opened the car door for her and she stepped out of the cream white car, her high heels followed by the rest of her body. She wore a marten-fur coat and see-through stockings, and her legs were long and handsome. One could pick her out instantly among her guards and aides.

The Taoist monks were performing the rites and laying out the offerings. White banners waved in the wind; the ceremony was grand and forbidding. Cassia knelt down and offered incense, *kowtowing* to her deceased parents.

Although she had avoided going into the town she was quickly spotted at the burial area.

Immediately the words 'Cassia has returned' echoed across the town.

Surrounded by her guards, she was able to finish her ceremony without being bothered. Yet a large crowd thronged from the town. Little girls ran to the front; their mothers, though not as crazy as the children, had stopped their sewing and joined them to watch. Cassia's guards tried but failed to stop the little girls from rushing up to clasp Cassia's hands. 'Miss Cassia, Miss Cassia, take me to Shanghai,' said one girl: 'I can sing the flower ballad!' Boys rushed in, too: 'I can sing well, let me sing to you. Listen, please!'

Her aides pushed the little girls away; some even fell to the ground. With difficulty they made their way through the crazed crowd. Li Yu and Xiu Fang sat with her in the back seat of the car and the two cars drove into the town, followed by the crowd of children. Cassia walked up the high street of the town, that one long street, to her uncle's house.

The grocery shop was open; everything was just as it had been when her parents were still alive, when she was about seven, running around her father, helping him with the bookkeeping. Occasionally she had hovered around her mother's knees. When she couldn't find her, her mother would call in a long, dragged-out voice: 'Cassia − Cassia come home!'

Cassia walked over. Her uncle and aunt saw her and looked scared. It was Cassia who greeted them warmly. She had come back to sweep her parents' graves, she said, and to visit relatives.

Her aunt said: 'So little Cassia has forgiven us our rudeness in the past; we are very grateful.'

'We are of one family, and you are forever my aunt and uncle.'

They were surrounded by crowds of onlookers. Cassia asked Li Yu to bring the presents in from the car. There were lengths of material, two top quality bottles of wine, a pair of golden earrings and a pair of golden necklaces. The neighbours shouted their praise: 'Cassia is indeed a thoughtful girl! A most generous girl!'

'She is the Number One Star in Shanghai!'

A five or six-year-old boy in a vest shot deftly out of the room and ran to the aunt. Watching Cassia curiously, he said in a clear voice: 'Ma, this auntie looks really pretty.'

'Such a lovely child. Is he my cousin?' Cassia squatted down and took the boy's hand.

The aunt patted the boy's head: 'She's not an auntie, she's your sister. Call her "sister"!'

'Sister!' the boy, behaving like he knew her, called out to Cassia in a soft voice.

Cassia bent down and slipped two pieces of silver into the boy's hand. 'I did not know I was going to meet you,' she said; 'Next time I'll bring you a special present.'

'Uncle, whenever you've had enough of the town, come to the city,' said Cassia, asking her uncle to take her to the village ancestral hall.

The hall was filled with the men of the clan. The guards pushed everyone else outside. The men had no doubt gathered specially to meet Cassia.

The head of the clan spoke, his voice loud and clear: 'We normally do not allow females to be present in the ancestral hall; but Miss Cassia is a hero among women, whose name has spread all over Shanghai. She's created luck for the clan and the whole of the Chen family thank her.'

The men clasped their hands in front of their chests in a gesture of sincere greeting. But instead of responding, Cassia simply knelt in front of the altar where the ancestors' name plaques stood. *Kowtowing* three times, she stood up and wrote a line in the donation book: 'Five hundred pieces of white silver, to assist in building the village school.'

The hall erupted in surprise and praise: 'Five hundred! Five hundred!' came the voices. Even the guards were temporarily distracted and the girls, who had been stretching their necks outside, took the opportunity to break through the barrier. They surged in, shouting and screaming.

Cassia lay in bed for two days after she returned from Chuansha. She was exhausted. She had no fever, but also no appetite. At night she couldn't sleep. Huang Peiyu wanted to find a doctor but she stopped him. She was missing her parents and she was just very sad.

Huang Peiyu sat on the sofa and lit a cigar, the ashtray on the windowsill. He was disappointed: he had wanted to take Cassia to the Lao Shun Teahouse and pop into the gambling room there. But she had smiled apologetically and said she had no wish to go out.

'When I'm a bit better I will go and watch how those big gamblers throw away their fortune in a single go.'

'Or watch how I win a fortune in one bet! Who would be so willing to lose if they have not had the opportunity to win so large a sum?'

'Of course, you understand it all best,' she said.

Huang Peiyu cursed vehemently: 'But some don't think like that, they say I gamble wildly and with other people's capital.'

'Those are people with mean mouths; you should just ignore them.'

'You are right,' Huang Peiyu said: 'The Qing Brotherhood still makes life difficult for me. Nothing big, just constant small squabbles. Though they do also say Qing and Hong are the same family. I think there are some outsiders who are trying to finish off both!'

Cassia rose, stirred by his words. She saw Huang Peiyu's hand rising, an elegant gesture. Leaning on the window, his voice calmed down. Ever since its humble bare-fists-holding-knives beginnings, he said, the Hong Brotherhood had always stuck to its principle of 'Fight the Qing and Revive the Ming', even if death claimed the lives of many members. But the Qing Brotherhood had always loved to mingle with the establishment. Ever since Li Hongzhang, the Qing Emperor's Minister of Trade established the Business Bureau to encourage commerce by the sea, the Qing Brotherhood had lost its support base. By then the Hong Brotherhood in Shanghai was still recovering; it had not yet gained full power. So the Qing took advantage of the situation to dominate Shanghai.

'So the saying:"Qing and Hong are the same family" is nothing but words, to help soothe both sides?' Cassia said.

'You've always been a clever woman. Now the Hong Brotherhood is within my grip, and as far as I can see it, Qing and Hong are only temporarily at peace.' At this Huang Peiyu extinguished his cigar and rose to leave.

At noon, three days later, Cassia took a carriage to the front of the Xishi restaurant. Madame Emerald's carriage arrived at the same moment. Both of them arrived punctually. Cassia looked much better now and following the fashion of the time, wore a plait tied up with a red ribbon. Madame Emerald wore full make-up and a silk scarf with many trimmings.

They sat down, and Madame Emerald took out a box, handing it to Cassia:'It's your birthday today. I have nothing to give you but this.'

'So that's why you want to see me!' Cassia smiled. She opened the box and saw that it was a jade bracelet, a present from Master Chang many years ago. Not believing what she saw, her eyes were immediately moist. Slowly she placed the jade bracelet on her right wrist:'Muma, this is so unexpected.You are so kind!'

'You forced it on me back then; now I am merely returning it,' said Madame Emerald.

They were both getting a little over-sentimental, as if trying to hide something from each other. They called for the waiter and ordered the restaurant's speciality: spring onion fried chicken and dried bean curd mixed with peanut. They also ordered a pot of Shaoxing rice wine in celebration.

'One cannot be an actress forever; sooner or later you'll have to marry someone,' Madame Emerald said, lighting up a cigarette: 'Come, have one, paper cigarettes are so much more convenient.'

'But I don't want to marry.' Cassia accepted the cigarette,

picking up the match and lighting it herself. She only pretended to inhale; she wanted to please Madame Emerald. 'I don't want to belong to a man. Besides, you yourself never married.'

'Don't you learn from me,' Madame Emerald said. She studied Cassia: 'Each time I see you I am convinced you will turn out better than me. You really can make something out of nothing.'

It has not been easy, Cassia told her. 'When I am free one day,' she said, 'I will get a teacher to instruct me in some foreign language. I have no one else to depend on but myself. It's lucky that I draw a bonus from the theatre revenue. I learned such business skills from you,' she continued. 'I would never be satisfied with working like a fool who is just given wages.'

'Lucky for me you weren't my Number One girl then: fancy me having to share profits with you!'

'Muma is making fun of me. But I have to support a large number of people. For the moment I can manage. Huang Peiyu has delivered on his promises. But I don't expect him to give me a penny more.'

'Well, us women...' – Madame Emerald changed the topic – 'we have to accept our fate. You cannot fight it. Take me, for example: I am a madame in a brothel. Those that I want to marry won't marry me; why should I seek out trouble by marrying someone I wouldn't want to be with? I gave up on marriage a long time ago. That's my fate and I am resigned to it.'

'I could say the same myself,' Cassia said.

Shafts of light hit their table as it started to turn dark and black clouds piled up in the sky. Time went by quickly. A sense of helplessness prevailed. But they had no intention of parting, as they picked at the peanuts on the plate. Just then Madame Emerald glimpsed Yu Qiyang walking in with a woman. The waiter led them up the stairs. She eyed Cassia, who turned and saw the pair. The woman wasn't very pretty, she had freckles, but she looked well-to-do.

Madame Emerald said: 'Let me go and get Yu here. Neither of

us have touched that little cockerel; perhaps he can help us out!'

This made Cassia embarrassed: 'I never knew you could make such fun of people.'

'He used to really like you.'

Cassia laughed: 'Stop it. What nonsense!'

'Am I making you unhappy?'

'No, why? Do you think I am not good enough for him, or him me?'

Madame Emerald knew she'd said the wrong thing and hurried to make up with Cassia: 'That's not what I meant.'

'You know it's impossible. I was born to sell my flesh; he was born to sell his fists. If we sell ourselves to each other, neither of us is worth anything.'

This made both of them laugh. They raised the teacups, clinked them together and drank up. But Cassia wasn't laughing inside. She was in no better position than when she had worked for Madame Emerald – serving men. And Yu Qiyang too was just as he had been before, a mere lackey for the Hong Brotherhood chief. Neither was a promising prospect.

Madame Emerald said: 'I've always had a feeling...' but she didn't finish her sentence.

Cassia glanced at her: 'Muma, speak either your mind, or say nothing at all.'

'You are a clever girl. Why should I waste my tongue?'

Cassia refilled their cup and looked at Madame Emerald: 'I often dream of Master Chang.' She raised her glass, 'Muma, his death is a source of deep sorrow. I need to find out the truth behind it, only then will I feel at ease.'

After she left Madame Emerald, Cassia sat in her carriage and felt gloomy. She took a roundabout route home, driving past Zhang Garden. She asked the driver to stop and walked into the garden. There were often garden parties here. The Western-style buildings differed from the Chinese ones that dominated the area. It made for a refreshing scene.

There were ponds floating with lotus leaves dotted around the garden. The trees were rare and expensive specimens. She walked over a wooden bridge; it all reminded her a little of the woods in Chang Lixiong's hometown.

Each time she came here, she thought of Master Chang, the first man in her life. Yet whenever Huang Peiyu was not with her, she completely forgot his existence. Huang Peiyu was an educated man; he should be even more reasonable and understanding than Master Chang. But she could never be sure what he really thought of things. Huang Peiyu could own her as he might own a rose in a garden: without real feelings.

He always wanted to be on top, pressing down on her. He would not tolerate any other way of making love. He'd bitten into the tattooed flower on her left shoulder until she screamed with pain. He'd come as he watched her face twist with pain.

Once, when Huang Peiyu noticed that she was not very willing, he told her he was putting up with too much in his daily business and wanted to totally relax when he was in bed with her. This she could understand. From then on, she had always made sure she served him well, from the time they had sex until he fell asleep. She tried not to feel anything, nor to show any resentment.

It wasn't as if Huang Peiyu had this sense of ownership only about her. He was just like that as a person. But precisely for this reason, the image of Chang Lixiong rose higher within her heart. She often imagined it was Master Chang in bed with her when Huang Peiyu was pressing down on her.

Now she understood: if one really loved a man, then at the height of happiness one would drift into a world of fantasy. When she was with Chang Lixiong, she nearly always fainted. In those few minutes she had very strange sensations. She remembered one such fantasy vividly: she was waiting for Chang Lixiong at the old ruined city wall. Willows were blowing softly in the wind and it was a long time before he turned up. Suddenly she understood she should take her clothes off. Just as she had expected, Chang Lixiong's arms embraced her from behind as soon as she had done this, nearly crushing her into pieces. Without a word he carried her and together they jumped off the wall and rolled downhill until they finally dropped into a pond filled with newly flowering lotus blossoms. Clasped tightly together, they became two drops of water upon the blossoms. Her feet kicked the leaves and the leaves moved up and down.

That month, in the old days at the Duchess Pavilion, she had spent almost every day in bed with Master Chang. One day Madame Emerald had broken in, bearing a bowl of soup. The net was not down and she glimpsed their love making. Chang Lixiong was on top and Cassia below, with a flushed face, her eyes avoiding Madame Emerald. But Chang Lixiong would not let her go; he acted as if he had not seen Madame Emerald. He was a strong man and he wrapped his arms around Cassia even more tightly.

'I've brought some soup.' Madame Emerald was embarrassed. Being a madame in a brothel, she didn't mind seeing such scenes. But the two were stuck together like glue; and she found it hard to swallow the fact that the man on top was Master Chang himself. Trying to get herself out of the embarrassing situation she repeated: 'I've brought soup.' His hands on Cassia's breasts, Master Chang said: 'Soup! Great; give me some.'

'There it is – on the table.'

'Where? I can't see it. I'm thirsty and I'm occupied. Feed me!'

Madame Emerald had no option but to come and sit by the bed and lean over Master Chang, feeding him the soup. He drank one large mouthful and passed the second one on, using his mouth, to the woman beneath him. The two carried on. Madame Emerald could neither leave nor stay. But Chang Lixiong's dramatic voyeuristic gesture made the heart of the woman below him beat like a drum. This time, the wave remained on the tip, until neither could refrain from shouting out loud, screaming alarmingly. The final overwhelming crush made them both breathless and sweaty. Before they released the tight grip they had on each other, their bodies had loosened and collapsed together. In the several minutes of faintness that ensued there was a long dream. Her heart was like the sky, with no centre and no edge. The sun filled the sea, wave after wave, never-ending. She smiled sweetly at this fantasy. Madame Emerald, who was used to seeing affairs of the heart, was dumbfounded at having witnessed this scene.

Afterwards Madame Emerald stopped her and said, in a sour tone of voice: 'You really had a good time, you little cheap slut!' Even later Madame Emerald would occasionally tease Cassia about it, saying in a strange voice: 'The satisfaction you had that day, if you only gave Huang Peiyu a third of it, his bones would melt into jelly.'

With Huang Peiyu it was like dragonflies dipping in the water. Apart from that first time at the hotel, when he was stimulated by their first contact, he hardly ever came more than once in a night. In order to please Huang Peiyu, and to make herself happy, she had tried her best: but she always failed. Her body was like a sick fish that could not swim at ease; she'd always fall before she reached the peak.

She felt a sense of loss in her heart. Her earliest sexual experiences had been too beautiful, too exciting. Ever since Master Chang's miserable death she had never been able to relive that wonderful experience. However much she murmured to herself 'I am doing this as a thank you to Huang Peiyu, he has been good to me,' it did not help; not even if she meant it sincerely.

There were not many people in the Zhang Garden. She walked into a pavilion and saw a building opposite, on the other side of the pond that was filled with people. The crowd even spilled out of it. She crossed the bridge and walked through them. A short-haired, bespectacled woman of fine and delicate features was giving a speech; most of the listeners were women, some of them foreign women.

The speaker was at most thirty years old, and her voice was clear and loud. 'This is a man's world. Men want women to be "talentless"; they say that's our "virtue". But what about us? We lack ambition for ourselves; we are short-sighted and weak-minded. We beg for men to be our masters. We are a bunch of good-for-nothing slaves, who would be miserable without a master!'

'Who's that woman?' Cassia asked a short-haired female student next to her.

But everyone was watching the speaker attentively, afraid to miss a single word. She asked again and the student turned, glimpsed her briefly, dismissed her wealthy women's clothing, turned away again and ignored her.

The speaker was getting excited: 'We must smash unequal male chauvinism! In society we must get rid of the principle of men ruling women, in the family we must smash the principle of husbands ruling wives!'

Cassia waited till she finished talking and then walked up to the speaker, who was still surrounded by the crowd. May she ask a question, she asked? A listener such as her must have been rare; the speaker nodded. Cassia said: 'Your speech was indeed thorough; but I don't understand why you avoided talking about sex? Tell me, shall we do away with men being on top, women only pleasing men?'

Surprised at this question, the woman carefully studied Cassia. After a long while she replied that this was a good question. 'Women should not be treated like mere tools for accommodating the sex drives of men. But we cannot point this out because to do so would bring criticism upon the women's liberation movement.' She was about to ask Cassia's name when some other audience members dragged her away to ask more questions. It was getting dark and Cassia could no longer wait, so she headed for the theatre.

But the woman she had seen on her birthday in Zhang Garden left a deep impression on Cassia. Little did she imagine that many years later the two would reunite again, to fight a battle against society.

The King's Theatre, an English-style theatre with stalls and boxes, and room for as many as a thousand audience members, would be completed in October that year. It would have the latest stage equipment, all of which would be ready for use for Cassia's new play.

At around 11am, Liu Ji, a man who had been invited to come over to talk about the opera 'Madame Butterfly' finished his speech. He played a gramophone recording of one of the more famous arias, 'One Fine Day'. Cassia sang with the record and followed the famous high note all the way to the top. All those present applauded her.

'It sounds wonderful,' Cassia said, 'but I'm not sure about the story. An Eastern woman waiting forlornly for a Western man? No, no.'

Mr Liu Ji was a man of medium height who wore a pair of glasses. Patiently, he said: 'It is not about waiting for a man; it is about the life and death intensity of the lovers' feelings for each other. "Madame Butterfly" is a very famous Western play!'

'Well I wouldn't play a character like that!' said Cassia. 'Not even if it is a famous Western play. I just don't like silly women.'

'Then let me tell you about Wilde's play, "Lady Windermere's Fan."'

Liu Ji had just returned from France after four years studying drama and had been recommended as a director for Cassia's Ruyi Troupe.

He had found it hard to accept the fact that even the so called 'civilised plays' of the time had men acting the role of women. But Cassia allowed men and women to perform on the same stage, not caring about others' comments. Her plays usually touched on common people's lives and the lives of people in Shanghai were getting more and more Westernised. No well-adapted Western play would appear forced here.

It seemed to him as if Cassia's troupe had been set up especially for him; it was totally beyond his expectations.

He explained the play carefully to Cassia. The whole story happened over a single day, the birthday of a young married woman. The husband gave her a fan as a birthday present and she suspected he was having an affair, until she discovered the woman she suspected her husband of having an affair with was her mother, for whom she had been looking for years.

'That's not a bad story in itself,' Cassia said immediately: 'But we have to change the names. Foreign names sound awkward and they would sound even more absurd when sung in Shanghai dialect. I am also not sure that we should pretend to look like foreigners. Why don't we just change everyone into Shanghainese? Make it a Shanghai story: change the title as well. Let's call it: "The Young Mistress's Fan."'

'That's a good idea!' Liu Ji said admiringly: 'I shall start adapting it tomorrow. Let's make the fan a sandalwood fan, and Mrs Windermere would be the young mistress; Mrs Erlynne a prostitute? No, a socialite. The lord should be a young good-for-nothing.'

Cassia added: 'The husband is a snob; and let's make the naughty lord a playboy who was prepared to sell the young mistress, who eloped with him, to a brothel.' She was getting excited by such a prospect: to get someone to adapt directly from a Western play was something she had never done before. 'When do you think you could produce it? All the words will have to be accompanied by tunes; why don't you write them out first and we'll try to fit tunes to them.'

'I will work day and night!' Liu Ji said.

Cassia immediately wanted to talk about money: he had originally been asked to come and talk to her about plays, not to adapt them. She asked what he thought of the Ruyi Troupe signing a contract with him and paying him ten per cent of the revenue from ticket sales.

Liu Ji felt it was unscholarly to talk about money so soon. He tried to be modest and decline, but thought to himself that the sum involved would not in any case be very big.

Seeing him hesitate, Cassia said: 'How about this: I feel it's unfair to ask you to risk anything. We'll pay you a one-off payment. So long as the words make sense and are rhythmic, we'll pay you a fee of 500 yuan.'

Liu Ji was delighted. An annual salary for a well-respected professor at this time was 200 yuan, an enviable amount. He was only just over twenty years old and he had never come across such a huge amount of money before.

He went off that day in high spirits. Cassia was a generous mistress to work for. The Ruyi Troupe had hired him as a literature advisor, they wanted to be enlightened. Each week he would talk to them about a story from Western drama, such as 'La Traviata'. To be paid 500 yuan for an adapted script which had not yet been written; it felt as if a pie had fallen from heaven. He was overjoyed. Later, he was to regret agreeing to this 'huge' one-off payment as the play became very popular and ran for a long time. The ten per cent would have resulted in no less than several thousand yuan. But since he had made the choice himself after careful consideration, he could not blame anyone else.

Ever since then, he became a fast friend with the generous and straightforward Cassia. He was almost a full-time art supervisor for the Ruyi Troupe. For the first time a peasant play of the Shenqu type had its own proper script and director. They used new-style set design and invited a lighting engineer to install new lights of many colours. The face of the Shenqu had changed totally; it was now famed as 'Shanghai Opera'.

Newspaper headlines such as 'Young Mistress intoxicates

Shanghai', announced that Cassia was leading a Shenqu revolution. 'The bonds between mother and daughter are unbreakable; the affection between husband and wife incredible,' said another. The new play, with its strange, enticing plot was sold out for one hundred days.

Cassia's grand dressing room was filled with flower baskets of all colours and scents. The telephone rang, and she said, 'I'm not answering it.'

Li Yu came over and picked up the phone. She listened to the person on the other line speaking, covered it, turned and said: 'Miss, it's Master Huang.'

Her hands holding a powder puff, her hair full of decorations, Cassia asked Li Yu to hold the telephone for her. She said sweetly to the phone: 'My old man, you must at least come and cheer me on once for the new play. I'm sure it will please you. I know – you are busy. Well, I'm going straight home after this. Of course I will miss you. I miss you every time I open my eyes and you're not there.'

She waved a hand and gestured for Li Yu to remove the telephone.

She knew Huang Peiyu was only paying her attention out of politeness. To him she was no longer as attractive as before and he had begun to pretend.

CHAPTER 14

Connaught Road was one of the smartest streets in Western Shanghai. Most of the concession areas had become centres of commerce, banking and industry, but some in Western Shanghai remained residential. Chinese parasol trees lined the road on either side, touching in the middle to create a thick shade under which few cars and fewer people passed.

It was two years since they had moved into Number 54. Cassia loved the peaceful surroundings. Once they had settled in, she sent Xiu Fang to go and buy twenty-two white rose bushes to be planted in the front and back garden. She said she'd wait until she was twenty-three, and then see what signs the roses brought.

She was twenty-four this year and all the roses had lived. Spring had now passed and they had grown well, with many blossoms blooming alongside the rosebuds. Branches were creeping up the wall. The rose bushes were flourishing and had bloomed in greater abundance than in the previous year.

'This house is fit for my mistress to live in now that there are roses here.' Xiu Fang was pleased with her newly-acquired gardening skills. She wore a soft, thin silk skirt with two wide 'trumpet' sleeves. It had been raining for the last three days and now the sky was deep blue. A cool breeze blew pleasantly on their faces.

At the street corner, two women got out of a black car. They sent the car back and began to look along the street for Number 54. It was evening and all the houses in the street had front as well as back gardens. There were no passers-by from whom to ask the way. It took them a while to find the house with its black, iron-barred gate at the front, and masses of small blue wild flowers that filled the empty beds. The roses creeping up the wall were already blooming magnificently.

The women, one strong and well-built, the other slender and elegant, saw the house number, pushed open the iron railings and rang the bell at the front. Someone inside asked, 'Who is it?'

'We're from Master Huang's house,' the strongly-built woman answered.

Xiu Fang opened the door just a crack but the woman pushed it wide open. Xiu Fang was about to protest when the strongly-built woman slapped her hard in the face and the slender one ordered: 'Get out of the way!'

The elegant and delicate set-up in the sitting room enraged the slender woman even more. 'Smash everything up!', she screamed. At her words the woman with a larger build began a frenzy of destruction.

The slender woman strode up the stairs, switching the lights on as she went. She saw the many photos of Cassia on stage which hung all over the corridors and rooms of the house. Finally, she stopped in front of the huge double bed, facing a large mirror. In it one could see the reflection of the three smaller mirrors which stood on the dressing table by the wall. The woman sneered and pulled out the drawers of the dressing table, turning them inside out. All their contents were thrown on the floor.

On the bedside table was a huge photo album, filled with Cassia's newspaper cuttings, comments and reviews. The woman caught sight of a page taken from a magazine, in which Cassia and Huang Peiyu were shown together with several other famous Shanghai personalities. The caption below them said:

'Shenqu Reform Society holds its first annual meeting; this picture shows stars and famous personalities of Shanghai.'

Cassia and Huang Peiyu were leaning quite close to each other.

Wearing a Western-style black evening dress and an expensive-looking necklace, Cassia appeared calm and sweet.

The woman went red in the face and roared. She began to tear at the photo album, but the pages were strong and were not easy to destroy. She had to go through it page by page, ripping the photos out of it as she did so.

Outside, she heard a car braking sharply. The bitch must be back, the woman thought, but without fear. She tore at the album even harder.

Several people rushed in. Before the strongly-built woman, who was a maid, could open her mouth she was smashed in the face and fell down. 'Sixth…' she shouted, trying to warn her mistress, but Li Yu had shoved a sock into her mouth. Cassia took one look at the broken china in the hall, walked to the kitchen and saw the same scene of devastation. Now she headed upstairs. Xiu Fang and Li Yu looked as if they were about to follow her, but she waved them away.

Sooner or later there would have been a clash. Yet she had not imagined that the women would come smashing their way in to her home like this. Cassia had thought it was the first wife who would be most likely to make the first move. As far as she knew the first wife had been chosen by Huang Peiyu's mother. She was close to Huang Peiyu and had given him three sons. Her family was famous in the north of Zhejiang. Huang Peiyu feared her a little.

The other concubines had been content to eat leisurely meals and play *Mahjong* all night, knowing only too well that none of them could monopolise Huang Peiyu. It was better for them if he had a woman outside the household than if he married again and brought her inside. So they did not bother making a fuss.

Only Lu Xianglan, the Sixth Concubine, minded. She had once been a famous Peking Opera star; Huang Peiyu's favourite. Two years ago, in order to make sure Lu Xianglan would be granted the title 'Queen of the Theatre', Huang Peiyu had another famous actress poisoned in a manner that ruined her voice. As a result Lu Xianglan became 'Queen' as she had wished. But as soon as she was married she was no longer allowed to sing in public, only at private functions. This was a deal they had agreed on before the marriage.

Cassia had been shocked when she got the phone call from Xiu Fang. She had called Li Yu and three other helpers, then rushed home.

If it hadn't been for the maid's screams, Cassia would have thought it was the first wife who had come. But as it was the Sixth Concubine, she must change tack. To Huang Peiyu's first wife she could perhaps explain everything clearly, but with the Sixth Concubine she must behave like a fool.

As she climbed the stairs she thought of ways to deal with the situation. As she entered her bedroom, she could hear drawers and cabinets being turned over. She pushed the door open and saw papers littering the floor, and the woman still trying to tear at the newspaper cuttings. Cassia said carelessly: 'Go on, tear it all, don't leave a single page out.'

Not expecting her to say such a thing, the woman froze, breathless with anger.

Cassia kicked the hard cover of the photo album, saying, 'Actually this album is not mine, it belongs to the old man. He asked someone to check through the papers every day and make this album.'

As if out of curiosity Cassia bent down and picked up a few broken pieces. She took a brief look at each, smiled and then discarded it. 'The old man liked to flip through this,' she said, 'but I don't care much about it. Give it a month or two, who would remember such news? The china, the antique vases, the furniture downstairs: they are not mine either; they're nothing to do with me. You might as well burn the whole house down, see if I care!'

'Cassia Xiao!' the woman shouted angrily: 'You are nothing

but a lowly maid who got lucky. How dare a dirty peasant maid from a brothel try and outdo me!'

Cassia sauntered over to the dressing table, kicking aside the scattered make-up that lay in her way. She sat calmly on the sofa by the window. 'You are so right, Sixth Mistress. How dare I compare myself to Lu Xianglan, Queen of the Theatre, a true lady from a fine scholarly family, one who is an expert in music, chess, calligraphy and painting? How dare the Dongxiang ballads be compared to the Peking Opera, which was personally favoured by her Majesty the Queen Dowager Cixi?'

Cassia's words of appeasement surprised the Sixth Concubine. 'You think you are clever with words, do you? You think you can use the bedroom skills you picked up in the brothels to allure men forever, do you?' The Sixth Concubine cursed loudly, 'The days of a whore are numbered!'

Now she was closer to her, Cassia was able to examine Lu Xianglan, the Sixth Concubine. She must have been about twenty-seven or twenty-eight years old. In the evening light she looked just like the beauties in the Peking Opera: there was no need for make up. She had long almond eyes, a cherry red small mouth and a melon-shaped face – she was a classic beauty. Needless to say, such a face would look absolutely charming when it was fully made-up. One could imagine what striking looks she must have had when she was younger. No wonder Huang Peiyu had wanted to marry her and had taken her home.

Perhaps she had thought about it all and knew that she could not be 'Queen' forever. Perhaps that was why she had agreed to leave her career behind and marry Huang Peiyu. When Huang Peiyu had married her, the banquet was supposed to have been the most luxurious and extravagant in Shanghai. Hundreds of tables were set; hundreds of stars of Peking Opera and Kunqu from the north and the south of the country were invited. For three days they performed together on a single stage to celebrate the marriage and satisfy the appetite of their fans. The newspapers said no such feast had been seen for well over thirty years, and the couple were congratulated on such a beautiful union. Cassia knew about this event, which had taken place when she was at her lowest ebb. Several times she had wandered by the Huangpu River and wanted to jump in.

The Sixth Concubine was breathless with curses: 'See how you arrange this room as if it's a brothel! The mirrors, reflecting you sleeping with men! You fox! Do you think you could own him?' Then she became tired and sat on the bed. 'You know what men need over a long time? They need elegance, they want taste. And you, where is your refinement, your elegance?' She picked up a cutting, peered at the photo on it and threw it in front of Cassia in disgust:

'Look at you, wearing that evening dress. You still look like a peasant girl in it. You spoil that nice dress. Go and look at yourself in the mirror!'

Cassia took no notice of the papers she had discarded. With sincerity, she said: 'I have no need to look in the mirror. I know I cannot compare to you. To be honest I am actually pleased to meet you. I have admired you ever since I was a child. I so wanted to see your plays, but could not afford to buy the tickets. And now you are sitting here right in front of me. It's good we have at last met.' Seeing that the Sixth Concubine was looking at her speechless, Cassia appeared even more sincere and earnest: 'I think perhaps you have misunderstood me. I never could possess a man, nor did I ever want to.'

'So you know your limits...?' The Sixth Concubine was at a loss at these words.

'Of course. We are not of the same class,' Cassia said.

'What do you mean?'

Cassia stood up, and approached the Sixth Concubine; then she said intimately: 'When the old man grows tired of me, he will go back to you. Just as Peking Opera is our national form of theatre and could never lose out to local ballads.' She lowered her voice:

'But today you have done wrong. The old man is coming over tonight. What would he say when he saw such a scene? Would he not think you are disgracing him?'

Suddenly frightened, the Sixth Concubine collapsed on the bed and began to cry.

'In my opinion you must leave as quickly as you can. The taxi I called has not left yet. I will ask the driver to wait for you. Go back to your house and leave your maid behind to help me tidy up. I will send her back as soon as we've done.'

The Sixth Concubine didn't stir. Cassia said: 'We are all women who wait on men. If I had married and become his seventh concubine, then I could perhaps threaten to take your man away from you. But I am nothing but a mistress: I can be sent away at a flick of his fingers.'

The Sixth Concubine stood up, took out a handkerchief and wiped her face, complaining as she did so: 'Why on earth did I agree to marry him as a concubine? I have lost my personal freedom, yet still I have to suffer at the hands of people like you.'

It was Cassia who helped the Sixth Concubine down the stairs. She motioned to her own maids and other helpers, who were waiting at the foot of the stairs, not to stir. She pushed the Sixth Concubine into the taxi and asked the driver to take her to the Huang household. She watched the car leave and returned to the house.

Xiu Fang and Li Yu took Cassia to the store room beneath the stairs, where she was shown the strongly-built maid, who had been tied up.

She thought for a bit, and then sent everyone away. A young lad began to pick the chairs up from the stairs. Li Yu told him to leave things for the moment.

When everyone had gone Cassia sat on the arm of the sofa and rang Yu Qiyang, who asked: 'What has happened? Why are you phoning so late?'

177

'Too late for what?' Cassia answered in bad temper: 'Yu, listen, tell the old man to come here quickly. The Sixth Concubine has come with some people and smashed the house up. She is about to burn the place down! Ask him to come now, my neighbour is going to call the police!'

Putting the phone down, Cassia went to the kitchen and found a cup. The teapot had been smashed but luckily there was some water in the bottom of it. Carefully she poured the water into the cup and drank it.

'Miss?' Xiu Fang came over, concerned.

Cassia did not speak. She put the teacup carefully back on the table. Smoothing her tangled hair, she asked Xiu Fang to bring a comb over and help her to put her hair back in place.

A little later, Huang Peiyu rushed in. He saw the rubbish-strewn floor, including the priceless Song vase, which was a little chipped. His face changed. He found the small missing piece on the floor and handed to Li Yu. 'Go and find someone to patch it up, though I wonder how much it's worth now it's been broken.'

He patted his hands together and saw the muddy footprints on the blossom-patterned green sofa. Shaking his head, he sighed.

Coming upstairs, he saw Cassia, dressed smartly and carefully patching up the torn newspaper cuttings. 'You've been frightened,' he said. 'How that bitch must have made you suffer!'

Cassia looked up and said calmly: 'Well, she's a woman after all, where do you find women who are not jealous?'

'The bitch is being totally unreasonable,' Huang Peiyu stamped his feet: 'I'm not going to put up with it!'

'You have to give her a chance to let off steam.' Cassia smiled at him with traces of tears in her eyes. As if making an effort to hide them, she stopped talking and bent down to patch up the photo album.

Huang Peiyu went on to check the other rooms. Their dressing room had been the worst hit; even his own clothes were thrown all over the floor. He went downstairs. The maid had already been untied. He said to the frightened woman, 'Do you want to go to prison?'

The maid opened her mouth and quickly shook her head: 'My lord, please spare me.' The servant knew how frightening Huang Peiyu could be. She had not imagined her mistress would slip away first, leaving her alone to shoulder the responsibility.

Huang Peiyu said: 'Then go back home to your hometown, and don't ever let me see you again. You are not permitted to go back to my house to fetch your things!'

The maid knelt down on the floor: 'Please my lord, please spare me!'

Huang Peiyu said: 'Did you hear me?'

The maid nodded.

'Then what are you waiting for? If you don't return to your mistress, I will not punish you further.'

The maid scrambled up, opened the door and rushed out.

Yu Qiyang had arrived by then and watched the maid stumbling out. Huang Peiyu found a single sofa on which there were no broken pieces, dusted off the footprints and sat down. Yu motioned for Xiu Fang and Li Yu to leave and waited for Huang Peiyu to speak first.

Only the two of them were left in the sitting room. They could hear the two maids cleaning the kitchen. For a long time Huang Peiyu didn't speak. Then Yu asked patiently, 'Master?'

'I fear the consequences if I do anything to her.' Huang Peiyu sighed: 'Even if I spent some money and drove this bitch out, they'll still report it in the newspapers. That will not do Cassia any good.'

Yu asked simply: 'Can you get her to leave of her own accord?'

Huang Peiyu said she would not leave unless she fell for some other man and took a large amount of money with her, which she would have to have squirrelled away somewhere. This cat was not the type to just up and go without a big fuss.

Yu laughed to himself: that wouldn't be easy. 'How could she fall for any other men when she spends her life inside your house?'

Huang Peiyu turned and pointed at Yu. 'You will do!'

Yu was frightened and protested quickly, 'People like us wouldn't know how to handle a bad-tempered diva of an actress!'

Huang Peiyu laughed loudly: 'Of course I know that. She isn't your type.' He lowered his voice and asked Yu to bend down towards him. Then he whispered: 'I'll give you one month to make her fall for you. Make her elope.'

Yu remained expressionless, as if he hadn't heard. Still bent down to Huang Peiyu, he gave no answer.

'Go and finish her off somewhere outside Shanghai. Do it neatly, don't leave any trace!'

Yu frowned and hesitated: 'I've never killed a woman before.'

'Neither have I,' Huang Peiyu said: 'But women nowadays are different, they are hardly like women at all.' He patted the back of Yu's hand. 'Let's make a start then. I'll reward you richly.' Seeing that Yu still looked reluctant, he said, 'Though if you are unwilling then I won't force you. You know me.'

Yu thought about it and said: 'Of course, boss, I'll do anything you order me to. But I don't think she'll fall for me somehow.'

'You know how to deal with women, I know that. There's no need to hide the fact.' Huang Peiyu praised Yu openly: 'And you always make sure they are attracted to you, but you remain unattached.'

'But she is your concubine...'

'Now she is the person I most despise.' Huang Peiyu stood up with a serious look on his face and said, 'So. You are clear what you have to do?'

'Yes, boss.'

That night, after Yu had gone, Huang Peiyu asked Li Yu and Xiu Fang to come to the sitting room and clean up. He went back upstairs and found everything already tidied up. All the pieces of the torn album were piled up together and placed on the table. All the smashed make-up was inside a cloth sack. Cassia emerged from the bathroom. She invited Huang Peiyu to go and wash. She had already prepared the hot water for him. Wearing only underwear, she walked softly to the window and drew the curtain.

Huang Peiyu felt the woman in front of him was simply too good to be true. She should cry and make a scene. She should complain and demand that he punish the Sixth Concubine. But she did nothing of the sort. It was as if none of this was anything she should care about. All that she cared about was that he ate well and slept. There'd never been such a gentle and understanding woman in his household. He had never come across such a woman before, alluring yet wise.

More than anything, Huang Peiyu loathed women who lost their tempers. They always seemed to become recklessly hysterical, no matter whether or not it was justified. That he'd found such a perfect woman as Cassia made him feel that he must have been a really good man in his past life.

Cassia walked up the corridor and turned back to him, smiling charmingly: 'Don't think too much about it. I'll be back in a second.'

Huang Peiyu said: 'Bring back a cup of tea.'

'That is exactly why I'm going downstairs,' she said.

~ CHAPTER 15 ~

One morning Cassia received an invitation to attend a fancy dress party at the American Consulate to mark the Mid–Autumn Festival. She couldn't make up her mind whether to go or not; she had been in a strange mood lately.

Women who worked in brothels had a way of avoiding pregnancy: one only needed to put musk paste on their lower bellies. But if one later wanted children, it became hard to get pregnant. This was a drastic way of ensuring that one had no descendents.

As soon as she started receiving clients at The Jade Pavilion, the madame had explained that if you became pregnant under these circumstances, it was not only bad luck: you would also harm the child.

'Think about it: if you're sure you're ready, let me know.'

She had told the madame she had made up her mind without hesitating.

Now Li Yu went to get a traditional doctor for Cassia, taking her cleaning cloth with her. As she went out she closed the bedroom door behind her, but then pushed it open again, with a mysterious look on her face. The day the Sixth Concubine had thrown a tantrum, while she was cleaning up in the kitchen, Xiu Fang had overheard Master Huang and Yu Qiyang talking about something.

'What did he say?' Cassia called her in immediately and made her shut the door, though there was no one else in the house.

'It's about the Sixth Concubine. Master Huang asked Yu to…' Li Yu glanced at Cassia and made a gesture with her hand on her neck.

The colour of Cassia's face changed: '... kill her?'

Li Yu nodded.

'Really?' Cassia walked to the window. The white roses outside the house stretched towards the glass window. They fluttered in the wind, as if flirting with it. She knew by informing Huang Peiyu of what the Sixth Concubine had done, she had made sure that she would not escape punishment. Perhaps he'd drive her away and cause a stir in the world of Peking Opera. But it was completely beyond her expectations that he could be so ruthless as to want to kill her, without any care for the affection he must once have had for her. Cold sweat appeared on her hands.

'Did Yu agree to do it?'

'Xiu Fang could not hear clearly,' Li Yu said: 'When Xiu Fang comes back, ask her for yourself.'

At lunchtime, Xiu Fang confirmed everything Li Yu had said. 'I was walking past and heard Master Huang saying all of these things, but Yu did not agree to it.'

Cassia smiled: 'Is that right?'

'I think Master Huang said that if Yu was not willing, then he would not force him.' Observing the habit of many years, Xiu Fang would not share a table with Cassia and only came up when Cassia had finished eating. Xiu Fang recalled the scene and explained that, fearing Huang Peiyu and Yu would discover her, she had withdrawn to the kitchen so was unable to hear every detail of their conversation.

Cassia grew worried. Xiu Fang advised her not to worry too much. Whatever happened to the 'Queen of Opera', it had nothing to do with her.

Xiu Fang was indeed a clever maid; she guessed that Cassia felt guilty about the situation. But Cassia suddenly realised that it was really Yu she was worried about. The Sixth Concubine was merely a mean little woman; but it wouldn't be good at all if Yu were to become involved in a murder on his boss's behalf.

Before they knew it, the Mid-Autumn Festival was upon them. On the 15th day of the eighth moon of the traditional calendar, even before it was fully dark, a luminous round globe had risen behind the gaps in the concrete buildings, casting a glistening light over the whole of Shanghai. Cassia started changing as soon as she finished her performance. She had hired a mask and a long white dress that swept along the floor.

The invitation said she could bring a partner. She thought about it and sat by the telephone.

At the other end, a woman answered the phone. Cassia asked whether Mr Yu Qiyang was in.

'No, he's not in.'

'When will he be back?'

'I don't know.'

She was about to leave a message but the woman had already hung up.

These last few days, Yu was nowhere to be seen; Huang Peiyu also had scarcely made any appearances. This was fine with her; she had been able to concentrate on her new play.

Now the American ambassador, sporting a Lincoln-style beard, was giving a long speech: the Americans are guests in China; even here in the concessions they were no one's masters. He was determined to be the good friend of Shanghai residents from all over the world, including the representatives from all walks of Shanghai life who were present today. This was just the beginning of a long relationship and he raised the wine glass with a Chinese toast he'd just picked up: 'On such a beautiful night, in front of such beautiful scenery, I wish everyone here to be as happy and healthy as the beautiful round moon!' His pronunciation was good, but the words he used were too formal, causing most to applaud blindly even though they didn't really understand what he was saying.

After the applause, he placed a feather-covered mask over his face. Many candles glittered around the dance floor. The band started to play and the waiter poured wine for the guests. This unprecedented fancy dress party was the grandest, the most frivolous of all the parties and social gatherings that Cassia had attended in Shanghai. It was an eye-opening experience for her, and also a bewildering one: among the Western costumes there were angels and devils and medieval knights, among the Chinese themes she could see Guangong the hero, Chang'er the moon lady, and a very proper-looking General Zhao Gong, all borrowed from stage shows. Most wore Western-style white fancy dress masks on their faces.

Cassia searched for Huang Peiyu. She thought he'd never bring his wife with her bound feet, so who would accompany him to such a party? Purely out of curiosity, she walked into the crowd. It was good that everyone was wearing a mask, as no one could recognise anyone else.

The curtains and walls were draped with colourful silks, like a stage. Holding her glass of wine she walked up the stairs, which were dotted with people. Even the corridor upstairs was packed. She had a feeling that Huang Peiyu hadn't come.

But she had to be sure, so she leaned over to look downstairs. A waltz had started and ethereal fairies and angels embraced, twirling around each other. Still she couldn't see anybody that looked like it could be him. She'd recognise him whatever he was wearing. Just then she heard two people talking behind her whose voices were a little familiar. She turned and saw a Chinese man, or at least someone in Chinese costume: a white-gowned monk whose face was covered, revealing just his eyes. He was whispering to a masked Catholic nun.

Cassia deliberately walked past them, looked up and saw the sign for the washroom. She entered. It was very dark inside and with the exception of the flush toilet and the wash basin, was arranged like a woman's boudoir. A lily in a vase in front of the mirror gave out a penetrating fragrance. She turned the tap on to wash her hands and felt someone behind her. She turned and discovered it was the monk, who clasped her tightly. She struggled. At that moment two people in skirts pushed the door open and the monk released her and hurried out.

Cassia hadn't recovered, but even then she knew it had been Yu Qiyang. It had to be. She followed him out and looked around, but couldn't see him anywhere. In one corner she saw a monk and seized him, flipping off his mask. It was a Westerner. She hurried to apologise and the foreigner laughed, feeling pleased with himself.

She asked herself why she was so restless. If Huang Peiyu needed Yu Qiyang to get rid of the Sixth Concubine, he would be sure to ask him to seduce the woman first, causing her to elope with him, to avoid placing himself at risk. This thought made her even more uncomfortable. She had no idea why she was so unhappy about this scenario.

All this had begun because of her! It was she who had caused all this trouble. Now she must take responsibility for it. It was she who had stoked up the fires in Huang Peiyu, though she had seemed calm herself.

'Have you remained well since we last met, Miss Xiao?' It was the nun. Such a pleasing voice as this could only belong to the Sixth Concubine: 'Are you looking for the old man?'

'What if I am?'

'He's busy tonight, so you'll have to make do with me.'

'So my instincts were right,' thought Cassia.

The Sixth Concubine was slender and attractive and the eyes that looked at Cassia were full of spirit. For a moment she felt envy. She was aware that there was no longer the same spirit or passion in her own eyes when she looked at people; they contained only shadows.

'Dance with me to this tune,' said Cassia, wanting to be the first to break the ice.

But the Sixth Concubine turned arrogantly away. 'I'm sorry

– but I can't,' she said. A man dressed as Robin Hood politely took her hand instead, and they stepped onto the dance floor.

A bright moon hung high above the big glass window, but she was no longer in the mood to dance now, and decided to go home. 'Damn you, Yu Qiyang!' She took off her mask and cursed. The housekeeper fetched her bag and asked her what she was saying. 'Nothing,' she replied. Her English had a thick Shanghai accent, but most Westerners in the city were used to this.

A man chased her to the big iron gate and called her back. 'Why are you leaving so early?', he asked. It was Liu Ji.

'I am not feeling very well.'

'Then I shall come with you.'

Cassia thanked him and the two walked out together. She thought: could the man embracing her from behind have been Liu Ji? No, it was not possible, she immediately vetoed the idea. She said: 'What a coincidence that you came to this party too.'

He told her that a friend was forming a new film company and had asked him to help set things up.

'You mean you want to dismiss me as a student?'

'How would I dare do that?' Liu Ji said. Seeing that Cassia smiled at this, he said that his cooperation with the Ruyi Troupe would carry on as normal.

Cassia was curious. Film? That was the sort of thing that street kids watched. They looked silly – but, she supposed, nothing lasted forever. Wasn't Shenqu originally once outside the mainstream? She said: 'Go and do it, then. If you have any problems, let me know and I will help whatever way I can. Come to Ruyi once a week: film might not be all that promising. You need to leave yourself a way out.'

Cassia's words were reasonable and understanding. Liu Ji was moved: 'Mistress Cassia is very thoughtful.'

But where is my way out? Cassia thought. I never have a way out. I only have myself to depend on. The edges of the moon were blurring. Tomorrow was going to be a grey day; it might even rain.

She had got along very well with this student who'd been abroad. They talked and laughed whenever they were together. But Cassia had never thought of him as more than just a friend. Perhaps she was a little in awe of him, this real scholar. Her temper was much too untamed; it was hard for her to fall in love with a man like this. Only underworld figures could satisfy her.

It was Tuesday, the only day in the week when she did not have to perform. The afternoon light was dark and the sky had a hint of grey. That evening she had only one appointment in her diary: dinner with the editor of the *Shanghai Times*. He was a famous writer in Shanghai and had agreed personally to write a feature on her. This was very prestigious. She opened her wardrobe and draped a red velvet scarf outside her long sleeved *qipao*.

Dinner time had not come yet, so she went to the Lao Shun Teahouse.

The teahouse owner was pleased to see her. 'It's Miss Xiao! Master Huang has just left.'

'It doesn't matter, I was only passing through.'

The teahouse owner was about forty years old, short and honest-looking. He made tea for Cassia, sat opposite her and whispered: 'Master Huang was angry just now.'

Cassia drank a mouthful of tea and listened, as he continued simply: 'His Sixth Concubine is often not at home.'

Cassia handed him a small packet with notes inside, and kept her voice low: 'A small token of my thanks.'

His voice was even lower: 'Thank you, Miss Xiao.' Feeling the weight of the bag, he puzzled: 'Why are there two payments this month?'

Cassia said she might not be coming here very much in future; that he might have to phone the theatre for her from now on. The teahouse owner nodded. She stood up and got ready to go, her voice neither high nor low: 'Today's tea is really not bad.'

'It is the new Longjing. If Miss Xiao likes it, then please take some home to drink.'

Just then Yu Qiyang walked into the teahouse. He saw Cassia and said happily: 'Such a coincidence! How is it that you are free to drink tea here?'

Cassia replied, 'But I thought you weren't living in Shanghai any more, why are you hiding here?'

Yu wore a long gown and seemed in high spirits. He made as if to block her path, asking why she was going just as soon as he'd arrived? 'Sit down, take a seat!' Cassia said apologetically to him that it was getting late and she had an appointment to meet someone at the Fengya Restaurant.

Yu walked her outside. After only two steps the sky darkened and he asked Cassia to wait a second. A minute later, he came out with an umbrella for her. Cassia took the umbrella and looked him deep in the eyes, wanting to ask him about the Sixth Concubine. But suddenly she felt unable to speak. It was such an awkward question, if it was nothing to do with him, and even more awkward if it was.

'Why is it that you keep so many things locked up inside you?' Yu said.

'It's nothing.' Cassia watched the cars passing on the road, 'It's thundery, but one can't tell whether it is going to rain or not.' Seeing that Yu was ready to return to the teahouse, she couldn't contain herself any longer. 'You aren't going to meet the Sixth Concubine tonight, are you?'

Yu Qiyang stiffened: 'I have no idea what you are talking about!'

'Listen to me, don't get involved.'

Yu Qiyang stretched out his left hand and patted her shoulder, as if to comfort her. She kept silent, so he faced her and said: 'It's not what you imagine.'

This surprised her. So he was not merely acting as instructed;

he had other plans. He was actually in love and had feelings for the woman! And now it sounded as if she was being jealous. She had secretly worried that the Sixth Concubine would take Yu's heart, now at last she was proved right. Normally he wouldn't even touch her hands, but now he patted her shoulders. This proved that he had nothing to hide from her. She said: 'I can see that you are completely crazy. But whatever you do, don't do it in Shanghai. It is for your own good that I said what I said.'

The two carried on walking; neither looked at the other.

'What if it was in Shanghai?'

'It would bother me.'

'What's it to do with you? Don't ask about things that don't concern you, don't say things you shouldn't.'

It was lucky she hadn't asked if it was he who pretended to be a monk, embracing her from behind. This man still refused to treat her properly; he still bore a grudge against her. 'Yu...' Cassia bit her lips and felt a strange bitterness in her heart. 'Do look after yourself. It's hard for both of us.'

'I thank Miss Cassia for her guidance!' Yu said sarcastically and turned to leave without saying goodbye. She couldn't help but look back at him, as he stepped away so unfeelingly. Wasn't he aware of her staring at him? All the dark clouds in the sky now twirled around her; even if there was heavy thunder, she wouldn't have hesitated about throwing away the umbrella he had given her.

She didn't enjoy her meal that night. *The Times* sent over two people: the editor and the deputy editor, who took notes. The editor was clever enough to see that she was distracted, that she kept staring at the pouring rain outside the window. He said: 'Perhaps we should just eat today and relax; let's do the interview another time.'

Cassia realised she was being unprofessional and insisted on doing the interview. Afterwards the editor ordered a car to send her home.

The rain stopped and water accumulated in the irregular slabs of stone.

When Cassia returned to 54 Connaught Road, Xiu Fang had already prepared the hot water using the boiler. Cassia started to fill the bath with water, turning the tap marked 'H', thinking that Yu Qiyang was sure to be in bed with the Sixth Concubine by now.

She didn't want to carry on thinking any more. From underneath the bed she fetched her soft-soled, embroidered slippers, decorated with a brown bird resting on a branch. She liked to wear them the moment she got out of the bath.

Suddenly she realised that she had never ceased to care for Yu Qiyang. Ever since they had been reunited, these last two years, he had always been in the back of her mind. When he had relationships with other women, she always minded. For a long time after each such encounter of his, her heart would ache. She had to rise above such feelings, because there could never be anything between them and both understood their own positions only too well. Neither would step out of line. They both relied on the Hong Brotherhood for a living; one step out of the place, and everything would be worse.

Such was fate, she thought. One on the top of the table, the other just below. She would have to make sure she never looked underneath.

She found that her eyes had become terribly moist and pressed a damp cloth to them. She wondered to herself: 'Isn't there anyone who truly loves me, and who I can truly love back?'

Over breakfast the next morning, Cassia learned that Yu Qiyang had left Shanghai after their meeting. That morning Xiu Fang talked constantly about the strange things Yu used to do. Cassia told Xiu Fang not to mention his name in front of her any more.

But Xiu Fang smiled mischievously. She walked over and took the bamboo cage from the kitchen window, acting as if she was about to set free the love bird inside.

Cassia stopped her: 'Master Huang sent that bird.'

'But it was Yu who brought it over. He must have chosen it.'

'Hey, you have a clever tongue on you!' Cassia was really annoyed this time, 'Do you really want to make me angry?'

Xiu Fang had hardly ever seen her looking so stern. Without a word she went to the garden and hung the birdcage on a tree-branch.

Cassia sent spies out, asking them to come back with more detailed news as soon as they heard anything. One afternoon, she had gathered from her sources in the Huang household that the Sixth Concubine had eloped with his private savings. Huang Peiyu had already reported this to the police, at the same time formally proclaiming that they were now separated. Then a month later she finally heard that Yu Qiyang had returned – by himself.

She only found out what happened many years later, from Yu himself. Perhaps they were the only two people in the world who knew. Yu sighed as he recounted the story to her, saying that a life such as his was not so easy to live.

The night was dark on board the ferry. Yu held the coquettish Sixth Concubine in his arms. It was all very romantic. They were appreciating the moon together on the rear deck. The Sixth Concubine leaned on him, intoxicated. He leaned down to kiss her and their bodies were clasped together for a long time. He took her hands and led her to the prow of the ship. Her hands clasped his neck; she tiptoed and wouldn't let him go. The peaks on either side of the ship seemed slowly pushed back, and a steep cliff rose straight from the surface of the river and into the darkened sky.

The deck was dark, but occasionally searchlights shot past. Catching a moment when the Sixth Concubine closed her eyes happily, Yu Qiyang brought out a bar made of pig iron, wrapped in a piece of cloth. With a swift movement he knocked her unconscious. Then, with one hand he held onto her as, using the other, he hung a rope that he had prepared earlier around her neck. Then he picked her up and threw her into the river.

When the searchlight returned, he had already turned around, and looked as if he was waiting for his lover who'd just gone to fetch something from the cabin.

The river was a glistening black, and one could only see occasional splashes of water beaten by the propeller.

Even years later, Cassia shuddered when she mentioned this. It was not that she was shocked at the detailed and flawless arrangement Yu Qiyang had made, it was that her own plays depended on tortured and sentimental love to move others. What Yu had done made her realise that the tears she had shed on stage were merely water moistening the stone on which real knives were sharpened.

Ever since then she found it hard to perform in sentimental love plays. But she could forgive Yu: only he knew whether he had real feelings for the woman or not; though even if he did, he still had to obey orders by killing her.

~ CHAPTER 16 ~

Wearing a white Western suit, Yu Qiyang hired a box to watch a performance of 'The Young Mistress's Fan'. Cassia was so startled on suddenly discovering him there that she forgot her words. Holding the sandalwood fan she circled the whole stage, without singing a single word.

Even before he left Shanghai, Cassia thought, Yu had hardly ever come to see her plays. Since his return, he'd never appeared either. Though at this point she didn't know how he had carried out Huang Peiyu's task, she knew he had accomplished it. Perhaps he'd even received a bonus for it and was now in such a good mood that he came to see her play! This made her feel even more restless.

Seeing Li Yu, who was watching backstage, gesturing to her in a worrying way, she immediately recovered and became 'the young mistress' once again, telling the playboy that she was ready to elope with him. The playboy seemed happy but as soon as the young mistress's back was turned, he didn't look so overjoyed. In the play it seemed there was no shortage of men who wanted to play with the young lady's feelings.

The 'young mistress' returned backstage and became Cassia again. Li Yu brought her a cup of tea. She asked for her lipstick to be re-applied and the make-up artist hurried to start work on her.

She knew she was not the person she used to be, and that she would not miss Yu Qiyang as fully as she had before. She had thought many things through lately.

On stage the socialite – the lover of the husband – arrived, and the playboy entertained her.

Cassia returned to the stage, becoming the young mistress once more. She sang a duet with the socialite, each expressing their own feelings. Finally the socialite sacrificed herself for love and departed from the city with a broken heart, so that the young mistress could return to her husband.

Waves of applause rang out. Cassia bowed on stage to thank the audience and looked over to Yu's box. He was not there any more. She was a bit disappointed: Yu was a little like the playboy in the play: he would come and go as he pleased. Women were cheap, she thought; even she could not free herself of this strange muddle.

It had taken some effort for her to succeed in not thinking about Yu, but today he had nearly ruined the play for her. This kind of thing had never happened to Cassia before. Her fans worshipped her and she always took care to ensure that the show lived up to their expectations.

But little did she imagine that Yu would appear as soon as she stepped into the dressing room. His knock was unmistakeable, a rhythmic '*tic*'.

Cassia guessed immediately who it was and shouted to him: 'What is it?'

Yu said, his lips close to the door: 'Master Huang said he'd come to Connaught Road tonight.'

Cassia kept deliberately silent. Huang Peiyu had been very unpredictable lately. He often treated her poorly, considering her less than he did his concubines at home. Now that she was his, he used her like old clothes, picking her up and discarding her as he pleased. Ever since the Sixth Concubine had 'run away from Shanghai with a man', Huang Peiyu had completely changed in terms of the way he treated Cassia. He started to notice other women and often went to the Pleasant Spring Pavilion. He visited Cassia less and less.

'I'm not even an old piece of clothing; perhaps I am nothing but a shoe cloth now?' She smashed the teacups on the floor: 'Go away, you running dog!'

Yu was still outside. 'What happened?' he said.

Cassia whipped the door open and, not caring she was only wearing underwear, shouted angrily: 'Go tell the Grand Master Huang, he can go to Si Malu, get himself a common street prostitute and take her to Connaught Road! I would rather stay at the theatre.' She slammed the door shut.

Yu Qiyang waited a minute, and then started knocking. Nobody answered. He knocked lightly again. Cassia came and pulled the door open before she returned to her seat before the mirror. Yu edged his way in and saw traces of tears on her face, which had messed up her make-up, while the handkerchief she used to wipe away the tears made her face look odd. Her hair, though, had been smoothed neatly, and she had dressed smartly. A long silk scarf was draped over her shoulders, beneath which was a purple evening dress.

'I was ordered to come here,' Yu tried to explain, but didn't know how to continue. He attempted a smile to soothe her, but failed.

Cassia took off the silk scarf and held it in her hand. She said, 'Do you think I don't know it is you who accompanies him to the Pleasant Spring Pavilion? Pretending you are talking business with foreigners, when you are actually seeing the prostitutes there. Don't think I am jealous! He's said several times before that he'd come over here to stay the night, but I waited and waited and ended up not even seeing a ghost. No telephone call, no apologies. Now, today, the thunder has sounded – but who knows where the rain's going to fall?'

Yu didn't speak.

Cassia refused to look at him but lowered her head and turned and walked out of the dressing room. She draped the silk scarf back around herself and said angrily: 'Come on then, what are you waiting for? Death?'

Yu drove the car. Watching Cassia through the rear-view mirror, he said softly: 'Your face.'

Cassia took out her make-up box from her handbag and looked at herself in the mirror. Yu turned on the indoor light to help her patch herself up.

The car drove straight into Connaught Road and stopped in front of Cassia's house. She walked out of the car and took her keys from her bag. But Xiu Fang had already opened the door and it was obvious to Cassia that Huang Peiyu wasn't there.

'Has Master Huang rung?' Cassia frowned and looked at the clock on the wall; it was nearly eleven o'clock.

'No, he hasn't.' Xiu Fang walked towards her room.

Suddenly Cassia had a strong intuition. She hurried to the door and opened it: Yu Qiyang's car was still outside. The white roses had already started to whither and the petals had fallen onto the steps. The moonlit night was cool as water. She thought for a minute, stepped a few steps forward, and waved at Yu Qiyang.

He looked up and saw her. Then he pointed at himself and then the house. Cassia nodded.

Yu hesitated for a few seconds, then opened the car door and got out.

The sofa cover in the sitting room had changed to a soft green pattern, which went well with the white of the curtain. The only light in the room was a table lamp. Cassia fetched Yu a cup of tea and then sat down.

'Why is it that there is less furniture?' Yu Qiyang was trying to find something to say.

Cassia stared into his eyes and said she had to thank the Sixth Concubine, who'd smashed everything up. She originally thought of adding some more, but changed her mind. It might be a good thing, she thought, to have less furniture.

'It's true. The room appears bigger.'

'You haven't been here for a long time,' Cassia said: 'More than two-and-a-half months.'

'Surely it's not that long.' Yu put the teacup down.

When Xiu Fang had first opened the door, Cassia noticed that the moon was at the corner of a nearby window. Now Yu was in the room, it had moved to the middle of the window. Cassia didn't glance at the clock on the wall, which said it was already 11.10 pm. She said to Yu: 'May I trouble you to ring your boss? At which brothel is he staying?'

Yu smiled and said: 'Which one would you like me to ring first?'

'Ring all of them, one after another!' Cassia threw the telephone book at him: 'Tonight you must be sure to find him. He is deliberately making fun of me. No, you don't want to make the call – so I will!'

'All right, all right, I'll call,' Yu said in resignation. He took off his Western suit and revealed the white shirt beneath, over which he wore a tie and the braces of his Western trousers. When he phoned, he sounded deadly earnest: 'Is that the Duchess Pavilion? I want Madame Emerald. Yes, to come to a tea party. Old? No, she's not too old, not at all, still a perfect beauty.'

Cassia burst into a laugh: 'Don't you tease the old lady. Another few years, I will be an old lady myself for you to laugh at. All right, ring the Huang household and ask them.'

Yu held the phone, but didn't stir.

Cassia said: 'Go on, what's the matter? If I rang the Huang household, I'd frighten them to death!'

Yu said hesitatingly: 'It's far too late. It won't look good if I ring him from here.'

Cassia suddenly understood. She raised her head to look at Yu: he had indeed turned out to be a clever young man, first rate in fact. His hair was smoothed backwards, not a strand out of place. He looked smart and handsome. She realised she hadn't looked at him properly for a long time. Just as she had said to Li Yu, she didn't think that much of him any more. Perhaps this was why she had dared to call him in and he had dared to come in.

Yu looked up at her, too. For a moment neither was able to talk, though both knew the words which were on the tip of their tongues. Cassia stood up and Yu also rose. 'I'll go and fetch your hot tea,' Cassia rushed to say.

Yu sank back onto the sofa.

Cassia was in the kitchen and suddenly remembered: if she was not wrong, then today was Yu's birthday. Li Yu had told the story of Yu's origins in perfect detail. What a coincidence!

Smiling, she brought out a tray with two wine glasses on it. A bottle of French red wine plus a plate of cakes.

Yu looked at her strangely. Her radiant smile seemed out of place.

'Come, let's make a toast to celebrate somebody's birthday!' Cassia said happily.

'Your birthday?' Yu looked pleased, 'No, it's already past. See what a bad memory I've got!' He slapped his own head: 'Heavens, today is my birthday!' he recalled at last and shook his head. This was a man who rarely remembered birthdays, she realised, and certainly never considered his own worth celebrating. But Cassia shared the same humble origins, so it did not seem such a bad thing to celebrate here his twenty-fifth year in this world.

'To the handsome youth of the birthday star!'

'No, no. To the everlasting youth of the great beauty.'

Cassia drank slowly, holding the wine cup. Yu did the same. Neither of them was good at drinking. She had dressed tonight for Huang Peiyu. After she had taken off the silk scarf, her bare-shouldered evening dress revealed her figure. At twenty-four years old, a fine age, she wasn't prepared to get drunk too easily: it would be only too easy to get drunk and to feel awkward when sober.

The clock struck twelve. Cassia kicked off her high heels and lay down on the sofa with her head resting on her hands. Slanting her eyes she looked at Yu Qiyang and said in a soft voice: 'Yu. If you dare not make a phone call, then what will you do if Master Huang entered the room now? How would you explain yourself then?'

Yu smiled uneasily. He licked his lips, put down the wine glass in his hand and reached for his jacket: 'I'll leave now.'

'So you want to escape?' Cassia stretched out a hand to gently squeeze the corner of his jacket; what if I don't let you run away?' she asked.

Yu looked at her and stood up hesitantly: 'The boss could come at any minute!' He did sound frightened.

'Absolutely right.'

The bottle on the tea table was still more than half full. Her eyes turned from the tea table to him and stood up: 'I want to give myself to you as a birthday present,' she said.

Yu lowered his head: 'No, don't...' He started to step away.

'Tell me, that day, at the American's fancy dress party. Was that you dressed as a monk, all in white?'

He didn't nod, but neither did he shake his head. He merely stood and stared at her foolishly. Two seconds later, he recovered and insisted again on leaving. But she had already come close and raised her face to gaze at him deeply: 'Huang Peiyu is a man, aren't you a man, Yu Qiyang?' She embraced him and rested her head gently on his shoulders.

Yu's hands still clasped his jacket, wanting to struggle free, 'You know Master Huang is the King of Shanghai.'

This angered Cassia. She pushed him away violently and turned to move a few steps away from him.

Seeing that he'd offended her, Yu grew anxious. Throwing away his jacket, he carefully stood behind her. They could hear each other's hearts beat and the 'tick-tock' of the clock. Cassia felt the air in the house freeze. She saw herself standing once more underneath the peach tree in the Duchess Pavilion. Moonlight shone on them and she closed her eyes, stepping back involuntarily. A mere step and she would be clasped together with him. She held his hand and turned to face him. Then she kissed him.

She had waited far too long for this, hesitated far too long. Now she did not want to let it stop. It was as if, by lengthening this kiss, she could make up, one by one, all the years they had been apart, the passion she released now had to compensate for all the years of frustrated desire. She moved another few steps and crushed him down on the sofa.

'Why can't you be the King of Shanghai?' She looked him in the eyes and said: 'As Queen of Shanghai, whichever man I fall in love with, he will be King.'

This seemed to remind Yu Qiyang of his own status. He struggled to free himself from her embrace and silently picked up the clothes on the floor. Instead of standing up to stop him, Cassia silently rose and covered her leg with a corner of her skirt.

Standing by the sofa Yu told Cassia with a sense of shame that Master Huang had many spies; that he would never hesitate when he wanted to kill someone. 'To get rid of you and me, for him, would be like strangling two caged birds.' Indeed, there would be no need for him to do anything, someone else would do it for him. He only had to arrange the setting, and make sure nobody asked any questions.

'Of course.' Cassia paused and thought for a while, then something made her say, choosing her words carefully, 'I have long had the feeling that there is nothing in the world that this man would not dare to do.'

Yu looked at her intently. Then he said, 'How much have you thought about it, I mean really thought about it?'

She started. He was still watching her closely. Finally she whispered: 'Then you too believe that he was implicated in Master Chang's death?' It was her woman's instinct and her love for Chang Lixiong that had made her suspect this all along, but she still wanted that final confirmation.

Yu nodded.

She stared at him, waiting for him to continue. Yu bit his lip. Finally it seemed as if he had made a big decision. 'I've known it for a long time,' he said. 'Yes, it was Huang Peiyu who arranged for the Qing Brotherhood to come and perform the assassination,' he sighed. 'But who is there to avenge Master Chang now?' he continued bitterly. 'Everyone in the Hong Brotherhood, from top ranking brothers down to the most junior members, have to make a living somehow in this city. There's a new "Emperor" and they've all switched allegiance.'

Cassia closed her eyes: the questions that had been in her heart for so long had finally found an answer. Of course, Yu would be interested in avenging Master Chang's death. Yes, he too had wanted to find out the truth. She hadn't misjudged him.

Yu continued: That night, eight years ago, after the gunfight with the Qing Brotherhood, he had not followed the other Hong Brothers in their exodus into the countryside, but instead tried to smash his way into the Qing camp, wanting to catch a ringleader for interrogation. Finding his desired target, and placing a knife on the man's throat he forced out the confession that there had indeed been instructions about shooting to death everybody but the man who drove the carriage.

That day, when Huang Peiyu had jumped on the driver's seat and driven the carriage out of the hail of bullets, Yu Qiyang and the Third Master had also attached themselves to the carriage, thus escaping with their lives. Huang Peiyu's brave act had made everyone admire him; now it turned out it was all a set up.

'What did you do with the man you caught?' Cassia asked.

'I had no way of getting him to the Chief Advisor! Our enemies were catching up fast,' Yu said despairingly. Now he recalled the situation – he had been forced to stab the informant to death, causing blood to splash all over him. At first he had wanted to tell her that, because he knew that she had wanted to avenge Master Chang's death more than anyone. That was why he had rushed to the Duchess Pavilion before daybreak. But in the end he himself had depended on Huang Peiyu to get him out of jail.

Yu's heart was heavy and neither said a word for a while. From the outside came the sound of two rattling carriages, one after the other. It made Cassia recall the night of the fight when that other carriage, and the mad, desperate sound of horses' hooves, disappeared into the night. Silence settled again on the room and Yu said, 'It was simple for Huang Peiyu. He took advantage of the rivalry between the two gangs. He got the gangsters to do his killings for him. Later he used his power in the concessions as a back up. In effect, what he did was conquer the Hong Brotherhood by becoming its Grand Master.

'Everyone obeyed him,' Yu continued, 'so who could I tell about the secret I'd found out? And what if I did tell someone? A single word out of place would mean death. Never mind people such as the Chief Advisor and the Third Master. Even I had to make sure I flattered the new boss, just to survive.'

'So, you are now content with being his lackey!' Cassia was silent for a long time, then her anger burst out with venom: 'You're like a mangy dog who'd suck the teats of any bitch who'll feed you. No – people like you are worse than dogs.'

'Whatever you say.' Yu was offended and rose, 'You have to admit Huang Peiyu knows how to deal with Westerners; they rely on him. He socialises with politicians and warlords, and as a result the Hong Brotherhood in Shanghai has prospered: it is to everyone's advantage.'

'You mean Master Chang was not as able as Huang Peiyu?' Cassia nearly jumped off her seat. She hated to hear him say this. It sounded like treason.

Yu held his tongue when he saw how her eyes shone when she mentioned Master Chang. He said: 'Cassia, Master Chang personally promoted me. How could I ever forget his kindness? But times have changed and even if we had avenged him, then what? How would we carry on living? What would happen to your troupe? Who would I be an aide to, to make a living?'

Cassia ground her teeth in anger.

Yu turned to leave the house, then paused at the door: 'Be very, very careful. Don't rush into things. Please listen to me!' He thought for a second, then came back inside the room and placed a hand on her shoulders. Looking directly into her eyes, he said: 'Whatever you do, consult with me first. Remember, if you can't trust even me, there is no one in the world that you can trust!'

The door clanged shut and Cassia walked slowly upstairs to her bedroom. She lay on the bed in a stupor. Suddenly something occured to her: how could Master Chang not have known Huang Peiyu was dangerous? He would have known it – but still he went ahead, sacrificing himself because he was sure this man could help him fulfil his dream of fighting the Qing dictatorship.

She had often wondered these last eight years whether it was possible that Master Chang had been driven to his death by Huang Peiyu. Today Yu Qiyang had confirmed her suspicions. When Master Chang died, he was covered in blood, yet refused to close his eyes. Was he trying to hint to her to pick up the gun in his hand? Did he know that one day it would be her turn to act?

She was a mere woman, how could she accomplish something men couldn't?

She turned and faced the ceiling, listening to the sound of an engine starting and watched the light of the car creep its way swiftly across the ceiling and then disappear. In the half-darkness her soft sobbing could be heard, mingled with sighs. 'Are there any real men left in Shanghai?' she murmured to herself.

Then, suddenly, she remembered the first moment she had met Huang Peiyu, eight years ago. Extremely nervous, Huang Peiyu had not glanced once at her, until finally when the extended version of the Seven-Star Formation was being laid out and she saw that he was about to pick up the wrong wine cup, she had unconsciously blinked once and the man had realised immediately his error and selected the right cup. As a result of this, Master Chang had believed the man was an important Hong Brotherhood figure. Later on, when they met at the Licha Hotel, Huang Peiyu had mentioned this as proof that Cassia had had feelings for him ever since that first meeting.

Now that she remembered everything, she realised it was her blink that helped Huang Peiyu to pass the final hurdle, to convince Master Chang that he was one of them, leading to his death! So she was the traitor who caused Chang's death. If she hadn't blinked and Huang Peiyu had made a mistake, then Master Chang would surely have driven the man away, or at least would have been on guard and would not have invited him to talk all through the night. The plot of the assassins would then not have succeeded, because before midnight most of the Hong Brotherhood was still at the Duchess Pavilion!

The sudden realization struck her like a bolt of sharp lightning, making her feel numb. It was she who had caused Master Chang's downfall! When she had blinked, she was merely showing off her excellent memory: Master Chang had asked Madame Emerald to teach her the rules of the Hong Brotherhood in two days, and she had remembered everything almost instantly! She was too young to know any better. That half-second of showing-off had killed Master Chang!

Now she felt an agony of remorse. Madame Emerald had once said she was a 'curse', a woman of 'bad luck'; she was right, of course, absolutely right.

Cassia was sweating all over and breathing heavily. She nearly fainted. When she recovered she thought things over and regained some clarity of mind.

There was only one thing to do: she had to heal this wound herself, otherwise she would not be able to carry on living.

When Li Yu returned from the theatre at ten o'clock the next morning, she discovered that the breakfast she'd prepared for Cassia had been left untouched. Normally Cassia was up by now, had washed and would be sitting in the garden having breakfast and some milk. Li Yu and Xiu Fang divided their labours. Li Yu would look after Cassia at the theatre and manage the budget; Xiu Fang's job was to look after the house, tidy the rooms and wash clothes. If Cassia ate at home, Xiu Fang would buy the vegetables and cook – one was responsible for domestic duties and the other for external ones. But whether or not Cassia was in the house or not, one of them was always there.

The two women got along very well and helped each other out. Perhaps it was because they enjoyed a generous salary, or perhaps it was because Cassia trusted both of them that they were never jealous of each other.

Li Yu took the milk upstairs. The bedroom door was wide open and Cassia was still in bed. She knew that Huang Peiyu would not be there. Whenever he stayed the night, he would get up early and be gone by now.

Cassia heard a sound, opened her eyes and asked: 'What time is it?'

'Still early.'

'I have a slight headache.' Cassia sat up and leaned on the bed. Her hair was in a mess, her eyelids swollen.

Li Yu touched her forehead, but fortunately it was not hot.

'I drank some wine last night.'

'But Master Huang didn't come last night.' Li Yu was clever: she guessed immediately.

'Yu was here.' Cassia continued. She'd never lie to the servants about these things. She couldn't anyway.

Li Yu turned: 'I'll go and fetch you some soup to sober you up, but drink this milk up first.'

Cassia said: 'You can think what you like.'

'You're always so considerate to Yu.'

Cassia drunk a mouthful of the milk and smiled: 'Not this time.'

~ CHAPTER 17 ~

After Cassia had taken the curtain calls, she came backstage to find the largest basket of flowers had been signed 'Huang Peiyu' and knew that this was his way of saying 'sorry'. But she still would not receive his phone calls, nor leave the theatre where she had been staying the last few days. She asked Li Yu to call him and say that she was not feeling well and that her period hadn't stopped yet.

Li Yu said: 'A Chinese doctor has been here and she's now feeling slightly better.'

The telephone hung up at the other end. Cassia said: 'Is he still meeting that prostitute?'

Li Yu said: 'I've checked, that woman had a chill and it affected her face, she cannot see visitors.'

Cassia knew that the reality was more complicated than this. Huang Peiyu had not been in a good mood lately. The Nationalist Party's Anti-Yuan Shikai campaign had failed dismally. Sun Yat-sen, the president of the party, had escaped to Japan. He had asked Huang Peiyu to raise a huge fund to support his revolutionary party for a 'third revolution'. Huang Peiyu believed Sun Yat-sen was acting foolishly and made excuses, saying he was having difficulty finding the sum. The two parted company over this. Some around Sun Yat-sen had already started to criticise Huang Peiyu, saying that he enjoyed the power and glory of an underworld godfather, was morally degenerate and a traitor to the revolution. He must be exposed. But Sun Yat-sen was a professional politician; he simply believed that Huang Peiyu had become a liability and should not be used again.

Had Huang Peiyu become a traitor to Sun Yat-sen? Cassia was

not bothered. To her it was simple: if Huang Peiyu had asked her opinion, she would have told him not to give his name to anything that would result in a handing over of the Hong Brotherhood's properties.

For she knew him. While he was studying in Japan, Huang Peiyu had joined Sun Yat-sen's Alliance Society, and was sent over to Shanghai with the specific purpose of mobilising the Hong Brotherhood into joining the revolution. But he had soon discovered that he now possessed a freedom within the Brotherhood that he had never had when he had been with the revolutionaries. In fact, it had become annoying to a man like him to play at politics, where one always has to espouse high principles.

He had once told Cassia that ever since he discovered the Brotherhood, he had become like a fish in water. The awkward ceremonies, full of contradictions and grammatical mistakes, made him feel superior. Members were not expected to believe in everything they swore an oath to, and he himself did so even less. The revolution was false; the only real thing was to live like a king and enjoy power. He was sick of Sun Yat-sen's overblown plans for the country. Now that he was the Grand Master of the Hong Brotherhood in Shanghai, he felt as if he owned all its property.

Anyway, it was unnecessary for Cassia to know about such grand causes as the revolution, she knew well enough what kind of creatures men were. She knew Huang Peiyu was utterly different to a hot-blooded character such as Chang Lixiong and despised him for it. She did not like capricious characters.

Li Yu put the basket down beside the dressing table. Cassia glimpsed into it and thought that by the day after tomorrow at the latest, Huang Peiyu would be sure to send Yu over to express his sympathy.

Just then they heard a knock at the dressing room door. Cassia said absent-mindedly: 'So soon.' She wiped her face clean and eyed Li Yu.

Li Yu left, her bag in her hand. It was indeed Yu Qiyang. 'My mistress has fallen asleep already. Mr Yu, will you please return another day.'

Li Yu closed the door.

'It is I who wants to see her.'

'The situation still applies, I'm afraid,' Li Yu said patiently: 'Listen to me. Don't go to her tonight. The mistress is not feeling well.' She dragged Yu Qiyang away.

'How long has it been since she moved here?' Yu asked.

Li Yu refused to answer.

Feeling helpless, Yu Qiyang had to leave.

Cassia heard everything clearly from inside the room. She did not want to return to that house. She had brought the low couch to the dressing room, and she slept there. She could sleep anywhere, after all. She was not at all attached to the luxurious house Huang Peiyu had given her. Here, after the play was done, it was actually quite peaceful. She flicked through a novel or two before she fell asleep and rested well. The next morning when she woke up, she could do her usual voice training, breathing exercises and practice walking again.

The next morning, as soon as she left the stage, Yu Qiyang rushed ahead to take her backstage so that she would not be able to prevent him from visiting her. He wore a suit and even his shoes were shining, but in spite of his good looks and smart appearance he looked very melancholic.

Cassia walked ahead of him in the corridor, acting as if she hadn't seen him. She entered the dressing room and he followed her.

'Acting as Huang Peiyyu's pimp again?' Cassia asked rudely.

'I heard you were unwell. I just wanted to come and see you.' It seemed the usually quick-witted Yu had lost his tongue; there were many things he wanted to say but couldn't bring himself to utter.

'You have seen all you need to see: I am well, and you may go and report to that effect.' Cassia no longer took any notice of him.

Yu waited a bit and then said that Huang Peiyu was waiting for Cassia in the dance hall of the Licha Hotel.

Cassia said teasingly: 'Just as I said: you're here as a pimp!' She told herself: Yu lacked backbone. Master Chang had once regarded him as his own adopted son: hadn't he passed on any of his manliness?

'Go and report to Huang Peiyu that I will come immediately. But I don't want you to drive me, I want him to send his driver to fetch me.'

'He is unlikely to do that.'

'Why not?'

'He would be sure to be suspicious and think we are trying to cover something up.'

'There's nothing between us,' Cassia said to the mirror. 'Rest easy, there's nothing between you and me. But since you are so afraid, this time I'll do as you say. Next time, ask him to send someone else. You wait for me in the car and I will be there after I've changed.'

The two sat in the car and didn't talk all the way there. Yu Qiyang lit a cigarette. Cassia took one for herself and lit it also, but she didn't inhale. The cigarette burnt itself out. It wasn't really that far, but they bumped into two stretches of roadworks and had to take a round-about route. The car drove for a long time and it seemed the two of them had reached a stalemate in their relations. Both of them looked pale and exhausted.

Yu walked Cassia to Huang Peiyu's table.

'Darling, I've missed you so much.' Huang Peiyu pulled Cassia into his arms and led her to the chair beside him.

'Aren't you angry with me, my old man?' Cassia enquired.

'Not at all, not at all. Women are entitled to lose their sweet little tempers once in a while, it shows you care about me.'

'But I don't care about you.'

Yu walked up to Huang Peiyu and said that he needed to leave as there was something that needed attending to at home.

'Why are you suddenly in so much of a hurry?' Huang Peiyu and Cassia looked at each other and smiled.

Yu said that his fiancée had arrived. Cassia was startled as she'd never been told that he had a fiancée; neither had Huang Peiyu. The two raised their heads and looked at Yu Qiyang, who explained that his late mother had once appointed the daughter of a fellow countrywoman to be his future wife. Now his mother was dead and the girl whom he'd never met had grown to be a twenty-five-year-old young woman. He had long forgotten about this but she was now all on her own and without any dependants, and she had come looking for him. If he did not shoulder this responsibility then he would not be filial and would not dare to face his long-suffering mother in the next world.

Cassia's heart went cold. So that was why Yu Qiyang had come to look for her several times but always hesitated about what he was going to say. Now he had taken this opportunity to speak up, with Huang Peiyu also present, she didn't even have a chance to be heartbroken.

'Then we must congratulate you,' she said to Yu, pretending nothing had happened. She poked Huang Peiyu: 'Mustn't we?'

Huang Peiyu understood immediately: 'Of course, Yu. I think a big celebration is in order. I'd like to arrange it myself.'

Yu humbly thanked him and said that he hoped Huang Peiyu would allow him a few days off.

That night Cassia returned with Huang Peiyu to Connaught Road. Before he switched off the light, Cassia spread a towel beneath herself, for fear of spoiling the sheets – the bleeding from her period had been ceaseless. The two didn't have sex and Cassia fell asleep after a short while. Huang Peiyu stroked her and his hands reached down to her thigh where he felt the paper-and-cloth belt. He reached inside the cloth belt. Then he went to the bathroom and looked down at his hands: there was indeed blood there. Now he could relax and return to the bed. After only a few minutes he started snoring.

The noise woke Cassia up, and for a while she couldn't sleep. Her eyes open, she stared at the ceiling in the darkness until she drifted off.

Yu Qiyang and she were at a church where several angelic children were singing hymns. Her heart was rising up and down along with the songs. A priest hosted the wedding ceremony. Cassia wore the latest fashionable white Western bridal gown, and Yu Qiyang wore a swallowtail suit. He exchanged rings with her and kissed her. A cameraman was photographing them, the flash was dazzling. She exchanged a sweet smile with him but when she looked again he'd become Huang Peiyu and the priest was Chang Lixiong, who waved the sleeve of his white gown to curse her: 'How could you be with a beast with a man's face?'

Frightened, she woke up and saw that Huang Peiyu was still snoring. She felt thirsty and got out of bed, went downstairs barefoot, and got some water.

Master Chang would never treat her like that, not even when he was asleep. She drank some water but still her mouth felt dry. So she sat on the sofa. The moon shone on her and she did not feel at all sleepy. She found a cigar in the drawer, lit one and smoked it. She forgot herself for a moment and drew her breath in, only to choke on it. Her right hand was a little numb and stiff. She pinched her right fingers with her left hand and only then did she feel her blood once again running freely.

She found a silk-wrapped cloth in the drawer and unwrapped it. It was a dagger – the one Chang Lixiong had given her.

Cassia held the knife, tears came to her eyes and she walked step-by-step up the stairs.

From the other side of the door she could hear Huang Peiyu scream. The door opened a crack and Cassia went in with a cup of water and gently helped Huang Peiyu up. He was having a nightmare. 'Pray it's not true,' he murmured.

For a long time after this Yu Qiyang did not come to the theatre, and neither did he drive to fetch her. One day she accompanied Huang Peiyu to the Lao Shun Teahouse. Third Master and the other senior Hong Brothers were all there, apart from Yu, whom everyone was making fun of. Someone said that Yu Qiyang was not getting out at all, but staying by his wife's side, and now all he could think of was his wedding.

'It's set for next Sunday.'

'I will personally be the host,' Huang Peiyu said to Cassia.

Cassia was all smiles and said she would be sure to send Yu a proper gift when he married.

'Just buy whatever you want and I'll pay for it.' Huang Peiyu had suddenly become especially generous. He was truly pleased about Yu getting married.

'Master Huang is always generous and kind to his staff.' The Chief Advisor nodded flatteringly. 'Yu's from a poor background and it is all Master Huang's doing that he's become who he is today.'

Huang Peiyu asked the driver to take Cassia to the Huada Company on Nanjing Road to buy things on his behalf. She went from shop to shop and saw an extremely handsome bed engraved with blossoms. It was made of chestnut, shining and smooth; it was the widest bed she'd ever seen. She tried to guess what Yu would think when he saw it.

The shop owner was ingratiating and straightened the bedding for her: 'If Mademoiselle likes it, why doesn't she go and lie on it?'

Cassia looked at the owner carefully: he meant it sincerely. She took off her high heels and got on the bed. It was indeed comfortable, like a big boat; she felt as if she was floating on the water, facing the blue sky. Her tiredness was overwhelming.

Cassia got off the bed and stepped back into her shoes. 'Sir, how much would you sell this bed for?'

'Two hundred.' The owner asked: 'Is it for yourself?'

Cassia suddenly grew red in her face – she hadn't behaved as if she was choosing the bed for others. She smoothed the bedspread and said that this was a little bit too expensive.

'If you like it, then have it for 180 yuan.'

'I do like it, and I will buy it. But for the moment keep it here. I will let you know when I'm ready for it to be sent.'

'No problem.'

Cassia paid by cheque. She smiled: all right, she'd gamble with herself and see who would eventually sleep on this bed. She went into a jewellery shop and bought Yu's bride a jadeite necklace and a pocket watch at the Hengdali for Yu himself. Finally she went to the shop next door and bought Huang Peiyu a pair of slippers and herself a piece of superior fine silk.

But she grew restless as Yu's wedding date approached. She spent one whole night awake. She asked Xiu Fang to send the presents she'd bought to Yu two days before the wedding, only to be told that Yu had postponed it.

'To what date?'

'He didn't say. Yu's wife is indeed perfect – one of a kind, with a flat face and chest, very stiff – and extremely ugly.'

'So long as she's a kind person,' Cassia said.

'She is kind all right and boiled me a bowl of egg noodles, with three eggs. I nearly choked to death.'

Cassia walked to the garden, opened the door of the bamboo cage and let the bird fly away.

Melancholy surrounded her. She said to herself: why am I like this? I shouldn't be so miserable. We both knew we never had a chance. Why am I torturing myself? She was getting more distraught now. It was as if a needle was pricking her fingers. Even if she didn't examine the wound, she knew very well that nothing could change. Thin raindrops streaked the glass window pane and a flash of lightning flew across the sky like a snake.

It was during this time that Cassia made a gramophone record for the Far Eastern Company. The few Shenqu pieces she recorded were sung with deep emotion.

The record became a collector's item for her fans. It was said that Cassia cried uncontrollably when she'd finished the singing and that the fans added their tears. Their hearts were broken more easily than their idol's.

Huang Peiyu had arranged with Cassia that after the show that evening he'd come personally to take her back to Connaught Road. It was now nearly ten o'clock and still there was no sign of him. She was feeling angry when the phone rang and Huang Peiyu's voice said: 'I thought I could finish my business earlier, but I am still busy.' From the speaker she could hear voices: a drunken game was going on and women's laughter could be heard.

'You go on being busy. Give me a ring tomorrow.' Cassia managed to continue sounding like she was in a good mood.

The phone hung up at the other end. Only then did she put the receiver down herself. She slammed it down too hard and the whole telephone jumped. She perched on the table; behind her there were two rows of stage photos, as well as some more ordinary shots of her. A fake antique wooden couch was placed near the window, not wide, but as long as a bed. It had two wooden arm rests, in the middle was a bamboo mat, and there was also a pillow and a thin quilt.

She liked to sleep here. The dressing room was not as wide or big as the bedroom in her house. There were many knick-knacks here, but Li Yu was competent and tidied everything up neatly. There was a lot of make-up on the table, and brushes, lipstick and face paints inside the drawer.

Cassia took off her costume – a vertically lined *qipao* and the fake pearl necklace. She smoothed her long hair and tied it up. She picked at the clothes on the clothes racks and couldn't make up her mind even after having been through both rows of them. In the mirror she could see through the semi-transparent silk underwear the line of her smooth stomach and back, the bare arc of her neck. It was as if a layer of brightness had glazed her smooth, clean skin.

A black Western-style dress trimmed with lotus leaves grabbed her attention. She remembered this dress had been sent by Yu, who bought it and sent it to the Licha Hotel after her first night with Huang Peiyu. She took the dress and put it on. Before it had seemed tight; now it was even tighter. She smoothed herself and was surprised to discover that her nipples had hardened. Suddenly she realised that tonight, she did not want to stay here.

She glanced at herself, a woman of twenty-four, still in her youth. She had fallen in love with a man when she was only sixteen and the man had said she was sex crazed; he worried that no one would be able to satisfy her. Indeed ever since then, and many years later, her body was always in a state of hunger; and she no longer experienced the sweet love of those years. She felt herself quickly getting old. If I love several men, I am still young. If I only love one man, I am already old; if I don't love anyone, I do not exist. She patted the back of the chair in confusion and despair. On such a lonely night, wearing a dress with the memory of a man – one who remembered her size – this already satisfied her. When she thought of him, she wanted him very much. She wanted her body to be in contact with his.

That night the wind was cool and the dew icy. She opened the door, entered and turned on a light. Xiu Fang rushed out; it was obvious she had just risen from bed and had just snatched up the first available piece of clothing. It was a man's jacket that hardly covered her.

'Miss, you said you would not return tonight.'

'Hurry back to your room. Make sure you don't catch cold.' Cassia knew Xiu Fang had summoned a boyfriend. She had had several boyfriends this year. Cassia never minded these things and only asked that they come and go by the back garden and never from the front gate.

Xiu Fang was never serious about her relationships but this was no fault of her own. Two years older than Cassia, a servant girl who had worked in a brothel, pretty herself and who happened to work for a good-natured mistress who never asked her about her private affairs: Xiu Fang went from man to man like a trotting horse.

Thinking of her own troubles, Cassia made a joke, intending to relax Xiu Fang. 'Hurry back. If a man gets too nervous he won't get hard! It can make him impotent for the rest of his life!'

Xiu Fang smiled: 'Not many men know how to please a woman anyway. But this stallion of a student, well, he's good-looking and has his uses...'

'Really?' Cassia felt herself cheering up a little, 'Is he? Perhaps I can see him?'

'If my mistress wants to. But I don't know whether he'll be up for it after your inspection.'

Xiu Fang was pleased; perhaps also delighted to have made Cassia happy after seeing her so gloomy. But when she started pulling Cassia into her room, Cassia grew a little jumpy.

Inside a small lamp was lit. The room was square with a bed and a wardrobe. A man was lying on the bed and, on seeing Cassia come in, he rushed to cover his face with a thin quilt. Cassia felt uneasy and said: 'Continue. Don't stop because of me.'

'Miss,' Xiu Fang smiled: 'You can see he's embarrassed.'

Xiu Fang flipped the quilts open and embraced the man: 'What's up? Why aren't you any good any more? Are you nervous?'

She turned and smiled to Cassia, 'See what I meant? One glance and he's useless.'

Cassia understood that since the man was in fear of the

mistress, perhaps she should try to relax him. She sat by the bed and stretched out a hand to smooth his back. He was only about twenty years old at the most and was indeed good-looking. After a while the man grew excited and started to make love to Xiu Fang.

Cassia watched and felt her heart beating fast. She remembered when she was herself in bed with Chang Lixiong with Madame Emerald watching. She had noticed Madame Emerald there and knew the outrageousness of their behaviour. But the more outrageous she felt, the more excited she grew. Her happiness had come and stayed for a long time that time; never in her life since then had she been so excited.

Xiu Fang's cry of pleasure during love-making was good to hear. Her face was flushed and her breasts firm and lovely. Undressed she looked even prettier, and she looked even more charming making love. The man cried out loud, 'I can't bear it any more, I can't!' and attacked her violently while Xiu Fang breathed deep and fast.

After they had finished, Cassia laughed and said: 'Good performance, there will be a reward!'

They sat up on the bed, the two naked bodies. Cassia examined them curiously. Now the three of them were much more natural with each other and Cassia understood a little of how Madame Emerald had felt that day.

She was feeling distracted when she heard Xiu Fang saying: 'Miss, may I wait on you while you change, and have a rest?'

'Help me undress you mean!' Cassia suddenly realised what her maid was suggesting.

But Xiu Fang obviously thought she may not have understood; she pulled at Cassia's sleeves, winked and smiled.

Cassia shook her head, having completely sobered up. She was mistress of the house. There was no way she could so lower her status. She recalled a line from the volume of ancient pornography *Jinpingmei*: 'A master must not lower his status and be intimate with his servants, or the order will be disturbed...'

She rose and slowly walked out of Xiu Fang's room. She walked upstairs alone but soon heard the footsteps of Xiu Fang behind her. 'Miss!' the maid called, worried she might have offended her mistress.

'Go and finish your business. It's getting late and I need to rest.' Cassia said.

Xiu Fang tried to grasp her hands but she turned, and cursed angrily: 'Cheap little bitch, what do you take me for?'

Xiu Fang froze with surprise; her steps going down were not as quick as those coming up. Cassia shook her head and turned on the bedroom light. She drew the curtain and felt miserable. 'The order of the master and servant must not be spoiled.' Madame Emerald had once said to her – she was so right: that year, it had been spoiled.

Lying in bed she felt that the room was too clean and too cold. An otherworldly atmosphere hung around it. Strangely, as soon as this thought came to her, her unbearable lust disappeared.

~ CHAPTER 18 ~

It was strange how her body seemed to heal itself after this strange sexual experience. The lingering illness she had experienced came to an end. Now she looked healthy. The Chinese doctor said there had been an imbalance of Yin and Yang, and it was a very accurate diagnosis. Of course, she and Huang Peiyu had always had sex, but for her it was about pleasing the man and she herself never took pleasure from it. Gradually she had forgotten that she was a woman herself.

Now she discovered that her sexuality was getting stronger. She was both pleased and worried.

The telephone rang and Cassia picked up the phone: it was the owner of the Lao Shun Teahouse; the spy she'd bought. The man was honest in appearance and was smart in his dealings. The telephone conversation didn't last long but when it ended Cassia drew out her handkerchief to wipe the cold sweat away from her face.

'The old fox!' she cursed. Huang Peiyu had sent people to spy on her; luckily that evening she had not done anything rash or stepped out of line. Of course she had been aware of Huang Peiyu, knowing he would test her just as he tested all his concubines. Perhaps even this new boyfriend of Xiu Fang's had been sent deliberately to test her by Huang Peiyu.

If this man were capable of having his own Sixth Concubine murdered, what would he do to any other woman who offended him?

She remembered once, only once, she had made Huang Peiyu unhappy in bed, and he had said only one thing: 'Don't you want to stay here any more?' That had sobered her up. She adored her fox-fur coat in the wardrobe; she was also getting used to the daily hot bath, and the white china flushing toilet was another luxury she cared about very much. This was her weak point. The widely spread rumour in Shanghai was that her exquisite skin was the result of a daily bath in milk. It was not completely unfounded: there was often at least a pint of milk in her bath.

She made a decision: 'I am shameless. Are such luxuries worth sacrificing my honour? I will discard this life, even if it means giving up the chance to have a bath!' And having made what she considered to be a solemn oath, she gradually realised she could live with herself again.

Cassia went out into the garden to prune the blossoming roses. Li Yu glimpsed her in the garden and came over to help her. 'Next spring, I must plant a cherry tree,' Cassia said to Li Yu, 'if I am still living here.'

Li Yu glanced at her and said, 'I am sure I would be able to eat these cherries; I would also give some to Muma for her to taste them.'

Some time ago, Madame Emerald had adopted an orphan. She kept the child to herself, never showing her to her old friends. Cassia knew that for Madame Emerald this was the 'secret treasure that could never be revealed'. She was very devoted to the girl and it was said that recently she'd even sent her to the foreigner's school to receive a Western education. Cassia took a bamboo gardening tool, smoothed a lock of hair and said to Li Yu: 'Go, quickly, send the child's New Year money to Muma. She will need the money; and don't forget to take her the sweets and new clothes I bought for the child.'

Li Yu said: 'Please miss, don't worry, I will arrange everything tomorrow.'

Cassia wanted to say something more but held her tongue.

The first half of November that year marked the end of autumn and the beginning of winter. Everyone relaxed; it was a good time of year for the entertainment business. 'The Young Mistress's Fan' had been on for a year and a month and still each performance was a sell-out. Everyone at The Ruyi Troupe was hoping for a good year and for big red pay packets full of money. But Cassia herself was fed up with 'The Young Mistress's Fan.' She and Liu Ji discussed ideas for new plays and picked at the many plays others had written specially for her. But she was never satisfied. Liu Ji said: 'Then I will have to write something myself. But my time is limited. We'll have to think of a way out.'

'Perhaps we could take an old costume play and change it to a modern play, Cassia said. As they say, 'Foreign bottles can contain local wine and old bottles can contain new wine.'

Liu Ji thought of something; he remarked that he had seen Yu Qiyang that day, 'That able young man from the Hong Brotherhood. Last week he mentioned to me that one of his friends, who has just returned from abroad, wrote scripts for the theatre.'

'You are going to meet Yu tonight?'

'It is his wedding night. Didn't you know?'

'Oh, I'd forgotten,' Cassia said, 'but I have to finish the play before I go and drink wedding wine.' Suddenly she felt restless inside. Yu had not informed her of the news. This was only right. She completely understood why he hadn't. She left Liu Ji talking to the others. As soon as she had left the exit door she went straight back to the dressing room. She asked Li Yu to guard the door well. She hadn't slept well last night and she wanted a good rest.

Worrying that she might sleep through, she left the door ajar so Li Yu could come and wake her.

The room had an English-style window with two wooden shutters. The light seeped through, tracing a pattern in patches. She felt restless on the wooden couch and closed her eyes, trying to sleep. The sunshine leaked through onto her body and face and after a few minutes, she finally drifted into a deep sleep.

Someone came knocking at the door. She heard the sound of the door closing. She heard footsteps, someone walked a few steps and then stopped. After a few moments they moved closer to her and she felt this person next to her. 'Li Yu, what's the matter? Oh, what time is it?' she asked, sleepy and confused.

'Still early,' said a man's voice.

Shocked, her sleepiness immediately left her: 'Yu? No, it can't be,' she told herself. 'Today is his big day, his wedding day; anyway he has almost forgotten about me.'

'It is me.' Still his familiar voice, a bit husky, still low.

She said nothing. Her right hand stirred on the wooden couch and held on to his big, strong hand. Her heart immediately warmed and with her eyes still closed, she said softly: 'Why are you here, ignoring your duties as the groom?'

He held her hands tightly and kissed her hair. Her eyes moistened. 'Don't...' he said.

She pushed him away: 'I don't want your pity. Go!' He said he wanted to see her before that damned wedding.

'I've wronged you, you should go!' She opened her eyes.

Yu Qiyang's head rested on her, his face close to hers: 'Don't you want me?'

'No, I've never wanted you!' Her voice was firm, but her hands wrapped around his neck, not listening to her reason.

Her face now bright red, she burst into tears: 'Of course I want you, once in a lifetime will do! Nobody can interfere with what I want!' Yu Qiyang sealed his lips with hers and would not let her continue. Suddenly she struggled free of his embrace and stood up. Raising her head, she looked haughty. Piece by piece she began to take off her clothes as he too stood up and started to strip. They stared at each other, and knew that they were challenging each other and meeting the challenge: they wanted to do the one thing they had not dared to do for so many years.

Nobody could stop them at this point, because they had started a race. Yu Qiyang watched Cassia place her hands behind her head as she took off her last piece of underwear. Her chest protruded like a statue and the breasts he had fantasised about for so many years were firm, the nipples standing up cockily, like warriors. Now that she'd taken off the last piece of underwear her naked body was tight and taut like an arch.

And he looked much stronger than when he was wearing clothes. His body was in good proportion and apart from a scar on the right hand side his chest was perfect. His hair was messy and his eyes were burning with passion; even his Adam's apple was pulsating. They looked at each other, standing motionless; then she moved closer to him. Suddenly, the two of them entangled like two rivers flowing into one. She grasped his back and dug her nails deep into his flesh and he grasped her hands as he pressed her down on the floor. The costumes and her daytime clothes were knocked down into a pile on the floor; they were crushed by each other. Sometimes he was on top but almost immediately he would be pushed down and she was on top. Neither wanted to be the one to initiate the entry, as if this would cancel out the long yearning they had had for each other. But the more they resisted the more they felt a desire to merge with each other's body.

He kissed her face and her firm, full breasts, then the birthmark that lay between them. She moaned softly: this pained her more than his direct entry. Her hips began to rise and fall.

But she would not let him enter her, and he would not allow her to hold his hard manhood. Whenever her hands grasped it, he'd remove them. He felt his swollen self pressed against her and moved along her hot, moist lips.

She could already feel the inside of her womb open and close and even begin to go into spasms. It was as if she'd already entered the state of happiness but still was unable to grasp anything tangible.

She was in such pain that she started to moan again. Her body suddenly sucked him in and the layers and layers of lips started to wrap around him, inch by inch she swallowed him. Her legs were in spasms, in a state of struggle, and he pressed them down, wanting to enter straight into the deepest part of her.

At that moment their bodies suddenly rose into the sky. Like two whales in the deep sea, there was a beautiful pause when they each stared at each other. They suddenly plunged into the ocean, sinking right to the craggy bottom where all creatures were stunned by their dramatic show and fled away, leaving the wide sea to them. When they emerged out of the water once more, they became two connecting curves, twisting into a spiral with their rising desires.

Her moans became screams and shouts, and her body crashed crazily into his, while he could only breathe and try to catch his breath, emitting a strange sob from his throat.

Suddenly she felt a mist form in front of her. She knew that the fantasy she'd waited for, for so many years had returned. She heard the sound of her own bones being crushed and scattered into powder. She closed her eyes gently and fantasised that this was all happening on stage. She was being watched by so many people and they were moved to tears by the couple's fulfilment. The thought of this brought tears to her eyes as well, and she felt that the bright, warm afternoon light was shining especially for them.

The sunshine filtered through the window onto their naked bodies. They lay flat on the floor. He turned and gazed at her, a strange intensity in his eyes.

She said: 'What's the matter? Never seen a woman before? A man who grew up in a brothel?'

'No –' he said, 'I've never seen a woman such as you.'

'What do you mean?' she asked curiously, looking at him.

He said: 'So composed and dignified on stage, yet so unrestrained in bed.' She saw that it was something that had long been on his mind.

'And isn't this what men want?'

'It is what I like. But other men like their women a bit more reserved. Even a prostitute must know shame and be shy, they do this to please a man.'

'I want only that you want me. Other men can go and find a shy woman!' she exclaimed and held him tight. The two kissed again. Afterwards, they could never remember how many times they'd made love. The whole afternoon they made love again and again, on and off, on and off; it was as if they wanted to make up for all the months and years past – and the months and years to come.

Someone was looking for Cassia outside and was stopped by Li Yu. Afterwards, worried that there would be more knocking, she fetched a stool and sat by herself at the door shelling sunflower seeds. She said to those seeking Cassia: 'My mistress didn't sleep well last night and is resting. She needs to perform tonight.'

The sun had moved from the wooden couch to the dressing mirror, turning slightly red. The number of times Li Yu had to refuse visitors increased. Yu Qiyang withdrew from Cassia's arms and started to get dressed. 'Cassia, I cannot come here often.'

Cassia's voice was very low: 'I know.' She didn't look at him but knew that he was being tactful. This was the first time, but it might also be the last.

Yu Qiyang sighed and said: 'It's fate.'

'I know.'

'And you don't blame me?'

'I could never regret an afternoon like this.'

'It's time to go.'

Cassia turned and put her head on the pillow, sucking a lock of her hair, listening to the sound of him dressing. The room was quiet and already there were the sounds of people and footsteps. Cassia knew that the sun must have sunk into the Huangpu River. How could Yu not leave? They were waiting for him to start the wedding! She turned her face around and saw that he'd already put on his tie and had bent down to tie his shoelace.

He combed his hair with his hands, found his jacket among the pile and put it on.

He walked to the door. She watched. Would he turn his head, she asked herself? He paused, and his steps were hesitant and anxious. But immediately he turned the key and went out. She turned back to lie flat on the bed. The ceiling was too high to touch.

'What are you worried about?' she called after him. 'It's not the end of the world. But go – just go if you have to. I won't hate you for it.' Cassia watched the remaining light of the sun reflected on the wooden couch and murmured to herself: 'I can live without you. I can do whatever I need to do without you.'

~ CHAPTER 19 ~

That night Yu was married. Cassia carried on with her show at the theatre. After the performance she went straight home without taking off her make-up. She found a bicycle and rode first by her house, then further and further afield. That evening many people saw a young woman on a bicycle, who dressed simply but was wearing heavy make-up. Riding past them, she was a flash of bright colour speeding past the parasol trees and foreign-style houses.

His wedding banquet was held at the Hushangxiang Restaurant. Apart from Huang Peiyu, almost all the senior members of the Hong Brotherhood drank to their heart's content. In order for the Brotherhood to have a good time, no business associates were invited. Huang Peiyu didn't stay until the end, but had to rush out to meet a man who had just returned from Japan. Madame Emerald was not there either, which surprised Cassia.

On the third day Madame Emerald, who was passing, dropped by the theatre to see Cassia. She looked slightly better than she had looked last time. 'There were people I did not wish to see there,' Madame Emerald explained. 'There are those in the Hong Brotherhood who do not treat Master Chang's women with respect.' Cassia smiled. There were probably even more who had the same view of her! She invited Madame Emerald to stay on and watch her performance in the evening but Madame Emerald said: 'Not today – next time. I have business to do tonight.' Then she changed the subject and said that she had been feeling very restless since her adopted daughter had been sent to the foreign school. She had been in twice to see her already this week.

Cassia smiled. This woman seemed to have made a firm oath

never to see her perform; she preferred to spend her time with a small child. She had been admirably consistent. Cassia asked when she herself would be allowed to see the child. But Madame Emerald kept quiet.

'Muma, please tell me!' said Cassia.

'It wouldn't be good for anybody...' she muttered.

'Please!'

But Madame Emerald changed the topic again and the two parted awkwardly.

Li Yu came to smooth things over and saw Madame Emerald off on Cassia's behalf. Cassia stood on her own in the corridor. A lizard jumped in front of her, nearly touching her nose. It quickened her heart rate. The lizard slipped in through a gap in the door and when she followed it into the room, she thought she saw a shadow crawling in front of the mirror, but when she got closer it wasn't the lizard. She searched for it everywhere but couldn't find it.

She thought of some old customs from home that she'd long forgotten, hurried to the window and opened it wide. Breathing deeply, she faced the western sky and knelt down and *kowtowed* three times.

That evening, in the car on the way back home, Cassia told Li Yu that she wanted to go and have coffee at the Licha Hotel. They sat in the ground floor coffee bar. A man selling lotus seed pods walked past the window. The street light shone on the pedlar and the bamboo basket in his hand. They passed their money out of the window and bought one *jin* of the pods from him.

The seedpods were green and white, tender and crisp, with a slight hint of bitterness. They sweetened as one chewed them. Li Yu's slender, beautiful fingers deftly opened the shells and picked out the seeds. Then she unpeeled them and put them one by one onto the plate.

Cassia drank her coffee and talked about the origin of the word

'Hong'. Master Chang had told her the day before he died that the character 'Hong'(洪) was taken from the character for 'Han' (漢), the name of the original Chinese race. This became Hong (洪) if you took out from the brushstrokes on the right hand side of 'Han' (漢) the elements 'Zhongtu' (中土) which meant 'central land'.' Li Yu's eyes brightened and said Master Chang was indeed a man of strong feelings.

They'd eaten the whole *jin* of seedpods up without being aware of it and felt refreshed.

Cassia took something wrapped in a silk parcel from out of her small handbag. Unwrapping the parcel she revealed a small dagger with a dark handle engraved with jade. 'This is what Master Chang used to defend himself. I always keep it with me,' she said. She passed it to Li Yu and said that if she looked at it in the sunlight she could see the four words engraved on the blade: 'Fight the Qing and Revive the Ming.'

She had been leaning close to Master Chang the day he'd given her the dagger. When he passed it to her, she had studied it, moving it back and forth, fascinated. Li Yu had been outside the door watching them and had seen everything clearly. Now Li Yu's nose crinkled up sourly and she turned her face away.

The next day, at five in the afternoon, it was time for Cassia to sit in front of the mirror once again. It was her habit to put on her costume first, then wrap her hair up and finally to apply her make-up. The phone on the table rang and she picked it up: 'Old man, how come I haven't seen you for several days? You promised you'd come to support me this week! You must come tonight!'

Words of explanation rang out from the other side.

'But what are you doing that keeps you busy till midnight?' Cassia moaned like a spoiled child, 'Yes, yes, I see, no need to explain. Some foxy spirits must have tempted you this time. You don't know what's it like to be waiting in an empty bed night after night. I can't sleep well if you're not here!'

Huang Peiyu explained that one of his men had lost his mind and killed someone. He had to send people along with money for burial and support, taking care of all arrangements involving the deceased. To be in the Hong Brotherhood meant having to gamble with one's life.

Cassia saw herself freeze in the mirror, and recrossed her folded legs. Li Yu entered and whispered something in her ears. She nodded at her and Li Yu went out.

'All right. Then I will forgive your missing the performance this time.' Cassia calmed down, looking in the mirror, and said: 'But you must come home tonight – you must not let me down this time, otherwise, don't come again.' She laughed and added: '...and if you come, this time I am going to kill you in bed!' She put the phone down and picked up some eyeliner. A plate of Western-style cake was placed on the dressing table. To refresh herself, she would usually drink a little coffee and have a piece of cake before she went on stage.

After the night's performance was over, Cassia sat in the taxi from the English-run Central Taxi Company. New Year was on its way and it was getting cooler fast. More clothes were needed. Cassia pulled up the collar of her fox fur coat and wrapped her sweet smiling face inside the white fur.

The car drove past a street corner, when suddenly another car charged out from a side street and stopped them. The brakes of the two cars screeched. Three men wearing long gowns and rimmed hats jumped out of the car, ran up and pulled guns on the driver and Cassia. They spoke in low, fierce voices: 'We are the police, checking for smuggled opium. Get out!'

The driver emerged with his hands up and saw Cassia being dragged towards the other car by the other two men. Cassia turned to the driver of the taxi: 'Tell Master Huang to teach them a lesson!' but immediately a black cloth was draped over her head and the car door slammed shut. The car drove away quickly and disappeared.

The driver trembled with fear and when he had recovered, he saw Cassia's floral shawl on the ground, quickly picked it up and returned to the car. He drove to the house on 54 Connaught Road, knocked on the door and entered.

Li Yu and Xiu Fang, upon hearing the news, started to sob. Huang Peiyu, who had already arrived and was patiently waiting for Cassia, was on his second round of tea. He came downstairs in his slippers, saw the floral shawl on the sofa and lost his temper. Holding it in his hand, he said to them: 'Stop crying, your mistress will be all right!'

He asked his aides to get more details from the driver and bring the telephone. He tried to contact many people but all were away. Li Yu brought tea but in his anger Huang Peiyu hit out at the teacup, knocking it off the table. Li Yu quickly fetched a cloth and squatted on the floor to tidy up. Luckily Huang Peiyu knew an opium den often frequented by the Chief Advisor, so he ran upstairs and fetched his address book. After a long search he found the number of the den.

The Advisor was indeed there. 'It just happened,' he told him.

'Make me another pot of tea!' shouted Huang Peiyu, slamming the phone down.

After a long while the Advisor rushed in. While the two were talking, Yu Qiyang arrived, with the Third and Fifth Masters.

They were in the sitting room. Huang Peiyu could neither sit nor stand. It was noisy inside the room. Someone suggested looking for the police, someone else suggested posting an advertisement, still others said there would surely be news from the kidnappers tonight or tomorrow.

Surveying the general chaos, Huang Peiyu looked severe: 'There's no point in worrying. Let's not tell the police first; let's wait a bit.' He picked out a cigar and lit one for himself, his hands trembling a little. Suddenly, the telephone rang and everyone in the room stared at it. The Third Master walked over and picked it up. He put a hand over the speaker and said to Huang Peiyu, 'It is the kidnappers.'

Huang Peiyu rushed over and took the phone. He could hear the thick, loud voice of a man: 'Master Huang, fifty gold bars, get them ready in two days, otherwise we'll cut Miss Cassia into pieces, bit by bit. We'll send an ear first, then her nose.'

Huang Peiyu roared: 'Nonsense! How dare you little thieves insult a person like me? How dare someone in Shanghai do this to me? Bring me back the hostage quickly, otherwise I will teach you a lesson.'

The man on the phone laughed and Cassia could be heard, crying for help: 'Old man, save me! Please, save me! Don't be mean with the money. Their knives are scaring me. Oh, my hair!'

The phone was cut off and Huang Peiyu looked at it, and then put it down. The cigar that he'd lit fell on the table next to it, still alight. He picked it up and inhaled.

Now that he'd exchanged the first round with his opponent, he calmed down. This was the sort of thing he had to deal with nearly every week, but it was the first time it had affected him personally.

Huang Peiyu said, 'Don't worry, they won't go anywhere. There are only a limited number of cars in Shanghai. In two days we'll find out who did it. Then we'll see what to do next.' He raised his head and looked at the men around him, giving orders: 'Don't leak the news to anyone! First, make sure we keep the driver detained!'

They heard a car drive swiftly away. Yu rushed out and immediately ran back in to say that the driver had driven away in the car. He'd slipped away while people were rushing around and nobody was watching him. Yu was going to chase him.

His hands still in mid-air, Huang Peiyu stopped Yu in his tracks. He asked instead that he ring the car company and stop them from talking. Tonight they must start searching Shanghai district by district; they needed a lead within two days' time.

But that night the news had already leaked out. Every newspaper seemed unanimously to run it as a 'stop press' story. The next day all newspapers, big and small, reported the event, with huge headlines:

'Miss Cassia Xiao, famous Shenqu star kidnapped by so-called "Concession police anti-smuggling team".'

Sitting in his meeting room at home, a pile of newspapers was placed in front of Huang Peiyu. He was about to read through them when the Third Master was led in by the housekeeper. 'Master,' he said, 'the police department of the Municipal Council rang to say that the foreigners have said the Municipal Council will not interfere with the domestic arrangements of the Master. He wanted to point out that as Chinese Governor for the Municipal Council he must never offer money to these bandits, otherwise security in Shanghai will be compromised.'

Huang Peiyu asked the Third Master to explain clearly to him which foreigner had asked him to send this message.

By now his wives had begun to shout and cry, even louder than the children. Some were knocking at the door, saying they wanted to see him. He roared at the corridor: 'Stop it, I'm fed up! She's only a rotten prostitute! Don't you worry; I'm not going to spend any money on her!' Immediately the noise quietened down. He said to the housekeeper: 'Take all these papers away and let the cursed woman rot!'

The housekeeper took the papers away. He was medium height, about forty years old, with a round face. Huang Peiyu had noticed his housekeeper had grown fatter. It seemed that everyone around him was fat, with an easy conscience. All the troublesome things happened to him!

The third day of Cassia's kidnapping was the day when Huang

Peiyu usually went to the Yongfeng bathhouse for his weekly bath. He asked the aides to prepare his car.

The car stopped at the entrance to a lane and the aides went in. Soon the Chief Advisor emerged in a long robe. After he got in, the car drove straight to the Yongfeng bathhouse. The owner saw Huang Peiyu and the Advisor and came up to greet them, leading them through the large and noisy bath room filled with white, fleshy forms, the masseur beating their backs with towels. The owner pushed a door open for Huang Peiyu and the Advisor, which led to a smaller bath about half of the size of the main one and full of hot steam. It was reserved for special guests only, and it had been arranged that this afternoon there would be no other people there.

Two young men of around twenty looked after them, carefully hanging their clothes, keeping an eye on the fabric so as not to spoil it. This was the yardstick by which their service would be measured. Huang Peiyu's coat was made of leopard skin and the Advisor's was made of marten fur, while he wore a tiger skin waistcoat. The two young lads rubbed hard at the backs of the Advisor and his boss. Without any clothes on, Huang Peiyu seemed thinner and older than before. In the bath, he sighed. Worried, he asked the Advisor: 'Desperate people see my purse and want my money; this is something I have long anticipated. But now the foreigners are involved. What shall I do?'

The Advisor's face and neck were full of wrinkles. His belly flapped loosely. But he was in good health. He listened but kept his silence. When they finished washing they went inside to lie down for a massage and pedicure. Only when he had lain down did the Advisor at last speak: 'Now, it is not your son or your mother, who has been kidnapped. It is merely a mistress. We shouldn't really worry about this, but Cassia is too famous in Shanghai and the newspapers are making too much of a noise about her for us to just forget about it.' The Advisor sent the young masseur to fetch his clothes from the hanger.

The Advisor picked up several newspapers folded together and pointed out to Huang Peiyu, on another couch, the headlines:

'Kidnappers blackmail famous figures in Shanghai.'
'Complex plots suspected.'
'Beauty in danger: where is the hero?'
'How could a hero not rescue a beauty in distress?'

The Advisor handed over a small piece of paper and said there was another, even worse one. Huang Peiyu took it and looked:

'Huang household revealed: not a single note to be paid; beauty does not need to be spared.'

'What is this all about?' Huang Peiyu asked.

The Advisor asked him to look at the main story and he quickly did so: 'This morning the Huang household received a parcel. Inside was a toe. It was confirmed by someone at the household that this belonged to Cassia, who has unbound feet. The Shenqu star will never perform again...'

Huang Peiyu lost his temper before he finished the piece: 'This must be from the Second Concubine, who has bound feet. That rotten woman, she always has bitter words to say. Doesn't she care about my reputation? I am going to drive away the lot of them.'

The Advisor said: 'Women are naturally jealous of each other, don't you lose your temper over that. Aren't there enough women in the world? All it boils down to is how to save your own skin.'

Huang Peiyu sighed and said: 'All my life I have cared only about appearances. It is true that if I don't rescue Cassia I will have no dignity left in Shanghai... If anything should happen to her, it should be after we've parted. Otherwise it is most awkward.'

'A gentleman must care about his dignity,' the Advisor agreed.

Huang Peiyu thought carefully and made a decision. He would not pay the ransom, for he must not offend the foreigners; instead he would find and rescue Cassia and shut the papers up.

The Advisor said that it was of the utmost importance not to offend the foreigners. Without order in the concessions, how would they be able to maintain their status in Shanghai?

'I'll find Cassia and pack her off back to her Chuansha hometown. How could Shanghai be so disturbed by one woman?' Huang Peiyu said angrily, gesturing for the servants to put his clothes back on.

Huang Peiyu asked the Advisor to go back home with him to finalise the details and they left for home after their pedicures were finished. As soon as they were home, and the servants had brought some jasmine tea, the telephone rang. The housekeeper ran in and whispered, 'The kidnappers!'

Huang Peiyu eyed the housekeeper. The latter immediately understood and asked the Advisor to answer the phone. But the kidnappers insisted on speaking directly to Huang Peiyu, who had no option but to talk. The words that he heard were clear enough: 'Warehouse Number 158, Ai'erke Road, Tilan Bridge, 7 a.m. tomorrow morning, we exchange goods.' Huang Peiyu was about to say something, but the other side said: 'No time to waste. Fifty gold bars, not a bar less. One bar less, we'll kill the hostage!' The phone went dead.

Huang Peiyu suppressed his anger and put the phone down.

'Let's take the gold bars with us, but get her out first,' Huang Peiyu decided, and asked the Chief Advisor to go and prepare the gold. He then asked the Third Master to get some men to go undercover somewhere near the adjacent warehouse. They must make sure they didn't hide too close to it, however, or reveal themselves too early. After Cassia had been released, they would follow the kidnappers and when they reached a remote place, capture or kill them and bring back the gold. He was sure that even the Municipal Council would not rebuke him for this plan.

The next day Huang Peiyu and the Chief Advisor rose early and drove towards the Tilan Bridge with two guards. A soft drizzle was falling and as Huang Peiyu and the Advisor arrived in the warehouse area with the gold bars, the Advisor immediately realised that something was wrong.

As soon as the car drove into Ai'erke Road, it became evident that someone was waiting for them. The Chief of the Concessionary Police, a man named Arsan who wore a red turban to signify his position, was waiting at the gate of the warehouse with some of his men. He saw Huang Peiyu's car, blocked the road rudely and asked them to stop.

Huang Peiyu gave orders for the car to stop. The Chief of Police waved for everyone in the car to get out.

He said: 'So, it is Mr Huang Peiyu himself. Come, I'll show you something.' Huang Peiyu and the Advisor followed behind and the Chief of Police opened the warehouse door. Inside were all the armed assassins he'd sent over, who had been arrested and locked in. It was not their fault that they had surrendered; officially they were Chinese staff working within the police force; they did not dare resist the orders of the Chief of Police – even a mere Indian one.

'Are these your men?' asked Arsan.

'Correct. They are my staff, Chinese patrols.' Huang Peiyu said arrogantly. Other Chinese might fear the Indian, but not him.

'What are they doing here?'

'Arresting kidnappers.'

'Then what is Mr Huang doing here?'

'I am here because I am in command.'

'It has been reported to the police that Mr Huang has brought gold as a ransom for the kidnappers. Will Mr Huang let me check his car?'

'Nonsense!' Huang Peiyu cursed, 'What right do you have to check my car?'

'Mr Huang, will you really not allow us to check?', asked the Chief of Police. Huang Peiyu pretended he hadn't heard a thing.

The Chief left, saying to Huang Peiyu as he did so: 'All right, sir, that's very clear,' then, writing in his notebook, 'If Mr Huang won't allow us to check his car, we can't very well do so, can we? We'll just have to record the matter in our report. We won't wait for the kidnappers, if you don't mind sir. But if you still believe they're going to turn up, by all means hang around yourself. You and your merry men. Goodnight, sir.' And he left.

The police car drove off and Huang Peiyu spat at it: 'Dogs!'

The Advisor pulled Huang Peiyu over and told everyone to get away. He pointed at several taxis coming towards them. 'You see the journalists arriving? How fast news travels.'

'Damn it!' Huang Peiyu roared, smashing his hat on the floor in frustration. These were not common kidnappers. He had underestimated them. They had calculated better than him and had swifter means of communication; they even used the newspapers! He sat in the car and it sped up and drove out at high speed, passing on the narrow road the cars with the journalists inside, appearing deliberately to want to frighten them.

Ashen faced, Huang Peiyu thought: I must think carefully who these people could be? They must have spies around me. There are traitors in the Hong Brotherhood.

Others in the car were frightened by his silence and kept quiet.

Huang Peiyu calmed down and his eyes glanced over the others in the car. After a long while, he said between clenched teeth: 'I am not going to be a common laughing stock! I will get to the bottom of this!'

~ CHAPTER 20 ~

Although his staff were working as fast as they could to follow up various leads, Huang Peiyu himself could not think of any way forward, and was already suspicious of several of the men within his team. He knew that what he had to do first was to expose the internal spy. Otherwise any progress would be wasted. As soon as the kidnappers heard anything they would change their plans.

Wanting to be alone, Huang Peiyu moved to the house on Connaught Road on the first day of the Chinese New Year. Just in case, he placed an extra two people on guard outside. Li Yu and Xiu Fang waited on him carefully and cooked well for him. They very much wanted to hear news of Cassia, but dared not ask. Huang Peiyu drank wine with every meal, and, like anybody who tries to dispel his sadness with drink, the result was he became more melancholic.

Lunch was nearly over and he was still drinking, and hadn't touched his food. He drank the best part of another bottle, asking himself: Who could it be? Don't they know how the Hong Brotherhood treats its traitors? That it would be a public punishment, where the victim would be cut to pieces, skinned alive and would then have his tendons pulled out? Each and every member of the Brotherhood would come and cut a piece of the traitor's flesh off, so that all were responsible for killing him.

In the nine years he had been Grand Master of the Hong Brotherhood, he'd only had to chair such an ordeal once, and he still felt sick every time he recalled that bloody scene. He was sure that if it was an internal traitor, it must be some reckless madman. Was it worth such a risk, for just a few gold bars?

He sat on the chair and put the chopsticks down. He thought

for a long time about his staff, feeling suspicious of every one of them; yet he could not put his finger on any individual whom he felt would have the guts to do something like this.

Meanwhile, the kidnappers hadn't rung for several days. Perhaps they were also celebrating the New Year. He gave a wry smile. His own celebrations were completely ruined.

Walking upstairs, the corridor was full of Cassia's stage photos, each gazing at him glamorously, each so beautiful and gentle, exuding tenderness and love. Possessing such a woman, he'd probably made every man in Shanghai jealous.

But now, lying on her bed, he felt strangely detached. It seemed her spirit was no longer there. She was no longer important to him. This woman had brought him too much trouble and caused him to lose face both at home and in Shanghai. He had to hide here all by himself. Huang Peiyu began to regret acquiring such a troublesome woman. The Sixth Concubine, a foolish pumpkin, had been thrown into the river and immediately melted into nothing; but Cassia was a tough woman – she would not go so easily.

He lit a cigar and told himself that he now knew what it felt like to be alone.

Suddenly the telephone rang downstairs and Xiu Fang ran in nervously, shouting: 'Master Huang, it is the kidnappers. They want you!'

Huang Peiyu rushed out of the room, barefooted. He thought, feeling jumpy now: an outstanding spy indeed! Wherever he was, the kidnappers followed him. He had told no one that he'd come here to Connaught Road, yet still he was discovered.

But as soon as the battle-by-telephone began, Huang Peiyu became excited. He sat on the sofa and said in a determined voice, 'You must know me, I mean what I say. I will not ransom a mere woman. If I were the kind of person to do that, the world would long have ceased to have heard of me. Anyway, she was only an actress, and I really don't care! I don't stay at home, I don't go to teahouses; I came here, because I don't really want to have anything to do with you.'

The man's voice on the phone was strange, seemingly teasing him: 'You are only pretending not to care. What you are really trying to avoid is parting with your gold.'

Huang Peiyu stood up on the sofa, his voice cold. He said he could easily pick up a handful of women like Cassia in Shanghai. 'Go ahead – cut her into pieces – see if I care! I said I would not ransom her, and I meant it. Besides, you know very well I work as the Chinese Governor of the Municipal Council, I cannot go against the law and ransom a hostage. No woman is so important as to cause me to give up the position of Chinese Governor of the Municipal Council!'

Li Yu, listening closely in the corridor, trembled with rage at his words. 'This man Huang, he is so utterly without conscience!' Xiu Fang pulled her into her own room.

After receiving such an uncompromising message from Huang Peiyu, the man on the other end of the line seemed to be changing his mind. For a long while he didn't speak; then, he came to a decision.

'All right, we know you are not prepared to ransom her; we're fed up with waiting, and would not want to harm Miss Cassia. Let's just say we caught the wrong person. We didn't realise how tough Master Huang could be.'

Huang Peiyu hastened to say: 'That sounds better. It's always better to untie a knot. If you let her go, we'll still be brothers and friends.'

'Miss Cassia is not in good health. We want to hand her back to Master Huang himself, to avoid possible hiccups. We don't want to be responsible for any problems.'

'What do you mean?' Huang Peiyu frowned.

'Your men are not to be trusted.' The voice sounded embarrassed: 'Several times we arranged to release the goods, several times someone spoiled it for us. We never imagined it would be so hard doing this business with Master Huang – have you no one you can trust?'

This was an attack on Huang Peiyu's weakest spot. He indeed trusted no one now.

Not wishing to pursue such a topic, Huang Peiyu said that he'd come to meet them himself.

'Tomorrow morning at six o'clock, we'll release the hostage. You go out of Dongchang Town to Pudong, go east past the memorial arch. There are two poplar trees in the winter wheat field, an area about as big as one li. No one will be about then; only Cassia will be there for you to pick up.'

Huang Peiyu said: 'That sounds good. It won't be possible for me to bring anybody to such a wilderness. Please rest assured.'

That evening, Huang Peiyu took five men including the Third Master and Yu Qiyang and sailed across the river to Pudong. The next day the group came to the suburb outside Pudong in the early morning light. They rented a peasant house in Dongchang Town and set up a careful watch from the window and the roof. It was still winter but getting warmer. When the wind blew on one's face, it didn't feel as cold as it had done a few days before. They walked out of the town, and there was indeed no one about. The previous night it had rained and a few soft raindrops were still falling.

Just as described, he saw the memorial arch and two slender poplars about one li ahead. The branches were not thick; they certainly couldn't hide anyone. A narrow path went diagonally past the two poplars. It was quiet all around, with no sign of any movement apart from two crows who cawed as they flew past, then stopped on the tree tops. The field was empty and there was no cover for any gunmen.

Huang Peiyu stuck a gun in his waistband and hid another in a holster around his leg. Smoking a cigar he asked the men on the roof to watch carefully.

Yu Qiyang held the heavy telescope and focused it several times: 'It's true that there is no one else there, only a woman, it is Miss Cassia. It looks as if she can't walk.'

Others also looked through the telescope, confirming: 'It does look as though she's the only one there.'

Huang Peiyu threw away the cigarette stub and said briskly: 'I'll go and fetch her and we can finish this whole thing.'

The men on the roof came down. The Third Master said: 'Let me go, the Master does not have to do this personally.'

Yu Qiyang said: 'Let me go; Master Huang must be very cautious.'

Huang Peiyu examined the two men. Although the possibility of these two betraying him was slim, he still would not trust anyone. He had thought carefully last night of each and every step involved in fetching Cassia. No one in the room knew that he wore a bullet proof vest, or that the inside of his hat had steel barriers which would withstand gun and knife attacks. Before any assailant could react, he'd have wrestled him to the ground.

He walked to the door and turned. He said, giving them no chance to protest: 'You all wait here. I will go by myself. I don't want anything to go wrong at this last stage.'

Huang Peiyu ordered his men to block the way out of town. In order to be safe, he sent two men up to the roof, holding guns and telescopes to observe the area in case of a surprise attack by gunmen. When everything was arranged, he set off down the road.

Past the memorial arch were the two slender poplar trees. He saw Cassia in the distance, standing on the track, her eyes blinded by a cloth, her hands tied behind her. Exhausted and tired-looking, Cassia seemed to have heard his footsteps and turned excitedly to him, trying with difficulty to walk towards him. Her face looked bloody. She slipped and fell down, then tried to struggle up.

Huang Peiyu saw immediately that this place was absolutely safe. Seeing Cassia again, especially in such a state, he suddenly felt a fondness for her. After all, this woman knew how to make him happy, something other women had failed to do. Besides, owning this woman he was able to be 'Lord of Shanghai': a hero must have a beauty.

This affair had dragged on too long and had damaged his reputation. But now everything could be resolved. In those few seconds, Huang Peiyu felt that he had perhaps been too cold towards Cassia, had caused her to suffer. He would look after this woman well, as he had promised to once before.

So he hurried along, and just as he passed through the two poplars, he triggered the wires of the bomb. In an instant fire shot up into the sky.

Cassia fell on the ground and clasped her head. A tree stump lay between her and the bombsite. Amidst the flames, dust and poplar leaves whistled over her.

Smoke filled the air, and for a while nothing could be seen.

Everyone raced over, shouting: 'Master! Master!' But even before the dust subsided they saw that Huang Peiyu's body had been blown to pieces, with the only remaining flesh hanging on the empty branches of the two trees. The head, still wearing its steel hat, had flown into the field. The iron body-armour had been blown into an odd shape, and trapped inside were bloodied ribs, empty of flesh. All present were used to bloody scenes but even their faces turned pale.

'By the powers of heaven, this is a diabolic way to commit murder!'

'How could the boss have been fooled by this?'

'What kidnappers could be mad enough to come up with such a deadly trap, to try and kill both the hostage and the Master?'

Yu Qiyang found Cassia lying on the ground, faint from the impact, covered in dust and drops of blood. Turning over her body, he discovered that both her hands were handcuffed and chained to an old tree trunk, and her eyes were blinded by a piece of cloth. Yu Qiyang quickly helped her remove the cloth from her eyes. Her hair had been roughly cut and her clothes were ragged, her face stained by the smoke. But on closer examination, she didn't have any deep wounds.

'Miss Cassia was indeed lucky.'

'To have escaped alive from the tiger's mouth, lucky indeed!'

Cassia's eyes were tightly closed, her lips blue. Yu gave her a few shakes but there was no response. Calling on his knowledge of Chinese medicine, Yu hurriedly pressed her 'tiger mouth' meridian point and finally she opened her eyes. Upon seeing the bloodied scene in front of her, she fainted in Yu's arms. The Third Master raised his gun and fired at her chains; only one bullet was needed for them to break.

A car drove over and they carried Cassia into it. They didn't dare to touch the scattered pieces of Huang Peiyu's flesh; instead they left several men behind to keep watch. The rest of them drove to Dongchang town to call the police.

In Lujiazui Dock, the car was waiting for the ferry. The ferry nearby was now powered by diesel, with much less smoke. Cassia leaned silently on the open window of the car. From time to time someone obscured her vision and she would close her eyes and rest, but when they moved away, she would watch the river again. The Bund on the opposite bank had been filled with row after row of high buildings. The ten li of foreign land was no longer just limited to ten li.

The river shook in the glistening sunshine. The anchor of the car ferry was released, the whistle blown and the ferry headed slowly towards the opposite bank.

The Chief Advisor was on the dock, lamenting the passing of Huang Peiyu. 'In 1887, the twenty-third year of the reign of the Emperor Guangxu, Master Chang re-established the Hong Brotherhood in Shanghai, and under the shadow of knives and blood. The third year after that the Kang Liang reform, which implicated the Brotherhood, and resulted in many arrests. It was again thanks to Master Chang, who was able to remain calm through all crises, that we were able to escape disaster!'

Both himself and Chang Lixiong were failed scholars, but though he lacked Chang Lixiong's strength or his skill in martial arts, the Advisor was nonetheless fluent in history and had studied both Buddhist and Taoist scripts as well as possessing the skills of divination. This was why he had become the Chief Advisor; his nickname was 'Little Zhuge', after the famous ancient strategist. Several grand masters had come and gone in the Hong Brotherhood, but though he was older, he could only assist and advise, not rule.

He counted his fingers: 'In 1907, the year before Emperor Guangxu died, Master Chang died; yet once again, thanks to Master Huang who was valiant and gallant enough to take over the Brotherhood, we were able to go through the chaos of the revolution unscathed. Who would have thought that nine years later, now, in 1916, Master Huang himself would have died an unnatural death. The history of the Hong Brotherhood is indeed one of many martyrs. How shall we manage now?'

The Chief Adviser was moved to tears, 'I glance around in the wilderness: where is the hero?'

CHAPTER 21

Yu Qiyang drove a Model T Ford with a soft top roof. Cassia sat by his side, wearing a red woollen sweater over her *qipao*, her hair rolled up in a bun, with no jewellery on. They drove along the Suzhou Creek and turned into a wide lane that led south with blossoming Chinese redbuds on either side, and stopped opposite an English-style house. There was a big yard, with a decorative iron gate at the front. A tall tree grew in the front of the house and inside children could be heard, singing English nursery rhymes, accompanied by the happy bustling sounds of a nursery school. At the gate a Western nun was on duty.

Cassia dared not open the car door. With her hand clasped to her chest she said: 'Yu, I am so frightened.'

'All these years, fearing that you might cause harm to Master Chang's flesh and blood, you've never dared to claim your daughter. Today is a day on which you should be happy!' said Yu Qiyang. But seeing Cassia's face was indeed pale, he smoothed her shoulders and said: 'Calm down. I will go and fetch them.'

He walked up to the Christian nun and said something to her. She went inside.

After a little while, a small gate opened next to the larger one and Madame Emerald walked out. Her temples were greying and she held a little girl of around eight years old. The little girl wore a Western-style school uniform and skirt. She had a bow on her plait and looked very spirited.

She saw Yu Qiyang and rushed affectionately to him. 'Uncle Yu!' she shouted.

Yu Qiyang lifted her onto his shoulders and walked slowly to the car.

'Where are you taking me? You promised we would go to Gaoqiao Beach again. You mustn't eat your words!'

Madame Emerald said: 'I have already told you that today we'll go somewhere else.'

'But I'm not going anywhere that's not fun,' the child said stubbornly.

They crossed the road. Opening the car door, the little girl saw Cassia sitting in the back seat.

Without a trace of shyness, the little girl climbed in, sat down and looked at her. In a bold and assured tone of voice, she said: 'I have seen you somewhere before. I must have seen you somewhere before!'

Madame Emerald, who was also crammed into the back seat said: 'Lily, you haven't seen her, this is…'

Cassia's eyes were already full of tears, but she held them in and kept her eyes on the little girl.

'I have seen her, I have.' The little girl shouted, 'I've seen you looking at me from the school gate. You are that passer-by who always looks inside! Are you a good person or a bad person? If you are a bad person I will ask Uncle Yu to kill you.'

Madame Emerald turned to Cassia with an accusing look: 'See! See! I told you not to do it, but you wouldn't listen!' But seeing the miserable look on Cassia's face, she stopped.

Impervious, the little girl patted Yu Qiyang's head, as he sat in the front next to the driver's seat: 'Uncle Yu, you did say that if I ever came across a bad person, you would be sure to help me beat them. Now, you mustn't go back on your own words.'

Yu Qiyang kept his head down in silence, biting his lips.

'Lily, stop it.' Madame Emerald became serious and held the little girl's arms, 'Look, who does she resemble?' she asked.

Yu Qiyang started the engine. He saw from the front mirror that Cassia's beautiful face had filled with tears.

'Who?' asked the little girl.

'You! Look carefully.'

The little girl studied Cassia's face closely. 'Well, a little bit. But she is prettier than me.' She pushed Cassia rudely, 'Hey, how dare you be prettier than me?'

Cassia said: 'When you are older, you'll be even prettier than your mummy!'

'Mummy? Grandma Emerald said my mummy had gone away to look for my daddy. My mummy's surname is "Chen" and I am called "Lily Chen", until I find my daddy.' The little girl talked incessantly. She leaned her small body over to pat Yu's head, 'Isn't that right, Uncle Yu?' Then she turned to hold Madame Emerald's hand: 'Isn't that right, Grandma Emerald?' It was plain that the little girl had a deep affection for Yu Qiyang and was even more indulged by Madame Emerald.

Cassia couldn't bear it any longer. She grasped the little girl, her tears finally flowing, 'Now mummy has finally found daddy and she has come back to fetch you.' She sobbed, unable to continue.

Yu Qiyang continued for her: 'Your father's surname is Chang, and he was called Chang Lixiong. He was a real hero!'

Madame Emerald was also crying now; she said to the little girl in a serious voice: 'Call her "mummy", this is your mummy. Your mummy has suffered a lot for you.'

The little girl remained silent and bit her fingers, her big eyes wide open. Finally she looked at Cassia and said: 'If you are really my mummy, then will you take me to see daddy?'

Cassia had already calmed down. Gently she used a handkerchief to wipe away both her own tears and those that were smeared on the child's face.

'Mummy will take you to see daddy. Tomorrow is Qing Ming, the 'Day of the Dead', we will go to sweep daddy's tomb and burn a little incense. From now on, you will use your original name, Lily Chang.'

Finally, the child rested her head on Cassia's arms. The car was going down a slightly busier street, where neon lights slowly emerged and blended into many other lights.

In the evening, Cassia took her daughter Lily to a photographer's studio. She sat on the right, her daughter to the left, almost as if they were still in the car. The difference now was that the two looked intimate, their expressions joyful. This must have been the most beautiful photo that was ever taken of Cassia. She was beaming with joy. Overnight she took on a new, more charismatic persona, through her love for her daughter.

After Huang Peiyu's death the Chief Advisor and the others became very busy, dealing with the investigation of the concessions police, helping the detectives to search for leads to the kidnappers. The Municipal Council's Chief of Police questioned Cassia several times.

Her replies were always very clear: her eyes were blindfolded and she was shut in a small room that was tightly-sealed. She could see almost nothing and all she remembered was that she had heard sometimes two, sometimes three voices, one of them a woman.

'What else was there in the small room? What was it like, what did you hear?'

Cassia thought carefully and said that there were tables and chairs, and a window, though it was nailed shut. She believed that she could hear water flowing outside. She was extremely thin, though the purple bruising that covered part of her body had gradually receded. Her hair was cut short just above her ears.

The Chief of Police demanded that the Chief Advisor and the Third Master should carry out careful examinations within the Chinese police team. But on the day of the incident, almost everyone had been within sight of each other, and it seemed it was impossible for them to have participated in the kidnapping and the murder plot. Besides, nobody could understand the purpose of the killing: there was only one possible motive: the failure of their plot to blackmail Huang Peiyu had driven them to come up with a venomous scheme to kill both hostage and victim.

The Chief of Police and several detectives arrived at the site. He asked his assistant to do a mock-up of the events using smoking firecrackers. The Chief threw himself on the ground swiftly to avoid being injured, but was still covered with tiny pieces of paper. The assistant thought Cassia was not above suspicion. 'See, you escaped,' he said.

'But I am an old soldier. I have been through the Boer War, I have escaped numerous cannon balls! How could this woman have my ability?' The Chief ground his teeth: 'Let's just say this Cassia was extremely lucky!'.

He had no evidence to suggest that this woman had participated in the plot. From the way the land lay, it seemed to be pure luck that Cassia hadn't been killed by the power of the bomb.

It had been rumoured that Cassia was a curse to men. Madame Emerald had specifically asked a fortune teller for advice; she was told that Cassia would be a curse to any man, some unlucky ones would die within two to three weeks of being with her, the best one could hope was to survive a few years! All at the Duchess Pavilion believed this fortune teller. None of the girls who did the entertaining wanted her as their servant, and so she had been forced to serve Madame Emerald, who believed herself to be so lucky that she could withstand such a curse.

It would be ridiculous for this foreign Chief of Police to believe such Chinese superstition! It was arguably true, however, that Huang Peiyu had lost his life because he had taken a woman as beautiful as Cassia as his mistress. And if Cassia was a curse to men, this was not her fault!

The Municipal Council showed 'deep sadness' for the 'untimely death' of Huang Peiyu, but it wasn't until two months later that Huang Peiyu's 'martyrdom' was formally declared. During these two months the Municipal Council had sworn to solve a crime that had been the talk of the town. But hard as they tried, they couldn't. It was not until the spring of 1917 that the case was closed. His death had occurred in an area that was not under the Concession's authority, and this was given as the excuse for the case to be closed – rather than because of any lack of ability on the part of the police. The police on the Chinese side were also happy to do as the foreigners had done and leave matters unresolved. It became one of the most infamous unsolved cases in Shanghai history.

It was now nine years since Huang Peiyu had obtained his firm footing in the concessions and become 'Lord of Shanghai'. Overnight he had become almost indestructible. His various opponents had tried several times to pull him down from his position as Chinese Governor but because of the Hong Brotherhood's power to preserve 'order' in Shanghai, and the fact that the alliance had become the foundation of power within the Municipal Council, they had to put up with him.

But with Huang Peiyu's death, the Hong Brotherhood lost its leader. A large number of debtors began to gather at the Huang household; some would not leave even when the Municipal Council was investigating the criminal case. Some even set up camp outside the household. This, too, became news in Shanghai. In the course of their investigations, the Municipal Council took the accounts of the Hong Brotherhood in Shanghai away from Huang Peiyu's house, but perhaps finally realising it was totally unnecessary for them to clear his debts, it returned all such documents.

Huang Peiyu's first wife had long been unable to hold her own; now she collapsed, spending her time in bed. The Chief Advisor took the key to the safety box from her. Opening it, his hands trembled with rage: the Hong Brotherhood accounts had been mixed up with those of the household ones, a situation of total chaos. He was in an impossible position and had no idea how to deal with the situation.

The Advisor thought about the matter for a whole evening: the Third Master was good at dealing with guns and knives, but not at sorting out finances; the Fifth Master used to be Chang Lixiong's housekeeper, and now, though the household had long been in decline, he remained there to help, so was obviously not a good candidate. Yu Qiyang was careful and smart, as well as being honest and reliable, so that even Huang Peiyu himself appreciated his support. Still, he was a mere aide doing other people's bidding; he had no formal position within the Brotherhood.

He circled the yard, ideas emerging one after the other but couldn't settle on any solution.

When he woke up the next morning, the Advisor's eyelids were puffy: he hadn't slept well. Before he was able to have breakfast a call came from the Huang household to say that even debtors from other provinces had heard the news of Huang's death and come over. What should they do? The first wife sent word that she would like the Huang's housekeeper to be in charge of this matter; should the Advisor agree, she would send him over to fetch the accounts.

The image of the round-faced housekeeper flashed through the Advisor's mind. He realised what the first wife meant by this suggestion. She was informing him that this was a matter for the Huang household alone. The interest of the household would have to come before that of the Brotherhood. The Advisor became angry, but controlled himself, telling the messenger: 'Tell the first wife not to worry, I will get someone to sort out these accounts.'

The Advisor put the phone down: his only option was to ask Yu Qiyang to help him deal first of all with the debtors waiting in the Huang sitting room. He sent for Yu urgently.

Yu lived quite a distance away. It took half an hour for him to arrive. He parked his car in a lane outside the Masi Nan Road and followed the messenger in. They drove to a *shiku* house, one of those half-Western half-Chinese dwellings unique to the alleyways of Shanghai. The gate was ajar and he pushed it open and went in.

The Chief Advisor, who was standing in the courtyard, rushed to pat his shoulders. The two sat down and the Advisor sighed and explained why he had asked Yu to come: He hoped that Yu would be able to untangle this mess.

Yu Qiyang took the account books and settled down to work. After only half a day he had sketched out a rough assessment. The Brotherhood assets that Huang Peiyu handled were over four million in the red and had almost all been sold to meet the demands of its creditors. The Hong Brotherhood was an empty shell, its capital insufficient to repay its debts.

The Advisor was deeply concerned. He said that the capital and debts of the Brotherhood should long have been separated from the personal finances of the Grand Master. How could Huang Peiyu have been as foolish as Empress Dowager Cixi: paying for the state's warships and the construction of a palace's private garden out of the same accounts?

Yu Qiyang gave a wry smile and said to the Chief Advisor, 'Wasn't it you who set this Emperor in place? To be honest,' he continued, 'Huang Peiyu didn't spend much of this money on himself. Most of his expenditure was political donations and taxes to the Municipal Council. There were also many obligatory 'gifts' that had to be administered in China: one always paid money to the most powerful. Idealists like Sun Yat-sen and Chen Qimei had accepted money to fund their revolution, warlords such as Feng Guozhang and Lu Yongxiang took money to fund their battles, even the foreigners in the concessions accepted money – it seemed Master Huang's status in Shanghai was purely sustained by donations to such powerful forces.

The Advisor stood up, so worried that he started to circle the courtyard again: 'But all Master Huang's debts were borrowed in the name of the Hong Brotherhood: how should we deal with that?'

Yu Qiyang gave a forced smile: 'When the Duchess Pavilion proclaimed itself bankrupt, it put its prostitutes and servant girls up for sale. But I've never heard of a brotherhood claiming to be bankrupt. A gangster for sale? Who would buy me?'

Several days later, Yu Qiyang finally sorted out the mess. The debts ran to at least two million yuan. When the Advisor saw this clear account of the problem, he told him not to say anything to anybody. To the debtors, they said that the Hong Brotherhood was creating a new Grand Master; that as soon as he was in position, all debts would be cleared.

Yu Qiyang had originally planned to take Cassia and her daughter to Fengya Restaurant that evening for fragrant and crispy duck. Instead he phoned Cassia to say that this plan had to be postponed; that he had something to discuss with the Advisor. 'If I am later than six o'clock, then go ahead by yourselves. I would still like to invite you out, but let's change it to a night snack at the Deyue Pavilion.'

When he had finished talking to the Advisor and finally had an opportunity to disengage himself, he took out his pocket watch and looked at it: it was nearly ten o'clock. He quickly rang Cassia.

'Never mind, Little Lily has already gone to bed,' said Cassia, a little annoyed.

Yu Qiyang said he'd still like to come and talk to her.

'Come talk to me sometime next week then,' Cassia said. 'Talk when we've sat down at the Fengya Restaurant. You made Little Lily unhappy, she said she wanted to hit you.'

'Isn't she asleep now? I'm not afraid of the sleeping Little Lily. I have something on my mind that I need your advice on.'

'Ah, when did you ever listen to my advice?'

Yu Qiyang put the phone down. The Chief Advisor walked into the sitting room and asked him to stay for a night snack, adding that the Third Master had also arrived. But Yu Qiyang took his leave quickly.

Lily had already fallen asleep. Cassia put her little hands beneath the quilt and closed the door gently behind her. On the corridor, she called for Xiu Fang, who was standing at the bottom of the stairs. 'Yes, Miss?,' she said.

'Prepare some light snacks and bring them to my room.'

Xiu Fang brought a tray with tea and cake. Cassia sat on the armchair and asked Xiu Fang to go and rest.

Believing they were going out to the Fengya Restaurant, Cassia wore a newly-made and layered long-sleeved *qipao*, appropriate for the cold season. She sat in the bedroom restlessly. She felt that Yu Qiyang must have a lot on his mind, otherwise he wouldn't have broken his appointment with little Lily. He was especially fond of the child, not least because she was Chang Lixiong's daughter.

She heard the sound of a car outside and walked to the window. It was his car arriving.

She went down the stairs and opened the door, where Yu Qiyang stood, looking exhausted. Speechless, they went upstairs one behind the other. Yu Qiyang went inside the washroom and when he reemerged even his hair was wet. Cassia smiled and handed him a dry towel.

'Are you hungry?'

Yu Qiyang nodded. Although he'd eaten something, just as she had guessed he was still hungry.

'I knew it.' Cassia showed him what was behind him.

On the tea table there was some hot tea and snacks. A sofa and a wicker chair were placed beside the dressing table. Yu sat down and ate the food, and then told her what had happened during the day.

'No wonder,' Cassia said, 'Huang Peiyu's first wife has sent another message to demand the return of the house. The messenger left word that if we could not return it then we must pay 60,000 yuan as compensation. I said this was impossible, as the title deeds were in my name. The messenger threatened to take me to court to sue me for fraud.'

Yu Qiyang asked: 'Is it possible that the title deeds could be fake?'

Did he think she could be that stupid? Three years ago, when she had got the house from Huang Peiyu, she had sent the deeds to the property registration office of the Municipal Council to have their authenticity tested. They were indeed genuine. After that they had been kept in a stainless steel safe at the basement of the Huamao Bank. She had only this property, plus the Ruyi Troupe, to support Lily's education at the foreign school. She also wanted to send Lily to a girl's school in America, and needed the money for this. She would never be careless like Huang Peiyu, acting as if the whole of Shanghai belonged to him!

'Even if we sold all of Huang Peiyu's properties we would not be able to repay the debts – but if all of the property of the Hong Brotherhood was frozen, it would be hard to know what to do with this house of yours, because many properties of the Hong Brotherhood were put under individual names, but the debtors will not easily let go.'

Cassia broke into a cold sweat: 'But I have long ceased to be a member of the Hong Brotherhood!'

Yu said that he wished the debtors could be convinced of this in court. He stood up, trying to explain the situation more clearly: 'We were all insignificant figures who had managed to grab small sums of money from the old man. Now that he is gone, the Hong Brotherhood looks set to collapse. But the influence of the Brotherhood could still be felt. It may be invisible, but it can still be used as if it was capital. Just like your reputation for being a sweet girl with a golden voice. Like the house, it is something one could use as currency – this merely depends on how one uses it.'

He pushed the teacups to one side, crossed his arms in front of his chest and said to Cassia: 'The Chief Advisor said the only thing he could say to the Brotherhood was that whoever could solve the financial predicament of the Brotherhood would be the new Grand Master.'

Cassia understood what he meant. She drank a mouthful of tea and held the teacup in silence for a while. Suddenly she was presented with a dilemma. Once again she faced another important battle in her life – if she did well, the position of ruler of the Hong Brotherhood would fall into the hands of someone she trusted; if she failed, the brotherhood would collapse, and so would she; while if some other Grand Master was appointed, her own fate would be unpredictable.

She put the teacup down and straightened her back on the wicker chair, watching Yu Qiyang: 'So you want to borrow money in the name of the Hong Brotherhood.'

'You are a clever woman, much cleverer than the likes of the Advisor. You know how Shanghai works. It would be far better to run a bank than to borrow money from one! If you borrow money you need to pay back interest, but if you run a bank, then you get interest. The Advisor said that all the Brotherhood had ever done was to rob banks; he said I was just daydreaming.'

Seeing that Cassia was still silent, Yu Qiyang paused. This battle of life and death was far more risky than any crisis they had faced before. Cassia frowned.

'Why are you so silent?' Yu could not contain himself any longer.

'Why shouldn't I be?' Cassia said angrily: 'Don't you think I know what you're thinking of? You want my house. Huang Peiyu's first wife failed to take the house, but you think you can, do you?'

'Cassia is indeed a clever woman,' Yu said with a hint of shame.

Cassia sighed: 'Let's suppose we can mortgage the house, which would only raise several tens of thousands. What's the use of that?'

Yu Qiyang's idea was to set up a bank, which would need only 250,000 yuan in capital to start up. One would need credit for running a bank; but the Brotherhood itself was credit. All the main businesses involved in opium, gambling and prostitution within the Concession were major customers who would only put money in a Brotherhood bank. The tradition had always been that other banks also put money in to congratulate a new bank when it was first established. The normal timescale for taking money out was two weeks. The Brotherhood would be able to make this extend to three to six months. This would give the Brotherhood bank enough capital to issue bonds, and to pay off loans with loans. In fact, if the Brotherhood was able to set up a new bank, its debtors would understand that the alliance was going strong and would not be in such a huge rush to demand repayment of their debts.

'All right,' Cassia said: 'I trust that what you say makes sense. But would the Advisor and others be willing for you to mortgage the properties of the Brotherhood?'

Yu shook his head and said: 'I know very well that the Advisor and the Third Master believe that this idea of mine is about seizing power; they will stand aside to see if I can succeed in setting the bank up. They themselves cannot clean this mess up; they can only pray for this crisis to pass over. That would be fine with me, so long as they keep their word: Whoever sorts out the finances, that person will be the new Grand Master.'

Cassia walked to the bed and held on to the netting that surrounded it. Sitting down, she watched herself silently in the mirror, her eyes moist, but voice firm: 'Alright, Yu. Since fate wants me to return to the days when I came empty-handed to Shanghai, then I will satisfy you and give you all that I own. This house, my Ruyi Troupe, the money I got from making records, and my jewellery: they are all yours. Even the money I have saved to pay for Lily's trip to America, that's all yours, too: altogether that should be about 100,000 yuan, the rest you'll have to go and sort out yourself!'

Yu Qiyang stood up and walked to Cassia. He gazed at the back of her. Suddenly he knelt down, held onto her waist and pressed his face onto her soft chest as tears rolled from his eyes.

Cassia saw that his shoulders were heaving and clasped him tighter to her chest, smoothing his head and shoulders. Time changes everything, despite human will. On this night of all nights, they felt they were once again the servant girl and boy of the Duchess Pavilion, two penniless children in the most piteous situation.

If this was their fate, then they would share it.

They could hear the beating of each other's hearts, feel pity and care for each other. However hard a task they faced, they would bare their souls to each other and share their problems. This was the most precious thing in the whole world.

'Everything will be alright.' After she said this, she, too slipped off the bed and knelt down with Yu Qiyang. They held each other and wept. Never had they cried so much. Before, she had always cried for her own sadness. Even when she shed tears on stage, she had feared messing up her make-up, and did not dare to completely let go. It was not in her nature to be so open with others.

They should not be two bodies that were separated from each other. However humble, however helpless, on this night, they were one. This moment of their new relationship locked them even closer together.

Afterwards, when they were lying on the bed, calm again, they embraced, looking into each other's eyes. The faint blue moonlight slipped through the window and spread over their naked bodies. At last Cassia said: 'Yu, Lily's future lies in your hands.'

Yu Qiyang's hands crossed with hers, he said that the bank was indeed set up for her. 'I think it should be called the Lixiong Bank – Master Chang's name still has the power to convince the people of Shanghai.'

~ CHAPTER 22 ~

***

People do not usually notice time passing unless they notice its effects on others. A clever little girl grows up into a sexy woman, and then people exclaim: has it really been ten years?

Yuan Shikai's fall from power, the power struggle between Zhi, Wan and Feng – the three factions of the North Ocean Army – Sun Yat-sen's death, followed by his lifetime dream, the Northern Expedition to rid China of its warlords and establish a Nationalist government, the subsequent coming to power of Chiang Kai-shek: even the shifts of power between the occupying warlords for the rule over Shanghai: from Feng Guozhang to Zhang Zongchang, Lu Yongxiang, Qi Xieyuan, and then Bi Shucheng...whether or not they won Shanghai, they left a large pile of dead bodies at the edge of the city. But all this was just like drifting smoke, here today, then gone forever. The Concession still prospered: Jewish jewellery shops, Japanese pharmacies, French cafés, White Russian brothels, German hospitals and more mushroomed in Shanghai. The citizens heard the artillery in the distance and only played harder at their games of *Mahjong*.

Only when you see people, do you notice how fast time has changed everything: people like this, driving an open-topped car through streets heavy with traffic.

Indeed, if one wanted to write about Shanghai in 1925, one would naturally describe the misery of the Qilu war between warlords; but then there were more tragic wars around Shanghai after this one: one should also write about the May 30th Movement, in which the murder of striking workers by Western forces triggered widespread protest; but then both the later revolution and counter-revolution were on a much grander scale; one should also write about the new skyscrapers that went up in Shanghai that year, but more buildings and greater buildings were built later so that the Shanghai scenery changed from the grand European look of a riviera to an American forest of skyscrapers.

How should we then determine the unmistakable flavour of 1925?

Only by one thing, and that is the people that I write about. You cannot transport them to any other time. The reinforced concrete will stand centuries into the future, while the same questions that gave politicians headaches will cause fresh pain year after year. But after this year – 1925 – people would no longer be the same.

I am not being boastful, not at all. My eyes brighten. Look, look how quickly it passes! A brand new, waxed and shining Chevrolet speeding wildly along the Bund.

★★★

It was around five in the evening on a Saturday in February, in the early spring of 1925. The sun had still not set. The car smartly dodged past pedestrians, who were also trying hard to escape from it. 'Damn you!' they cursed: 'Crazy!' The car drove past the front of the Xinhu Theatre, where neon lights flashed the words:

'Cassia takes the lead in the famously passionate show, "An Orchid In An Empty Valley."'

The car didn't stop here, but turned sharply into a narrow lane where it halted with a squeak in front of a small gate. The driver stepped out of the car, slammed the door, and took off the typical male driver's get-up: a leather peaked cap and dark glasses – but even without lipstick this person's lips looked shiny and fresh; the driver was a girl. She wore a leather jacket.

She opened the door. When the guard saw her, he clasped his fists together in respectful greeting and she walked past him with her head held high, her eyes hardly registering him at all.

Two male actors stepped out to breathe fresh air, talking and joking, one of them lighting a cigarette. They saw the young girl in the leather jacket but like all the other 'artists' they only glanced at her once: this was the backdoor used by all actors and actresses.

The young girl, who seemed to know her way about well, passed down the corridor swiftly. Those whom she encountered on the way called out to her affectionately. She threw the women flying kisses; she waved her hands at the men. Shenqu music and singing seeped out from the stage itself. At the end of the corridor the girl pushed open a door to find Cassia's trusted maid Li Yu.

Li Yu saw that Lily Chang was wearing men's clothes. Now that she'd taken off the leather jacket, her waist, tightened by a wide belt, appeared thinner; her legs longer; her chest more prominent. Li Yu said respectfully: 'Miss Lily, I heard that you're back; that you've graduated from high school in America.'

'Of course! And so I am free!' Lily patted Li Yu's face, though Li Yu was even older than her mother. 'Where's my mother?'

'On stage,' Li Yu said. 'This afternoon she had her first performance, and many have come to congratulate her.'

'I've heard: all rich Shanghai millionaires.' Lily made a face. 'That's why mother couldn't come to pick me up. But anyway, I'm not used to being met by women.' She sat by her mother's dressing table and saw herself in the mirror: a seventeen-year-old girl whose hair was tied up, looking like a boy. The room contained many of her mother's stage photos and as she looked, she began to grow interested in them. The dressing room was big, at least thirty square metres in size. By the window stood a low wooden couch and a tall, old-fashioned redwood mirror; the glass inside could be adjusted within the frame. On top of the mirror was placed a man's black leather hat. A lemon tree in blossom grew in a pot by the couch, while by the wall there were three rows of clothing rails, stacked with various dresses; props were piled up around them.

Lily picked up a newspaper and started reading. It said that 'An Orchid In An Empty Valley' was a love story, a tragedy about two women fighting over one man. Lily threw the newspaper aside, and felt mild interest. She must go and watch it one day! She pulled out the drawers in the dressing table.

'Miss Lily,' Li Yu said, tidying the teacups quickly away: 'The curtain is about to fall: I must go and help. Your mother doesn't usually allow people in here; she worries they might mess her things up.'

'I know, I know,' Lily said, 'but won't mummy trust even me?'

'Your mother only fears that she might not be able to find things where she left them.' Li Yu had already reached the door. She glanced back at Lily, who was fiddling with the make-up. She walked out reluctantly.

Lily rose to flip through various stage costumes and *qipao*. She took off the leather trousers and tried on a handful of different outfits until finally she found an especially bright sleeveless *qipao* deeply cut into the thighs and shoulders. She put it on and it fitted well. Looking at the mirror she felt pleased. Letting down her hair, she held Cassia's stage shots against her own reflection in the mirror. Then she sat down and began to apply make-up, copying the photo. Rouge and eyeliner began to litter the area around her.

Li Yu returned with something in her hands and Lily turned and stood up. Li Yu said 'Miss...' absent-mindedly. She set about rearranging the props she'd brought back. Suddenly she seemed to notice something and looked at Lily more carefully, her mouth open wide: 'You, you... Cassia?' she was so startled she fainted on the floor, dragging the objects down with her.

Cassia was in the corridor, talking to several acquaintances who were on their way to the dressing room to congratulate her. As she asked for their continued support, she glimpsed several journalists coming her way, wanting to interview her.

'Please, wait just a second, while I finish taking off my make-up.' She smiled. Just then, she heard the strange sounds from the dressing room. She hurried over and opened the door.

She was startled to see herself, about ten years younger, sitting in front of the dressing table and looking back at her. Cassia felt as if she was in a dream. But then immediately she understood what was happening. She walked over and clasped Lily: 'Lily, my lovely daughter, you're back! You look so grown up!'

A tall magnolia tree grew in front of a two-storey house on Jessfield Road in the French Concession. Evergreen vines climbed over the wall. Cassia had lived here for about ten years.

After Huang Peiyu's death, his first wife had several times brought people to the house on Connaught Road, trying to take it back. On the most frightening occasion they had brawled outside the house and broken down the door. All the male members of the Ruyi Troupe turned up to help their boss and the two sides had fought each other. The concessions police came and Cassia produced the title deeds with her name on. The police declared it was illegal to force one's way into residential buildings and tried to arrest the first wife's men; she was forced to leave.

But after that Cassia began to feel that the house was full of too many old memories. She decided to sell it and buy a new one. A German business couple, left without work because of their country's defeat, wanted to return home and were eager to be rid of their house in the Concession. The price was good and Cassia bought it.

The Great War had created havoc in the Western economy, but in the Far East things were looking up. Shanghai property prices had doubled in a few years. Though she sold and bought houses, Cassia didn't need to touch her share of the Lixiong Bank, but instead had capital of her own.

The house was redecorated before they moved in, so that even though from the outside it looked modest and plain, inside everything was shining new. The rooms were wide and spacious and there was an attic for extra storage. The back garden was bigger than the front garden, with trees growing tall into the sky.

On the right at the top of the stairs were Cassia's bedroom and dressing room. The first room to the left was Lily's bedroom, which was kept empty even when she wasn't there. There was a sofa and a low couch in Cassia's room, as well as a large bed, which lay in the middle of the room: the wedding present she had bought for Yu Qiyang, the carved bed she had seen in a shop. It had looked big in the shop; it looked even bigger now it was in the room. But it was indeed comfortable.

It had been arranged that at noon all the directors of the Ruyi Entertainment Company would go to the Carlton Cinema. Liu Ji, who had now become a famous film director, had promised to come to introduce proceedings. Lily heard Cassia open a door and ran out of her room. She wore blue dungarees and knee-length boots, resembling at once a Shanghai factory worker and a cowgirl in a Western movie. 'Lily, what are you doing at home? I thought you'd be out shopping,' Cassia turned back as she made her way to the car carrying an umbrella.

Lily ignored her and stood by the gate, looking at the sky and the soft rain. Cassia's car started and Lily rushed over and opened the door herself, 'Mother, I will go with you.'

Cassia laughed and said, 'Listen to yourself! I invited you to go and you wouldn't and now I am about to leave, you want to come too. In future if I want to go somewhere I will forbid you, and when I don't want you to come with me, I will hurry you along!'

Lily laughed, too. She jumped into the car and only then did she answer her mother: 'Mother's too clever, that's why her daughter has to pretend to be a bit stupid!'

About a dozen people were seated in the cinema. Most directors had probably brought their families with them, as there was quite a crowd in the room. They shook hands and nodded to each other, then the cinema grew dark and they began to watch the rough cut of 'Orchid in an Empty Valley.' They had borrowed the cinema before the start of its usual afternoon show. One-and-a-half hours later, the film finished and the lights were turned on. Liu Ji rewound the film spool. The curtains went up and fresh air filled the room.

Wearing a long gown, Liu Ji pushed his glasses up his nose and walked onto the stage where he began to talk at length. The film was still in the process of being edited, he said. 'When I directed it, I paid special attention to close-up shots; I concentrated on the actress's eyes, her tears. Her upturned face was the most beautiful thing, very much suited to the image of her character, a long-suffering mother. This kind of close-up shot cannot possibly be achieved on stage.'

Liu Ji had already made three films. He started in the Bright Star Company, then transferred himself to the Blue Shadow Company. Liu Ji said he did not wish to hide the fact that he wanted the Ruyi Entertainment Company to buy Blue Shadow, which had just finished making this rough cut of 'An Orchid In An Empty Valley,' but which was heavily in debt and would find it hard to carry on. It wanted to sell the film along with the company. It already owed fees to the Ruyi Entertainment Company for copyright in its scripts, so naturally Cassia was the first person that came to their mind when they thought of selling up.

Liu Ji tried to promote the deal enthusiastically: 'Mr Tang Bihong has made a big investment in "An Orchid In An Empty Valley," and had originally anticipated making a 100,000 yuan profit. And Yang Naimei, the lead actress, was the pure young girl called "Yunqian" from "Soul of Yuli". This time she played the role of the bad woman, Rouyun. Her name alone will guarantee success.'

Lily started talking quickly: 'This Yang Naimei is not so good.'

Liu Ji said, 'Yang Naimei is having trouble at home; her father feels that what she did was an insult to the family and was ashamed. Now father and daughter are estranged.'

Lily said to Cassia: 'If I were to act in a film, would you sever your relationship with me?'

Cassia smiled: 'Quite the opposite, I fear you might not want me as a mother if you became a big star.' She turned to Liu Ji, 'If the film is put on, who would want to come and watch my Shenqu version?'

Liu Ji stepped down from the stage and approached them. He told Cassia that the two would have a complementary effect, each advertising the other. They each had their own audience. People would want to watch such a play in the theatre several times. Neither would take an audience away from the other. The theatre had relatively small costs and was guaranteed a profit, though not a large one, while the film needed bigger investment, with a greater risk, but would also bring in bigger gains.

Once again Lily was getting impatient: 'But I don't believe we will lose, if only you let me act in it! I can compete with Hollywood stars! You know I don't have a good voice – mother always looked down on me for that – but film does not require one to sing, nor to talk.'

'Don't be silly. It takes a pile of money to make a film. I have no such money,' said Cassia, stiffening. She felt Lily's American style was too unreserved. She had wanted the girl to study further in Europe, and become 'a lady'.

Lily said: 'But you have, you have! You invested 40,000 yuan in the Xinhu Theatre.'

'Well, things like the theatre depend on your Uncle Yu for support. Otherwise we'd be very much taken advantage of.'

Lily was pleased and smiled: 'That's fine, then. I will ask him to come and take charge of the Ruyi Film Company. He wouldn't dare say no!'

Suddenly a man's voice rang out from behind, 'Of course nobody dares say no to Miss Lily!'

Yu Qiyang was sitting in the seat behind them. They had no idea when he had entered. Over the past few years, he had developed a full beard, which he kept nicely trimmed, and wore a long gown. He looked like a mature man, with a steady and calm countenance, knowing his own power. Nonetheless, several bodyguards stood close by.

Lily rushed over and hung herself on him as if she was a child. 'Uncle Yu, where have you been? I've been waiting for you for so long! I just knew you would agree that I make films with you.'

'Yes, yes, go on, let's make films!' Yu managed to struggle free and looked with surprise at the Lily Chang that he no longer recognised. After a long while he turned and said to Cassia: 'Sorry, I have been looking after some business and only got back to Shanghai today. How wonderfully Miss Lily has turned out after these few years.'

He walked up to the front to join Cassia and Lily followed him, her arms in his.

Cassia felt the need to chastise him: 'Yu, don't make idle promises. Lily is no longer a child.'

'Hey!' Lily said: 'How dare you go back on your word!' She turned around and said something she used to love saying to Yu when she was a child: 'You promised!'

Yu Qiyang smiled and was about to pat her head, but, realising she was no longer a child, he withdrew his hand. He asked Liu Ji: 'It seems you understand the background of these companies. Tell us why Bright Star prospered and Blue Shadow had to sell?'

'The risk is indeed big. Over the last few years there have been too many "one-film companies". It is not easy to make a film, but it is even harder to succeed at it. The main reason for Blue Shadow's failure is lack of finance; scripts and actors were only secondary factors,' Liu Ji said. 'When Bright Star started, it had no problem with scripts or actors. But they had only 40,000 yuan in capital and found it hard to finish making just the one film; they had to owe the actors salaries. But after making "An Orphan Rescues His Grandpa," they made 8,000 in Nanyang alone. Copies were sold all over the country, making a big profit and recouping several times the original investment. Everybody said "The Orphan" had rescued the company.'

'But nowadays things are different again. There are so many companies in competition with each other.' Cassia saw that everyone was concentrating only on the positive side and cut in: 'Films are being rushed out. Relying on a film like "The Orphan" to rescue the company is a gamble, and you know I never gamble!'

But Lily immediately replied: 'But more people are coming to the cinema. You see how Hollywood has made Los Angeles rich.'

Everybody looked at Yu Qiyang, for he was the financial expert, Shanghai's first banker as well as the Grand Master of the Hong Brotherhood. His word alone counted.

Yu Qiyang thought for a moment and then said: 'I think we should take over Blue Shadow. You have a finished film that only needs some editing – the "Orchid In An Empty Valley" – and you could establish the Ruyi Film Company on the basis of that film alone. I would be able to raise 80,000 by floating shares, there shouldn't be a problem there. But I'll only do it on these conditions: one, that Cassia personally manages the project, as I don't trust anybody else; and two, Liu Ji, you must poach some talents from Bright Star for me.'

Lily cut in: 'Three, you must make Lily Chang the lead.'

But Lily had pushed too far this time and her jokes did not go down well. Seeing Yu Qiyang and Cassia hesitate, Liu Ji tried to smooth things over: 'Tomorrow I will take Lily to the Bright Star film studio and ask the director, Zheng, to try her on camera. Perhaps she is star material, you never know.'

Lily jumped for joy: 'I am a star, I am a star!'

Cassia said unhappily: 'But do I still act in Shenqu plays? We were about to rehearse the new play! I was about to invite someone to put tunes to words, add Western equipment to the band and make Shenqu into "Oriental Opera" – in a word, can I still pursue my own acting career?'

Trying to make peace, Yu Qiyang suggested that she could still carry on with her theatre projects, and only take a little time out for the film. For a moment voices echoed all around the cinema as everyone contributed their opinions.

Lily was talking excitedly to Liu Ji. Cassia stood up abruptly and walked to the balcony. Nobody noticed her disappearance, except for Yu Qiyang. He followed her over. Cassia said anxiously to Yu: 'Do you know the reason I spent years having Lily educated and then sent her to America was because I did not want her to become an actress like me? I asked her to stay at home after she came back from the States, and then I was going to send her to Europe to go to university. Yet she won't even meet the son of the mayor at my request. She really hurt me.'

Yu patted her back and said that whether she wanted to be a lady, a rich married woman or a scholar, it was all up to her. 'Your daughter is your treasure; if she didn't want to meet the son, then it was good the meeting never happened: she might have offended him if it had.'

'Well, let's not pursue the topic; it's her own choice,' Cassia sighed: 'If she is destined to act in films, I will help her as much as I can. But does this mean my own stage career has to end?'

Yu comforted her and said there was plenty of time for her to do both. But it was surely too tiring to sing on stage for three hours a day? Perhaps she could go on stage every other day, or only on Saturdays and Sundays, and play hard-to-get a little?'

Cassia smiled and said: 'But what about the money? You will need thousands.'

Yu smiled: 'You should have asked this a long time ago: How about this proposal: let's say Lixiong Bank issues you with an 80,000 interest-free loan, to be cleared over three years. If you make a profit, it's all yours. Now are you satisfied?'

Only then did a smile come to Cassia's face: 'It seems you are willing to do anything for Lily. Whenever did you lend the Ruyi such a sum?' She leaned on the balcony and thought carefully: 'You think money comes easily, but I will still have to pay back the loan. If we fail we all lose face. How about this. This Ruyi Film Company, I want you to be the Chairman of the Board. The Shanghai business world is tough and only you can keep a grip on the situation.'

Yu said thoughtfully that the income of the Shanghai Brotherhood had long switched from opium, gambling and prostitution to banking, cigarettes and shipping. 'Now it seems we should also get a foothold within the entertainment industry. If Shanghai starts to spend on entertainment, then the rest of China will follow.' He said he'd taken a trip to Nanjing, Hefei and Jinan and all of those cities called themselves 'Little Shanghai', following Shanghai fashions closely. 'Films? The Hong Brotherhood can definitely do films!'

Cassia began to relax: 'If you treat the company as your own business, then I won't have to worry. I am not a member of the Hong Brotherhood; I worry I might not be considered suitable.'

'So long as Shanghai remains, the Brotherhood will survive.' Yu Qiyang said as he turned to see Lily looking animated: 'You should be pleased that your own daughter is as pretty as you were when you were younger, and even more lively and sociable.'

Cassia didn't look at Lily, but instead raised her eyes to Yu. He reached out a hand and rubbed her shoulder and she immediately took hold of his hand, pressed it to her waist and turned to look at him.

Against the bright background of the window, the two shadows pressed together tightly, intimate. After all they hadn't seen each other for two weeks. It seemed their relationship was now quite open, so much so that nobody seemed surprised.

~ CHAPTER 23 ~

'You remind me of a fish,' he had once said to her.

She was in the garden drinking a glass of milk, watching the goldfish swimming happily back and forth in the pond, while she remembered his words. He liked to kneel by her side when she bathed, washing her body this way and that, until finally he himself was all wet and had to strip off and join her in the bath.

The weather was nice today, the temperature rising, warm and sunny. She returned to the sitting room and rang Yu. The Board of Directors were meeting at four o'clock this afternoon, voting to decide about the Ruyi Film Company. She wanted Yu Qiyang to come home before the meeting.

Soon Yu Qiyang's car arrived and Cassia waited for him, half-reclining on the low couch, wearing everyday clothing, looking relaxed. She heard him open the door with his key and greet Li Yu. Soon his footsteps rang on the stairs. Cassia didn't get up until he was in the corridor. She stood behind the door and waited. As soon as he reached the door she stepped up and clasped him, walking backwards with him. As they walked she took off his jacket and dragged him onto the big bed.

Surprised, Yu asked: 'You can't wait until night time? You want to make love in the afternoon, too?'

'You are too good to keep for the night time!' Cassia let go of him and took off her own clothes.

'I've been away too long this time. I shouldn't have done that.'

'So how can I let you go today? You are the rabbit who's given himself up to a tiger.' Cassia laughed: 'By the time I finish the play it will be deep into the night, and you, I never know where you'll be, besides which you have an ugly wife at home.' She

274

pulled down the curtain and flipped open the white quilt that had already been arranged. But before she was able to lie down, she was picked up by Yu Qiyang and thrown to the middle of the bed. His face, darkened by the sun, watched her with lust and a mature man's attraction seeped through his naked body. Suddenly he clung to her more tightly than ever before, with Cassia beneath him.

'You know my marriage was arranged by my mother before either of us was born. We put filial piety above all things in the Brotherhood, so I had to go through with it.'

'Divorce her now!' Cassia was about to say, but still she couldn't say the words out loud. This matter had been with her for so many years and she had thought about it time and time again. The thought itself was torture enough. She could not think too clearly about it, as she could not bear to face the reality. She had a gut feeling about the situation.

She had only ever been to Yu Qiyang's house once, for something urgent that needed to be discussed with him face-to-face. It so happened that he had a cold and couldn't get out of the door.

His wife was extremely respectful to Cassia, saying she was her admirer, a fan. She produced tea, then peanuts, and pressed Cassia to stay for a meal. But she'd never leave them alone. They could only discuss business and were unable to say anything about their feelings for each other. After their discussion, Cassia rose and said goodbye, and the woman walked her to the end of the street.

Now Cassia pretended she didn't hear what he had said. She stroked him and leaned up to look at him more clearly.

'I know what you like,' he said, 'don't worry, time's not up yet.'

They laughed and collapsed together on the bed, both as excited as ever before. She let him take off her skirts and unlace her. Her upper body was revealed, and her belt hung from her waist. All the time Cassia was aware that she was being watched as well as having her breasts touched. It made her dizzy, so she closed her eyes and remembered the first time he had been in her dressing room: he had stroked her breasts, first gently cupping the right one, then stroking the left one. When he touched her nipples, she had moaned and wanted to press his hands to her chest, but the hands had already gone one step further, slipping down to her waist and thighs. She struggled instinctively, but her body had already surrendered to him.

She closed her eyes so she couldn't see him smile. Just then he penetrated her urgently. She pulled his arms and he stroked her face, his hot tongue wrapped around her hardening nipples; suddenly she felt dizzy.

'If we carry on, I will need to have a bath, then get made up; there is not enough time...' she murmured to herself, and her hands loosened.

'We'll stop here today then.' He sat up and so did she. But once they saw each other's naked bodies, they started to get excited again. They clasped each other and kissed passionately, rolling on the bed.

After a long while, she asked him whether he had fainted.

'What about you?'

'I did, I was nearly paralysed.' She revelled in the happy moment.

'I felt almost paralysed myself,' he sighed.

She looked up and saw that the hands of the clock on the wall pointed to three o'clock. She brought Yu Qiyang back his clothes and went to the wardrobe to look for clothes of her own. They were the two biggest shareholders in the Ruyi Company. The matter to be voted on was really their decision. But still they had to go through the procedure, and so many people were waiting. She found a *qipao* covered in blue blossom.

He stopped her, 'Don't put it on yet, let me look at you again.'

'We've known each other for so many years: you've looked at me enough.'

He cupped her face in his hand and looked into her eyes and said: 'No, never.' The two were pinned together again and immediately they felt their souls shuddering, with shivers spreading over the whole of their bodies.

'Come on, it's a quarter past three.'

He shook his head, 'How is it that when we make love it is still like the first time? It's amazing.'

'How indeed?!' she kissed him passionately, 'I am still not letting you go.'

Their bodies joined together again, and both looked at the clock helplessly, then laughed out loud, embarrassed. Ten minutes later, they were in the car. This time Cassia drove, her hands on the steering wheel, her eyes on the road. 'We must have been together for ten years?' she said.

Yu Qiyang looked at Cassia with deep affection and said, 'Yes, it has been ten years. Since 1915.' He noticed the confidence and deftness Cassia showed as she turned the wheel, and the car made a big left turn. He said with conviction: 'You are more than thirty years old, but still getting prettier and prettier! Your waist is still so thin, your nipples are still so hard, your face is still so soft. You are prettier than ever before.'

Cassia laughed: 'We're in the car, don't say any more. You'll make me feel lascivious, again. You yourself are a worse flatterer of women than ever before.' She narrowed her eyes and looked at him, then immediately to the road. She stopped laughing and instead seemed to be thinking deeply. Finally, she murmured something, as if to herself: 'After ten years we're still together; that alone is good enough for me."

~ CHAPTER 24 ~

In the dance hall, the stylish general and the glamorous dancer did a fancy foxtrot, the dance that was currently so popular in America.

This was the opening scene of 'The Flying Heroine', the first film the Ruyi Film Company had made. Liu Ji was both director and screenwriter. The camera man was the famous Yang Zhizhong, who used to work for the Bright Star Company. The film was edited by Li Shikang, who had been a special effects designer in America, working with such famous American directors as D.W. Griffith. The film's editing technique was outstanding, comparable to the most advanced in the world.

The lead actress was of course Lily Chang. Before the making of the film, Liu Ji had asked her to take on small roles for several film companies, and now she was quite familiar with the camera. The male lead was the famous Zhang Hui, poached from the Bright Star company. He was renowned for both his looks and his masculine prowess, matching the beauty and vigour of Lily.

Before the film was publicly shown, the tabloids had reported that this Lily Chang the Ruyi Film Company wanted to promote was the daughter of the 'Queen of Shenqu'. Another tabloid paper was even more thorough and discovered that the new rising star was the posthumous daughter of Chang Lixiong, Grand Master of the Hong Brotherhood. Suddenly Lily, who had been totally unknown, had become a hot topic. *The Entertainment* even carried an exclusive:

'Lily Chang, just back from America, employed by Hollywood; will return to the States after filming "The Flying Heroine."'

Cassia walked down the stairs in her pyjamas, holding a newspaper. She said to Xiu Fang: 'From now on, buy the papers every day.'

Xiu Fang was dusting the sofa with a feather duster, 'Of course, I will go and buy a notebook to collect the cuttings.'

Satisfied, Cassia smiled and straightened the candles that stood on the mantelpiece above the fireplace. From the big mirror above she glimpsed the glorious Western-style chandeliers in the hall.

At the shoot, Lily was losing her temper. She gave Zhang Hui a stern look: 'You are so stupid, you obscured my face.' Cassia looked at director Liu Ji, who called 'Cut!' before approaching her to explain: 'Miss Chang is right. Let's do it like this. Look how the camera pulls closer and adjusts its angle to make Lily's eyes, which are full of affection, more prominent.'

The camera was focused on Lily's eyes, which were indeed full of affection, looking at the man. She said something.

Her words appeared on the screen: 'Will you marry me?'

The general paused in his steps before the tune had finished. He lowered his head and looked saddened as he walked back to the edge of the dance hall. The dancer followed him and the general held her hands, saying earnestly: 'Excuse me Miss, a revolutionary leader cannot marry a dancer.'

In the background, couples were continuing to dance. The heartbroken dancer sat alone by herself and shed silent tears.

This was a sentimental film. Cinema audiences of the time loved to watch sad plots such as this, in which they saw that even the most attractive female stars could suffer everyday pains just like them; they would shed generous tears of sympathy for her. When the preview screening was shown at the film company, even Cassia had to wipe her eyes with her handkerchief. Lily, who sat by her side, happily embraced her mother and noisily and exaggeratedly kissed her cheeks. 'You see! You see! I did it. I did it!'

But Lily's fame was not based on the sad feelings she inspired, but on her so-called acrobatic acting – not the old-fashioned sort of performances seen in traditional plays; she didn't think much of those. She had worked hard to get Cassia to invest in this film because she had wanted to show off the sporting skills she had acquired whilst studying in America. It could be said that the film was especially designed for Lily Chang, to such an extent that no other actress could act in it.

War broke out. The deputy chief of staff rushed into the dance hall and saluted the general: 'The warlords and the imperialists are about to bomb us!'

People screamed and dispersed, the general and the deputy chief of staff rode back swiftly to their headquarters.

Loudly, the general issued his commands: 'Withdraw immediately!'

The troupe was retreating.

Just then the dancer jumped on a white horse and rode off in the other direction. Sweeping past open pastures, she wore a combination of a black pilot's uniform, a protective pair of glasses and a red scarf which burned like a flame on the black and white screen.

They had worked day and night to make the film. When it was shown, colours were added to a few specially made copies. This was the idea of Li Shikang, the special effects designer, supported enthusiastically by Cassia, who hired workers especially to do this.

In a corner of the editing room, the workers were painting each roll of film red. Several tens of thousands of rolls needed to be painted in this way. At first they had thought they'd taken on an easy job, but after two days their hands were so sore they had to keep massaging them. Some complained: 'It's all Mistress Cassia's idea, and now we suffer for it.'

But Cassia wanted personally to test the effect of this 'colour film'. Whenever she had time she'd walk in and glance through the room in a stately manner, saying: 'Paint carefully, make sure nothing goes over the edges. Everything must be done by the day after tomorrow!' She sensed the unhappiness on their faces but still she would not comfort them. 'If you don't like the work, say so. I can find someone else. I need the copies in two days' time, only then will you be paid.'

The workers kept silent and quickly reached for their little paint brushes as they continued working. They were lucky since in the film, the girl's red scarf was always waving around, so that even if the paint did go over the edge it only increased the sense of movement.

Lily Chang drove off especially to bring Madame Emerald to see the show. She had always had a good relationship with her 'grandma', who had looked after her when she was small. Madame Emerald would not watch Cassia's plays, but she would not disappoint this favourite child of hers.

When she saw the airplane coming towards her from the screen (this film was set in some imaginary war of the future) Madame Emerald was so alarmed that she closed her eyes and touched her chest, exclaiming '*Aiyaa*!' She nearly had a heart attack and wanted to leave. Cassia stood up to cover the screen and bent down to reassure her, saying: 'Muma! Don't be frightened. The film is not for real. If there's anything scary in it I will cover your eyes – but you must watch Lily's scene, it's coming up!'

The red-scarved girl, who had in an earlier sequence jumped off her horse onto the wing of an enemy's aeroplane as it took off and made her way into the cockpit, now used both hands to grab the joystick. The plane started to fly in a hazardous manner, shooting up alarmingly into the sky, then turning at an angle and falling straight down. The foreign imperialist devil piloting the enemy plane, whose face happened to be distinctly Japanese, seemed shocked. The red-scarved girl wrapped her feet around the neck of the enemy pilot, and knocked his hands with her fist. She pulled suddenly at the joystick. The plane gradually slanted until it turned a somersault and flew over an empty field, its wing juddering from left to right. The red-scarved girl caught hold of the joystick and hung in mid-air as the pilot, who had already been thrown from the plane, clutched desperately at her leg. The two hung together in mid-air and the plane flew upside down towards a large city, obviously Shanghai, as one could see from the sinuous lines of the Huangpu River and Suzhou Creek. Down below the townspeople were running around in the streets pointing up at the spectacle in the sky.

On the screen the red-scarved girl twisted her leg and kicked the pilot off his chair. The enemy pilot turned somersaults as he tumbled down from the sky, falling amidst the forest of buildings and walls below.

A subtitle flashed onto the screen:

'Try this – Chinese Kung Fu!'

When this sequence of scenes was shown in the cinema, the audience would scream: mothers put their hands in front of their screaming children, though they themselves couldn't stop screaming; many were so frightened they closed their eyes; there were even reports of people fainting from fright; men who were afraid of heights became breathless at the sight of the realistic aerial special effects, causing the cinema to issue warning posters:

'This film is extremely thrilling; the cinema will not take any responsibility should anyone die of fright.'

This only made everyone want to come and test their pluckiness, which increased ticket sales.

The red-scarved girl straightened the joystick and the plane gradually turned the right way up. She sat back in the pilot's seat and flew the plane right over her enemies on the open plain below; she dropped bombs and explosions came one after another onto the screen as her enemies flew up in the fire, their limbs struggling weakly.

When this sequence was shown at the cinema, there was always applause all round, with the audience wildly shouting and cheering, the atmosphere heated and celebratory. It was a silent movie, so there was no need to stay quiet.

The Westerners in Shanghai, who had tended only to watch films imported from the West, also came to satisfy their curiosity after hearing how splendid this film was.

'But this is simply too ridiculous! Isn't it propaganda for the radicals?' said an Englishman.

An American woman beside him said: 'This woman, Lily Chang or whatever her name is, she is quite lovely, I want to meet her.'

The Englishman said: 'This is the Chinese Mary Pickford you're talking about. In America you wouldn't be able to get near such a big star.'

'Don't be silly!' the woman said indignantly, 'This is China, darling. Anybody can become a celebrity. Even me.'

The Englishman's instincts had been sharp. The Ruyi Company's 'The Flying Heroine' was truly radical propaganda in the context of 1925. In Shanghai in the latter half of May, demonstrators used the film to cheer people up. Whenever they walked past cinemas showing the film, they would cheer and shout. If the film just happened to have finished and the audience was making its way out of the cinema, they would head straight for the streets and join the demonstrators, their patriotic fervour greatly strengthened, shouting loudly, 'Down with the imperialists!'.

At the crossroads between Nanjing Road and Yuqiaqing Road, the concessions police aimed high pressure water jets at the demonstrators, crushing many to the ground. But some sporty-looking girls, whose wet clothes clung tightly to their bodies, would follow the example of the 'flying heroine', climb the machines that produced the water and wrestle with the driver and operator for control of the jets.

That summer was the season when this bold new star Lily Chang was at her most popular. Travelling among the demonstrators, Liu Ji, who witnessed these Shanghai women who dared to fight and take precedence over men, the lines of whose bodies were revealed clearly by the water clinging to them, and who felt no need to cover themselves, couldn't help thinking of Delacroix's famous painting, 'Liberty Leading the People.' The men defending the Parisian streets had been greatly inspired by the stiff and prominent breasts of the Goddess of Freedom; they had dared to fight to the death for the cause.

Several years later he began writing novels in which a series of revolutionary female characters had beautiful, large healthy-looking bosoms.

***

Even when Cassia was sitting opposite me, in later years, the figure that had charmed Shanghai still remained; so that even I, a woman, blushed when I saw her. I asked her what magic she used to stay so young and she merely smiled, looking almost shy.

Lily Chang did not inherit Cassia's clear, soft voice, but she did have her figure. Her waist, hips and bust were of Western proportions; especially her breasts, which grew more and more pert on her youthful body. Unlike Cassia, there was no pressure on Lily to bind her chest.

The female nudes in traditional Chinese pornographic pictures reflected the sexual fantasies of Chinese men. Almost all of them were fleshy columns whose figures went straight up and down. A beauty was someone who was slender, whose nipples were two hastily drawn dots. There were numerous poems and also prose on the subject of beauty, but as far as female figures were concerned, there were only a few clichéd expressions such as 'intoxicating chest', 'soft and slender waist', or 'her breath warm and her figure soft'. It was as if the writers had never really looked at the figure of a woman properly.

Ever since a 'Chinese-style' figure such as Cassia's had emerged, women with similar figures had begun to appear in the paintings of Chinese artists, as well as appearing in real life.

How did Chang Lixiong fall for Cassia? How had he been so charmed that his soul nearly left his body? I wasn't able to find the answer to this question until I read carefully Liu Ji's earlier novels. Through these I realised how modern influences emerged in Shanghai; only then did I understand. All the female leads in his 'Red Rose', 'The Gulf Trilogy' and 'The River' possessed 'devilish figures' with full bosoms and slender waists.

Liu Ji had become China's Delacroix! I do not doubt that when he wrote the novels he was thinking of Cassia.

It was absurd to think that breasts had become the symbol of the spirit of the age, the new excitement for a new era. Yet such a view was suggested by the Chinese themselves.

So an outlaw hero like Chang Lixiong, living in a Shanghai where Chinese and Westerners mingled, had unconsciously embraced the not yet fully-formed spirit of the new era. If the reader will allow me to be sensational for a moment, then I'd say that Chang Lixiong had started this fashion in love. Those Shanghai citizens who had fallen in love with Lily Chang's healthy, strong female body in 'The Flying Heroine' had fallen in with the fashion Chang Lixiong had set eighteen years earlier. Neither Liu Ji's novels nor the advertisements in the *Good Friends of Shanghai* pictorial appeared until the end of the 1920s, when the B(Bust), W(Waist) and H(Hips) of the female bodies had already started to be exaggerated. The novels and the pictorials were in effect twenty years behind Chang Lixiong's tastes.

***

The plane was swooping down out of the sky above the headquarters. It nearly touched people's heads; then suddenly it pulled up again. Seen from above the aeroplane, the ground was sometimes big, sometimes small. The general shaded his eyes with his hand and watched.

He asked: 'Who is this flying general?'

The plane finally landed and the red-scarved girl jumped on the wing and then jumped smartly down. The general and his aides stepped up and saluted the hero. The red-scarved girl took off her hat and goggles and the general was startled.

'It's you!'

The red-scarved girl charmingly extended a hand to the general.

'Now will you marry me?'

The general knelt down on one knee like a Westerner and kissed her hand.

'I ask mademoiselle to agree to marry me.'

The final shot in the film was a man in a Western suit with his arms around a beautiful woman who wore a white wedding veil. The two looked at each other with deep affection. Their heads drew closer together. At the point when the two lips were nearly touching the words 'The End' appeared and the film ended.

Everyone stood up; they applauded for a long time. The men cheered; the women wiped their tears away. Watching from the box, Cassia, Yu Qiyang and Lily Chang embraced excitedly.

The audience began to disperse, but someone spotted the people inside the box and screamed: 'Cassia, Queen of Shenqu!' 'And Lily Chang!' Others filled the corridor until they blocked the exit. Women especially wanted to approach Lily and Cassia and touch them. Yu Qiyang commanded his men to come quickly to protect mother and daughter. They crowded into the car and crowds surrounded it as it drove slowly out.

Near the front of the cinema, the whole wall depicted Lily Chang, her face as glamorous as a dancing girl, dressed in a pilot's uniform, looking handsome and fit, quite unlike other innocent-but-helpless looking film actresses of the time. For a while the 'Lily Uniform' – a military jacket – became a symbol of the braver young females.

The sky was not yet dark, but already advertisements in colourful neon light had begun to flash:

'The Ruyi Film Company's unprecedented production: "The Flying Heroine," led by Lily Chang.'

In the car, Cassia held onto Lily and said: 'You are even more popular than me when I was young! Dear Lily, you make me feel so happy!'

Yu Qiyang turned from the front seat and said: 'The Ruyi Film Company will make a lot of money this time!'

Lily patted his head just as she had done when she was a little girl: 'You only think of money! I want to co-operate with Hollywood ånd make big films! With my English, my beauty, and my first-class acting skills, no one in Shanghai can compete with me! Absolutely no one!'

'Steady, steady.' Cassia said excitedly: 'We'll carry on making films and make you as hot as can be, and also make sure we make enough money! I only pity my poor Ruyi Shenqu Troupe, who I haven't been around to look after for a long time.'

~ CHAPTER 25 ~

Li Yu saw Cassia sitting quietly on the sitting room sofa, something rare these days. She approached her with some freshly-prepared Biluochun tea. Cassia, deep in thought, looked at Li Yu, then drew back into herself. Suddenly she asked Li Yu: 'Were you going to say something to me?'

Li Yu was startled: 'No, no.'

Cassia peered at her, then turned to glance at the purple pagoda blossoms outside the window, the blossom vibrant and beautiful, the colour so soft and tender it felt as if one more look at it would make it decay and fall. Li Yu brought over a plate of the sunflower seeds that Cassia liked. Cassia looked at Li Yu again and said: 'If you have something to ask, don't hesitate. What's the point of holding a dumpling in your mouth without swallowing it?'

Li Yu stood embarrassed: 'The mistress is indeed wise; how do you know I have something on my mind?'

'I am the monkey king reincarnated; I can see exactly what's going on inside you. Come, sit down. Words kept hidden inside won't attract anyone's interest.'

Li Yu looked thoughtful and sat opposite Cassia on the sofa: 'If the mistress has a few minutes, then would she care for some local gossip?'

Cassia laughed: 'Local gossip? How could there be any gossip around here. I don't think anybody would know if their neighbour was alive or dead.'

'No, not around here, but stories from the old city.'

'You are good at telling stories Li Yu, so I trust it will be a good one.'

'They say it's all true.' Li Yu said earnestly. Her eyes on Cassia,

Li Yu began to talk.

A street pedlar selling dumplings walked the same route every night, rain or shine, selling midnight snacks. Business was good. One family along the street always bought from him: a couple living above a cigarette shop. It was not convenient to go through the back of the shop to reach them, so the wife would always open the window on hearing his voice and drop down a basket containing two bowls and two jiao to pay for the dumplings. The street pedlar would put the hot dumplings inside the bowl and the couple would pull up the basket. From outside the window, the woman could be seen sewing and the man leaning at his desk, reading and writing. The two would affectionately eat their midnight snack together, then draw the curtain and go to bed.

Cassia's hands, originally on the edge of the sofa, smoothed her own cheeks. She listened attentively as Li Yu carried on: 'So, two bowls of dumplings each night: it carried on for about ten years. To have such business, though small, made the pedlar happy. So one day, when he walked past the cigarette shop in daylight, he asked what did the couple upstairs do, and the man in the shop said: What couple? The man died of an illness about five years ago; the widow upstairs lives alone.

'Oh,' Cassia said, 'so this woman misses her husband and insisted on buying two bowls? You see I am an actress, but still you made me cry.'

Li Yu said: 'So this pedlar could not bear it and from then on he would not go down that street.'

'Oh no,' Cassia said, 'if tragedy affects the dumpling seller to the extent that he won't sell dumplings any more, who on earth will come and see our plays?'

'Don't worry, there's always people like me who'll come and cry at your plays. I'm such a fool.'

Cassia thought carefully about the story. 'But the street pedlar shouldn't really have seen it as a tragedy. The woman is actually happy: she and her husband loved each other when he was alive and she still loves him when he is dead. But if all you wanted to tell me was this sad story, why were you so hesitant just now?'

Li Yu's started to blush. 'I am thinking of getting married.'

Cassia nearly jumped off the sofa: 'I thought it was odd! Now it turns out you want to share dumplings with someone. Your lover must be nearly fifty? But if you marry him, your salary would not be enough for him to continue with his gambling.'

'It is because we are getting older that we want to marry. We want to reward ourselves for being together so long, and to celebrate our relationship.'

'I don't think much of this opening story! But when is the wedding? I want to give you a really good present,' Cassia said, '...but you must not leave me.'

Embarrassed, Li Yu said, 'The crazy old man has asked me to set up home with him. As the mistress hardly ever goes out to the theatre at the moment, I thought I might be allowed to go free.'

'You hope I shall never sing again?'

'Of course not. I just thought that before long the old man's gambling addiction would be sure to return and then I would be able to come back here to look after you.'

Cassia said reluctantly: 'All right, let's just say that I'll give you leave for your honeymoon. With regard to your man,' Cassia said, 'I will invite him over here to play *Mahjong* and make sure he loses so miserably that he has to sell you to me.'

'Good idea,' said Li Yu, laughing loudly, relaxed: 'he will never be your match.'

Li Yu walked away, but Cassia watched the maid who had looked after her for so long disappear and suddenly felt a nameless melancholy. The story of the two bowls of dumplings lingered in her mind like a sad tune, making her feel restless. As if cursed, she knew now she could not be peaceful again.

Yu Qiyang returned from the provinces and Cassia sent a car to the station to fetch him. But first Yu had to go to the bank; only when he had finished his business did he come to see her. He said that no matter how busy he was, tonight he would make sure he came to Jessfield Road. Lily was shooting with the Ruyi Film Company in Shandong. She liked the current film 'The Heroine' very much; the script for it had been especially written for her by Liu Ji. In style it was an American Western, the heroine shooting with both hands while riding on horseback. The company had driven to the Haikou District where the Yellow River delta sands could stand-in for the Gobi Desert.

Cassia brewed a pot of tea for herself. She knew Yu was sure to come if he said he would. No matter how late, he would not go back to his own home. He had said that home was not home, it felt more like an inn.

She went to the kitchen to cook a few of his favourite dishes and then waited for him. Calm and quiet, she wore a white shirt and a black skirt, her hair tied up high, and no jewellery. The moon was bright and the wind soft, the leaves of the French parasol in the street outside whistled softly in the wind; the moonlight was rubbed into pieces and scattered on the street.

Yu Qiyang's car came over and Xiu Fang went to the door. The car was parked in the drive, its lights switched off. Yu stepped out, wearing a white Western suit, and a tie. Cassia stood in front of the window and watched his familiar figure enter the house. She swiftly patted some powder on, straightened her clothes and glanced at herself in the mirror. She was thirty-five years old now; her daughter was eighteen. In the small town she had come from, it would be time for her to prepare to be a grandmother, but the woman in the mirror really looked as if she was only about twenty-five or twenty-six.

The sound of Yu's footsteps came up the stairs.

Cassia stood at the top and watched him walking up. She took his jacket and fetched some tea for him. Yu felt odd; his eyes searched the quiet room.

Cassia said that she had asked Li Yu and Xiu Fang to have an early rest; that she herself would accompany him downstairs to have some food.

'There's no need for food, I've just finished entertaining.' He sat on the soft low couch and pulled Cassia to him. Both their professions involved working at night; for a long time they had not had a chance to sit and enjoy a quiet moment together.

Standing in front of him, she said affectionately, 'When I saw you for the first time Yu, you were the humblest little servant, so worthless that you waited on prostitutes.'

Yu laughed: 'Of course. When I first saw you, you were a mere servant girl who was not even fit to sleep with the guests; they said you could not even become a common prostitute.'

His hands clasped around her and the two embraced; stroking each other, kissing, they moved to the bed.

'But now all of Shanghai is yours!'

'And all over China people admire your beauty and talk about you.'

'We've known each other for nineteen years,' she said.

'It's nearly twenty.'

She drew back by the bed and kissed him between the legs. He stroked her face and started to moan. The sky became darker and the leaves of the trees waved in the wind outside the window.

Yu sat on the edge of the bed, facing the mirror on the wall opposite him. It had been changed from oval, to square, then oblong. Now it was a rhombus. In the mirror he also saw his own face, parts of the bed behind him and also that she had risen to sit on the bed. He glimpsed the half of her shoulder that was exposed outside her shirt, the shoulder with the tattoo of a cassia flower. He closed his eyes. She faced the other mirror, which had never been changed, and smiled at the man who once more opened his eyes. The green trees outside the window were waving rhythmically. They were reflected in both mirrors, the one on the left that was constantly being changed unlike the one on the right that was forever the same.

She was about to stand up when he threw himself down onto the bed. He stripped off her underwear.

They were already clasped together. She held on to him out of habit and swept all the pillows and cushions off the bed and onto the floor. To the accompaniment of the creaking bed, she saw the woman through the ever-changing mirror, her face red and shining, her eyes jet black.

She was still the same girl of ten years ago, yet she was even more womanly. Her body trembled in hunger, her black hair shook. Her breasts still stood erect as if in fright; she could even feel the spasms of flames shooting across her skin, wave after wave moving from the small of her stomach and gathered in a certain point in the lower part of her body, swollen and painful. He bent down and kissed her there, and she turned on her side to look at the mirror. It had only been a matter of seconds, yet now she was not able to recognise herself. She struggled and wanted to turn, but felt the mosquito nets pressing down on her face and chest like a real net. She couldn't breathe; it was as if her heart nearly stopped beating. She grasped his back with force: 'I'm going to die: don't you pity me?'

He held her face and looked at her: 'I cannot live either.'

'Come quickly inside me, Yu.' Her feet kicked him excitedly. 'All right, I'll come.' He flipped her body around, and entered her from behind. She saw the sweat on her face in the mirror and his hands wanting to turn her face back to kiss it. She could feel the ramming down below, causing her whole body to go into spasms, making her ever tighter down below.

His hands came from behind, tightly clasping her breasts. The sudden new stimulation caused her to scream and she felt his speed catching up with hers. The two erupted like volcanoes, suddenly jumping to the ninth heaven.

'Come on!' he shouted.

'I'm there!' she shouted back.

She was full of joy and melted into a blinding light. Together they reached the peak of happiness, and were left covered in sweat.

'Me too!' he shouted, 'There, there…'

Their heavy breathing gradually subsided and slowly they returned to reality. She said breathlessly: 'Don't leave me too quickly!'

He said: 'I won't.'

There was no sound in the room. Even the mirror was covered with the steam from their bodies. After a while, she didn't know how long, as if just coming back from death, Cassia stirred in the bed. She was surprised that after so many years her reactions were getting stronger and the fantasies that came to her at the point of happiness were getting more and more extreme. The enjoyment afterwards, akin to collapse, happened more easily. As time went by, she should have become more placid; she should have taken things less seriously; but no, on the contrary, her desire to enjoy happiness became stronger and stronger. She wanted to be with Yu Qiyang every night.

This sense of dependence made her fearful: she really didn't want to lose this man. She reached out a hand to the cup on the cupboard by the bedside, drank some water and handed the cup to him. 'Yu, in another twenty years I will be an old woman. You won't want me then.'

Yu Qiyang drank the water and placed the cup on the floor. He smoothed the long hair that lay scattered over her shoulders and said, 'No, you will only get more and more beautiful. I have only you in my heart. Everything of ours is mixed up together: our capital, our careers. Without the Ruyi Company's success, the Lixiong Bank would have been unable finally to stand up in the world. Without the Lixiong Bank, the Ruyi Company would find it difficult to keep going. The company cannot do without the bank and the bank cannot do without the company. Since there is no way the two can be separated, the people involved must be chained together.'

Cassia didn't say anything, but looked into Yu Qiyang's eyes: 'You have only me in your heart?'

'Of course, I have always felt like this. I have never hidden the fact that, as a man of the world, I have some affairs, but you know of each and every one of them; these encounters only serve as stories to amuse us. I've never taken any of them seriously and neither have you.'

Although she was the model for a cigarette company, Cassia rarely smoked: she had to protect her voice. Only when the character she was performing required her to smoke would she pretend to. The cigarettes she had at home had been prepared for Yu. Now, believing that he might be in need of it, she took one from the cigarette box on the cupboard by the bedside, lit it and passed it to him.

He took it and continued: '…and none of those women have dared to be jealous of you.'

Cassia leaned on the pillow, sat half up and laughed. After her mirth, she said: 'Neither of us wants to be separated. We are more and more loving in bed and more and more happy in general. We never tire of each other. So why don't you marry me?'

Yu Qiyang never imagined she would say such a thing and froze.

'You are unwilling?' Cassia hesitated, then said: 'But surely you can't be?'

She had not expected Yu to react like this at all. She had thought he might not agree immediately, as after all there were many other things to consider; or perhaps he would make a joke of it and then change the topic so that they could talk properly about it later. He had always been smart and quick-witted; he knew how to deal with difficult situations.

But this time she was wrong. Yu Qiyang was unprepared for such a question. It seemed as if his brain had stopped working; as if he was struck dumb by her words. She felt embarrassed. Perhaps it was a deliberate decision: that he did not want to sound undecided on such a topic, and wanted to give her a direct answer.

Cassia could only speak her mind with all sincerity: 'Actually, for many years I have been waiting for you to ask me that. I decided that, if you didn't ask, then I would.'

Yu sat up in bed, smoking heavily. After a while he rose, still naked, and walked to the other side of the bed to fetch the ashtray. Watching him, Cassia also sat up and said gently: 'It seems you disagree. Can you tell me the reason why?'

'I have a wife at home, you know that.'

'That's not a reason. Which other great Chinese hero has refused to divorce their humble first wife to marry a prettier, smarter one? Sun Yat-sen? Chiang Kai-shek?' She saw that Yu remained silent, and said: 'All right, if you don't want to get a divorce, that's fine, too. Which Grand Master in the Brotherhood has not had three or four wives? I will be your concubine, will that do?'

Yu put the cigarette out and dressed in silence. He put on his tie, remaining silent all the time. Cassia's face grew ever darker. She felt strangely suffocated, but still couldn't help saying that she would not stop him having affairs or marrying a younger wife. She was nearly in tears.

Yu could not bear to look at her. Looking the other way, he said: 'Cassia, it's not about that. It won't do for us to get married.'

'What is it about then? Do you love someone else?'

'You know that you were the favourite woman of both of my masters. You were the woman I fell in love with at first sight when I was young, the woman who helped me to be who I am now, who shared all my hardships. I could not bear to leave you for any of these reasons! I have never met another woman who really stirred my heart; only you will always move me.'

Hearing his words, Cassia jumped off the bed, kissed him wildly and said: 'Then why don't I stir you all your life? Wouldn't that be good?'

'Yes, yes, I like to hear you saying it. It makes me happy. But that's different from marriage. To be really blunt, you know people like me cannot have…' He paused, unable to continue.

'Have what?' Cassia nearly shouted, 'Go on!'

Yu couldn't find the word; he knew he shouldn't say it, it wouldn't be fair on Cassia and he didn't mean it either, but he couldn't find any other words. This was a commonly held stereotype, something that was beyond his own ability to choose.

'A dominant wife,' Yu finally said. He had prepared the explanation as well: 'You are far too powerful and far too strong as a woman. I head a brotherhood which can kill; although nowadays such deeds are hardly ever called for, those working for me are hardly refined gentlemen. If I marry someone who could appear to dominate me, then I won't be able to sustain my position in the Brotherhood.'

Cassia burst into tears. 'You! You are so heartless. I endured everything for you. I sacrificed my money, my life, my soul, and you: how did you repay me?' She spoke hysterically, as if she had lost her mind.

Yu held her tightly and she bit into his shoulders, crying aloud: 'I will kill you if you don't marry me. Huang Peiyu didn't marry me, and I killed him!' He placed her on the bed and held her until she calmed down.

'Kill me then,' Yu said, visibly stirred. He bent down to kiss her tears.

'Why,' Cassia sat up: 'You think I dare not do it again?'

Murdering Huang Peiyu was the riskiest thing Cassia had ever done in her life. Even those involved still could not tell how everything had been planned and how the traps had all been set.

It was Yu Qiyang, of course, who had watched Huang Peiyu's every move. His little group of die-hard followers were only doing what he asked them to do. No one knew the whole picture; each only did the specific task commanded by Cassia.

Their situation then had not allowed for much hesitation: Huang Peiyu would not be able to keep a mistress such as Cassia forever; it would be even less likely for him to allow his men to steal his woman. On Yu's wedding night, when Huang Peiyu failed to see Cassia, he had asked Yu: 'Hey, why isn't Cassia here?' It was a simple enough question, but cold sweat had soaked through Yu's vest in response to it.

They didn't have any ambition to be in charge of the Brotherhood, but they understood that, once Huang Peiyu was gone, there would be a new Grand Master and new possibilities. Nevertheless the sum of all his calculations was not sufficient for Yu to take such a risk as this. He hesitated for a long time: he had seen the cruel way the Brotherhood dealt with its traitors; he did not want to end up like that. Even if they escaped punishment by the law, they would find it hard to escape the wrath of the Brotherhood.

But Cassia had cornered him: 'Huang Peiyu is the "Number One Traitor in the Brotherhood". If you can be sure he is completely dismembered, then I will give up my plan.'

Yu had been unable to find any words to answer this.

She said she was not sure of success. Perhaps she would die together with Huang Peiyu: if so, that alone would be enough to avenge Master Chang. This moved Yu Qiyang: this little woman was braver than he was. He didn't know of the huge pain that tortured her: that it was her stupidity that had caused Master Chang to fall into Huang Peiyu's trap. If she did not cause Huang Peiyu to die miserably, then she would never know peace in her own heart.

The bomb in Dongchang Town was Cassia's idea. Nothing else would be sure to kill Huang Peiyu, who was good at protecting himself. Although it was Yu who had bought the dynamite and fuses from the quartermaster of the retreating army of Lu Yongxiang, he felt it was all too dangerous; he didn't agree to the plan for a long time.

Cassia had foreseen that the trees would be able to shelter her. But at the second the bomb exploded, no one could be sure of escaping unscathed. Indeed the distances involved were in themselves proof that the kidnappers had wanted to kill both of them.

When the shockwave of the explosion had passed, Cassia, who had only pretended to be wearing a blindfold, had swiftly found the leg chains they had prepared, chained herself and clicked on the handcuffs – all whilst covered by a cloud of smoke. This was hard, but she had always been deft with her hands and had practised for many days beforehand. Everything at the scene had suggested that she was innocent. Even if the tree trunk had saved her life, she had needed to be extremely careful with her eyes and her body. Even a professional soldier with considerable fighting experience would find it hard to do what she had done, let alone a woman whose hands had been cuffed behind her back and feet bound together, a woman was supposedly unable to move. Her escape alive, surely, was purely a matter of luck. The disciples of Sherlock Holmes from the Municipal Council, however suspicious, could find no evidence. Since his death, some of Huang Peiyu's die-hard associates had continued to search for someone on whom they could avenge his death, but had failed to find this person.

***

Such a terrible secret would never have been discovered; not even I could have guessed at it.

So how have I come up with all this? On what basis can I make these accusations? My evidence was what Cassia herself said to Yu Qiyang: 'I've killed Huang Peiyu.'

Could there be any other phrase franker than that?

Put on the spot, Cassia had to admit the truth to me. But she still did not give me any details, for fear of incriminating others. After all, it was not something that could be done by just one or two people. If someone wants to solve this case, famous in the history of the Shanghai Hong Brotherhood, or if Huang Peiyu's great-grandson wants to avenge his great-grandfather, let me proclaim here: What I have written in this book cannot be used as evidence. They should still hire professional detectives and find evidence that could be sustained in court.

Cassia was an actress, after all. Even in matters such as kidnapping and murder, she could behave as if they were real and be convincing enough for Huang Peiyu to be taken in.

Her ruthlessness in the matter must have made Yu Qiyang a little fearful, especially when he thought about marrying such a woman. Yu Qiyang's instinct was right: home was a place in which one could not hide. Perhaps he sensed that such a unique woman could only be a curse to her husband?

★★★

On the evening that she never wanted to remember again, she had pushed him away and buried her head in the pillow. He had patiently and tenderly smoothed her shoulders. After a long time she raised her head and said calmly: 'It was me who was unreasonable. You were right. I have asked for too much.'

Yu sighed, stood up and said, 'Let us both think about it carefully. With so many factors to consider we must be completely calm when we decide what to do.'

He put on his Western suit and went to wash his face in the bathroom. It was late. He would never normally leave Cassia and 'return home' at such a time, especially as today his wife did not even know he was back in Shanghai. There was no need to go back, but he felt he could not stay there.

He emerged from the bathroom, walked up to the bed and said to Cassia: 'It's time for me to leave. You should rest.'

Cassia didn't restrain him, but she put on her slippers, picking up a nightgown, draped it over herself and accompanied him down the corridor. The two walked down the stairs gently and in silence. It was not until they were at the gate that she spoke:

'You've broken my heart, but I believe that true love will find a happy ending!'

Yu Qiyang didn't reply; these words sounded like something from a play. But he looked at her and stretched out his hands. Holding her tightly he embraced and kissed her, as if in apology. Then he turned, opened the door and went out to the car. She stood motionless and watched like a puppet as the engine started, the lights went on and the car drove off.

Standing there, she regretted having been hasty. She had forgotten herself. So long as Yu Qiyang still loved her, she shouldn't worry. Gradually, step by step, she would be able to cover the distance of the many mountains and rivers that stood between them. He would not desert her; yet now she needed to concentrate on making up for her misdemeanours.

But she simply must succeed. She believed she could do it – if she could risk all to murder a Grand Master of the Brotherhood, she could risk all to love one. Just as they had been twelve years ago, her feelings for Yu were dangerous, yet it was precisely these dangerous feelings that made her understand her own heart.

Left alone to face the darkness that lay behind the street lamp, tears filled her eyes and she tried hard to not let them fall. She was used to acting out other people's emotions and portraying their broken hearts; now that it was her turn, she knew that there was no question of her acting out this misery, it was all too real.

~ CHAPTER 26 ~

Cassia was backstage, taking off her make-up. These days she hardly ever had the opportunity to go on stage. Performances were almost a hobby. The theatre made a big fuss on the days she did perform there, advertising the event especially. Some of her older fans had a special love for her 'Xiao style' of singing, as they found its deep and enduring qualities intoxicating. They wanted to hear her sing in this manner again and again. Some also loved the personas she adopted on stage; they felt her portrayal of young married women was especially charming and sweet. If they did not get to see this, they were left unhappy.

She received a strange telephone call that day, which, as was the custom, was received by Li Yu. The man insisted that Cassia herself come to the phone, saying that it was about a very confidential matter. In a bad mood Cassia took the phone. A middle-aged man's voice said: 'We know all about the ugly things you've done.'

'Extraordinary!' Cassia said sarcastically. She had received many strange phone calls before and did not take them seriously.

'You've been a common prostitute!'

'I've been your ancestor!' Cassia slammed down the phone.

Half a minute later, the phone rang again. Cassia refused to pick it up; she knew it was the same man. But she wanted to hear what he had to say and asked Li Yu to listen, which Li Yu did before passing the message on to her:

'Ask Cassia to take out 20,000 yuan, otherwise the evidence will be made public.'

Cassia said: 'Tell him he'd better pay 20,000 himself – for a security guard: before he has time to show this evidence, he'll lose his head!'

On the way back in the car, they laughed at this. But Cassia had an inkling that this man wasn't just calling her bluff. His price was far too high for that.

The man went on to demand money several more times, the sums involved getting smaller and smaller each time, until finally it came down to 300 yuan. Cassia knew how to deal with such blackmail and refused to pay the man any attention: if she paid up once, he'd only come and bother her again.

The one thing Xiu Fang did every morning without fail was to buy all the available newspapers, taking cuttings of any coverage of Cassia's plays. Now she had to make cuttings for Lily as well, so Cassia could flip through these when she had time. Xiu Fang had at first found it hard to read the papers, but now she did so whenever she had time and found it interesting.

Cassia had asked her to keep all the articles, whether complimentary or critical, and so after eleven or twelve years, several thick booklets full of them had accumulated. Cassia could even recognise certain famous writers from their style.

During her interviews with journalists, she would recite some of these sentences, exciting and flattering her interviewers: what they had written could actually be recited and passed on, like words of the great poets! If this famous celebrity thought so highly of them, they were more than willing to write about her, to make all sorts of titles up for her, to call her the 'most remarkable woman in the last 300 years of Shanghai history', or 'the high priestess of the Shanghai art world.'

But the day's *Entertainment* carried an article which caused Xiu Fang to blush and her heart rate to increase.

'Famous and beautiful Shanghai celebrity originally a prostitute; humble origin of this spinster of the acting world exposed!'

The article said that art was intended to educate by

303

entertaining while teaching people to behave well. Mixed standards had developed in the theatrical circles of China, and things had to be improved. Recently it had been revealed that a leading female Shenqu star had originally been a second-rate prostitute; that she had never regretted her origins and had often put on plays that were obscene, doing her best to seduce and corrupt others.

The article was signed 'Lian Cheng', which was obviously a pen-name.

Xiu Fang hid the newspaper. Cassia asked: 'Where's today's *Entertainment*?'

Xiu Fang didn't raise her head. There was no newspaper that day, she told Cassia.

'Nonsense. I have been waiting to read it.'

'So you know already?' Xiu Fang said in surprise.

'I knew it would be today that the snake would emerge from its cave.' Cassia took the newspaper from Xiu Fang and read it carefully. 'So this is it. You made a big fuss over this? Take it away.'

She rang Liu Ji, saying that the Bright Star Company was behind *Entertainment*, who published the article; *Entertainment* was originally produced by writers from the Bright Star company. Now that the Ruyi Film Company had stolen some strong actors from Bright Star, the remaining female stars there – women such as Le Dandan and Ouyang Feng – had been angered by Lily's sudden rise to fame. Cassia told him she didn't think much of them attacking their rivals in this way.

Liu Ji promised to try and uncover the truth; he would try to smooth things over before any names were named. Cassia indicated that if they stopped here and went no further, she would pretend she hadn't seen anything.

Entertainment was published twice a week. That Saturday they published a 'reader's letter'.

'Mr Lian Cheng's article has really hit the bull's eye. Many wise people have long loathed the corruption in the art world of our country. Leading figures such as Cassia Xiao come from obscene, lowly professions; their habits remain obscene; they do not have any self respect and are proud of their scandalous practices. If they are not exposed, no reform of art could be completed; if not disposed of, no righteousness could be established.'

Cassia held the newspaper and thought for a long time. If it had named no names she would not do anything; even if people guessed it were her, she would have left well enough alone. She'd leave it for others to comment. But now the newspaper was forcing her to speak up; she needed to consider what to say.

Then Yu Qiyang phoned her. He was more worried than her; he had already consulted the legal advisor of the Lixiong Bank. The advisor had suggested she turn to the law: the court of the concessions used English law, and in a libel trial, according to that law, the burden of proof was on the accuser; the accused did not have to disprove anything. As it was rarely easy to produce hard evidence either way, the English law favoured the plaintiff.

The next day, Cassia placed an announcement in the *Shenbao* newspaper:

'*Entertainment* has over several days slandered me, the writer of this note accusing me of having a low and obscene background. This accusation was purely a fabrication; a libel has been committed. I am bringing a suit at the concessions' law court, claiming loss of good reputation to a value of 30,000 yuan.'

But *Entertainment* was prepared. It immediately responded with an announcement of its own: 'Cassia was originally a common prostitute, this is a fact based on hard evidence. We will fight the case in court.'

All this to-ing and fro-ing in the media had become big news, and for a time newspapers carried such unsightly headlines as:

'Colourful flag of female celebrity raised high!'
'Woman's charmed life disappears; her charm remains!'

Yu Qiyang was now very angry; he was worried that it would be hard for Cassia to appear in public. But Cassia's biggest worry was how all this might harm Lily Chang. Lily herself, however, threw the papers aside and didn't think much about it. For Lily, news was not news if it did not appear in Shanghai's English language newspapers. She thought it funny, however, and several times, while they were eating, she actually laughed about it. This made Cassia feel relaxed about it in turn.

To her surprise, however, both the Shanghai art world, and the city's women's organizations issued declarations, denouncing *Entertainment* for holding artists in contempt. Instead of denouncing the Chinese Governor, who was originally a bandit, or the Chief of Police who was originally a hooligan, it targeted actresses with malicious gossip and insulted their personalities with news of a pornographic nature.

Cassia had always believed that her colleagues in the art world were jealous of her; that the virtuous figures of the women's movement looked down on her, especially after her advertisements for Hardeman cigarettes, with her much too tight, much too revealing foreign skirts, and the seductive words she used in the advertisements: 'I've inhaled all sorts; only he is the best.' For many years the gossip about her had been ceaseless and its tone had been much like that taken by *Entertainment*; sometimes it was more malicious still. But now that such matters had been made public, everyone united to fight with her, at least publicly. She felt comforted by this.

During this time Cassia received many letters from her audience. The majority were posted to the theatre; a big pile arrived every day. She had to bring them home and asked Xiu Fang to go through them. Many men sent letters that were both obscene and insulting; Xiu Fang would burn a basin full of them. Sometimes Cassia would catch a glimpse of these; they made her feel that men were indeed made of mud: their sexual fantasies, whether written down or drawn, were all so similar and so sickening. But the fan letters from women were especially interesting. The majority worried that she might not be level-headed enough over this; that she might even commit suicide; they tried to comfort her in all sorts of ways. This was because she had acted in too many plays which involved her committing suicide, and her audience was worried that she might do as her characters did.

She asked Xiu Fang to reply to the comforting letters. Xiu Fang wrote better letters than she did nowadays.

Yu Qiyang came several times to spend time with her and saw that she remained upbeat. He felt he had been over-protective. They discussed the matter. The opponent wouldn't be able to produce any evidence. Perhaps many who had known the second rate prostitute she had once been would suspect that this was the same woman as the well-respected actress Cassia Xiao, but that was not hard evidence. The only person who could act as a witness would be Madame Emerald, who had already been to see Cassia. Someone had gone to her with a huge sum to try to buy her participation as a witness, Madame Emerald claimed, but she had cursed the man and sent him away. She would be willing to curse these rotten turtle eggs again in court if need be.

One day a woman rang to say that she was the lawyer Gu Yuyin; that she had returned from studying in England and had her own practice in Shanghai. Cassia had heard of her name and knew she was both famous and important. Gu Yuyin felt very aggrieved on Cassia's behalf and was willing to defend her in court. They made an appointment to meet in Dongkang Restaurant. When, in the restaurant, Cassia saw the bespectacled, middle-aged woman walking towards her, she immediately looked familiar. The woman also said that they must have met somewhere before.

The two sat down and instead of discussing the topic at hand tried their hardest to remember where they had met before.

Finally they remembered at almost the same time. Gu Yuyin was the female speaker who had preached equality with men in the Zhang Garden. Cassia was the young woman who had asked her a strange question. The two laughed happily.

Cassia said: 'I am sorry my question was so blunt.'

'No, no,' said Gu Yuyin, 'the question was very much to the point. I have never been able to forget it. But in Chinese society, none dare to ask such a question; even in the West it can only be discussed in an academic context. My estimate is that even in a century it will be hard openly to discuss such a question in China!'

The reason she wanted to act in defence of Cassia, Gu Yuyin went on, was to defend women all over China. She wasn't even interested in the question of whether Cassia had been a prostitute or not. The publication of such an article was dirty water thrown over all women: if it's not a scandal for men to have three wives and to go and see prostitutes, why then had women to be so closely scrutinised by society? She would not even charge Cassia a fee: she wanted to fight for the equality of women.

Gu Yuyin was getting excited; Cassia felt she was perhaps being a bit too idealistic; that she was not suited to dealing with the nastier elements among her opponents. But Gu Yuyin's enthusiasm made her hard to refuse. And the principle on which Gu Yuyin was fighting was one of which she approved.

On 24 September 1926, the fifth year of the Republic, the case came to trial in the law court of Shanghai's foreign concessions. The case had been hotly discussed in newspapers for almost a month, attracting the attention both of officials and of ordinary people. On the day the case opened, the front gate on the Jiujiang Road, where the court stood, was crowded with journalists, Cassia's female supporters and spectators passing-by. The road was packed: there were thousands of people in the crowd. The police, reluctant to pull women demonstrators away, had to divert traffic instead.

When the lawyer Gu Yuyin and Cassia appeared together, the supporters shouted: 'Miss Cassia will be sure to win! Sure to win!'

Lawyer Gu wore a professional lawyer's uniform and Cassia wore a plain blue *qipao* with no jewellery or make-up. She looked elegant and calm, like a female worker, a weak woman. She passed through the crowds, shaking people's hands. Many grasped her hands and cried.

The people from *Entertainment* took stock of the situation and realised that if they passed through the crowds, they would be sure to be attacked, so they entered the court through the back entrance on Hankou Road.

The gate at the entrance to the court was closed and no coverage or attendance by journalists was permitted for the duration of the trial, as English law dictated. The crowds outside waited patiently for three hours. An organization calling itself the 'Association for the Support of Cassia' distributed tea and *mantou* bread.

Finally the gate opened again and Cassia walked calmly out. She left it to Gu Yuyin to announce to the waiting press and public that the court had made its decision. *Entertainment* had committed the offence of libel, with 'particularly malicious intention'. The plaintiff's demand for defamation to a value of 30,000 yuan was reasonable and was upheld. Another ten newspapers who had reported the same story without checking their facts and mentioned Cassia by name as well as using such words as 'second-rate prostitute' and 'common prostitute', had committed the offense of spreading a libel. It was up to the plaintiff to decide whether to prosecute them or not.

The supporters outside the gate shouted: 'Victory! Victory!' and lifted Cassia up as if she was a victorious hero.

The next day the newspapers carried the long defense speech given by the famous lawyer Gu Yuyin. It read like an impassioned declaration of equality.

***

All researchers of Cassia's life have treated this case as an important event. But they only limited themselves to the newspaper reports of the time. When I studied the case, I felt there were many omissions in these reports. It took me a great deal of effort to dig further: I begged a friend's friend, who eventually agreed to allow me access to the inner archive room of the Shanghai Archive Bureau, where complete sets of all the court records in the concessions were kept. I spent several days among the shelves and boxes of archives, until I found the written record of the debate of this case held in court.

It turned out that not much of the trial was to do with Gu's speech. The defendant had persisted in demanding that Cassia confirm whether or not she had been a prostitute.

Lawyer Gu asked the court to confirm that personal experiences were matters of privacy that had nothing to do with the case, that there was thus no need to respond to such a question. But Cassia indicated that she would be willing to answer the question, and stated that she 'never had been'.

The lawyer for the defense asked her about her experience at the Duchess Pavilion. Madame Emerald, formerly the owner of the Pavilion, gave evidence that Cassia had been a servant girl at her establishment. All prostitutes at the Pavilion who received guests had to have bound feet, a Suzhou accent and be able to sing the 'Ping Tan'. Cassia possessed none of these attributes and so it would have been impossible for her to be a prostitute there.

The defense lawyer then asked about Cassia's experiences after the Duchess Pavilion and both Cassia and Madame Emerald were adamant that she went back home to work in the fields.

The lawyer asked for a witness, a woman whose surname was 'Cao', who claimed to be the madame of the Jade Pavilion. She said that eighteen years ago, in the autumn of 1908, Madame Emerald, the owner of the Duchess Pavilion had sold a young girl to the Jade Pavilion. This girl had been a working prostitute there for as much as four years, until finally she returned back to the countryside because of illness. She identified this person as the woman here called Cassia. However, both Cassia and Madame Emerald denied having ever met the woman, let alone recognising her.

Then the defendant's lawyer produced his so-called firm evidence: the sale certificate with which the Duchess Pavilion had sold the young girl to the Jade Pavilion at this time, with the fingerprints of Madame Emerald, Cassia herself and the woman called 'Cao'. The defendant's lawyer demanded that the court used this document as evidence and asked for an expert to check the authenticity of the fingerprints.

Cassia could never imagine that she would have left such a document behind eighteen years ago. For a moment she did not know what to say. But Madame Emerald stood up and denied that she had ever pressed her fingers to such a certificate. She said the Duchess Pavilion would have never been involved in something as illegal as human trafficking.

Madame Emerald's words inspired Lawyer Gu. She asserted that the court must never recognise as legal evidence the legitimacy of this document. If such a document was deemed reliable, then all the relevant parties would have violated the laws of the Concession. The Jade Pavilion was in the Concession and the court had a responsibility to arrest immediately and prosecute the owner; the case would then become a criminal case. As soon as her words were out the opponents fell silent. It had never occurred to them that such a document would not be recognised by Concession law.

The judge, in summarising the case, pointed out that the document for the sale of humans was itself illegal and thus could not be used as effective evidence. But since it had been over eighteen years go, and the time for retrospective prosecution had long expired, there was therefore no case for criminal prosecution.

And since *Entertainment* had not produced any effective evidence to prove that the accused had once acted as a prostitute, the judgment had to be that *Entertainment* had published two articles, one after another, committing the offence of defamation, and because its accusations had been especially vile, it should pay a hefty fine.

This judge, who'd also studied abroad, wore the wig of the English Crown Court and a black robe. Upholding justice in a Chinese court according to English law, he looked severe. He of course knew what both the crowd outside and wider public opinion wanted to talk about.

Whether or not the judge's deliberation was affected by 'modern consciousness' or by public opinion, or what the psychology behind this judgment was, I have no way of knowing. But I have guessed one thing: the document was illegal, and that gave the judge a very good reason for following the general opinion of the times.

★★★

Cassia won a complete victory. As she left the court she declared that she'd donate the entire 30,000 yuan compensation to Shanghai Peiwen Women's Night School, the aim of which was to improve the status of labouring women. *Entertainment* was unable to pay the fine and filed for bankruptcy; it put all its capital up for auction. Lixiong Bank bought the newspaper for 15,000 yuan and relaunched it under the name *New Entertainment*. The whole trial was big news, the talk of Shanghai and the entire country in September 1926.

On the night of the victory, Cassia and Yu Qiyang ate crabs specially chosen from the Yangcheng Lake and drank the Wang Baohe Restaurant's own brew of rice wine. Yu Qiyang asked: 'Do you know who organised the "Association for the Support of Cassia"?'

'How could you hide it from me?', said Cassia. 'I thought of it a long while ago and just wanted to see whether you too would come up with such an idea.'

The two were extremely happy; before long they became intoxicated, and started boasting to each other. Cassia said that someone from the Gobi Desert in the north had told her that the Mongolian herdsman there knew there was a woman in Shanghai who could sing good songs; that as a result she had become a general and now they would like to invite this female general to come and try her voice at the grassland's singing competition.

Yu Qiyang said that what he had heard was even more interesting: the Paoge Brotherhood in Shangan, which counted as a branch of the Hong Brotherhood, had sent people over to enquire whether it was true that the Shanghai Brotherhood had set a young boy up as a Grand Master and appointed his mother Cassia to be the Queen Dowager.

Cassia listened to the story with a smile on her face, but inside, she felt her heart grew heavy: nothing could remain this good forever.

Those newspapers who had not chosen their words carefully and who had repeated the gossip now came one after another to apologise to Cassia, hoping that she would not sue them too. 'If you portray me in a good light from now on, I won't mention it,' Cassia merely answered.

She knew that however much white paint she applied, her own history would never be as white. She guessed that the majority of Shanghai people believed that she had indeed been a prostitute and simply wanted to cheer her on in the battle.

She knew one thing: that city people nowadays were like children. They would soon forget this and get involved in some other new event. So long as the entertainment journals papered over the old Cassia with the new one, the old Cassia would disappear into history.

★★★

'I write biographies', I said to Cassia, 'and so I must state the facts; and cannot only say what you would like to hear.'

But Cassia acted just as she had done in the past: 'That won't do. When I say you can't, you can't. I had to do so many things against my will that even now when I think about them it still pains me!'

Through a gap in the curtains I glimpsed the masses of foreign words on the neon lights in the distance, and felt a strange sensation. Each time I argued with Cassia, it always felt as if I was making life difficult for myself. 'All right,' I said, 'I give up. Let's talk only of food and drink.'

After several days she asked me: 'How are you getting on? Any progress?'

What I was thinking, and eventually said out loud was that the bad things she had done fascinated me far more than the good things, and I suspected my readers would also be interested in learning about these 'bad deeds'.

Then she sighed and said helplessly: 'Then you must write about them.'

The mere fact that she told me with such excitement, vividness and joy what she had got up to in her bedroom – otherwise how would I ever have known – showed that this was not an ordinary woman.

But I also felt that this woman had long understood some of the dirty secrets of this world. She had once sung the following doggerel through a stage character:

'Some say I am pretty,
Some say I am ugly,
Whatever they say, they add to my longevity.

Some say I am good,
Some say I am bad,
Whatever they say, they add to my prosperity.'

When Lily heard this she laughed loudly, turning it into an English version on the spot:

'Good publicity
Bad publicity
Any publicity
Is good publicity.'

Later on, the famous actress Ruan Lingyu killed herself in protest at the newspapers publishing her affairs in and out of marriage. The news shocked the country. Cassia took a wreath to the funeral. But afterwards she said to me: 'This woman was born at the wrong time. Perhaps she wanted to be a martyr! To kill herself just because "gossip is fearful"? Only those who have fought their way out of a predicament worse than the fate of beggars know that the only fearful thing is when no one talks about you. Only silence can kill!'

Another time, when we were having a longer chat, she grew more animated: 'If ever a journalist accuses me of being a whore, I will slap him and make sure his face carries a red mark, so that he can produce it as evidence and shout: "Look, I've been slapped by a whore!"'

Such words startled me. I even wondered if I had been one such fool of a journalist, taken advantage of by Cassia. But I had become her good friend and as a result I could only think good things of her. And since we both agreed that all facts should be stated and nothing should be left uncovered, then I will tell you one more thing, something else that happened in the year 1926. Too many things happened that year, so let me tell them to you slowly.

~ CHAPTER 27 ~

On the first evening of autumn, a chill came into the air as soon as the sun slipped behind the clusters of buildings. For several nights it was windy and showery. The mornings grew colder.

One morning Xiu Fang pulled open the curtains on the ground floor. The magnolia tree in front of the house glistened in the morning light and the pretty-looking Chevrolet was likewise polished and shining.

She noticed a peasant couple, neatly dressed, and accompanied by a fourteen-year-old boy. They nervously pushed open the iron gate and walked up to the house. They looked to the left and right and glanced curiously at the car. Drops of water hung from the leaves, and the ground was still wet. With their straw hats in their hands, they knocked gingerly on the door. It seemed they were not familiar with the door bell, though they had some idea of its function. The uncle tried to press it, the sound of the bell itself startled them.

Xiu Fang opened the door and looked at the three people. 'Who do you want?' she asked.

'We are looking for Miss Cassia. I am her uncle.' The man tried to sound confident: 'Her real uncle.'

'Come in then,' said Xiu Fang, 'come in and sit down,' adding that the mistress hadn't gone to bed until midnight last night as she'd been performing. 'She will not get up until noon. You've come a little bit early.'

The uncle hesitated: 'Let's go then,' he said, 'and walk around a bit, and come back in the afternoon. Let's not trouble her now.'

The aunt, however, remembered to unpack the presents they had brought in various sacks, things such as peanuts and water chestnuts, and handed them to Xiu Fang. She asked Xiu Fang to accept these humble offerings. The mademoiselle liked cleanliness, they were sure, and they were embarrassed they could only give her grubby country stuff like this. The couple's behaviour was far too humble; they looked as if they didn't know where to put their hands and feet. Xiu Fang felt awkward herself, but she said 'Fresh produce is really delicious. It's really quite rare to have some.' She then saw them off.

Xiu Fang put the sacks in the kitchen and walked upstairs. She heard Cassia washing, knocked and went in. Cassia sat at her mirror, brushing her hair. Xiu Fang walked over to help and said: 'Mistress, you are up already. Your uncle and his wife and child have just come to see you. I have asked them to come back in the afternoon.'

Cassia looked surprised: 'Really?'

'They brought some country produce and I have put this in the kitchen. They are country-looking people, with a Chuansha accent. His nose was quite pointed, his wife's eyebrows a little bit upside down, oh, and the boy must be about fourteen, he's quite good-looking. Quite an honest looking family.'

Cassia said: 'That's them. My aunt and uncle. You must have seen them when we visited before.'

'I forgot. How time flies!' Xiu Fang used the rose water she'd made herself to smooth Cassia's long hair, then passed the comb back to her mistress. She opened the window. The bathroom was quite spacious, and now that the window was open, the birdsong in the yard sounded even louder.

Cassia was so restless that she broke the comb, the teeth piercing her fingers and making her bleed. Xiu Fang hurried over: 'What's the matter?'

Cassia sucked at the blood. 'Nothing. It's just I haven't seen them for so many years. This afternoon I need to go and sort things out at the Ruyi Film Company. Someone is coming to buy the rights to one of our films; I won't be able to see my uncle and aunt today. You look after them for me and give them a chance to settle in. They will probably feel awkward staying here, perhaps it's better to arrange for them to stay at an inn. Find a nice clean one and give them some money to spend. Tell them I will go and see them as soon as I have time.'

Xiu Fang said: 'That's all easy to arrange. So long as you're not still angry with them.'

Cassia laughed and said: 'What is there to be angry about? My parents died when I was only seven, it was thanks to this aunt that Madame Emerald took me away. Otherwise I would never have been able to sing and work in Shanghai. These country relatives hardly ever visit. You settle them in first and let them have a good time.'

In the dressing room of the Xinhu Theatre, Cassia was getting ready to go on stage; she had her eyes closed. Just then Yu Qiyang pushed the door open and came in, saying that he'd come to watch the new play 'The Suffering Lover', and wanted to see her first. Smartly dressed in a Western suit, he paused at the door, took off his hat and held it in his hand. He was concerned about the big scene going on outside. 'A lot of people have come to cheer you on,' he said.

'All the newspapers are here. I'm so involved in film now that I haven't acted in a new play for a long time. Now, I am glad you are here; I have something important to discuss with you.' With a serious expression on her face, Cassia said, 'A journalist is coming in a few minutes, and then we won't have time to talk.'

When he had sat down, Cassia took his hat and put it on the table. 'Yu,' she said, 'do you remember something you said before?'

'I have said many things,' Yu Qiyang said, hearing the roughness in her tone of voice and feeling a little uneasy. 'You won't be like Lily and say that I can't go back on my words?' he said, laughing.

'Not this time you won't,' Cassia said. 'You said that from now, whenever a situation arises that involves blood and killing, you won't let me, a woman, participate.'

'Well,' said Yu, 'I'm not having you setting off any explosions again, if that's what you mean. Dead right you shouldn't be involved.'

'As it happens, a little something has come up. If you don't want me to be involved, then what must I do? Ask you to help me?'

Yu Qiyang looked serious. 'What is it?'

'My aunt, uncle and their son have come to find me in Shanghai – the three of them.'

'That's easy. Don't see them.'

'I have asked them to stay at an inn; it so happens that Li Yu arranged for them to stay in the Xinglong Inn, the place I stayed in when I first started up the Ruyi Troupe and singing local ballads.' Cassia turned and watched Yu Qiyang in the mirror. 'Needless to say, the grocery shop in the countryside has closed and they want money from me. They've been here three days already, though I haven't seen them, and they won't talk of leaving.'

'Give them some money and send them off.' He saw the look on Cassia's face and added: 'It's fine if you don't either, really, country relatives are always troublesome.'

'It's not about the money,' Cassia said: 'When I recall how I was ill-treated when I was young, all those beatings and all the hard labour I endured, and them finally selling me to a brothel... Ever since my youth I've made an oath that one day I'd take my revenge on them.'

Yu was a little surprised and stood up: 'You are someone who was always destined for big things. Why think like a peasant? Give them harsh words and send them back home.'

'No. I have to get my revenge.'

'Is it really necessary?' Yu was getting impatient; he was about to leave.

'My parents were killed by them. The two of them died one week apart. The uncle told me they died of strange illnesses. Blood spilled out of their mouths, noses, eyes and ears. They looked horrible,' said Cassia.

'That's different, then.' Yu Qiyang had to stay and find out more: 'Do you have proof?'

Cassia shook her head and said: 'For more than ten years they wouldn't come to Shanghai to find me; now when they are desperate for money they come for me. That must mean they have dark secrets; that is proof enough.'

Yu remained silent. 'Are you a judge?', Cassia asked, 'Why do you need proof?'

Yu asked her what she wanted.

Cassia's face darkened: 'Help me to deal with this couple...at least cut off their right hands! The child has nothing to do with it, you can let him go.'

Yu listened but said nothing. He picked his hat up and walked to the door. Outside the door, someone called: 'Miss Cassia, another ten minutes and you are on.'

Cassia pretended she hadn't heard this. She walked up to Yu Qiyang, saw the dark look on his face, and stopped. For a moment the atmosphere in the room was tense. Then she asked: 'Are you willing to help me or not?'

Yu didn't say anything.

'Cut off just the thumbs, then, not the hands. Will that do?'

Yu Qiyang remained silent.

Cassia went to the window. 'If you won't do it, then I will never perform again.' She took off the costume she was wearing.

'What are you doing? All the journalists are waiting. Don't be silly!'

'When have I ever been silly? If the play fails it's my failure. It's nothing to do with you. You just watch me make a fool of myself!' She picked the cotton wool up from the table and smeared her make-up, putting red and black smudges across her face.

Yu let his hat fall to the ground. Grasping her hands, he said: 'All right, I promise!'

Cassia gave a smile that was at once charming and sad.

'You are about to go onstage,' Yu said. 'I will go down and check that everything's all right. But you must understand that the Shanghai brotherhoods are no longer criminal gangs. They're now businessmen's clubs.'

'I don't believe you never resort to guns and knives.' Cassia picked the hat up from the floor, handed it back to Yu Qiyang, then called to Li Yu and asked her to inform everyone backstage that the performance would be postponed for a quarter of an hour.

'Only if it's a dispute that cannot be resolved without resorting to arms.'

'Well this is such a dispute! There is no room for negotiation. You think it's a small matter, but for me it is big. If I let this go then I will no longer be deserving of my name. If you don't help me, I will still find a way to ensure they disappear in Shanghai.'

'Go and arrange it then. Just let me know when the time is right and I will get someone to carry out the plan.' Yu pulled open the door and left without a backward glance.

He felt his footsteps grow heavy. Cassia was normally such an able woman; how could this matter make her behave like all other women, short-sighted, sentimental and unreasonable? He did not understand her; he decided to ignore her. He would talk to her again when she calmed down. He was an industrialist and banker now; he was not willing to get involved in senseless and bloody affairs. No man would treat an irrational woman without caution. Not so long ago, Cassia had been discussing marriage with him. She knew he had not made up his mind on this important matter. Then why should she initiate an argument like this one, which would ruin everything? Perhaps his hesitation had made her desperate through disappointment, so she was resigned to her fate, determining only to let him see the pain she felt. Perhaps, to her, that was the only fair course of action.

Whatever her reasons, it was something only foolish women would do; women like the Huang household's Sixth Concubine. How could the silly girl be so callous about a matter of life and death?

But after this unhappy meeting Cassia never again mentioned her uncle and aunt to him. The two of them had many phone calls about all sorts of things, but they never again talked about this matter. It was as if it had never been raised.

★★★

If both of them had really forgotten, that would have been so much better.

★★★

Two months later Yu Qiyang read a story in the newspaper that the Xinglong Inn had caught fire in the middle of the night. It was a wooden building on the edge of the old city and it had burnt like a paper box. Nobody could go near it. The fire engine came and tried to put the fire out, only to find everyone was dead – the innkeeper and all the guests, eight people altogether. No one had escaped alive.

Yu Qiyang knew of course that this fire had not been started by accident. Surely Cassia had sent someone to do it. But her intention could not have been to kill eight. Didn't she know anything about arson? That you should only pour petrol over a building after you have killed and set light to the bodies of those you wanted to be killed? And once the fire has been started, that you must shout the alarm, ensuring that all the bodies of your victims were burnt and the evidence destroyed, but others in the building had the chance to run away?

Perhaps whoever she had found to do this was inexperienced? Or something had gone very wrong? He threw the newspaper away. He wouldn't ask her about it; he only felt lucky that he had had nothing to do with it.

★★★

If Cassia seems like a bad woman to you, this then is surely the worst thing she ever did. But if even the police of the Municipal Council couldn't establish what really happened, and not even Yu Qiyang could find a clue, then whoever could?

But I had an even better way of finding out what had happened than Yu Qiyang. I could ask Cassia directly. I did ask her: 'If she believed herself to be a hero among women, I put to her, then why couldn't she tolerate poor country relatives? How could she be so desperate for revenge that she didn't mind the death of innocents? Eight lives! How could she live with this on her conscience?'

Cassia stiffened up and wouldn't say anything.

I said, 'You have to say something about this. A biography is a trial before history; I am checking facts, not writing novels. If you did this, why don't you take this opportunity to explain things to me and thus rid yourself of the heavy burden on your conscience?'

I pushed her hard on this, and she became very angry.

If I had asked Yu Qiyang, he would have been sure to say that this was the first time in his life that he had lied to Cassia. He had never actually asked anyone to do anything about the uncle and aunt. This matter was totally her responsibility. I told Cassia what I thought.

Cassia's face suddenly looked ashen. She did not look like someone who had been through countless highs and lows, and could withstand anything. Cassia said she had always believed he had sent someone to do it, that they had messed it up. That was why she had never dared mention it.

And nor had he. The two avoided the subject and gradually

grew distant. This incident was the beginning of so much that went wrong. Now, as she talked about it for the first time in many years, she realised it was a misunderstanding: that this affair had nothing to do with either of them.

She began trembling all over. 'Yu must think I am ruthless. The sort of woman that one should not get close to! You know, I never really wanted to assassinate these people. Nor did I even care about revenge. I'm a woman, and Yu Qiyang had annoyed me. I was angry with him, so I said something that I knew would anger him. Don't you understand? I never ever wanted blood on my hands.'

Suddenly she looked as if she wanted to cry, as if she had suddenly perceived the truth about herself, that she really was a curse to men – Master Chang, Huang Peiyu, and yes, even Yu Qiyang, whom she loved. Here's the irony, though. Yu Qiyong, by this logic, should have suffered the same fate as the others, but fate in this instance was on her side. Yu Qiyang did escape, because the three lives of her uncle's family were sacrificed instead of his. Perhaps she and Yu were destined never to be husband and wife; this miserable affair had instead been allowed to destroy the ten years they had spent loving each other.

And that day she understood for the first time that it was she herself who had separated the two of them.

Fate had suddenly revealed itself, as sudden and as fierce as thunder; just as it had done years earlier, when she suddenly realised that it was she who had sent Master Chang to his death.

***

For a long time after this affair, Yu tried to avoid embarrassment by doing his best not to see her alone. She made no attempt to see him either, so as to avoid a situation where he should feel she knew all his secrets. Their relationship started to become formal, superficial.

One night Yu was staring at the ceiling when he suddenly thought, if my own parents had been killed, what would I do? Once such a question had come up, he found he couldn't face it. He had never thought of it that way before. He never knew who his father was; he only had a very faint impression of his mother. He felt he should forgive Cassia.

But even if there were opportunities, there was no way they could resume their love affair: a crack had appeared on fine porcelain. If one ignored it, the crack would gradually grow stronger; when one touched it or rubbed it with one's fingers, it would break, pricking the skin, making one bleed. The fire at the Xinglong Inn might have been due to other causes; the death of Cassia's family might actually have had nothing to do with either of them. The hotel had always been a fire hazard. It probably had been an accident. But that of course never occurred to either of them, so they blamed each other.

Cassia and Yu had been wronged; they had both suffered punishment for this, adding a further twist to the winding path of their fate. What was the point of all this?

~ CHAPTER 28 ~

Zhang Hui, the actor, appeared at an unsuitable time and got out of the car. Those who had seen 'The Flying Heroine' would remember him as the tall, handsome general. He had jumped ship from the Bright Star Company and ever since making this famous movie, had cultivated the carefully trimmed beard the general had worn in that film.

Zhang Hui walked around for quite a long while, asking a few passers-by the way. Finally he entered a lane in Masi Nan Road, stood in front of a *shiku* house and carefully checked its number. Then he knocked gently at the door. The knocking pattern he used was a special '3-1-2'. He repeated it three times, then paused to listen.

After a long time, someone inside asked: 'Who is it?'

'The Eighth Master's guest,' he replied.

The gate opened and someone guided Zhang Hui in. It was a big house with unusually high walls. No neighbour could see inside. The winter jasmine and the pear tree that leant by the wall had both blossomed. He determined there and then that the spring of 1927 would belong to him.

Zhang Hui was led around two corners until they reached a spacious room which was arranged like a sitting room. The Chief Advisor of the Hong Brotherhood sat there, still looking healthy, if now elderly with white hair. Next to him sat the younger-looking Third Master. The two turned to stare silently at the visitor. More people sat behind them. There was no sound in the room and they all stared fiercely at him.

Having never imagined that he'd see a roomful of strangers all wearing Chinese-style black jackets, at first Zhang Hui was at a loss, not knowing what to do. Then, imitating what he had seen in old plays, he clasped his hands together in greeting and said: 'Masters, your humble student Zhang Hui greets you.' The two men remained silent.

Zhang Hui offered a package wrapped in red cloth with both hands: 'It is a small present, I am afraid.' He walked up, wanting to place it on the table between the Chief Advisor and the Third Master. Someone stopped him, took the red parcel from him and unwrapped it on the table, layer after layer, revealing a single gold ingot.

The Third Master glanced at it, not bothering to check its authenticity. Fiercely, he said: 'We don't accept presents without knowing why.'

'Please, don't be angry Master!' said Zhang Hui.

The Chief Advisor raised his eyes and said slowly: 'So you'd like us to do something for you? Please don't be mistaken, because we never do anything that involves killing or robbing people.' Having said this, he wanted to drive the man away.

Zhang Hui responded quickly: 'I came here on behalf of the people, to offer you a way of getting rid of evil.'

The Third Master laughed so loudly that Zhang Hui's ear-drums echoed: 'You think we need advice from someone like you? We get rid of evil on behalf of the people every day of the week!' Now he suddenly came close to Zhang Hui, his eyes fierce. Though Zhang Hui was taller than he, he was forced to take a step backwards. The Third Master said: 'Isn't this because Lily Chang has dumped you, and now you want revenge?'

Zhang Hui blushed. His inner thoughts had been penetrated and he might as well confess: 'She humiliated me in public. A gentleman can be killed, but not insulted. I need the Chief Advisor to be my avenger. I am prepared to do anything.'

The Third Master was about to speak, but the Chief Advisor stopped him, stood up and paced around the room: 'You are bold indeed. Do you not know that she is the daughter of Chang

Lixiong?'

Zhang Hui again replied quickly: 'I know that, but it is not Lily Chang that I want to target, it's her mother. This is why I have come to you. Please let me know what condition I must meet in order for you to help me?'

The Advisor let out a breath. 'Well, well. They do say: "A real man would prefer to break rather than bend." Very good. Obviously you are a hot blooded man eager to wreak his revenge. What do you want us to do for you?'

'Kidnap this Miss Lily. She is too beautiful; don't hurt her, just blunt her arrogance. Get her mother Cassia to come and negotiate, and then kill her. With only Yu Qiyang to back her up, Lily will no longer be as proud. I will reward you abundantly when this business is done. Will three gold bars be sufficient?'

'Hey,' the Advisor asked, his interest raised: 'What else do you know about the inner secrets of the Hong Brotherhood?'

'Everyone knows that Cassia is the strongest woman in Shanghai, the undisputed Number One,' Zhang Hui said with conviction: 'Without Cassia, Yu Qiyang would be nothing! And without Yu's money, Lily will no longer be a star. Rest assured, the martial arts skills she shows in her films are constructed from scissors and paste, they are all fake!'

The Third Master and the Advisor exchanged a glance, then laughed loudly. The Advisor waved his hands and said: 'All right. We will be sure to get rid of evil on behalf of the people, and this deceiving, false star! First, go away. When the time's right we will tell you where to go, with how much money, and what weapons to bring.'

'But I don't know how to kill,' said Zhang Hui, trembling.

'We'll do the killing!' the Third Master roared: 'There are thirty-two tools of torture and forty-eight ways of killing; we've used all of them many times.'

'Then I shall rest at ease,' said Zhang Hui, his courage boosted.

'The three gold bars have to be paid up front. This is your enemy, who has nothing to do with us.'

'But one always pays after business is done,' Zhang Hui objected, wanting to bargain.

The Third Master jumped up: 'When will this business be done? When we chop off Cassia's head and hand it to you? Do you think we are crooks, who will promise anything?' He took the heavy gold bars from the table, held them in his hand, and laughed: 'Ha! Three gold bars and you want to buy the life of the "Number One Beauty in Shanghai". It's a good deal for you!'

'All right, then, I'll get them. I believe you,' Zhang Hui said.

'Whoever heard of the good men of the Hong Brotherhood going back on their word? Just make sure that you yourself don't regret what you are doing!'

When Zhang Hui went out, the laughing stopped. When the juniors went off on their own business and there were only the two of them left, the Advisor said: 'Number Three, do you really want to carry out this act of vengeance?'

The Third Master sat down, smashing the table with his fist as he did so. Indignantly, he said: 'Back when Master Huang Peiyu died, I should have been offered the Brotherhood's Number One post, but Yu grabbed it. Yu was backed by this woman, and he dragged the foreigners in the concessions to help him become the Chinese Governor of the Municipal Council. These are the only reasons why he is Grand Master.'

'Number Three, I advise you to be not so indignant. Ten years ago, when Master Huang passed away, the Brotherhood was heavily in debt and it looked as if we would not be able to manage. It was decided then that whoever was able to sort out our finances would be the Grand Master. Yu and Cassia dared to risk their lives and all they owned to set up the bank, a most desperate act. When the debts Master Huang incurred had been sorted out, it was I who resisted giving Yu the official ceremony that would have appointed him Grand Master. They didn't force us into a public ceremony, even though it would have recruited more disciples.'

The Third Master stood up and said that no matter whether the ceremony took place or not, everyone considered Yu to be the Grand Master of the Brotherhood, the Number One celebrity in Shanghai! The situation could not be tolerated. 'This damned pair have borrowed our name for their own benefit! They are fakes!'

The Chief Advisor sighed. 'We are still collecting protection fees in the old-fashioned businesses of opium, gambling and prostitution; we haven't changed in decades. We are not destined for big things. The old hierarchies of the Hong Brotherhood don't seem to be working: those two run banks, exchange bureaus, shipping and film companies, using only their own abilities. These are not the traditional territories of the Hong Brotherhood.'

The Third Master said angrily: 'Chief Advisor, I see you are getting older and weaker. They are the Number One celebrities in Shanghai and we are resigned to eating their leftovers. You can bear it, but we old brothers can't! We must at least blunt the sharpness of this damned pair. I have told you before that I suspect Huang Peiyu was killed by this woman's plot.'

'But didn't we suspect Huang Peiyu of setting a trap so as to kill Chang Lixiong? Huang Peiyu used all the Brotherhood's money to purchase power; what good did he do us?' The Chief Advisor shook his head and sighed: 'You must understand in Shanghai nowadays you only have money if you have power, and whoever has the most money is the real Grand Master. Even if we killed Cassia and Yu Qiyang, without money we'd still be nothing! If everyone then saw the Hong Brotherhood was empty inside, what would we do then?'

The Third Master said: 'Do we then have to suffer in silence? At least we shouldn't allow them to flash the sign of the Brotherhood!'

The Chief Advisor laughed coldly: 'But I've never heard him use the Brotherhood's name; he simply doesn't deny it when others say he is the Grand Master. We can do nothing about that. If someone said you were the Grand Master of the Hong Brotherhood, I'm sure you wouldn't deny it either.' Seeing that the Third Master was still indignant, he went on: 'All right. Let's borrow someone else's knife for this task and demand payments from this damned pair. But let's think carefully about the steps we are willing to take, and the aims we wish to achieve.'

He paced the yard, his hands behind his back, murmuring to himself: 'A strange place, Shanghai. All the talk of brotherhood and friendship dissolves into schemes and plots, attempts to stab each other behind the back. Even the brothers can turn against each other.'

The soft yellow of the French parasol tree was made invisible by the glare of the street lights. It was almost midnight on that same night. Lily Chang's car was parked by the roadside. She jumped out of it, her high-heeled shoes stepping onto dead leaves, wearing a white fox fur coat, with a very thin knee-length skirt underneath it. She pushed open the big iron gate.

She hurried out into the front garden, its magnolia in bud, used her key to open the front door, and ran straight up to Cassia's room and pushed open the door. She saw Cassia sitting with her head down by the low couch with a wall lamp by her, its dimmer switch turned down. 'Ma!', Lily called affectionately.

Cassia raised her head and smiled at her daughter: 'What happened, Lily? Why are you here at such a late hour? Why don't you stay in your own flat?'

'*Aiyah*! These silly men are really tedious!' Lily sat on the bed, bouncing on it several times: 'That man believes that, because I kissed him on screen, I would have to go to bed with him in reality. What would I see in such a pale-faced little man? I want to marry someone as famous as Charlie Chaplin.'

'You do have high hopes!' said Cassia, mocking her.

'Every time I go to the dance hall I am surrounded by large crowds of men, and they fight over me, and it always ends miserably. In a few days' time I am going to Mount Huangshan to shoot on location. If I can't play to my heart's content for a few days before I leave, what is Shanghai for?'

Cassia was a little bothered now: 'What do you want me to do?'

'Get rid of these people!' Lily demanded, stamping her feet.

'How?'

'Kill them all!' she continued, with a fierce look on her face; then suddenly she laughed: 'Or at least get them all to go away! Let me get on with having a good time, enjoying the dance.'

'So you only want to frighten them and make a scene!' Cassia laughed, and pointed at a man who sat quietly in the darkness on a sofa. 'This man would be good at such things.'

Lily turned her head in surprise and saw Yu sitting there, smoking. She rushed up to him and began to hit him: 'Hey! You are so bad, so bad! You were watching me making a fool of myself!'

Yu stood up and asked Lily not to be so naughty. 'Ask your mother to hold a family party for you,' he said. 'It will be safe and grand and all the important people of Shanghai will be invited.'

Cassia said unhappily: 'I said I'd do that ages ago, but she wouldn't have it. She wants to go to the dance halls and show off.'

Lily exclaimed: 'So you see, mother alone knows my heart. All I want is to go to the Paramount Dance Hall every day! Yes, Paramount!' she cheered. 'Since mother wants you to go and frighten them, you must come too!' Without waiting for Yu to answer, she added: '7.30 p.m. tonight then, it's fixed!'

Cassia and Yu Qiyang, who had both been wearing a stiff expression on their faces, couldn't help but laugh at her excitable behaviour. Lily jumped and sang, before fetching her bag and starting to walk out of the door.

Cassia said: 'I'm afraid that perhaps I shouldn't allow you to run wild like this. Hey, Lily, when are you going to agree to study in Europe?'

'I know you want me to personify all the elegance and sophistication that a European education should deliver, but mother, I am like a midday sun in China, why should I be a boring lady?'

'Go to England to study Shakespeare; come home and reform Shenqu.'

'*Aiyah*! Films are the art of our times. Drama is old-fashioned and out of date,' Lily Chang said: 'We have argued about this so many times. Let's not argue any more. It's so boring.'

There were more Chinese people than Westerners in the Paramount Dance Hall, where Chinese and Western men and women mingled. Some Chinese men and women were partnered up with Westerners, their arms raised high, their actions exaggerated.

Lily came through the door, wearing a red dress. She flipped her fox fur coat to the doormen. It seemed she was a regular here, that she knew her way around. She walked through the hall in the middle of a tune, her body soaking up all the liveliness. The dance hall was filled with loud whispers; many dancers glanced over to her; some even went out of step. Only the band was professional, still keeping time to the waltz.

Lily sat down by a table and the waiter ran quickly over to her. She was about to order drinks when a man came up and told the waiter to settle the bill with him. She picked up the cigarette on the table and put it in her long smoking pipe, and another man appeared to light it for her. Just then the music finished and more men hovered around her table, trying to attract her attention.

Yu Qiyang walked into the dance hall wearing a hat. Among these handsomely attired men in their Western suits he seemed stiff and old-fashioned, with his black Western suit, brown tie and black waistcoat. His appearance was not remarkable. For a thirty-eight-year-old man, he seemed elderly, his expression cold, while all around him were handsome young men. Someone said: 'It is Master Yu!' and everyone turned to look, their whispers sweeping through the hall like a wind through a forest. 'It's indeed Master Yu! It's him!'

Yu Qiyang smiled and stepped slowly over to Lily's table. The crowds respectfully parted for him. Yu didn't seem to notice anyone, and no one dared to greet him. He sat next to Lily, put his hat on the table and drew out a cigarette. In a few minutes, all the men had disappeared from the table and many women, including several foreign women, had gravitated towards it.

The music started again and nobody came to invite either of them to dance. Lily stretched out a hand to Yu Qiyang and he smiled and took it.

Yu's steps were steady and small; he was just able to follow Lily's fancy movements. Lily whispered in his ear: 'See these silly hooligans! They all slip away when they see you.'

Yu Qiyang also smiled: 'Who isn't afraid of death?'

Lily nearly bit his ears: 'You really are a strong man!' she said, and pressed her face to his sideburns.

Yu was a little embarrassed. 'How could I be?', he said. 'The "flying heroine" is the truly powerful one!' He tried holding his body away from Lily, but Lily hung both her hands around his neck and looked at him with affection. Yu turned his face away and avoided Lily's eyes. Everyone in the hall saw that Lily Chang was embracing and dancing with the famous Master Yu; everyone whispered in low voices, guessing, gossiping. Lily felt intoxicated by the excited speculation of the crowd.

The piece finally finished, they politely clapped the band and returned to their seats. An aide walked over and whispered to Yu, who in turn indicated that they should go outside and talk. He rose and told Lily not to go anywhere, 'Wait for me, I'll be back soon.'

It was several tunes later when Yu returned to the dance hall, and Lily had already danced a number of times. This time around the jealous men had not dared to compete openly for her attention, but she was still surrounded by men, both Chinese and Western. When they saw Yu, however, they dispersed again; though a few tried to make conversation: 'Master Yu is in a good mood today.'

Yu Qiyang smiled, but still wouldn't engage in conversation with anyone. When the next piece started, he pulled Lily up. But this time he allowed Lily to clasp herself tightly to him, and whispered something in her ear. Lily's mouth opened wide, her eyes also, but she soon recovered her calm and the two continued to dance affectionately.

When the tune finished, Yu Qiyang escorted Lily back to the table. He picked up his hat, looking as if he was about to leave. He called for the waiter and paid for the bill, giving a large tip, and smiled: 'I'm getting old, I can't play any more. I'll go first; you stay behind and play some more.'

After a while, claiming she was also tired Lily said thank you to one after another of those who had been most attentive and well-behaved among the men who had been pursuing her. The waiter brought her coat and she walked downstairs to the front entrance of the dance hall. Her car was already parked outside. She pulled open the door and got in. One foot on the accelerator and the car shot forwards. But another car was parked on the other side of the road. It also started and soon she saw that the car behind was following closely.

She drove into the busy city centre, the car still following closely.

She grew nervous and drove fast; the car behind also speeded up. The two cars raced over the Bund and drove quickly westwards along Ximo Road. Suddenly she turned sharply into a small street and the car behind, not expecting this, sped past, braked suddenly and drove back against the streams of cars amidst protesting horns, until finally it was in a position to follow her into a small dark street.

It had driven only a short way when two bricks were suddenly thrown from the side of the road, smashing the front windows. Soon, more bricks were flying. The car braked sharply, coming quickly to a standstill. Suddenly the street lights went out on both sides of the road. Four people stormed out of the dark, the two at the front holding daggers and the two behind carrying guns. But they didn't kill anyone; they simply pulled open the car door and pulled someone out.

Those who remained in the car started to draw their weapons, but someone commanded from within: 'Withdraw! Don't shoot!' Meanwhile the figure who had been pulled from the car was kicking around wildly and shouting; but its driver reversed swiftly, not caring that the car door was still open.

The door bumped into a telegraph pole by the roadside and flew away. Broken glass was scattered everywhere. The side of the car sparked as it drove close to the wall. But the driver was skillful at manoeuvring out of tight spots and they managed to get out of the little street, the tyres squealing as the car sped away and vanished without a trace. Only the man who had been pulled from it remained, on the ground, moaning.

Someone flashed a torch on him and found out who it was: the actor Zhang Hui, who always played heroes. 'Hey, what rotten luck!' came the voice of Lily Chang, 'Half a night's trouble and all we caught was a silly turtle!'

Someone pulled Zhang Hui off the ground, saying: 'Miss, step away, disappear among the lanes!' Lily didn't understand, but someone pulled her away to a yet darker side lane. When she had been moved a certain distance away, the torch was turned off and a heavy fist landed on Zhang Hui's ribs. He cried out sharply and collapsed to the ground, where a kick landed on his ribs, making him scream. Now more kicks fell on his face, and a fierce voice instructed: 'Don't make a sound. One more sound and you're dead!

Another kick hit him in the ribs, and this time Zhang Hui kept silent, clinging onto his chest in pain, not daring to make a sound.

Now they heard footsteps, and another voice warned: 'Miss, don't come near.' When the torch flashed on again, it shone on a swollen and bloodied face. In a low voice, one of the men asked Zhang Hui: 'Who was in the car just now?' Curious, Lily edged closer and glimpsed the face. The sight frightened her so much that her lips turned blue. She turned her face away.

'I don't know them,' Zhang Hui moaned. The answer came from between the gaps in his bloodied teeth.

'Then why were you in the car with them?'

'A friend came out of the dance hall and said I could have a lift.'

'Liar!' Another kick, and Zhang Hui nearly fainted with pain. But the man was careful not to beat any really sensitive parts of his body. 'Who was it really? If you don't speak I'll cut off your nose.' The metal edge of the knife pressed coldly against his face and Zhang Hui shivered with fright.

'Don't use the knife!' Now, finally, Zhang Hui confessed: 'A man called Number Three.'

That was enough. There was no need to continue with the questioning. The torch was extinguished again and this time the knife was used. A flash of light and Zhang Hui's face was slashed. He fainted and the man doing the beating threw his last words at the man on the ground: 'If you report this to the police, you will be the first to go to prison. You are the one who plotted this kidnapping.'

Lily's car drove swiftly out of the lane. Now it was Yu Qiyang who drove. Behind him was another car, the car which had been hidden here; now it was escorting them in case they were ambushed again. Lily glanced back at the man lying on the ground and asked in a frightened voice: 'Is he dead?'

Yu didn't say anything, but one of the two men at the back answered: 'No, he isn't dead. But the cut on his face will make sure that his pale face will always be disfigured.' The man sneered: 'He won't play a general any more though. Perhaps he could specialise in hard men and baddies!'

Lily wrapped her arms around herself, trembling with fright. Suddenly she cried out: 'I am so frightened. He surely won't spare me. What shall I do?'

Yu Qiyang said: 'No, he will never dare to approach you again as long as he lives.'

Lily acted as if she didn't hear. 'Killing people is so horrible. So horrible!' she kept saying.

'This has nothing to do with you. Don't be afraid, it is me they are after. I am fully responsible for this.'

Lily still couldn't stop her snuffling. 'So horrible! So bloody! So horrible!' She tore at her red skirt and covered her face with her hands.

Yu Qiyang watched and said to his men: 'All right, send a signal to the car behind. We'll go first to Number 3 to have some tea and calm her down.'

Number 3 Jianameng Road in the Concession was a *shiku* house, with three bedrooms on two floors around a courtyard. It was one of Yu's party's secret hiding places. Yu felt that they had been lucky that his source had so swiftly apprised them of the situation, allowing them to be in a position to destroy his opponents' plans from the outset.

'You've all worked hard,' he said to his men: 'Everyone who doesn't actually live here should go home and rest. Tomorrow I will reward you.'

He led Lily into the hall on the ground floor and pressed the light switch. Two slender, green, healthy-looking plants, one big, one small stood in front of the window. Lily still had her arms wrapped around herself, trembling. Yu asked her to sit down and went to get her a cup of tea, smiling. 'A heroine who dared to fight a pilot mid-air, but who could not bear the sight of blood. Your mother stood up to protect your father amidst a forest of bullets; even when she herself was shot, and covered with blood, she remained still and calm!'

Lily didn't hear anything. She sank onto the sofa. Her face was pale, she was still in shock. Yu brought the teacup to her lips.

Lily took the cup and put it back on the table, grasping Yu tightly: 'I am so very frightened.'

'What for? I'll protect you.'

'I know, I know,' Lily clasped him even harder. 'I want a real man like you to protect me. Only then will I no longer be afraid.' Yu smoothed her head: 'Fine. Your Uncle Yu will always be your uncle.'

'I want you to be with me forever,' said Lily, raising her head and looking at him.

'Of course, forever,' said Yu, smiling: 'How could I not protect you forever?'

'I don't mean that...' Lily clasped him tighter, and pressed her lips to his, 'I want you to sleep next to me every day.'

Yu pushed her away quickly, 'Lily, don't be silly. I am your uncle. I watched you grow up.'

But Lily grasped Yu Qiyang tightly, and when he pushed her away she came back to him, speaking quickly: 'There is only one person in my heart and that is you. I just want to love you. I don't think of anybody else!'

Yu managed to struggle free, and moved Lily's arms to rest against the sofa. He drew out a cigarette: 'Lily, you are far too excited. Driving in your car like that, in order to attract them you were too nervous; you've never seen fighting before. Just calm down and everything will be all right.'

Lily Chang began to see what he meant. She drank some tea and was silent for a while. Then she smiled apologetically and saw that Yu was looking at her tenderly. Only then did she move closer to the arm of the sofa and say to him: 'Uncle Yu, I have calmed down. Now I can talk to you in a calm state of mind. Don't think I am being hysterical. I am not like that! All my life, ever since I was a child, I have only ever loved you, and you are still the only man I love. This is something I am completely clear about. It is not an impulsive thing; it is something I have thought about for many years. I am already eighteen years old, no, I am nineteen, an adult; I am not a spoilt child!'

'Lily, that won't do.'

'There are many more couples with bigger age gaps!' She stood up again and spoke slowly to Yu: 'If I want to love a man, I will love him! No one can stop me!'

Yu evaded her passionate look and smiled with embarrassment.

'What are you laughing at?' Lily was only a step away from him now. The light in the room shone on her face, which had become extremely beautiful in the hot flush of her excitement. 'Another woman said the same thing once,' said Yu.

'Which other woman?'

'Your mother!'

Lily narrowed her eyes at him: 'Do you think I am a little fool, that I don't know what is going on between you and my mother? But you've never married and that shows me that my mother has never really won your heart. She keeps pushing me to go to Europe to study, practically chasing me away. Why? Is it so that I can't be with you? She wants to destroy the feelings between us!'

Yu wanted to smoke, but found there were no cigarettes left. He turned: the courtyard was not big, and the moonlight spread generously over it. Cassia had talked about sending her daughter to Europe even before Lily returned to Shanghai. This present scene was created by him. It was he who had made it possible for Lily to be a film actress in Shanghai. He felt he'd wronged Cassia, and wanted to clear the whole matter up. But he also felt it was all very silly, and hardly knew how to explain it. He wanted to say that Cassia was the only woman he had ever really loved. He also wanted to denounce Lily's suspicion of her mother's aims as a childish indulgence. But still he could not think of the right words, and now Lily's arms were around his neck.

'My mother is a woman. Am I not? Am I not prettier? You held me when I was little, why don't you now?'

'Stop it!' Yu was getting annoyed now. 'Your mother wants me to marry her!' he said bluntly.

Lily's face turned white; she let go of her hands and stamped her feet. 'And you agreed?' She burst into tears. 'You are lying to me, aren't you?'

Yu Qiyang said seriously: 'I am considering it. Lily, stop being silly. I will take you home now.' He continued to look as severe as he possibly could. 'I am indeed seriously considering the matter of marriage to your mother, so don't you be foolish!'

It was past midnight and the light in Cassia's residence in Jessfield Road was still on.

Lily hurried upstairs, her face pale. Cassia walked out of her bedroom, wearing a dressing gown. It was obvious she had not been asleep. She asked her daughter what the matter was.

Lily strode into her room at the other end of the corridor without a word and slammed the door shut.

Yu stood at the bottom of the wide stairs, his face dark.

Cassia walked down the stairs. 'Yu, what's the matter?' she asked him.

'They really wanted to kidnap Lily. But Number Five sent a message in advance and we ambushed them. We caught a small fish, the actor. He said it was plotted by the Chief Advisor and Number Three. They'd get Lily first, then you.'

Cassia nodded and said: 'It all seems to have turned out as we'd expected. Thank you for protecting Lily.' She walked down the stairs: 'Is Number Three hurt?'

'We didn't shoot, but his car was a bit damaged; perhaps he

is nursing a scratch from the broken glass. We only got to teach Zhang Hui a lesson; we don't think he'd dare report this to the police.'

Cassia said, 'That's good, no wrong done there.' She walked to Yu and took his hand: 'Yu, both the Advisor and Number Three are your elders, so you must show some generosity and make sure the brothers will not harbour any resentment. Share some profit with them. You must suffer a little because you are the Number One. This whole thing about Lily has been too close to home. It's better that we don't make a fuss.'

Yu didn't say anything. He didn't like the fact that Cassia was lecturing him like this. He said: 'But they hate you, this was obviously aimed at you.'

'That's good, then,' Cassia said. 'It seems they are not foolish people.'

Yu was so angry he wanted to walk out. After a few steps he thought about it and felt he shouldn't be so impulsive. Cassia always talked to him like this, for more than ten years she had talked to him without thinking much about her choice of words. It was only in the last half-year or so that he'd begun to find it so irritating. But he always tolerated her, never arguing. Perhaps he should just let it go this time as well.

'Well then, whosoever ties the knot must also untie it,' he said.

Cassia walked a few steps and stood opposite him. Looking at the strained expression on his face, she said tenderly: 'Perhaps it's better that I sort this out. This is all to do with hurt feelings among the older brothers in your organisation. If you go and the discussions turn sour, we won't have any leeway at all.'

The morning sun shone on the lane that Zhang Hui had visited. A car stopped and Cassia got out alone and started looking for the *shiku* house. She knew the secret knocking code, rapped '3-1-2' three times, then waited silently.

Someone watching through a spy hole in the gate saw that it

was Cassia alone, without guards or aides. She could hear footsteps, someone rushing away as if to report this. Soon the door opened. Cassia went in and saw a number of fierce-looking people, armed with guns and knives.

Cassia walked across the courtyard, stood in front of the grand hall and greeted everybody there in a loud voice, neither humble nor proud: 'I am a mere woman, not fit to enter the hall; so I greet all the Masters from here, at the bottom of the steps. We all shared food from a single pot once upon a time, but lately I have had fewer opportunities to learn from you all, and this is my fault. Now I salute you and hope that you will forgive me.'

The Chief Advisor and the Third Master were both sitting inside the hall. The Third Master's forehead was wrapped in bandages. Cassia said: 'I do apologise that some brothers were accidentally injured.'

The Third Master said: 'Yu arranged for the ambush, commanded the beating and even used knives against me. What on earth happened to our brotherly feeling?'

'I know about what happened last night,' said Cassia. 'Someone was indeed hurt, but it was not anyone from the Brotherhood, merely a mean person who wanted to turn brothers against brothers. The rest is all a misunderstanding. I, Cassia, will admit my fault again. It was nothing to do with Yu. It was I who arranged security guards for my daughter; I take full responsibility for what they have done.'

The Chief Advisor coughed and cleared his throat. 'I didn't think Yu would dare do such a thing!' he said finally.

'Of course not. Yu is extremely respectful of his senior brothers and his elders,' said Cassia. 'He asks me to say on his behalf that he would very much like to invite Number Three to manage the fish markets on Fuxing Island. A small gift, just to show good feelings.'

The Third Master stared: 'What, he wants me to sell fish?'

The Advisor quickly stopped him, 'Steady steady,' he said.

'I am talking about the whole of the fishing industry in the East China Sea. There are three million people in Shanghai who eat fish,' Cassia said: 'the daily revenue from the fish markets in Fuxing Island...'

The Advisor shoved the Third Master. 'Let's not talk about money,' he said. 'Why should money matter among brothers? Now Miss Cassia is indeed a generous woman, and thinks of the global interests of the brotherhood. In future all of us in the Brotherhood must indeed help and support each other.' He waved a hand and someone fetched Cassia a chair. The Chief Advisor's tone of voice softened as he spoke to her: 'Miss Cassia. Even when Master Chang was alive, you were our Number Seven. We are all one big family.'

'Thank you, Chief Advisor,' said Cassia: 'Let's not spoil the Brotherhood's rule: 'Men will sit and women will stand.' I am merely asking the elders to forgive my daughter and guarantee her safety from now on.'

'Hey!' exclaimed the Third Master: 'That little witch swaggers around the streets day in, day out. How will anyone be able to guarantee her safety?'

'Indeed,' the others chimed in; 'we can't guarantee it.'

Cassia smiled, saying, 'Actually, both you and I know that if the Brotherhood wants to guarantee someone's safety in Shanghai, they can do so. My daughter won't stay long in the country; she will go abroad to study and marry, so we are only talking about a few months.'

But the Third Master would not give in: 'You are talking about a few months? I can't even guarantee her safety for a few days. We won't touch a single hair on her head, but what if someone else set their eyes on her, what could we do then? Heaven knows how many men in Shanghai have set their eyes on her.'

Cassia was prepared for such difficult words. She reached into her bag, brought something out and walked to the table where the Chief Advisor and the Third Master sat. 'I want to show you something: a photo taken on Lily's eighteenth birthday last year.'

The Advisor took the photo. It seemed to have been taken in a church. It was a shot that showed a tremendously charming woman standing next to Lily, who was dressed like a princess in a fairy tale. The woman was handing her a present, and behind them stood Cassia wearing a Western-style dress. A priest stood by them, holding a bible.

The Chief Advisor and the Third Master stared at the photo, looking confused. Cassia said: 'This respected guest is Miss Song Meiling.'

'What does it mean?' The Third Master didn't understand.

But the Advisor remembered something: 'Miss Song's father Song Yaoru was a senior brother in earlier years and a good close friend of Master Chang.'

Cassia said: 'The Chief Advisor is indeed knowledgeable of all the Brotherhood's affairs.'

The Chief Advisor was not stupid. He knew that the Chief General of the Northern Expedition Army, Chiang Kai-shek, was about to marry this third daughter of the Song family. News of their engagement had just come out. Today Cassia had surrendered to the brothers so fleshy a gift as the fish market on Fuxing Island, and he must honour her for that. She really did deserve thanks! The Advisor stood up suddenly and clasped his hands in salute to Cassia, saying: 'Even the Song family have remembered to look after the flesh and blood of Master Chang. This is indeed the good fortune of the Hong Brotherhood! From now on we will all follow the command of Mistress Xiao.' He called to the men: 'Come brothers, come and apologise to Mistress Xiao!'

Everyone in the courtyard bowed, their hands clasped in salute to Cassia. The Third Master also raised his clasped hands to her: 'I am a foolish man and have been rude. Will Mistress Xiao please forgive me!'

Cassia spread her hands in front of her. She entreated the elder brothers not to be so polite. 'We were all brothers of Master Chang.

To be honest who would have known what would become of the Song family? But of one thing I can be sure: if we in the Hong Brotherhood cannot ourselves share happiness together as well as hardship; if we fight among ourselves and become a laughing stock, then the Brotherhood will surely collapse. Don't forget the Qing Brotherhood has always had a deep hatred of us, and are now stronger than us in the French Concession! As a mere woman,' she added, 'I don't know what else I can say, but trust that the elder brothers here can see things clearer than me; isn't that so?'

The little group nodded in agreement and came to make up with her one after another. The tense atmosphere had disappeared, and everything was peaceful. Suddenly, Cassia was at a loss: these brothers were a bit too easy to conquer. There was no heroic air among them, not even an edge of wildness. As the Hong Brotherhood's new Grand Master, Yu Qiyang was perhaps a bit too soft. If a business man such as Yu Qiyang could operate as leader of the Brotherhood, the world must indeed be a peaceful one. But if at any point the world called for a merciless hooligan, perhaps then the Hong Brotherhood would fade from the Shanghai underworld.

★★★

How right she was. A couple of months later, on April 12th, the Qing Brotherhood gained the upper hand because of their role in the incident ever after known as 'The Shanghai Massacre'. They made a pact with Chiang Kai-shek and the nationalists, then they did their dirty work for them, purging Chiang's former allies, the communists, tricking them out of their hiding places and beheading them. Afterwards a grateful Nationalist Party ensured that it was they, not the Hong Brotherhood, who ruled Shanghai's criminal underworld.

Flipping through the hundreds of biographies that have been

published in recent years about the chiefs of different sects – Huang Jinrong, Du Yuesheng, Zhang Xiaolin – Cassia sneered: 'These unimportant figures of the Qing Brotherhood, they were merely bold in terms of doing bad things. I have never thought much of them. Why were they so honoured by history?'

But before I was able to answer, she laughed at herself: 'I am an actress. How could I forget that the characters depicted on stage are all one thing or another, either tremendously upright, loyal heroes, or utterly evil bastards?'

Quick-witted and wise, she had saved me from attempting an explanation.

I merely said that those were only superficial books, aimed at a mass market, just something to flip through after eating and drinking. I wanted to write the real truth about the brotherhoods in Shanghai.

'Don't you comfort me,' Cassia laughed loudly: 'It's rather fortunate that I did not sink as low as they did.'

~ CHAPTER 29 ~

Yu Qiyang hurried anxiously to Jessfield Road. Before he even sat down, he asked: 'Has the mistress come back?'

Xiu Fang shook her head.

'Have those people come back who were with her?'

Xiu Fang said she hadn't seen the car coming back; that the lunch she had prepared had gone cold; she had taken it back to the kitchen to reheat when they returned. She was about to go and fetch him a cup of tea, but Yu Qiyang stopped her; he hoped nothing would have gone wrong, he said. But if something had, then someone would surely come quickly back to report. Since no one had come, perhaps everything was fine.

'I hope the mistress is alright,' Xiu Fang voiced her concern.

'Be patient,' Yu said, then laughed at himself for not being calm enough.

Yu sat down, and Xiu Fang brought him tea. As he took the tea from her he heard Lily's voice coming from upstairs: 'Uncle Yu, my mother's not here, but I am. Come and talk to me if it's not too much trouble.'

Yu had no choice but to go upstairs. Wearing a silk dressing gown, waiting for Yu, Lily was reclining against her bedroom door. Seeing him pause in the corridor, she smiled innocently: 'You're not going to refuse to talk to me from now on, are you?'

'Why should I?', said Yu, 'You are my very own niece. I am old enough to be your father. I watched you grow up!'

'Yes, your niece has grown up. When my mother fell in love with my father there was a thirty-four year age gap between them! She dared to love then, why shouldn't I now?' Lily leaned closer: 'I'd never imagined my uncle would experience a moment of cowardice.'

Yu smiled: 'I'm no coward!'

'That's what I like to hear!' Lily clenched her teeth in determination and grasped his arms, surprising him and pulling him inside the room. As the belt of her dressing gown came loose, the garment fell off her. She was wearing nothing underneath. 'Do you like what you see?'

'No, no, don't! Especially not here!' Yu grew anxious now; he had never imagined that Lily would make such a move, especially in such a place and at such a time.

'Are you worried my mother will come back?' Every part of her body exuded the glamour of youth. Lily grasped hold of Yu's hands and placed them on her pinkish-red nipples. 'You are already attracted to me, see how fast your heart beats. Uncle Yu, I want you to want me. Go on, take me like a man. I was born to be your woman, and I love whom I want to!'

Yu was so worried that he didn't know what to do. Lily pulled him down on the bed so that he was on top of her. 'I just want to love you, with no fear of anything!'

Yu tried to avoid touching her naked body, but he had no option if he was to separate himself and get rid of her. The more he pushed, the more Lily grasped his hand and pulled it between her legs. He didn't know how to react to such forced intimacy.

Lily said fiercely: 'I just want "Mistress Xiao" to realise one thing: She is very powerful and can command many things, yet there are still some things over which she cannot be the boss!'

Her words struck him to the heart. Yes, he had lately resented Cassia, and for the very reasons Lily had stated. But still, she was his niece! Even if they weren't in fact related, he had always treated her as if she was. He could not carry it through. Carefully he avoided touching her body and tried to think of ways of escaping from her, while being careful not to make any sounds that the servants might hear.

Cassia returned to Jessfield Road with a look of happiness on her face. The nervous look on Xiu Fang's face as she opened the door surprised her, but she was far too happy to really take it to heart. She sat on the chair next to the telephone. 'Miss…' Xiu Fang said timidly.

But Cassia didn't look up. Xiu Fang called again. 'What is it?' Cassia asked, 'Wait till I've rung Yu.'

Xiu Fang lowered her body and whispered something into Cassia's ear, pointing upstairs. Her mouth wide open, Cassia stood up and shook her head in disbelief.

Xiu Fang grew anxious and whispered again: 'It's true, it's true!'

The colour of Cassia's face changed in an instant. She had no idea what she would encounter or what kind of reaction would be appropriate. Her face turned red, and for a long time she sat there, frozen. She had spent all her life being decisive, but she had never imagined she would have to face such a situation.

Finally she recovered her composure.

Suddenly she raised her voice and spoke clearly: 'Xiu Fang, I'm back. Get me some tea, will you?'

Xiu Fang, hearing Cassia using the voice she only ever adopted on stage, looked frightened, her face turning pale. But Cassia stood up and continued, her voice even louder, even more than her stage voice: 'Yes, Biluochun tea. Send it to me upstairs! Yes, send it upstairs.'

No sound came from any of the rooms upstairs. Cassia stepped loudly, slowly and deliberately up the stairs, making sure anyone up there would understand that they need not panic; that they should come out and greet her. That way everyone's face would be saved. But no one came out.

Cassia bit her bottom lip, fearing she would say the words that got stuck in her throat. Were these two people so stupid that they didn't understand she was giving them all an opportunity to escape this awkward situation?

She stood halfway up the stairs, and said in an even louder

voice: 'Oh, Yu's here already?...and Lily's at home as well, is that right?'

Still no one emerged. Perhaps they had been scared stiff by her loud voice, or maybe they had thought she was being threatening, wanting to show her anger?

'So Yu's in Lily's room!' Desperate now, she cried out loud: 'Lily, Yu, here I come!' Each step she took, she felt a pain shooting at her heart. Her legs wobbled, and she found it hard to move. Finally she was in the corridor above the stairs. She dared not walk the final few steps to Lily's room.

Just then, Lily's door was pushed open, but nobody emerged. Instead the sound of loud love-making could be heard. Lily screamed in exaggerated ecstasy: 'I love you! I love you! I just want to love you!'

Cassia froze on the spot. She could neither go in nor go back. She was totally at a loss, her face was as pale as a dead person. Then blood spurted from her mouth and she fainted on the floor with a loud thud.

***

Now I've touched on the most miserable part of Cassia's life and even my own hands tremble as I write this. But perhaps I should worry more for myself, because if I am not careful, I might end up in an even worse situation.

I might well write about the things they'd done that were not honourable. Who can swear that everything they have done in their own lives has been honourable? And if their descendents should hear of these things, and do not like the sound of them, then I might well be sued in a Chinese court, having committed the crime of 'defiling the reputation of an ancestor'.

For example, what Lily Chang had done was far from honourable: she was practically raping someone she had always called 'uncle' and who was about to become her stepfather. Such things should be kept quiet. If I had to appear in court as a defendant, how could I prove this actually happened? The plaintiff, on the other hand, could easily prove that it hadn't.

Never mind the three to five years of lawsuits, and the final verdict of my being banned from writing for a hundred years, and the payment of a large fine; the lawyer's fee alone would cause me to lose weight without effort. I would have to suffer the miserable fate of being both sued and accused of stirring all this up as part of some cheap 'marketing ploy'. Now readers, since you've already reached this penultimate chapter, you must know the embarrassing situation I now find myself in.

Many people have suggested that I put the usual disclaimer on the first page:

> 'All characters in this publication are fictitious. Readers are requested not to believe that they are real.'

I asked a lawyer friend to have a look at the manuscript and he said that such words were like saying: 'There is no money here,' while burying the money right underneath the sign. Such phrases do not necessarily mean you are exempt from the law. If the court passed judgment that you had violated the reputation of someone's ancestor, such an announcement would only be seen as a way of trying to cover oneself up.

I thought about it a lot and began to get angry. I decided to write a new clause, in the spirit of the imaginary sign reading, 'There is money here.' If any readers should neglect such an unprecedented announcement, made on the first page of the book, then I should repeat it here again:

> 'This book is purely factual; the characters and plots are all based on real events. Please note that the author is well prepared for anyone who thinks that they are being slandered.'

I didn't show the clause to the lawyer again. Whether I encounter luck or disaster, I cannot escape fate. Why should I be so cowardly and frightened? What's more, if I did not dare to write such things, the book would be untruthful, and that would be the greatest loss.

But Cassia said to me, 'You are a mere narrator, you are only recording what I told you. If anybody should be held responsible, it is me, Cassia. Why should you care about the nerves of those who had nothing to do with any of this? You said you had no fear, and yet you wanted to abandon the story just at the point when I collapsed at the top of the stairs?'

Her words reminded me of what I have always believed: that God sympathises with writers who write what they feel. By writing about Cassia, I became a hot-blooded woman myself. I have the responsibility to be frank, to write only the truth. So now I must tell you how she got over those heartbreaking events.

**

Cassia was given a private room in the Christian-run Tongji Hospital. Flowers were piled up in the room, trailing down either side of the corridor, sent by people from all walks of life. Most were from her fans. The strong fragrance of the flowers overpowered even the smell of disinfectant.

Outside the hospital a grandmother and granddaughter were kneeling on the ground, burning incense and praying to Buddha. They had been there for a long time and would not leave when asked. They were fans of Cassia's, praying to Guanyin the Goddess of Mercy to let them be ill instead of her. The hospital had to call the police in to remove them forcibly.

An elderly nurse entered Cassia's room. 'Miss Cassia, there are far too many flowers already, and still more are arriving. What shall we do with them all?', she asked.

'Throw them away, throw them all away,' Cassia said, lying on the bed, her face looking tired and her voice cracking: 'Flowers are not medicine, they cannot cure anything.' She sounded despondent.

'The doctor said you simply collapsed from exhaustion, with extremely low blood pressure, though that is temporary.' The nurse said kindly: 'You will get better soon. You have the best voice in Shanghai. Will you forgive me if I tell you I have been your fan since I was a child and consider myself extremely lucky to be able to look after you here?'

Even when she was a second-rate prostitute, Cassia had never felt so completely crushed as she did now. She had never collapsed in such a humiliating fashion. She simply wanted to sleep, but had continuous nightmares. She was twelve or thirteen years old, planting rice seedlings in the fields, working so hard that her back was nearly broken. Even in the busy summer months, her uncle and aunt would not recruit an extra hand to help them, so it was just the three of them. When her work was finished she was covered in water and stained with mud. She lay exhausted in the muddy water and leeches crawled all over her legs. Frightened, she pulled at them, but the leeches simply stretched themselves longer and dug deeper into her flesh. She remembered that she should pat her legs to try and remove them, but still the leeches refused to come off. She raised her head, looking for help, but no one would even look at this small girl, with leeches stuck to her flesh, sucking her blood.

After three nights in hospital Cassia still did not feel any better. Every day she slept, yet she would dream, half-asleep and half-awake, the same nightmares recurring again and again. She seemed to hear someone talking, there were many words, but they made no sense. Only one sentence stayed; it was when a man's voice said: 'But she is our daughter, after all.'

She woke up, and knew that the man was Chang Lixiong. She hadn't dreamt of him for such a long time. It was always the same, whenever she was ill, or faced disaster or a crisis: she'd dream of him.

Tears ran down her cheeks, though she didn't want to cry, Master Chang did not like her to cry.

'From now on, you must never see Lily again!' Madame Emerald had spoken to her in a severe voice, all those years ago, and asked her to swear an oath. For many years, whilst her daughter was growing up, Cassia had not dared to go and visit the girl, but in order to pay for her upkeep, she had merely handed over the money she had earned by selling her body. Even when Lily went to school Cassia still could not see her, it had been terrible! Now she was able to go and see Lily whenever she wanted to, as free as a spirit. Who could restrain her soul? Should she go and push open that iron gate that was so tightly shut?

Finally, she pushed the gate open, but the sound it made was too loud. She woke again, her mouth full of bitterness. She turned.

'Miss Cassia, there is a girl at the door wanting to see you,' the head nurse said. 'I asked her name and she refused to give it to me. Another fan, I suppose. She was here a few days ago, too. Today she waited for a long time and we asked her to leave; she left, but now she has come back again, wanting to see you.'

Cassia felt herself start to panic and asked what the girl looked like.

'She looks just like that very popular film star, the one called –'
Cassia sighed deeply and said, 'Let her in.'

'But you've not allowed anybody in for days, not even journalists!' the head nurse said, surprised.

'How could I refuse a film star?' Cassia gave a wry smile, 'or even someone who looks like a film star.'

In a short while Lily rushed down the corridor. Before she reached the door she cried, 'Mama!' and was about to leap onto Cassia's bed. But suddenly she paused, clutching her bunch of flowers. She didn't know what to do. She watched her mother's expression closely.

Cassia simply looked at Lily without any expression. Lily grew worried. When a forced smile emerged on Cassia's face, Lily still did not know what to do and stood there, shivering slightly.

Cassia stretched out a hand and whispered: 'Lily.'

Lily threw the flowers into the air and rushed to embrace her mother, bursting into tears. Cassia held her and rubbed her shoulders gently; she felt oddly suffocated, but she did not cry. 'Mother... I... I am so sorry!' Lily cried.

'Don't say anything.' Cassia held her shoulders tightly, but turned her own face away. Trying to sound calm she said: 'Don't say anything. Mummy knows everything.'

Lily cried more heavily: 'Ma, you must forgive me!'

Cassia thought how remarkable it was that, as soon as she dreamt of Master Chang, she got her daughter back.

The head nurse rushed in. It was obvious she knew now who this young girl was. She said a car was waiting in front of the hospital to take Lily back to a film shoot – she had been away for a long time and must be taken back. The messenger had already asked for her twice, which was why the nurse had to come in. Lily ignored her: 'Mother, I am not going to go off and shoot some damned movie. I want to stay here with you!'

Cassia held her daughter's hands in front of her chest and said: 'Listen to your mother: you must go. Your career is important.' Lily was forced to leave, but kept looking back as she walked away.

Later that evening, Cassia was lying down, exhausted. The head nurse came in, felt her pulse and checked her blood pressure. Speaking gently to Cassia, she said: 'You said you wanted to drink some rice congee. Your maid has brought some. Drink it while it's still warm.'

Cassia struggled up but the nurse immediately said: 'Don't move, let me feed you.'

'Rice congee is indeed delicious!' Cassia murmured. The only time she had been close to death's door, she had asked for a bowl of rice from the innkeeper. For someone whose life was cheap, rice congee had been life's elixir. She watched the nurse walk out with the bowl, closing the door behind her. For the last few days, she had been supported by medicine, eating no food at all. Her head hurt badly. The room was completely soundproof and she couldn't hear any noise at all from the corridor outside. She felt as if a long time had passed.

The door opened again and the head nurse came in and said to her mysteriously that a man had waited for a long time outside and refused to leave when asked. 'He wants desperately to see you, just a few minutes will do, he said. But when I asked his name, he refused to give it.'

'Another visitor who wouldn't give their name?' Cassia said.

'He has a beard, quite tall, and wears a long gown. He looks like a – '

'A what?'

'A travelling salesman.'

'Ah...' Cassia's head suddenly hurt less. She turned to look at the window, at the parasol tree, its arms looking oddly human. Staring at the leaves, she said lightly: 'Actress, businessman, I suppose I've got to see them all.'

Confused, the nurse said: 'Didn't you say you did not wish to see anyone?'

'Just this one businessman. It must be quite exhausting coming all the way to Shanghai to do business!' Cassia turned and said to the nurse.

Yu entered, looking tired. He held no flowers, but carried a bag of lotus seeds. There was no particular expression on his face and he said simply that these were last year's lotus seeds, brought by someone from his hometown, that they were especially nutritious when boiled with chicken soup.

Cassia looked at him with a blank expression on her face, and he looked at her. Suddenly he grasped her hands, then quickly withdrew. But she held him tightly and said: 'Yu, I was afraid that you would not come to see me any more.'

He was overcome with embarassment. She wanted to sit up, and he hurried to help her, fetching a pillow to support her back. 'How could I stay away?' he said. 'It was I who brought you here to the hospital, but then I was unfortunately called away by the Chief Advisor. Now I'm back.' He looked at Cassia and put his hands on hers. 'The Advisor invited me to inspect all the docks along the Yangtze River. The trip is to announce formally to them that I am now the Grand Master of the Hong Brotherhood in Shanghai.' He smiled: 'It's something he should have done twelve years ago. Of course they did it because there would be some benefit to them, too. They are simply trying to trap me with such a title.'

Cassia smiled. 'Then I congratulate you on finally becoming Grand Master,' she said.

Yu Qiyang said: 'Everyone knows that the real Grand Master is you, Cassia. Only you can resolve all the disputes among the factions. Throughout our journey, the Advisor kept saying that you were both courageous and wise and saw immediately where the problems lay. He was totally under your influence; he said they all promised to follow your commands from now on.' Suddenly he paused, and couldn't continue: 'Cassia —'

Cassia shook her head, 'Just sit with me for a while. Don't talk about other people and other things. I am not interested.'

'You are right. Let's not talk about others,' Yu said hesitantly: 'Let's talk about us.' He placed both his hands on her shoulders, his face reddening slightly: 'I have thought about it all very carefully. I cannot live without you. It was the saving of my own face that I worried about before; I worried about what others might say. But without you, I am just an empty shell.' He seemed to have thought about these words for a long time, they were sincerely meant.

She listened, and tried to stop herself from crying. He said a lot more then, and finally: 'Therefore, regarding the possibility of marriage, I want to ask: if you, Cassia, would agree to be my wife —'

She stretched a hand out to cover his mouth: 'I've never asked for such a thing, so please don't mention it again...'

'Listen to me.' He drew out an elegant blue velvet box and opened it. The inside was lined with satin in the same colour, and perched on top was a shiny golden ring.

'Yu!' Tears finally filled her eyes but she brushed them away, refusing to let them fall. She tried to smile, taking the box in her hands. Not wanting to continue the topic, she said she had a wish, and would like him to do something for her. Would he be willing?

'Anything, just tell me what it is.' He picked up her hand and held it to his face.

Withdrawing her hands, she said: 'Lily is going to Mount Huangshan to film on location tomorrow. The warlord, Sun Chuanfang, is now fighting the Southern Army of the Nationalists in the south of Jiangsu, and Huangshan is not far from the battlefields. Whichever army is defeated will instantly turn to banditry and cause chaos, which will be taken advantage of by bad people. I am worried for her. Since you are now the Grand Master of all the docks along the Yangtze River, I ask that you take another trip, to protect her, just this once. All right?'

'I can send my most trusty aides to be her guards,' said Yu.

'No, no. I am still worried. Last time someone only half-heartedly wanted to blackmail us, and even then there were nearly deaths involved. The Third Master was right. Too many people have set their hearts on Lily. Outside Shanghai, things are even more unpredictable. You must protect her this time, promise me.'

He didn't know what to say, and sighed deeply: 'You must understand that this is not an easy matter. Lily is not at an age when she will listen to what I say. I am afraid!' Indeed, he now feared Lily more than he feared anybody.

'I don't believe that. If one is suspicious, then one hesitates: like Huang Peiyu, who died worrying about offending this or that person and ended up with nothing, not even a place to lay his own dead body. You two...' – Cassia spoke resolutely now – 'I can't bear to lose either of you. If one of you is killed, then I am dead, too.'

These two people, Yu and Lily, were the only people close to her heart. Only these two could make her cry, make her risk everything, make her sacrifice everything. 'Lily is sick of making films and will go to Europe to study. When that happens we will no longer have to worry all the time, but until then, you must be there to help.'

Yu looked a bit awkward: 'I think it's best that I keep my distance from Lily. This girl is not able to control herself.'

She might as well be blunt: 'Rest assured, I understand better than most what passes between men and women. You and I are both experienced in the ways of love. What is it that's so difficult to think through? If you really feel Lily is so lovely that you cannot resist her, then why should I, Cassia, stand between the two of you?'

Many years back, Madame Emerald had not tried to stop Master Chang from getting involved with Cassia, and he had been eighteen years older than her. Could she not be as generous as Madame Emerald? She recalled clearly now: indeed, when Master Chang fell in love with her, he was over fifty; and Madame Emerald, who was forty, had already been his lover for twenty years. Imagine how miserable Madame Emerald must have felt! She could never have imagined this before, but now it was her turn. How heaven tortures people!

When Yu disappeared, she buried herself in the pillow and her tears flowed. She looked so unhappy that the head nurse couldn't bear to witness it, so she went outside, stood by the door, and began to cry herself. Cassia's body jerked in spasms and her hands grasped the pillow close to her face, allowing more and more tears to fall on it, as if it was a special container for them. She knew now that she would never marry anyone in this life. She wept at her own fate. The man that had been by her side a few minutes ago, holding her hands; it was she who forced him away, to a place she could not reach. As soon as he was out of the room, she began to miss him. She knew that she had been cruel to herself by forcing him to leave her, to lose him forever.

She remembered every word she had said: 'However much I make through films, none of it is enough to buy my daughter back once I have lost her. I am prepared to sell the film company. It is not such a good thing that Lily becomes famous so suddenly.'

'I know you miss the stage. You don't like doing business.' He had become once again his old, considerate self.

But it was too late. She had already made up her mind. 'That might not be the case,' she said: 'I was so very poor when I was young; if we invest in this industry...'

Without thinking, he said: 'That's a good idea. Let's do it together.'

'No, what you said before was right. I cannot be your assistant, and naturally I cannot be your boss. So why don't I be my own boss? Why can't I be the first female investor in China?'

Of course she could, he said. He felt like applauding her. He'd known her twenty years and still didn't have a high enough estimation of her. It was at that point that Cassia placed the blue velvet box back in his hands: 'It is for this reason that we cannot marry.'

This provided a better excuse for both of them. She would always remember that moment, when his face turned ashen, as if a layer of white frost had covered him. She pretended she hadn't noticed and said again: 'We cannot marry.'

After she had said this, she sensed that there was someone walking past the two of them; someone holding a black umbrella and walking through the rain. She recovered and looked again, there was no one in the room holding an umbrella. Outside though, the rain started falling ever more heavily, each drop getting bigger, pitter-pattering against the window pane.

***

The person holding the black umbrella was me. I had walked past Cassia's window, and had heard everything. I had waited for three days and three nights, wanting to go in and see her, but had failed to do so. Finally, though, I got to see what I had been waiting for.

I saw Yu walking out and the rain soaking straight into his collar. But he refused to get in the car; he sent it away. He wandered disconsolately in the rain.

He reached the middle of the bridge where the Sichuan Road crossed the Suzhou Creek and paused. He put his hand into his pocket and took out the blue velvet box that had been declined by Cassia. He opened it and took out the gold ring with his right hand. He looked at it and then threw it into the dirty Suzhou Creek. The blue velvet box slipped from his hands and fell to the ground. He walked off, his feet treading on the box and leaving it crushed.

I could understand his gesture: he could not throw Cassia into the river, as he had with the Sixth Concubine; but at least he could make a resolution to throw away this feeling of entanglement. It might not be anger; perhaps he just felt ashamed that he could not be as resolute as a woman, in matters concerning the heart.

And as I gazed at him, disappearing in the rain on the other side of the bridge, I felt that I too should feel ashamed.

~ CHAPTER 30 ~

A week later, Li Yu came to take Cassia home. It was all her fault that Xiu Fang had been left alone to deal with an impossible situation, she told Cassia.

Cassia comforted her, saying: 'It's nobody's fault, not least Xiu Fang's. It is just fate.'

Her home on Jessfield Road was clean and tidy. Li Yu and Xiu Fang wanted to help her upstairs, and she smiled: 'I'm all right, really, I can manage. Help me when I am really struggling!'

She opened the wardrobe, wanting to change into something more comfortable, and glimpsed Yu's clothes: a pile of underwear; two sets of Western suits, one black, one white; three ties. Suddenly she felt something hard in the pocket of the jacket on the white suit: it was the pocket watch she'd bought for him at Hengdali's on Nanjing Road. She opened the lid and found it was still ticking, as if nothing had happened since.

The scent of night blossom floated down the corridor and she walked into her bedroom. Leaning on the bed against a pillow, her eyes on the round bronze mirror, she asked: 'Has anything untoward happened here?'

Xiu Fang replied that there was nothing urgent. 'We have dealt with most things and you can catch up on everything when you've recovered.'

Li Yu, who had returned to work for Cassia once more, brought ginseng and chicken soup, made sure Cassia drank it, and that her mistress then lay down. Only then did she tell her that she'd gone to visit Madame Emerald that morning, but found that Madame Emerald had gone back to live in her old house in the Duchess Pavilion.

'Wasn't that house converted by Muma into an inn ten years ago?' Xiu Fang asked curiously.

Cassia nodded; she knew about this.

'She's kept a room for herself there.' Li Yu turned, put a pair of embroidered slippers by the bedside, and said: 'And now she's moved in permanently.'

'Is she so nostalgic? Well, I suppose her days at the Duchess Pavilion were the best of her life.'

'She said her days were coming to an end and she had moved back there to wait her time.'

'Is she dying? She's only just sixty.' Cassia was startled, and counted with her fingers. She remembered Madame Emerald had just turned forty when Cassia had been fetched from the countryside to the Pavilion; now twenty years had passed, so Madame Emerald would only just be sixty years old. Why would she think of dying?

'She didn't look well at all, so perhaps she has good reason,' Li Yu said.

Cassia put both hands on the bed and sat up. 'Really?' she said. Li Yu had once told her that no woman in this profession lived for long. Now, it seemed, even Madame Emerald could not escape her fate.

Li Yu looked serious. 'I fear that she might die at any moment.' Cassia knew Li Yu was always level-headed about such matters; that she would not exaggerate. She was, after all, older and wiser than Cassia herself.

'Then get ready, I want to go and see her,' Cassia said: 'I hope we're not too late.'

Li Yu had not imagined that Cassia would be so anxious.

'But surely you can't go so soon?' she asked.

'You yourself said just now that she might die at any minute. What if she is gone before I see her?' Cassia said: 'After all, it's been twenty years. I owe so much to her.'

It was dusk, and the Duchess Pavilion, now completely devoid of bustle and empty of its amorous atmosphere, felt lonely and melancholic. Years of neglect meant that the paint was peeling on the wooden columns and cracks and holes had appeared between the walls and floorboards. Moss and wild grass grew rampantly in the gaps between the flagstones in the courtyard. A so-called 'inn', the Pavilion had few customers other than the occasional small-time businessman who had to stay away from home. A faint cloud of smoke floated out from the kitchen, and the doorstep was blackened from years of dirt.

Cassia climbed the creaking stairs to the first floor. Walking along the passageways, she suddenly stopped: the room she had once shared with Master Chang was no longer there. In its place were two small rooms with separate doors.

She walked past slowly and, peeping through a gap in the corridor wall, saw that the peach tree was also gone, and the fish pond was now a washing bowl.

Once upon a time she had lived here, listening to the alluring Jiangnan music being played on strings and woodwind instruments, played by beautiful women in colourful dresses who sang softly as they plucked at the strings. How she had admired their elegance; how pleasingly the housekeeper called the names of the girls being invited out to dine! 'Your eyes are like those of a cat's; they look soft, yet lack the shyness that a girl should have.' Madame Emerald had once said these words to her sixteen-year-old self in this very corridor.

Now all this was gone. Not much later, perhaps, even this once-glorious shell would be replaced by concrete buildings. She turned away miserably and walked directly to the rooms Madame Emerald had once lived in. She still remembered the glory of the Phoenix Hall.

All the furniture in the sitting room was gone, and it felt empty. Even the paintings and the chandeliers had gone. The bedroom door was ajar; she pushed it open gently and walked in. Madame

Emerald lay in a bed, half of which was hung with old netting, and obscured her. The room was dark and Cassia went right up to her, pulling the net up and hooking it out of the way. She stood in front of Madame Emerald and watched her quietly.

The white-haired Madame Emerald struggled to open her eyes, then smiled faintly: 'Why have I recently felt there is something missing in the Pavilion? Now I know – it was you, Little Cassia!'

She took Cassia's hand and asked her to pull the curtains open. A shaft of light shone in, a ray of the setting sun, but it only added to the room's melancholic air. 'The light...turn the light on...' Madame Emerald whispered, breathless.

Li Yu and Xiu Fang came in from the corridor and went in search of a light switch. Cassia walked back to the bed and sat beside Madame Emerald, who asked Cassia to turn her face towards a ray of light and looked at her for a long time: 'Cassia is still beautiful. You are a woman who never grows old!' She smoothed Cassia's face, 'Still so soft and white! You must be thirty-six already!'

'I will get old,' Cassia said. 'Madame, tell me, tell me truthfully: What should a woman do when she gets old?'

'Little Cassia,' Madame Emerald said, 'you are the cleverest person in the world, so I will be honest with you. When a woman starts to get old, she must withdraw herself so that she doesn't become an embarrassment. But for you it is still far too early. You have not only stopped time, you have actually retained your youth.'

'But when does a woman start to get old?' Cassia murmured, almost to herself: 'I am not talking about appearances. I mean, when should a woman admit to herself that she is ageing?'

Madame Emerald knew what was going on inside Cassia, it seemed. Grasping her hands, she said slowly: 'It is when she starts to pity herself.'

Cassia was silent for a long time. Finally she said: 'Thank you, Muma. You are right.' She walked over and fetched a wooden comb with its teeth missing and said: 'Muma, I would like to comb your hair.' She helped Madame Emerald up, and leaned her against herself as she combed her hair.

'Fetch the mirror,' Madame Emerald said to Li Yu. Xiu Fang lent a hand, as the mirror on the dressing table was quite heavy. The two held the mirror up so that Madame Emerald could see herself in it.

Cassia held Madame Emerald's messy hair in her left hand and combed it with her right hand. She tied the hair up in a bun. Her hands touched the folds of the wrinkles in Madame Emerald's neck. Glimpsing Madame Emerald crying silently in the mirror, Cassia handed her handkerchief to her.

'These are tears of happiness!' Madame Emerald murmured.

'I know, Muma,' Cassia answered softly.

'Is Lily well?' Madame Emerald turned and looked into Cassia's eyes.

'I so want to see her again. I know she is out on location. I know she can't come.'

Cassia held Madame Emerald's arm tightly. She was about to cry, but she held her tears back. 'Lily will be sure to come and see you. She's closer to you than she is to me. Sometimes I get very jealous, you know.'

'My dear Cassia,' Madame Emerald's voice may have been weak, but her tone was serious: 'There is something...something I want to say... I beg you to forgive me,' she spoke so fast that she became breathless.

'Muma, slowly. Come, lean on me, make yourself comfortable.'

'I took the joy of motherhood away from you. Lily gave me such happiness: it should have belonged to you. Can you forgive me?'

Cassia could no longer control her tears. Madame Emerald passed her the handkerchief. 'Dear Cassia, can you forgive me?'

'Don't say any more, Muma, it was you who I should thank for looking after her all these years.'

They spent a day and a night with Madame Emerald. Afterwards Li Yu and Cassia returned to the house on Jessfield Road, leaving Xiu Fang behind to look after her. The next morning Cassia returned to the Pavilion. She called Madame Emerald's name, but heard no reply. Placing her hand underneath her nostril, she could feel no breath. It seemed Madame Emerald had slipped away just before daybreak.

Cassia put pieces of the bark of the fragrant aquilaria tree into cotton sacks, soaked them in the water and rubbed them until the water became frothy, then she wiped Madame Emerald's body with the fragrant water. Then she changed Madame Emerald into a new set of white clothes, with white shoes. This was a cruel spring. Cassia felt breathless, and opened the window. She saw lightning flash across the sky. 'It's about to rain!' she murmured. She turned to ask Xiu Fang if Madame Emerald had said anything during the night.

Xiu Fang thought about it, and said that Madame Emerald had requested that she be buried in her hometown of Songjiang.

Wearing mourning clothes, with a thin linen thread around her headscarf, Cassia smoothed the lining of the coffin in front of her. She wanted to cry but no tears came. Madame Emerald must have so badly wanted to be buried next to Chang Lixiong. She had never said this out loud, because she knew it would be a difficult thing to achieve.

'Muma, did you think I wouldn't ask on your behalf?' she whispered, kneeling down next to the coffin.

The aides managed the funeral well. The Master of Ceremonies placed rice into the right side of Madame Emerald's mouth, shouting: 'One thousand *shi* of rice, you shall not starve!', and then into the left side, shouting: 'Two thousand *shi*!'. Finally he placed rice inside the middle of her mouth, shouting: 'Three thousand *shi*!'.

The Chief Advisor and the Third Master had also arrived. They sat down and discussed where she should be buried. The Chief Advisor immediately vetoed Cassia's suggestion, saying that there was no way Chang Lixiong's family would allow this to happen. Madame Emerald would never be allowed anywhere near the Chang's ancestral burial land. 'That won't do at all!', he said resolutely. 'She was a mere prostitute!'

Cassia's face turned pale, and after a long while she said: 'Then how about burying her on the hill opposite Master Chang's tomb. Will that be acceptable?'

There was a hardness in her tone of voice, and the Third Master kept silent. But the Chief Advisor said: 'More importance is attached to the burial place than to the houses of the living. Master Chang died so unexpectedly; if he had to face a filthy prostitute, that would mean disaster. The Feng Shui of the Hong Brotherhood would be ruined, and the Qing Brotherhood would gain an upper hand.'

'The burial plot has already been bought,' said Cassia, standing up: 'There are so many tombs on that hill, who can tell the fortunes of all those who are buried there? How can you be sure there aren't any prostitutes there already?'

'But Madame Emerald is different,' the Chief Advisor insisted.

'Why, in what way different?' Cassia began to adopt a more aggressive tone of voice. 'Go on – say it.'

Someone waiting outside was getting impatient; they started to blow a car horn loudly. The Third Master roared angrily: 'What's the hurry?'

But the Chief Advisor stood up and walked off, shaking his head helplessly.

She was not even allowed to be buried opposite Master Chang's tomb, just because she had once been his lover.

Cassia burst into tears. Should she buy another plot next to Madame Emerald's, so as to be prepared? Who would try this hard to get her one when her own time was due? Perhaps she would not be so lucky.

The Xindu Hotel, situated on San Malu Road, was a skyscraper. There were many in the city centre, but this was one of the first to be funded by a Chinese-dominated company. Though a German architect had been employed, the famous Rong Building Company had been contracted to build it.

The Xindu Hotel combined hotel, leisure facilities and offices to rent. Cassia's company had rented quite a lot of space there, and she had reserved for herself a room on the top floor with a view of the whole of Shanghai.

The opening ceremony was enormously grand. Several hundred guests came to celebrate, from all walks of life and many nationalities.

'Now let us invite Madame Cassia Xiao, director of the United Financial Group, and China's leading industrialist, to cut the ribbon,' proclaimed the hotel manager.

Everybody on the three floors of the great reception hall watched and flashbulbs popped. Cassia wore a hand-embroidered silk satin *qipao*, with a diamond necklace glistening from her neck; she looked radiant.

'Such a ravishing beauty!' the guests commented.

'She can conduct business and sing, how extraordinary!'

'They say she is the only woman the mobsters of the Shanghai underworld will pay any attention to.'

'Such a person could only exist in Shanghai!'

To an uproar of applause, she cut the red ribbon, which was placed not across the front door of the hotel, but across the entrance to a strange iron and steel construction that stood between ground and first floor.

'This automatic stairway, called "Stepping into lucky clouds" was specially commissioned in Germany. It is one of only a handful in the world!' proclaimed the hotel manager. He pressed a button and *bam*! the strange thing began to move; those who stood nearby stepped back in fright. He invited guests to step onto the automatic stairs, but no one was willing. This thing looked too monstrous; it looked as if it could swallow people up.

Cassia nodded elegantly, then said: 'I will be the first.'

'Presenting Madame Cassia Xiao, the first person in China to "Step into the lucky clouds!"' bellowed the manager.

Cassia composed herself, trying not to show any fear. She stepped onto the machine in her high-heels and slowly rose amidst the terrifying noise it made. Everyone around her cheered as she rose higher and higher.

The band started playing and the party began. Now many people queued in front of the new escalator, wanting to try it. Some made a fool of themselves, falling this way and that; some screamed, still others would not dare to step from it and had to be pulled off. The hotel manager and his staff made themselves busy looking after the guests, trying to avoid an accident.

When everyone's attention had been drawn to this new plaything, Cassia slipped to one side. The lift took her to the top floor; she pushed open a side door in a corridor and stepped onto the roof.

The whole of Shanghai lay beneath her. This was no longer just ten miles of Foreign Concession land; it was the biggest metropolis in the Far East, with a population of three million people. Skyscrapers rose high, laid out across hill after hill; never had such a spectacle been seen in China.

On the other side, across the grand Huangpu River, Pudong could be seen on the opposite bank. Here there were still fields remaining, only just beyond the shipping yards and warehouses immediately by the river edge. The same sun shone on two totally different worlds; both spread out without limit.

The view was indeed grand, but it seemed not to move her at all. 'Shanghai is indeed big,' Cassia murmured to herself, 'but why isn't there someone I can love among these three million people?' She felt a sadness creep over her.

She had discovered that as she slept her hands were clinging tightly to a cold pocket watch. When she was in bed, a pillow often slipped to one side of her, and she pretended it was someone next to her, someone who gave her company. A feeling of desolation came into her heart. The morning after she had left the hospital, she had been woken early by the ringing of the telephone. It was Yu Qiyang, who had already escorted Lily to Mount Huangshan. Hearing his voice, her whole body tightened.

'We need to talk,' he said.

She tried hard to calm herself, not allowing herself to give in. She refused him again. When she put the phone down, she felt as if she'd dreamt the whole thing. Yu would never come back to her side now. She had lost him forever.

How far away the horizon was. She looked closer, at the layers of roofs below her, a mixture of dark tiled Chinese houses and flat-roofed Western ones. She moved to the edge of the balcony and peered directly downwards, at the streets full of people and cars, at this living world that was forever moving and stirring. What were they busy doing? Fascinated, she took off her shoes and socks and raised one leg over the railings, riding on the back of Shanghai. She gazed down again.

The roads below appeared to sink even lower; the drop was sudden. She fantasised that another world lay beyond the deep chasm below, a world where the heaviness and trouble that weighed upon her no longer existed. It was the Shanghai she had first seen as a sixteen-year-old girl from Chuansha, straining to carry the sedan on her shoulders. Pausing at Lujiazui Dock, she had gazed longingly across the Huangpu River at the city of Shanghai.

There below the grey and black of the roofs were the earliest joys she had known, the joy of the life that she and Master Chang had shared in bed. She closed her eyes and thought of Lily, her dearest daughter. She seemed to hear the first cries Lily had uttered when she came into this world. She had held the newborn Lily tightly, tears streaming off her cheeks. 'We will never be parted,' she vowed. But little Lily was taken away by Madame Emerald, who forbade Cassia from seeing the child.

When she was sold to the Jade Pavilion, Cassia has been as good as dead. She had missed her daughter so much that her hair began to fall out and blisters appeared on her lips. She couldn't sleep at night. She sometimes went to the Duchess Pavilion just to try and hear the voice of the little girl on the other side of the gate. But of course Madame Emerald would not keep Lily there. After she found out that her daughter had started at the Christian school, her feet somehow carried her there, even though she knew well enough that she would not be allowed to see the child. The place itself gave her comfort and life. How could she live without her Lily? 'Lily, mummy misses you so much,' she would whisper to herself.

Now she brought the other leg over, so that both her feet were stuck outside the railings.

She saw her own bare, elegant feet, stepping over the whole of Shanghai. Downstairs the party was in full swing: she could hear music clearly, as if it was nearby. She stood up and danced a few gentle steps along the stone edge, following the rhythm of the music. The allure of the deep chasm made her steps extra light. She had not felt so light-hearted for a long time. The sky was endless and the earth was wide; now she could truly be free.

Suddenly, she gripped the railings hard, asking herself in fear: 'You shameless, big-footed girl; are you pitying yourself?'

Someone on the top floor saw Cassia walking outside the railings and rushed back to the building, shouting: 'Mistress Xiao wants to jump from the building!'

A group of people rushed breathlessly up, headed by the hotel manager. He searched anxiously beyond the railings but could see no one. He rushed close to the railing and looked straight down at the streets below. There were many people there and it did look as if something had just happened. A blood-red setting sun was falling into the city through the gaps between the skyscrapers, its light dazzling.

He looked again, more carefully, and realised they were only crowds trying to get into the hotel.

Bewildered, the hotel manager approached the man who had shouted the alarm, but he couldn't explain what had happened either. The hotel manager sent his staff to search everywhere. 'Check Mistress Xiao's bedroom on the top floor!'

There was nobody there either.

They kept searching anxiously, until finally they found Cassia in the dance hall downstairs. She had changed into a white *qipao* trimmed with silver. She walked towards the banqueting hall, her breasts firm, her waist slender and soft.

Many people both Chinese and Western, surrounded her there. The Western-attired waiter in his tie brought her a drink. She held a glass of champagne; she had rosy cheeks and looked radiant, just as she had looked when ten years earlier she had caused a sensation on entering the Licha Hotel. She had nothing then, apart from the *qipao* she wore, which had been bought on borrowed money. There had been many obstacles in her life; yet she had really lived. Now the whole of Shanghai knew her, idolised her; she was both wealthy and powerful. And yet she had become someone without love, even her beloved daughter Lily was absent; her heart empty, with no flame of passion; she knew not where her life would lead.

So many people came to see her at that grand banquet. They took turns toasting her, and from time to time someone would kneel down in front of her, saluting her with their fists raised high above their heads. Her aides, guards and other subordinates, including the Third and Eighth Masters stood faithfully in one corner of the banqueting hall. The waiter brought a tray full of delicate *dim sums* and the music suddenly changed from gentle to passionate.

***

I know, of course, dear readers, that you are getting impatient. You want to know how I ever got hold of Cassia herself, how I have come to be such an intimate friend of hers, how I have been able to talk to her at such length.

Shanghai is still there, and so are those buildings, and so many women like Cassia! But how time has changed! Humans are the most fragile things; it is they who will disappear all too easily.

I have seen Cassia's shadow several times: once on Nanjing Road, she stood idly gazing at a shop window, looked thoughtful, then disappeared. This is hardly surprising, there are not many good things in the shops these days, only false promises. Women such as Cassia scorn such promises, she was a down-to-earth Shanghainese and disliked exaggeration and falsity. As regards to 'fashion', well, she created fashion, rather than followed it.

Another day, a spring rain fell continuously and the whole of Shanghai was enveloped in the scent of blossom. She cast her eyes down and watched her hands as they sat in mine. She knew, of course, why I had kept silent after I'd read her palm: it was plain that there were many paths on her lifeline; that although one's palm could change over time, anything that was not meant to be kept secret would not be kept secret.

All right. Now I am going to end this book. What happened to my characters after the spring of 1927 is something everyone in Shanghai knows. These events have become part of Shanghai's history; you don't need me to tell you about them. How many industries did Cassia set up? Would Yu Qiyang eventually become her lifetime companion, with or without a formal ceremony? Did Lily go to Europe and become an expert on Shakespeare? Will mother and daughter be reunited?

But still, you would like to know my professional secret.

Or perhaps you will say: I understand, you are a poetess.

I did indeed write poems, when I was at university in Shanghai. Someone saw me once sitting in the café outside the campus. One cup of coffee and two hours later I had filled four pages with my bold ramblings.

It is poets who are the most adept at lying, according to Plato; although Shanghai is still a little way off from the ideal society he envisaged, almost all its poets have been exiled.

I thought I might use some fictional techniques, but truth is the most important principle of biography. Perhaps to write it like this is not showy enough, but I had to be faithful, to myself and to history.

And I know that I must let you know, before the book ends, how I came to meet Cassia, and how I came to know so much of her private life, and of her unspoken thoughts.

All right, I will tell you about the moment that I first saw her: a moment I have passed over deliberately.

★★★

She was walking down a cold, desolate street. She couldn't understand how what had once been an incredibly busy road at night could now be so quiet. It felt as if she was the only person there. Banners still hung outside the buildings, colourful lanterns were displayed, bearing the alluring names of various girls, but there were no customers to be seen. The only sound came from the building with the two red doors. Here laughter could be heard and she seemed to hear the voices of Master Chang and Yu Qiyang. She heard Madame Emerald's voice calling to her: 'Come on, Little Cassia, come in, what are you doing there, hovering outside the door?'

Master Chang was dead, and so was Madame Emerald. These were people who were no longer with her. Yu, of course, he was still alive, but in her heart she had already given him a funeral. She had always had him in her heart; he had been present there ever since she first set her eyes on him. She had never loved anyone like she had loved him. She was prepared to sacrifice herself for this love.

She stood at the door, unwilling to push it open. She turned her back to the door and tried to calm down. Only then did she turn again and look inside.

She saw that she had a big belly. Madame Emerald had asked her to come back here so that she could help her give birth. Very soon after, just as Madame Emerald had predicted, she went into labour. By the time the midwife rushed in, she was already struggling, sweat and tears mingling all over her face. 'Push! Push harder!' the midwife shouted.

She was in extreme pain, and shouted for help. Li Yu and Xiu Fang were both by her side now, helping her. Madame Emerald waited impatiently at the Phoenix Hall. Suddenly she heard loud, clear crying: 'It's a girl, what news!'

Madame Emerald rushed over: '*Yaa*! Master Chang's daughter!'

Cassia fainted. She felt her soul leave the couch and walk towards the corridor. Down the stairs it went, and pushed open a big gate. Now she stood there, just as she did now, feeling that the night had never been so dark or so blue. When the final call of the night watchmen had faded, people started to emerge: pedestrians, street pedlars and women: women of all kinds, all professions and in all quantities; even professional women. And writers such as me.

She smoothed her own face, still so soft and so vivid. She knew she must set off. She walked out and joined us. She knew I had been waiting for her.

~ POSTSCRIPT ~

Several years ago, I lost my job working at a magazine. I had been a dedicated journalist, working for this same magazine, ever since I graduated from university, but it was precisely this dedication that landed me in trouble. The details are complicated but recalling the experience now, it strikes me that a woman like myself would probably have had to leave sooner or later and that it was only thanks to the generosity of the editors that I was not fired earlier.

On the day I was fired, it felt as if I had been struck by lightning. I was plunged into a really difficult situation, suddenly becoming a child deserted by society: no work, no money, no friends. I could not afford my rent; I would imminently become homeless.

Instead of packing up my few pieces of luggage, I collapsed on the bed, turned the light off and left this noisy, competitive world by going to sleep. Little did I imagine that that night would mark a turning point in my life.

Waking up in a cold sweat in broad daylight, I touched the small desk that stood by the window. It was a little damp, moistened by the morning dew perhaps. But looking in the mirror I saw that my face was a healthy red. A fortune teller once told me that my fate was strong, that I did not need to avoid evil; though he did also say that evil would not avoid me.

'You cannot get around it,' said the woman in a dream I once had, winking at me strangely: 'Why not look around, and if you find it, grasp it!'

I opened the window. The day was as quiet as night. There was a wall immediately outside the window, but stretching out I could see a turning, beyond which was a Western-style house, its

379

walls filled with climbing roses, their scent alluring. I had noticed my surroundings before, but it was only now that I saw there was something quite striking about them.

I stood by the roadside and looked at the empty playground beyond the wall. I asked the old doorman about this place, and was told it was a professional training school. It was empty now, since it was the summer holidays. Had it been a drama school before, I asked? Yes, the old man answered in surprise, but not many people knew that. Seventy years ago, a famous actress had bought this land and used it to establish the first drama school in Shanghai. Every morning at about this time, pretty young girls and boys gathered there to practice singing and dancing, doing ten somersaults in one breath.

I asked him more questions: 'How could an actress be so rich? Where did she get the money from?'

The old man smoothed the back of his head and said he was not sure. Then, with a start, he said to me: 'If you are lucky, you might bump into Mr Liu Ji, who knows everything about this part of town. He lives around here, and often walks around the area.'

'Really?' My eyes brightened. All Chinese people know the playwright Liu Ji, just as all English people know Shakespeare.

So now I forced myself to get up early each morning to jog in the playground of the old drama school building. Finally, one day I saw a man there, with silver hair and a Chinese Mandarin jacket made of very fine silk. He wore a pair of cloth shoes and, though thin and dependent on walking sticks, he appeared stylish and elegant.

I walked towards him. Of course I recognised a person as famous as him. Later, whenever Mr Liu Ji mentioned the day we first met, he always said that I frightened him as I ran up to him: 'Mr Liu Ji, do you know who you reminded me of when I saw you here?'

'Who?'

'Her!'

'How do you know about her?'

'She told me.'

I was talking about 'Her'; the woman in my dream.

Mr Liu Ji smiled and stretched out a hand:'Little girl...' I am not in fact a little girl, but I suppose I was to someone whose hair has turned completely white, 'Little girl, we are indeed connected.'

He lived in Fumin Road, not far from there, and had long stopped working. For such a master of his chosen profession, a rare national treasure, there was of course no talk of retirement. I feel lucky to have known such a near-legendary figure.

It was then that I decided to settle down and find another job. A popular magazine, whose editorial department happened to be based in the west of Shanghai, agreed to employ me for a year. It would be decided after a year's trial whether I would be employed permanently or not. The staff at this magazine concerned themselves only with making a living, and thus everything there was simple. I found a studio flat in an old house nearby where the rent was cheap and moved there.

The second time I met Mr Liu Ji was at his house. Now that I knew him a little better, I discovered that Mr Liu Ji was not at all like an old man. Although he walked a little stiffly, his hearing and eyesight were still good and his sense of humour was infectious. There was a woman by his side who was not much older than me. She listened coolly as we talked. At first I thought she was his granddaughter, but realised later that she was his youthful wife. She never looked at me properly and at first I only ever exchanged a few pleasantries with her.

At the beginning I was slightly troubled, suspecting that Mr Liu Ji had accepted me as a student only because he was interested in me as a woman. But as time passed, I was greatly influenced by this old man and felt I had learned a lot about the real essence of life.

He rarely talked about his scholarship; he mostly liked to gossip, especially about the affairs of men and women. If I had written down everything he had told me each day and published just a small part of it, I am sure all the professors of modern history would jump in surprise: the great and grand men of revolutionary literature had done things in their youth that were even more extreme than what goes on in the literature of today's young people.

★★★

New Good Friends, a weekly publication, was situated in an old Western-style house, its corridors and offices draped with reproductions of Shanghai publications of the 1930s. Though this lady's magazine, full of pictures, was not really to my taste, I knew well enough that it was at the top of the entertainment industry. I would force myself to do my best.

One day, when the Chief Editor walked into the room where we journalists worked, he told us that the magazine's biggest regret was not having been able to secure an interview with Danyi, who was known as the 'Number One Petit Bourgeois Female Writer in Shanghai.' He asked whether any of us could think of a way of getting an interview with her. The other two journalists turned to look at me, as they had both tried but been refused. It was my turn to try my luck.

'I'll give it a try,' I said reluctantly.

The Chief Editor indicated that if I could succeed then I would be paid a handsome sum.

After he left, my colleagues told me that it was not just bad luck that they had been refused. This is what they said:

'I saw that there was nothing real about Danyi's face, it was all make-up!'

'She must be nearly fifty, they say her mother used to write for the old *Good Friends,* used to work with Zhang Ailing, the famous writer.'

'This woman thinks she is Zhang Ailing reincarnated: why would she reveal herself to you?'

In fact I felt pleased. Danyi was Mrs Liu Ji. Even if she didn't want to honour me, she'd hardly deny herself such an opportunity for publicity. I knew by instinct that she and I would talk at length.

Just as I had predicted, Danyi indeed asked me to come out and chat.

She wore a *qipao* in the new style, and very heavy make-up. But her skin was fine-looking, and her nails varnished with the latest brightly coloured, shiny polish. According to her, her maternal grandmother had been married to a bank manager before the Communist liberation, and owned a large blue three-storey house in the French Concession.

We sat in a café on Ruijin Road. She boasted about which European city she had bought her dress in, and what Parisian perfume to use in which season, telling me her feelings about her visits to various European countries. This was exactly what my boss had wanted me to write about, and I couldn't understand where my colleagues had gone wrong.

I knew that at the end of the seventies, Liu Ji had suddenly become a 'rare cultural relic', receiving many invitations abroad. In twenty years, he went all over the world, Danyi always at his side, until recently when he was not really up to it any more. But I had been wise not to mention Liu Ji.

'The Number One Female Petit Bourgeois Writer in Shanghai.' I asked her straightforwardly about the origin of such a title.

'Of course, I do not call myself that,' she smiled. 'But I am not ashamed of the title either,' she added, lightly. 'It's just that the title has been made to sound common by the "little sisters" of today.' The waiter came by so I ordered beer and Danyi ordered iced coffee before she continued: 'It's not possible to fake class or taste. Only after three generations of wealth, can you lay claim to possessing taste. The Americans have been rich for a hundred years, and still they are vulgar! Nowadays it's fashionable among petit bourgeois women in Shanghai to watch American soaps, to read magazines such as yours, which is indeed common.'

I held my beer glass and quickly noted down her words with the other hand. Suddenly, she was alert, asking me: 'But you don't look as if you are from Shanghai.'

I nodded. Indeed I wasn't. Then she judged my character, simply by using the Western horoscope.

She asked me when my birthday was.

It turned out I was a Virgo.

'People born under this sign have an insatiable appetite for mystery, suspense, danger and even violence,' she said. 'Their curiosity might lead to creativity, but on the other hand it might lead them to disastrous extremes and leave them in helpless situations. If a Virgo pursues art, she becomes a perfectionist, almost ridiculously so.'

Danyi told me these things and I knew exactly what she meant. I must admit that her fortune telling was perfectly accurate: as the daughter of a Yangtze sailor, I was forever behind the times.

'At least you were not born in Shanghai,' Danyi said in a voice that could not be argued with.

This shot the arrow straight to the bullseye. Nothing was the same on the other side of the river. I was not born to be a Shanghainese.

Danyi also said that she was surprised that a woman like me was interested in the subject of the petit bourgeoisie. I grew nervous: did she know something? Before the local bourgeoisie spread like parasites, Shanghai had been dominated by women of stronger voices and actions; these were, for me, the real Shanghai women. But how could she know about this even before I had written a book of my own?

A little while after I had got to know him, Mr Liu Ji had to be admitted to hospital. He had a nurse deliver a letter to me, asking me to come and see him. It was a grim afternoon, his thin face looked even thinner and there were dark grey shadows beneath his eyes. I suddenly realised that he would not live for long. It seemed he had waited for me for a long time. He pulled off his oxygen mask and sat up. I tried to stop him, but he silenced me with a gesture.

The dying man's words were meaningful. He said them without introduction: perhaps he sensed that I knew the context. He said intellectuals such as us could never fully live in the modern world. Only ordinary folk could live in the present, where flushing toilets and modern baths were a part of everyday life. No revolutionary or political movement could change that.

He opened his mouth wide and wanted to laugh, but he couldn't. The pathos: the intention to laugh was there, but the ability had gone.

Shanghai is materialistic. Modern Shanghai is a collection of material things. How could you think in the abstract when you sit on flushing toilets in Shanghai? I laughed on his behalf.

It seemed he had waited all this time for me to fall into the trap that his words had laid. Now he asked me to fetch his canvas bag from beneath the bed, from which he drew a big brown envelope. Inside were many yellowed and fragile-looking newspaper cuttings, all about a Shanghai opera singer: Cassia.

Seeing that I looked surprised, he narrowed his eyes and said slowly: 'I know you can write, and I know also that you write about unimportant things. But if you ever want to write something interesting, then write about Cassia, the most remarkable woman I ever met.' Suddenly looking tired, he leant back on his pillow. The nurse rushed over and put the oxygen mask back on him, and his daughter signalled for me to leave.

That afternoon was the last of our meetings. He died not long afterwards.

But what he had entrusted me with really saddened me. I did research on all sorts of things: the history of drama in Shanghai, cultural history, economic history. I even went on the internet and searched using 'Google' and 'Baidu', but I could never find a name such as Cassia. I consulted some cultural figures of old Shanghai, who had indeed heard of such a name, but she was known as 'a bad woman', 'a female mobster', 'a good-for-nothing woman', some even called her: 'that obscene woman of the Shanghai underworld.' Nobody could provide me with detailed information.

So I felt unsure of what Mr Liu Ji had entrusted to me and I didn't really try very hard to follow up the story. Not long after, I again became dejected, feeling listless, going to work just to get paid, writing about how fashionable people kill time; and after work I drank in bars, watched DVDs and surfed the internet aimlessly. It felt as if nothing really mattered. Then I quarrelled with our Chief Editor over a small matter and though he didn't mention the word 'fired', I felt it was too demeaning to carry on living like this.

It was then that I remembered Mr Liu Ji's request. So I asked the magazine for leave and gave up a few days' salary to sit in the library and look carefully through newspapers from the beginning of the Republican period. If a woman's reputation could be as bad as this, she must have done something the society of the time couldn't tolerate, something perhaps even today's society would not be too pleased about.

'Where there's a will, there's a way.' My daily digging among the mass of papers resulted in a rich body of material. Cassia's life attracted me like a magnet, so much so that when I went near this material I could barely pull myself away.

There were many stories about Liu Ji's youthful love life; indeed, he had quite a reputation among the literati of the 1930s. But he had always moved in New Art circles.

Later on Liu Ji became a celebrity, a famous figure in Chinese cultural history, a heavyweight of left wing theatre. He had never been an official, and yet he was wiser than many of the officials who threw their weight around. He knew how to protect himself and suffered no more than anyone else in the political upheavals of his day. After the Communist liberation he no longer wrote anything, though he was a member of numerous film and drama committees and attended meeting after meeting of the Political Consultative Advisory Board. Some called him 'The Father of Modern Chinese Drama.'

Now that he was famous and considered to be important, nobody mentioned his earlier cooperation with the Ruyi Troupe, and he himself refused to elaborate on it.

Liu Ji didn't usually mention anything if it was awkward; and anything that he refused to mention must be extremely awkward indeed.

I am sure that deep inside his heart, Liu Ji had secretly fallen in love with Cassia, though he lacked the courage to express it. My proof is this: when he had entreated me to write about Cassia, after calling her 'the most remarkable woman I ever met,' he also added: 'and the most beautiful,' in a softer voice, as if he feared offending someone.

Perhaps he didn't want his wife Danyi to hear it, even though she was not in the room with us at the time.

But it was this half-swallowed statement that stirred me. Perhaps deep inside I felt a slight jealousy. Liu Ji had been linked to numerous female stars in his life and Cassia was indeed beautiful, perhaps the most beautiful of all. Still, she was never referred to as the 'Number One Beauty of 20th Century Shanghai'. Liu Ji's words of praise were obviously a subjective, sentimental expression.

We had known each other for more than a year by the time he died. During that period the only time he talked about his scholarship was when he boasted about how he had translated the word 'modern' into the Chinese language. At that time he had to come up with his very own translation. He transliterated the word, coming up with '*Mo'deng*' and it became fashionable. What he was really thinking of was actually the lascivious woman named 'Prakriti' of the Buddhist scripture 'Shurangama Sutra', who seduced the Buddhist disciple Ananda, nearly spoiling his virtue.

Modernity was the female seductress who spoiled one's virtue, just like a certain fashionable woman of the time. Saying he had a sudden inspiration, he came up with the translation. Now it seemed as if there was a more profound meaning to it.

Then he burst into a hearty laugh, so loud that I feared he might not recover from it.

I am a hundred per cent sure that the modern woman he had in mind was Cassia.

On the first day back to work after my break, I submitted my piece about Cassia to the Chief Editor. Our magazine's market was the white collar petite bourgeoisie. There was a special column that introduced the legendary lives of the stars and celebrities in the past, and I believed that my biography was both literary and full of strong characters.

Coming out of the office, I deliberately walked back home via Liu Ji's house, feeling a little melancholic. I felt as if he was still alive and was waiting for me to finish writing about Cassia. He had introduced her to me. His study faced the garden and watching the curtain of his study window waver in the wind I felt like telling him that I myself had finally found Cassia, after many ups and downs. I had been lucky that she had been in a good mood when I called, so she had picked up the phone and talked to me.

If only Mr Liu Ji's soul knew this, he'd be so pleased. However, I also knew that Danyi still lived there, and there was no need to disturb her, so I walked past their door.

The Chief Editor called me to his office with a stern look on his face. My colleagues had already started gossiping even before I reached his office, gloating over my possible misfortune.

In dedicating myself to the writing of this biography of Cassia, formerly 'Queen of Shenqu', I had begun to care less and less about my appearance. This had not escaped my curious colleagues.

When I handed in my manuscript, hoping the magazine would serialise it, the whole building knew about it.

The Chief Editor closed the door and said directly: 'It's well written, but there is no way that *New Good Friends* will publish it. Prostitutes, the underworld, murder: these subjects are unacceptable. Cassia can hardly be called a life model.'

Heavens! I took a deep breath. A little taken aback, I asked: 'Hasn't every former star in Shanghai had biographies written about them, one after another? Ruan Lingyu has several – and there is a film about her!'

The Chief wanted to appease me. He poured me a cup of tea. He re-iterated the fact that *New Good Friends* focused on petit bourgeois fashion, its readership were white collar urban females. Cassia's life story would alarm them too much. 'Besides,' he continued, 'if all women were like her, there wouldn't be any peace, would there? Let's just settle for peace.'

'You are saying that if one frightens the chattering classes there won't be peace?'

He laughed: 'Your words make me uncomfortable, but yes, that is what I meant.'

'Perhaps it is rather that you are worried you'd lose money!' I felt like saying. But I couldn't. I depended on this magazine for a living, so I could not afford to get on my moral high horse. I took the manuscript and made my way out, but the Chief called me back: 'Are you thinking of submitting the piece to other magazines? Let me tell you something more then.'

Surprised, I turned and waited. It felt as if I had gone back to the magazine that had first fired me and got myself into fresh trouble. But this Chief Editor was a so-called 'young and up and coming talent'. He only cared about money. *New Good Friends* had made so much money that he was the rising star of his generation.

'The person who will feel most threatened is Danyi. I won't repeat what she says, but I believe she would protest to any magazine who dares to publish your writing.'

It was stupid that I hadn't even thought about this possibility. I grew angry: 'But what would she protest against?'

'I am merely repeating her own words just now. Of course it is totally up to you whether you publish or not. But I must tell you, for your own good, that although Mr Liu Ji has passed away, Danyi herself has many contacts among the literati.'

Every chief editor meant well, so they claimed, even the chief editor who virtually operated as a 'thought policeman' at my former magazine pretended he was being considerate when he fired me.

But that was all. Cassia had never shied away from being who she was, so I burnt my bridges.

I didn't feel that the petit bourgeois women would have time to feel angry; the most they could do is dislike my piece. But I knew that the way Cassia lived her life would offend a large percentage of male readers, who might be so angry that they would want to burn my writing. I didn't expect everyone to have as generous an outlook as Mr Liu Ji.

So no magazine dared to serialise my manuscript, and no publisher dared to publish it as a book either. In anger and protest, I put it on my blog, one section a day, one chapter a week. Once a week I checked the entries with Cassia before publishing them on-line.

An English student called Johnny read the blog and found me as a result. His Chinese was good and he was extremely clever, he was studying for a PhD at King's College, Cambridge. When he wasn't expressing his opinions on matters to do with China, he was extremely gentle, and sometimes shy, like a schoolboy.

He was writing a thesis entitled: 'The Oedipus Syndrome in Modern Shanghai,' and, assuring me that his ideas were to be treated extremely seriously, he insisted on a meeting. He sat next to us in an Internet café, peeping surreptitiously at Cassia. It was quiet there, we were the only three present. Johnny went online and both Cassia and I ordered coffee.

Later on, he sighed to me: 'Oriental women always look so

young.' He said when his paternal grandfather arrived in Shanghai, he had written in his diary of encountering a glamorous Chinese woman in a hotel, whose beauty he could never forget. That was why Johnny had wanted to learn Chinese. Once he came across the ocean to Shanghai he had been immediately fascinated by the beauty of Chinese women. 'How many Chinese women are as beautiful as Cassia?' he asked me.

His words of course insulted me. It was obvious that he did not count me as a beautiful Chinese woman. We had met many times and he had never made such a comment before. But I really have no reason to be angry with him. All men, Chinese or Western, are unreasonable.

I knew very well that I had fallen in love with Cassia and that this would affect the objectivity of my writing. But I really couldn't help myself. I felt that a woman's beauty was not just for men. Cassia had always had more female fans than male; why should I be an exception?

I received a phone call from a colleague, saying that the first page of the current *New Good Friends* carried an announcement from 'Madam Danyi'. Its content was not straightforward, but it did say that I had hinted in the biography of Cassia – serialised in my blog – that Mr Liu Ji and Cassia had had an affair. 'How could one of the founder members of Chinese modern theatre, a standard-bearer of left wing cinema, have been involved with an underworld female good-for-nothing?' it asked.

Danyi's statement read: 'This is the greatest of insults to our country's revolutionary art tradition.'

I put the phone down, my face pale. I was only publishing online, not in print. Just as the Chief Editor had predicted, I had not been able to find any magazine willing to publish this biography. But even so, each time I posted a chapter, I felt nervous. More people wrote to condemn Cassia than praise her, and the words of accusation directed at me were even fiercer.

I knew what Danyi was waiting for. She was waiting for the book to be formally published, then she could sue both the publisher and myself in court. To try and sue me for an online publication would have been counter-productive. It would also be hard to work out what kind of defamation payments were appropriate.

In China, people are still entitled to sue for 'defiling an ancestor's reputation' as far back as three generations. It seems I will never have a peaceful life!

Indeed, the phrase 'Chinese mafia' gave people pause. Why would I want to write about thieving men and obscene women? Besides, this was a world that a woman should leave well alone. My book was bold, but not because I was writing about the underworld.

Chinese officials have always had an air of formality, they are pretentious in their talk, unreliable in their actions, and make a lot of fuss while they achieve little. They treat women, especially, as second class citizens; Chinese society's attitude to women makes me angry, makes me want to smash things.

Whereas the people of the underworld were courageous enough to be responsible for their own actions. They had principles.

When I was eighteen years old, I made a resolution to be a poetess, and so naturally I wandered into the underworld. But instead of becoming good at martial arts, I learned how to write alternative poetry.

Many female heroines emerged in that underworld. There are many different kinds of brotherhoods and all would tolerate figures such as Madame Emerald and Little Cassia.

Now you understand why I had to write such a book. And since writing it, I have become a feminist writer. My own fate is just as unknown as Cassia's and when once again I sit down with her, perhaps we'll be able to work out an ending for ourselves.

~AUTHOR'S NOTE ~

My debt to Shanghai

My family are all natives of Chongqing, growing up by the side of the mountain and banks of the river, watching the clear water of the Jialing River and the dirty water of the Yangtze River passing by. We all laughed, sitting huddled around a small transistor radio, listening to the local comedy acts, called *yanzi*. But one member of the family was different from the others, and that was my father.

My father was drafted and sent to Chongqing by the Nationalist Army during the Japanese War. The local Chongqing people called him a 'down river person'. My father had never learned to speak a passable Chongqing dialect. He was a man of few words and only spoke when it was absolutely necessary. When he did speak it was in the dialect of Tiantai and Ningpo, very much like Shanghainese, a world away from that of Chongqing. Only I could understand father, so I volunteered to be his interpreter when necessary, and as a result picked up a few rusty Shanghai expressions.

Father had always wanted to travel downstream to the land of his birth, to the large wide plains where the Yangtze enters the sea. But he was only the pilot of a goods boat, home on sick leave. At home he cooked and did housework, feeding his six children with very limited resources. He was the lowest of the low in society: what dreams could he have? The only thing he could do was to watch the river when he had a free moment: a man was not allowed to shed tears of homesickness.

But my father was a man of great heart. Local bullies saw that he was gentle and teased him, making me, a small girl, so enraged that I wanted to throw knives at them; but father did not resent these people. Whenever they needed help, or wanted to borrow some salt or rice, he'd give it to them; if they didn't return what they had borrowed, he never asked for it back. Once a family home further down the hill caught fire and father rushed down with a fire extinguisher; and when the fire was out he came back with a blackened face and torn clothes.

I visited his tomb this year and brought with me lilies and my book about my upbringing. After burning the paper money, I burnt the book. The flame burnt fast: father had to read quickly in the other world. My spirit went with it, and as he read the book I told him everything. Blood ties are important, but father and I had a deeper affection than that. Though he was not my natural father, he was the man I loved most. His kindness and compassion meant that a girl like me would not descend into the depths of hopelessness. His existence ensured that I never completely gave up on the world.

Father had a wish: that when he died, his ashes should be returned to his hometown. My mother, brothers and sisters did not want to do this for him, as they feared father's soul would not be able to get back to Chongqing if it was returned home. So when I came back from London one year, we chose a hill facing the Yangtze River, so that his soul could travel downriver to his hometown, and then return.

But somehow I had to fulfill my father's wish. At the end of the 80s, I went to university in Shanghai and learned an inauthentic Shanghai dialect, causing me to suffer at the hands of street pedlars there. Even on buses I was often given the wrong directions, with the conductor saying impatiently: 'An outsider, she doesn't know anything.'

In recent years I have visited Shanghai several times for book signings, and Shanghai journalists are surprised and pleased to hear that I can say a few words in the Ningbo dialect.

Even so, there was always a distance between Shanghai and

myself.

But as a novelist, I have a skill obtained through years of practice: I am able to let my characters fulfill the wishes of my father: to have grown up in Shanghai – taking risks there, meeting success and being defeated there.

I feel as if my father in the world beyond would like this story; that he would allow me to live in Shanghai on his behalf.

Coming from Chongqing to Shanghai, I was seen as just another peasant, as all outsiders to Shanghai are, like Little Cassia was. There's nothing wrong in that: not everyone in Shanghai has to be a merciful Buddha.

But I want to ask myself: how did this modernity, the pride of Shanghai, first develop? This question made me imagine what it would be like to grow up in Shanghai.

My mother's first husband was head of the Paoge, an underworld organization. Once upon a time he held great power in Chongqing, but he was also a womaniser. My mother finally escaped him.

When I started preparing to write this book, I wanted to write about how a revolutionary became an underground figure. But I soon found out that what I really wanted to write about was a woman like my mother. How her big unbound feet took her from the countryside into the modern world. How she landed in sticky situations and sank into hell, and how she emerged from hell and came back to the world.

Hence this 'fictional biography'.

By the time I had finished the first draft, the peach blossoms had fallen, blossomed and fallen again. I wanted very much for my father to know that I had spent a year-and-a-half fulfilling his wish.

I returned to Chongqing this year. On the night I visited his tomb, I dreamt of my father. Against a background of glorious peach blossoms, he said these two lines of a poem in his Tiantai dialect:

'I've been away so often that hotels feel like home, and home like a hotel. Who will ask me: are the blossoms at home just like they used to be?'

This strange, obscure language woke me up. Did my father's soul really accompany me as I wrote?

I look out of the window. The day is breaking. Just as father said in my dream, the peach tree has indeed come into bloom.

Acknowledgments

Liu Hong would like to thank her husband, Jon Cannon, who played a fundamental role in this translation.

HONG YING

K: THE ART OF LOVE

China, 1930s. Julian Bell, son of the Bloomsbury set's Vanessa, is newly arrived in Peking. In search of fresh experiences, he encounters the beautiful, intelligent and deeply erotic Lin Cheng. Though Lin is wife to a university professor, their passionate assignations blossom into an affair.

Schooled in the ancient Taoist arts of love, Lin instructs Julian in the ways of the East. But if society won't tolerate this union between Occidental and Oriental can their love possibly survive?

Based on a true story this is a tragic tale of romance, betrayal and sexual desire set against a backdrop of conflict and war.

'*The Art of Love* is written with a wonderfully intense simplicity - full of poetry and grace' Andrew Motion

'A lively book in its portrayal of liberal Chinese intellectual life before the multiple catastrophes of war' John Lanchester, *New York Review of Books*

'The book's strength comes from Ying's skilful management of the theme of East meets West . . . readable, clever and spare' Tibor Fischer, *Erotic Review*

He just wanted a decent book to read ...

Not too much to ask, is it? It was in 1935 when Allen Lane, Managing Director of Bodley Head Publishers, stood on a platform at Exeter railway station looking for something good to read on his journey back to London. His choice was limited to popular magazines and poor-quality paperbacks – the same choice faced every day by the vast majority of readers, few of whom could afford hardbacks. Lane's disappointment and subsequent anger at the range of books generally available led him to found a company – and change the world.

'We believed in the existence in this country of a vast reading public for intelligent books at a low price, and staked everything on it'
Sir Allen Lane, 1902–1970, founder of Penguin Books

The quality paperback had arrived – and not just in bookshops. Lane was adamant that his Penguins should appear in chain stores and tobacconists, and should cost no more than a packet of cigarettes.

Reading habits (and cigarette prices) have changed since 1935, but Penguin still believes in publishing the best books for everybody to enjoy. We still believe that good design costs no more than bad design, and we still believe that quality books published passionately and responsibly make the world a better place.

So wherever you see the little bird – whether it's on a piece of prize-winning literary fiction or a celebrity autobiography, political tour de force or historical masterpiece, a serial-killer thriller, reference book, world classic or a piece of pure escapism – you can bet that it represents the very best that the genre has to offer.

Whatever you like to read – trust Penguin.